Meaning Less

This book is dedicated with love to my parents, Leonard and Elaine Oates. For inspiring my love of literature, my curiosity in life, and my passion of spirit, I am forever grateful.

sands press
Brockville, Ontario

Meaning Less

A Novel by Brad Oates

sands press

sands press

A Division of 3244601 Canada Inc.
300 Central Avenue West
Brockville, Ontario
K6V 5V2

Toll Free 1-800-563-0911 or 613-345-2687
http://www.sandspress.com

ISBN 978-1-990066-20-7
Copyright © Brad Oates 2022
All Rights Reserved

CHAPTER 1
The Day it Started to Rain

A cold rain battered the streets of Edmonton, Alberta. It slammed down in great unrelenting cascades onto the pothole-ridden pavement, and assaulted the foggy windows of the #4 Bus which carried Jeffrey Boggs. He'd caught the transfer from the LRT station near the university—a tedious journey from his claustrophobic office at SALIGIA Inc. downtown to the dingy and dark confines of The Black Dog on Whyte Ave.

At least it isn't snow, Jeff thought. Positive affirmations were an important daily habit, he'd been told at some point, by somebody he didn't care to recall.

Still, Edmonton didn't get very much as far as summer goes, and rain felt like a terrible waste of the season's final days.

Today was as good as over the moment this bullshit rain started. He recalled hearing the downpour even above the wailing demands of his alarm clock, and how he'd seethed the moment he realized he'd left his patio window open the night before. A panicked run to his living room revealed a long, sour-smelling wet spot on the mangy carpet. "The landlord will love that. Oh well, not like I was getting my deposit back anyways."

After only five minutes awake, Jeff had already been miserable.

Maybe tomorrow will be better. He forced a sharp smile across his long, aquiline face. He didn't really believe it though. It was already

9

mid-August, and 2026 had been a grim, cold, and disappointing year thus far on all fronts. Save for a brief couple of weeks back in May when the sun had shone bright and warm and all the world seemed right, little else was worth remembering so far.

Sometimes, it seemed every year was a little bit worse than the last. Fewer worthy stories, worse weather, and more bad news. To top it off, each one passed a little faster. That was inevitable, of course, when each day was so similar to the last. The dark clouds that hung so often over his city were fitting companions to the dreary days—always the same cycle, always the same disappointments. Jeff woke up wishing he was asleep, dragged himself into a job that noticed him only when there was blame to dish out, and then went home to wait for it to start all over again.

On lucky days like this one, he stopped by one of the many bars near his apartment for a few drinks with a friend. "Sometimes, I think my reliability is becoming a liability," he'd quip. That or something like it. All the complaints blended together over the years, and what sharp wit Jeff might have pulled off in his phrasing was dulled by overuse.

That's okay. It's important to get it out once in a while. It was another useless platitude he'd picked up somewhere along the way.

Sometimes, people would advise Jeff to quit. Friends, therapists, strangers at bus-stops…the opinions always went the same direction. But Jeff knew what they didn't—the world was changing, and the corporations were the only gods left. It hardly mattered which one he served, his fate would be the same. SALIGIA, as awful as it was, could at least afford to pay a competitive salary.

It was a bleak way to look at things, but he'd been lucky to land the job ten years ago, and nothing since then gave him any hope of the market improving. The demands got heavier, the overbearing bosses grew more cruel, the alleys filled up with those who'd lost their grip, and the desperate need to hang on to whatever semblance of control was left to him became the only thing that pushed Jeff out of bed in the mornings.

In his thirty-six years of life, he still recalled with crystal-clarity the best moment he'd ever had.

He'd been eight years old, attending elementary school in a quiet neighbourhood on Edmonton's south side.

It was lunch recess—the longest and best recess of the day—and he was out playing tag with his classmates. Freeze-tag in fact, which was certainly a fitting choice in the festive white chill of the Canadian December.

Jeff could still hear Katie's screech when David snatched the toque from her head and sprinted with it to the far end of the tall, red, sliding board.

"Give it back!" screamed Katie, and took off after David like a bullet.

She grabbed the slide's handrail to anchor her turn, flying around the corner as she reached with her other hand for the bright, red-and-white maple leaf hat carried by the retreating David.

David, recognizing he could never hope to outrun the lithe young Katie for long, extended his arm and launched it forward in a wide arc.

The maple-printed wool sailed through the chilly air—suspended for a moment as if in a dream amid the sparkling crystals of ice and snow dancing down to the playground—before it was caught up by Imran.

"Pig in the middle, pig in the middle. Katie is the piggy!" yelled David, and a choir of laughter accompanied the song as it was taken up by the rest of the wild young boys. "Pig in the middle, pig in the middle. Katie is the piggy!"

"My mom gave me that. It's mine! Give it back!" Katie raged, and through the polished white steps of the sliding board, Jeff saw tears trembling in her brilliant, brown eyes. A drop just on the edge of her eyelid hung for a moment, and shone like a sun amid the pinprick stars of the falling snow.

"Piggy, piggy!" chanted the boys. The wool hat flew from Imran, to Scott, to Liam, and back to David. Katie's tears flowed freely now, and her pursuit began to slow.

"Piggy, piggy!" Again the hat took flight, high over the top of the sliding board, and down into Jeff's own hands.

"Piggy, piggy!" the others chorused, and Jeff balanced on the balls of his feet, a terrible trepidation seizing his fragile young soul. Even then, with the eyes of all the boys—and Katie—on him, he felt clearly the import of the choice he had to make. It was heavy and hot, like the old quilt his mom would wrap him in when he was sick.

"Throw it to me," called David. "Let's get it up on the roof!"

Slowly, Jeff rounded the slide, turning away from the boys and coming face to face with the angry yet utterly flabbergasted Katie. She was taller than they were, and her dark hair cradled her face in a way Jeff never could quite forget. Katie had stopped running by then, and stood trembling with broken fury. Her hands clenched into little pink balls, and she stared wildly at her attackers with eyes like daggers. They stabbed back and forth between the boys, then finally lowered and held upon the cold, frozen ground as Jeff approached.

"Here." He felt the warm wool caress his young hand as he held it out to her.

As Katie slowly lifted her eyes to his, he saw the veil of her tears draw back, and somewhere deep within the onyx lakes of her pupils, a sacred white fire sparked to life.

Jeff felt it flicker up in his own eyes too—he remembered it all so clearly even now.

Her pink hand brushed his as she took the hat, and she smiled as she pulled it eagerly down over her red-tipped ears. Then, out of nowhere, she threw her arms around Jeff, and all the world was them, the hat, and her warm tears on his cheek.

"You're my best friend," she said. Jeff knew that it was true.

That was the best moment of his life—when the world seemed fair, and what he did mattered.

He recalled it vividly as he listened to the bombastic torrents of rain beating like war drums on the tired old roof of the bus. It was long ago, but he thought about it often. Things were so different now. Nothing he did at work meant anything, and the rest of his day was no better. He got by, and he kept his head above water, but there was no great purpose behind any of it. Nobody really cared, and nothing really mattered.

Not like it used to.

Has the world changed since then, or is it something else that changed?

It took a stranger ringing the bell for his stop to shake Jeff out of his fruitless reverie and haul him moaning back into the drudgery that was his daily life.

Hopping through the middle door of the bus, he landed with both feet in an ankle-high puddle—immediately soaking through his shoes and down to the flesh. "Damn it," Jeff yelled, then grimaced as a mom with one arm around a small child hurried by with a scornful glare. "Sorry," he called after her.

He doubted she heard, or would have cared even if she had.

The pouring rain brought out the smell of the dying grass and fallen leaves in the gutters. This mixed with the ubiquitous smell of weed that hung constantly over Whyte Ave to create a dizzying potpourri. Jeff took it in gladly, thinking back to times long gone as he hurried along under the dripping eaves.

The Black Dog was only just ahead, and Jeff shook his sopping feet as the rain pressed down upon him—promising that the rest of his body was more likely to match their wetness than his feet were to dry.

Once inside, the familiar smell and creak of each step warmed him from within. Jeff always preferred these smaller, independent bars—the ones with sticky floors and crusty regulars. They were few and far between these days. Most bars in the city were giant corporate sports lounges with hockey on the screens, jerseys on the walls, and cheap, piss-tasting beer in the taps.

He spotted his friend, Edward Slane, already sitting at the long, narrow stretch of table which gazed out the open windows onto the busy stretch of Whyte Ave. He had one beer in hand, and another set out beside him. Eddie was a good friend.

"Hey," said Jeff, taking a seat beside Eddie and grabbing his beer.

"Hey, bud!" Eddie looked him up and down with a wry smile. "You appear especially Lennon-esque today," he said, and ran a hand through his own well-combed hair.

Jeff laughed. He was business casual as usual, but at this point he'd untucked his shirt, and his shaggy hair and relaxed posture meant Eddie's assessment was fair.

"So, how did it go with Marcy?" asked Eddie.

Jeff grimaced. Marcy was Jeff's direct supervisor at work, and one of his least favourite people anywhere. Lately, he'd been complaining—to Eddie primarily—about her near-comedic inability to understand even the most basic details of a project's timeline. Regrettably, she was also rigidly enthusiastic about piling on more work in answer to even the simplest question. It was like the end stages of a long Jenga game, Jeff had told Eddie two nights prior. A few drinks later, he swore to confront his manager, Nadia, about the situation.

"It didn't go quite how I was hoping," he answered sadly.

"Remind me what the problem was again?" asked Eddie.

Jeff sighed, and took a quick sip of beer. He tried not to complain too much, and even focussed on being grateful as often as he remembered, but his job had a way of getting to him sometimes.

"It really boils down to a failure of communication, but Christ does it get annoying. Get this—right now I'm working on two major projects. The first is called The Liveable City Initiative. We're being contracted by a major condo developer who wants the entire city to know about the new developments they aim to have for sale next spring. It's a full engagement project—which means busses, billboards, park benches—you name it, they want their info there. It's my job to guide the initiative team along and make sure they meet the developer's goals, while respecting SALIGIA's own interests along the way."

"Fantastically dry," said Eddie, "but it sounds simple enough."

"One would think," Jeff agreed.

"So, what's the other project?" asked Eddie.

"That's just it. My other major project right now is The Clean City Initiative, which comes from the City Council. They want to reduce the clutter on our park benches, busses, and highways, and create a less 'ad-driven' city."

"Shit," said Eddie. He raised his mug in an empathetic toast.

"Yeah," said Jeff, and met his glass with a solemn nod. "Marcy's been riding me about both projects. When I'm successful at one, I'm obviously falling behind on the other.

"To make it even worse, SALIGIA's time-tracking computer

system needs a stated initiative topic for every meeting and every minute—so Marcy will only ever talk to me about one initiative or the other, never both." Jeff ran a hand through his wavy brown hair.

Eddie laughed long and hard.

"There's no way to win," Jeff lamented.

"It's almost Tartarean," said Eddie.

"What?"

"Tartarean…of or pertaining to Tartarus. It was my class word of the day today."

"You're depraved."

"Yet you're the one trapped in this cyclical nightmare."

"Oh, it gets better. Last week, I was asking a simple question, and Marcy gave me another new project. The City Branding Initiative is an inquiry into why the City has so little branding. They expect that a significant marketing push will be in order—which will only add to my headache."

"'City of Champions' isn't cutting it anymore?" Eddie joked.

"Apparently not."

"So, what did you do?" asked Eddie.

"I told her I didn't have time for this with the other two pulling the soul out of each other. Naturally, she told me there was no way around it, because the initiative had already been officially designated to me in the SALIGIA system. Then, she signed me up for a six-hour time management course."

Eddie was in stitches now, and didn't seem ready to continue for a good while. Jeff drank in sad silence. He watched a wet, hunched man make his way down Whyte, begging for money, smokes, or company—Jeff couldn't be sure which.

"You're kidding me with all this though, right?" Eddie finally managed.

"Hell, I wish. So, I finally had enough, and decided to message Nadia about how out of touch Marcy's supervision is."

"And?"

"Well, Nadia made the call a lot quicker than I thought. I now have a new supervisor."

Eddie gasped. "They fired Marcy?"

"No," Jeff frowned. "They assigned me to Francis. I have two supervisors now."

"Fuck right off!"

"I swear it's true. I wouldn't believe it either if I were you. Working in a high school must be a breeze compared to corporate life."

Eddie gave Jeff a strange look, but didn't push the issue.

"Wow, I don't even know what to say to all that." It seemed Eddie was telling the truth, as, for a long while he sat silent, and together he and Jeff stared out the window, watching a few strangers struggle by—too foolish, unfortunate, or desperate to stay indoors.

The bar was slowly picking up, as small trickles of smarter people made their way inside to escape the storm without. The Black Dog had a musty, cool feeling at the best of times, and a wet wood smell that Jeff always maintained should be the chief fragrance of any good bar—along with stale beer and old liquor.

Across the street, an old woman stepped off a westbound bus, directly into the raging water of a swollen storm drain. She nearly fell, but was caught by the man behind her and helped up onto the curb. For thanks, he took an umbrella in the eye as she stumbled once more, and finally stood leaning against the wall of the bistro directly across from Jeff catching her breath.

The scene was a perfect picture of life in Edmonton. Life before the snow, at least.

"That's so messed up," Eddie rejoined after finishing his beer. "What are you going to do?"

Jeff took a long swallow— his drink was nearly empty too, and he hoped Eddie would stay for one more at least. "Well, haven't I ever told you what my father used to say to me?" he asked.

Eddie raised one eyebrow at Jeff, an eager smile pushing at the corners of his mouth.

"He'd say to me, 'Jeffrey, life's not fair.'" Jeff finished his beer, and set it roughly down upon the long wooden ledge that served as their table.

"Is that so?" Eddie asked.

"It is indeed," Jeff confirmed, happy for the prompt. "See, I hated that expression for years—the first half of my life really. Then one day, maybe the third year of university if I recall—"

"I can scarcely imagine you do, if I recall that year correctly," Eddie interrupted.

"Be that as it may," Jeff continued with a chuckle, "I was having a particularity awful day at one point, and heard myself thinking about how unfair it was. Then I heard that old refrain in my head, 'life's not fair', and it all made sense. I realized that if things were going to get better, it would be up to me. Complaining and self-pity have never gotten anyone anything besides maybe addictions and an early grave. I solved the problem that day, and I've remembered the lesson ever since."

"That's a damn fine outlook my friend—I might test that out on my students. Let me grab us another round, and you can tell me what you're going to do to change things in that ridiculous tower you work at." Eddie swung himself up from his seat, trotted down a short set of well-worn steps, weaved through the army of barstools littering the floor, and finally leaned up on the long, black bar.

Ridiculous tower, that's putting it lightly, thought Jeff.

The Edmonton skyline had never been world-renowned, but there had always been a handful of vantage points known to locals where the natural beauty of the city's long, winding River Valley could truly bring a sense of pride to a prairie-born heart. The SALIGIA tower had changed that to an undeniable degree. Bigger than anything else around by more than half, it was huge, jagged, aggressive, and black as jet. It seemed to grow up overnight, as SALIGIA maneuvered itself into a new market and promptly scooped up the vast majority of media rights and contracts.

The corporation was a goliath, and the rapidity of its growth was well-reflected in the labyrinthian sprawl of its management. Nothing got done without treading through a quagmire of redundant, maddening double-checks, red-tape, and inefficiencies. This was all punctuated by a general disregard for the well being of its employees beyond their ability to generate profit.

Jeff was just below management, and that made the sight of the tower—which was hard to miss from anywhere in the city— particularly aggravating. It took up every view, reminding him even on days off that it owned him, and would use him up, and leave him a resentful husk if he wasn't careful.

"This should even us up from last weekend," said Eddie, sitting back down and sliding over a dark pint of Guinness. "So, what's the plan here buddy? You'll have to tread carefully, I imagine."

"I will at that," said Jeff. "To be honest, I'm not sure what to do yet. I can't change the way the office runs, and I certainly can't hope to find a job anywhere else that pays half as well. It's tough right now, but it could be a lot worse… or so I've been told.

"I guess it's a bit of patience and extra grace I need right now— which, by the way, this Guinness is certainly helping with! Besides, there's always the principle of regression to the mean. Things are brutal right now, but they'll even out and get better eventually. They certainly can't get worse at any rate." Jeff took another drink, set his slender arms along the sticky black wood of the counter, and stared into the tempest outside.

Eddie took a swallow of his own. "Well, that's a more agreeable outlook than I expected. You really think you can keep your course steady and just wait for change to happen on its own?"

"I don't know. It's complicated. A steady job is nothing to scoff at in this economy. I can handle things for now, it's just…" Jeff took a long drink and shrugged, making no effort to complete his thought.

"Just what?" Eddie pushed. "Aborted self-expression isn't your style. What's going on?"

"It's only 6:00 p.m. Eddie, no need to trawl such depths just yet."

"Well, I'm genuinely curious, but you know I can't stay late on a school night. So, if you're getting to something…"

"Well, I guess I always just believed there had to be some underlying sense to all of this. You know, that beneath all the bullshit in this world, there must be some kind of meaning."

"Well, don't we all find our own?" asked Eddie.

"I get where you're coming from. You've got everything you need, everything you've ever dreamed of. No doubt that comes with exactly the sort of meaning I'm talking about. But it doesn't have to be dependent on others, does it? Families are great and all, but there must be some way to find meaning without finding it in someone else, right?"

Eddie sipped at the thick beer, but said nothing.

"I hope that doesn't sound harsh," Jeff went on. "I'm not trying to offend. Whatever works—whatever helps anyone get what they need—I support, as long as it's not hurting anyone else."

"Without their consent, of course," said Eddie.

"Without their consent," Jeff agreed. "I'm pro-just-about-everything, and I think it's a wonderful testament to our times that there are so many different roads to happiness these days. You know I'd never deny that, right?"

"Certainly not," Eddie confirmed. They'd known each other since their third year of university, and Jeff knew Eddie understood him in a way few others had ever even claimed to.

Jeff took a moment and finished his Guinness as he stared out into the rain. It showed no sign of slowing. "I guess I'm still just waiting to find my own meaning is all," he continued. "Maybe it's not in work. Maybe it's not in family, or art, or any of those places everyone else seems to find their passions—but it's out there. It has to be. I can put up with the bullshit at work, don't worry about that. I just hope that, sooner than later, I can find something that makes all the other stuff worth it. That's all."

Eddie finished his own beer, and pushed the empty glass up to touch Jeff's with a gentle clink. "I get that buddy, I'm sure you will. You're a good guy, things will turn around soon enough. In the meantime, can I offer you a ride home?" he asked, standing up and pulling a light windbreaker snug against his neck.

Jeff stood and opened the door for his friend. Having no jacket with him, he tucked his hands resolutely into his pockets. It was only seven blocks to his house, and he figured that, despite the awful storm and the growing chill, a bit of exercise and fresh air might do him well. "I'll make it, thanks," he said.

With a quick handshake, Eddie dashed off and slid into his car. Pulling away, he waved to Jeff as he drove off down the tree-lined block.

Jeff waved back until he lost sight. Then, he stepped out from the doorway onto the wet sidewalk, joining the rest of the fools, the unfortunate, and the desperate.

Leaning into the cold wind and the rain, he began his long walk home.

CHAPTER 2
A Day at the Office

"How long are we expected to wait?" asked Jordan.

Fair question, but the answer should be obvious, thought Jeff.

Jordan was a Team Lead like himself, and had been for only four months fewer than Jeff. Jeff admired his ability to speak out against SALIGIA so openly, although he questioned the effect it would have on his long-term employability.

Still, it was going on sixteen minutes now since the "Supervisory Consultation" meeting was meant to begin, and there wasn't a single supervisor to be seen. Everyone else was packed tight around the table, waiting for their bi-weekly opportunity to check in with management and learn what unexpected, senseless new direction their work would take.

Of course, with no supervisors, the meeting was pointless. It succeeded only in keeping them away from the tasks they were assigned, and for which the absent management team would ultimately hold them solely accountable.

"We wait as long as it takes. Can you imagine the reaction from 'the Brass' if they turned up to find a single one of us missing?" answered Rian. As overly-cautious as Rian tended to be, she had a good point.

'The Brass' was an old military term which had come into favour among the non-management workers at SALIGIA to refer to their gilded superiors—so often perceived as the puppet-masters of all their woes—who were despised, yet worshipped accordingly. The rest of the team, those who existed in the powerless purgatory below the Brass, were called 'the Tins.'

"Imagine what we could've got done in this time," Jordan fumed. "Hell, look around and calculate the money being wasted on a meeting whose very purpose is foiled by those who arranged it. Every second week this happens!"

"Isn't there something we can do together before they arrive?" It was Janice speaking this time. Janice was new, and it occurred to Jeff that he'd never seen anyone—at SALIGIA or elsewhere—try so hard to catch up, yet remain so overwhelmingly behind.

"The purpose of these meetings, Janice, is to receive updated statements of direction from management," said Adra. *Ever the bootlicker.* Jeff did his best to avoid Adra whenever possible. "Without that," she continued, "anything we try to do right now will be an outdated waste, and if you turn in something that's not based on current market realities, it can be far worse than turning in nothing at all, because they will rightly think you don't understand your projects."

Jeff lifted his coffee to his lips, determined by the steam that it was still too hot, faked a sip for good measure, and set it back down alongside his notepad and pen. He could think of a dozen places to jump into the debate, and twice as many strong stances to take on this familiar conundrum boiled below the calm surface of his mind, but his ten years of experience allowed only one thought to bubble up. *What's the point?*

Janice scratched her head for a moment, and a deep line marred her freckled face. "Adra, you and I are both working on the City Branding Initiative with Jeff, can't we discuss that while we wait?"

Jeff respected the youthful naiveté Janice still displayed on occasion. She'd only been with SALIGIA for two months now, and clung to some desperate belief that sense and logic would prevail if only she worked hard enough.

It would get her in trouble sooner or later, Jeff knew. "Janice, before looking at the City Branding Initiative, we have to get Marcy's updates on the Clean City Initiative. We can't go forward on either until then," he explained.

"What about my Green City Initiative?" interrupted Jordan. "Francis is going to want movement on that. Hey, isn't he your supervisor now too, Jeff?"

"Well, yes, but that's not really relevant. The Liveable City Initiative still needs confirmation of intention from the condo developers about their plans to build in the River Valley, so those two are at loggerheads. We'll need to hear from both Francis and Marcy to clear it all up."

"I thought Marcy was your supervisor?" said Rian.

"It's best not to ask questions like that," said Jeff. Everyone except Janice nodded their agreement. She just frowned, and took a timid sip from her coffee mug.

Reaching the end of his patience already, Jeff excused himself to the washroom, hoping the scene would be less absurd upon his return.

Stepping out the door, he turned right at the old, stained coffee machine which had been out of order for six months at this point—and pushed eagerly into the washroom.

Like everything else at SALIGIA Inc., the washrooms were considered state of the art. The moment Jeff finished his business, a great loud swooshing sound went bouncing back and forth between the pristine white walls, and a surprisingly sparse jet of water exploded against the porcelain bottom of the urinal, splashing over the rim and across Jeff's leather shoes.

"God dammit," he said. Sadly, he was more than familiar with the inevitable routine he'd been caught in once again.

Crossing the bathroom to the sink, he reached for the paper towel machine.

Nothing happened.

Waving his hand back and forth under the tiny green light caused a whirring sound, and a slight slip of paper towel wheeled its way out. Tearing it away, Jeff waited until the light—red now—switched back to green after several seconds, and repeated the motion four more times until he had amassed a stash of paper towel sufficient to dry his shoe.

He bent down to begin, but this motion was detected by the mechanized faucet, which shot a furious wave down into the sink, over its edges, and across his shirt, pants, and shoes. Jeff groaned, grabbed more paper towel, and set to drying off.

When he was finally finished, he placed his hands neatly beneath the nozzle of the sink. The light shone red, and nothing happened.

"For fuck's sake, do I miss taps," he said, waving his hand like some demon-possessed karate master until finally, another sharp jet of water exploded out, soaked him once more, then stopped. The light was flashing red again, meaning it would be another solid minute until the water masters saw fit to bless him with their bounty.

Jeff brushed his hands together briskly, and reached for more paper towel. This time, it seemed determined to withhold—no doubt using some complex SALIGIA-made algorithm to conclude that more than enough towel had been dispensed that day.

With a long sigh, Jeff accepted he'd have to make do, wiped his hands miserably across his pants, and walked back to the conference room.

Still, it was only the Tins around the table, and Jordan was rambling on as Jeff took his seat. "Well the Green City Initiative, one way or another, will require a reduction of clutter and an increase in natural green spaces—studies have indicated that it's vital to the health and wellness of the population, and that's not something that will just go away."

"You know," said Jeff, "I'll have to install a lot of signage for the Liveable City and City Branding initiatives, I could look into making those green. That way everyone wins."

Jordan grinned. Adra and Rian rolled their eyes.

Janice frowned. "Wouldn't that kind of defeat the point?" she asked.

Around the room, eyes bounced off each other, and Jeff wondered who would be the first to offer Janice the corporate insight she so clearly needed.

With that, the door of the big white conference room whooshed open, and the scent of fresh ground coffee and shoe polish filled the air. Marcy and Francis pushed through first, each hustling to be first through the door, which resulted in an awkward, bumping motion as they both spilled in together. Behind them, talking loudly into a Bluetooth headset about things that would undoubtedly impact them all shortly, came the manager, Nadia.

She was short, and had the slight frame of an adolescent dancer. Her cool demeanour was a blade of ice however, and she wielded her authority like the impenetrable shield it was. Her dark hair fell straight to her shoulders, and her smile held the threat of a coiled viper.

The room fell into a terrible, heavy silence as the Brass took their seats at the head of the long, dark table.

"Status?"

It took a while for Jeff to realize that Nadia was no longer speaking into her headset. Instead, she seemed to be demanding to know what they'd been working on in lieu of being able to work on what they were meant to be working on.

The dreadful pall of silence grew all the weightier, and all eyes turned down to the polished surface of the conference room table.

"We were just waiting for our project updates," said Janice. Then, battered by a barrage of incredulous expressions from the rest of her colleagues, she slouched down in her seat and chewed her pen nervously.

Nadia frowned—a withering, noxious frown undoubtedly perfected at some secret SALIGIA retreat none of the Tins could ever hope to access. "Waiting? Is that what we're paying you for?" she asked with a picture-perfect sneer.

Again, all eyes stabbed towards Janice, trying desperately to convey to her that most questions were best taken as rhetorical. She took the hint.

"I suppose that's to be expected," said Nadia, the seething frown never leaving her face. "Fortunately, SALIGIA can help with that. An Independent Working Workshop will be running from 3:00-5:00 p.m. starting next Wednesday. It's a seven-week course, and attendance will be mandatory. I believe it will be essential in helping all of you keep up your work ethic without this need for constant supervision.

"Of course, you are all presumed to be high-functioning adults, and this really shouldn't be necessary, but it will be freely provided by SALIGIA as a courtesy nonetheless. I look forward to observing your increased productivity. The results will be covered with each of you at your upcoming Supervision Sessions, which will be pushed up as a result of this lapse."

Jeff could hear his teeth grinding, and was impressed that not a single one of the Tins allowed themselves even a quiet groan in protest.

"Well, let's get started then." Marcy stood up, and moved over to a large whiteboard displaying all the active initiatives. Each initiative was headed by one of the supervisors. Nadia presided over them all.

Marcy was a tall, big-boned woman with rust coloured hair and squinty eyes. As she jotted notes under the initiatives she was leading, Jeff wondered what bet Francis lost to so willingly submit to Marcy taking the lead. Usually, they competed like rabid dogs over every little scrap Nadia tossed them.

"Today," continued Marcy, extending a long silver pointer towards her illegible scribblings on the board, "I want to focus on the Liveable City Initiative, as the deadline has been advanced considerably."

"How considerably?" asked Jeff, pulling at his collar and staring into his coffee. He noticed Jordan slouching down into the hard, sharp back of his chair. His projects would be off the table for discussion for the foreseeable future now.

Marcy popped the cap back off her marker, and began scribbling frantically on the whiteboard. "The River Valley development is officially a go. I'll need a full report, including cost breakdowns, by the end of the next week."

Jeff didn't care that his head literally dropped to his chest. The report—without costs—had previously been due a month from now.

Nadia pressed a button on her digi-pad, and finally looked up from it for a moment. She stared straight at Marcy, who froze on the spot, then flinched. A dark cloud blew across her beady eyes. She reached slowly into her pocket, and pulled out her own digi-pad.

Silent a moment, she stood staring at it as Jeff chewed his lip and wondered if the rainstorm which had started yesterday and thundered on through this morning was showing any signs of stopping.

Finally, Marcy reached up, rubbed a line off the board, and wrote over it. "End of this week," she corrected.

"The end of this week?" Jeff meant for it to be an exclamation of protest, but the sight of Nadia standing at the head of the room like a scorpion poised to strike forced a quick cost-benefit analysis in his brain, and it came out more as a polite request for confirmation.

"That's right," said Marcy, and turned back to the board with her pointer. "What's your current strategy for this initiative? I need to know the primary marketing tools you're looking at, projected audience, projected engagement, and estimated budget for my External Management meeting this afternoon."

Jeff took as big a swig of coffee as he felt he could possibly get away with. When he'd delayed as long as he could, he proceeded carefully. "Marcy, you told me last Thursday to put those projections off in order to weigh the impacts this initiative would have on the Clean City Initiative."

Nadia clicked her tongue, but kept her eyes locked on her digi-pad. As far as Jeff was aware, Nadia never sat, and though she was a physically small woman, she towered nonetheless over the sitting Tins and supervisors alike. Marcy frowned, a pitiful and desperate smear of momentary panic. "Jeff, the topic on the agenda right now is the Liveable City Initiative. You know very well that we bill our clients by time spent, and we cannot in good faith talk about the Clean City Initiative until it is brought to the agenda. Is it the current topic on the agenda?"

Nobody said a word. Jeff's toes twisted in his polished brown loafers, and he began to claw at the particleboard underside of the table as if trying to escape Shawshank.

"Janice?" Marcy called.

Janice—who clearly remembered just then that as the junior member of the team, she was responsible for updating the agenda and recording the minutes—nearly jumped out of her seat. Grabbing her pen, she bumped her coffee thermos and sent it crashing off the table and spilling across the floor. She stared furtively down at her obviously blank page, nodded, and looked up. "No. We're talking about the Liveable City Initiative right now," she choked.

"That's right," said Marcy, staring at Jeff matter-of-factly. "And clean that mess up," she finished, glancing back towards Janice.

Janice hopped up from the table and sprinted out towards the bathrooms for paper towel.

Francis sat still in his executive leather chair—grinning manically and undoubtedly relishing that it wasn't yet his turn to present.

Jeff heaved up his eyebrows, fortified his upper lip, and gazed towards Marcy, who was only half-watching him at this point, and half-watching Nadia. "Well," he said, "I can manage a good estimate of those projections by the end of the day if necessary." He braced himself for what was to come.

"The end of the day?" asked Marcy, nearly breaking her neck in her haste to seek Nadia's confirmation.

Nadia didn't look up from her digi-pad, and gave no discernable reaction.

A crash shook everyone out of the tense moment, and Janice exploded through the door with seven individual pieces of paper towel in her hand, as well as two bundles of printing paper. She had a small cut on her forehead, and her modest blue sweater was soaking wet.

Fucking bathrooms!

Janice hurried over to the coffee spill. She quickly used up all but two of her paper towels, then spread large stacks of paper over the remnants of the spill.

Marcy, still sputtering nervously, finally ventured to take back the room. "Fine," she declared with a jerk of her head.

Jeff exhaled, and sank back into his seat thinking of hammocks, rainforests, and weekends.

"Well then," continued Marcy, clearly feeling quite proud of herself. "I suppose that concludes the Liveable City Initiative's time on the agenda."

Again, a nervous hush took over the room.

Jeff glanced over at Janice, who was successfully pushing several separate piles of coffee soaked paper into one large, oozing stack. With the last two pieces of paper towel, she began to corral the escaping streams of coffee.

I wonder if she regrets that giant thermos now, Jeff thought. She was a scatterbrain, but Jeff liked Janice. At any rate, he hadn't yet found any cause to dislike her. She was new, and seemed a bit distracted to say the least. But she did her best to remain friendly, and in her two months of work so far, he'd never heard her say a bad word about anyone.

He hated to see her suffer, and could tell it was coming a mile away.

"Agenda!" he mouthed to her, faking a drink of coffee to conceal the effort from the Brass.

Janice sprang up, speeding over to her seat. Her first three steps created an audible splashing sound, and Jordan failed to stifle a quick chuckle.

Nadia clicked her tongue.

Marcy, nearly melting into the floor, was losing her composure. "Janice!" she called in a tone that might have been worth a note to HR. It would have inevitably been filed away a thousand feet below the tower, and never mentioned again.

"The Liveable City Initiative has been concluded on the agenda at 9:45 a.m.," Janice said first in a whisper, and then a second time, only slightly louder, but with a strange vibrato to it that made it almost musical.

Jeff smiled. That was one down.

"Onto the Clean City Initiative," declared Marcy, wiping all traces of the previous discussion off the board. "What have you got for us Jeff?"

"In order to comment on the Clean City Initiative in any meaningful way, I'll need to know the scope of the Liveable City Initiative—at least how many billboards will be involved," Jeff braced himself even as he said it.

Marcy gasped.

This in turn made Jordan nearly choke trying to contain his laughter. Adra and Rian gaped at Nadia, who showed no reaction.

Once everyone regained control of themselves, they all looked back up at Marcy. She seemed ready to finally scrap the rules on corporate violence—which was only permitted through implied threat and misapplied authority—and tear out the eyes of anyone she could reach.

"So, you have nothing for us on this agenda item?"

The room grew cool—the voice had been Nadia's. She wasn't looking at her digi-pad now. She was looking right at Jeff, who might have sworn just then he could see his breath.

At the mention of the agenda, Janice shot up straight as a ruler. Then, obviously tracing Nadia's eyes over to Jeff, she slowly leaned back, trying to align her position with Jordan to disappear from Nadia's view.

Occasionally referred to as 'backgrounding' by the Tins, this was a common trick that worked best using either of the Team Leads as cover. This was true not only because they were in the best position to receive deflected blame, but also because they were the tallest of the Tins. Jordan was the only one taller than Jeff on the floor, but suffered none of the gangly awkwardness Jeff so loathed in himself.

Realizing he was still expected to answer Nadia, Jeff shuddered. He wondered how much time had passed since she asked the question. Too much, no doubt. If he tried to bullshit his way through some kind of update, he'd inevitably tie himself into an unescapable knot, and likely end up with some twisted new dynamic added to the already painfully complex project. But the Clean City Initiative was primarily an effort to reduce corporate advertising in the city, and the Liveable City Initiative was a request from a client to canvas the city with corporate ads.

In the rare moments when he had time to reflect on his work, Jeff saw two possibilities. One was that the Brass could not understand how inversely connected the two initiatives were. Far worse, it could be that they understood all this perfectly well, but had designed this dystopian reporting system in order to avoid providing answers they knew they couldn't honestly give to people so low in the hierarchy.

More and more each day, Jeff suspected the latter.

He hoped the chill in the air since Nadia spoke had frozen time as well. Otherwise, he'd definitely stalled too long at this point. *I bet it's turned to snow outside*, he thought. *That would be just perfect.*

Swallowing hard, he finally spoke. "Not at this moment."

Silence.

"I can talk a bit about the City Branding Initiative, although that does share many of the same complications. The social media aspect is progressing nicely though."

Janice scribbled furiously.

Jeff wished there were windows in the room. He was convinced now that the rain must have turned to snow. A day like this could only end in a freezing walk and miserable bus ride.

Nadia looked over to Marcy, whose neck twitched slightly to the side before she spoke. "We are meeting with the City Council later this morning to hear some updated directives," she seethed. "We don't need any discussion on the City Branding Initiative until we've received our new mandate. Until then, don't offer up any public dialogue on logos, branding, or bylines. We may be going external for that."

Oh, fuck me, thought Jeff. "I passed the briefing to you last week—I've got a public engagement forum booked to discuss City Branding possibilities in the Victory Room this afternoon—we've got 250 confirmed attendees."

Nadia's glare nearly lifted Marcy off the ground. Her back arched like a demon-possession as her eyes rolled absently. "Marcy, that is not going to look good. You need to handle it. Meet Francis and I in the Executive Hall to prep for the Council meeting once you're done. Go."

Marcy turned as if on a pivot, and sped out the door.

Jeff, Rian, and Adra sipped their coffee. Janice reached for hers, remembered her embarrassment once she found it empty, frowned, and proceeded to continue scribbling in her notebook as if creating a manifesto.

Francis shifted uncomfortably, trying his best not to check if Nadia was looking at him now.

"Can I ask a few questions about the Green City Initiative?" asked Jordan.

Francis did nothing to conceal his frustration, but Nadia spoke before he could muster a reply. "I am afraid it is past 10:00 a.m. now Jordan, and we are going to have to wrap this meeting up."

Jordan couldn't help himself. He was a bit of a hot head, and in Jeff's opinion hadn't yet learned how to ride the waves in order to save the ship. "But I haven't received updates on any of my projects—I need some news!" he blurted. His face grew bright red under his dark crest of hair, and his lower lip trembled.

Fucking amateur, thought Jeff.

"Jordan," Nadia hissed, "perhaps if the team had not kept going off agenda, we would have had time to answer some of your questions. As it is, you will need to find those answers on your own. Please bring your findings to the update meeting next week.

"I have no doubt the upcoming Independent Working Workshop will be of special relevance to you. Please submit weekly learning reports to Francis once it commences."

Jeff could see the shimmering heat rise from Jordan's broad forehead. It was a brutal consequence, but a predictable one. Jordan put his work before his well-being, and should have known better.

If it's snowing, I'm going to wait inside, Jeff decided. He hoped it wouldn't make him miss the bus. It usually did.

Suddenly Janice yelped—a terrible, high-pitched noise that made everyone jump except for Nadia. Her ice-cold nerves would never allow such a reaction, even if she hadn't been staring straight at Janice as it happened.

In fact, Jeff soon surmised, it was her gaze which elicited Janice's yelp.

"The meeting is closed as of 10:04 a.m.," Janice murmured. Her face was downcast with a potent cocktail of remorse and dread Jeff knew all too well.

"I meant," said Nadia, "did you or did you not record all deviations from the agenda? You know very well that any reference to the agenda or deviation from the agenda requires a notary confirmation from the Agenda Recorder."

"I'm sorry, I missed them," said Janice. "All this agenda stuff just gets overwhelming sometimes."

Jeff gaped, and felt his collar tighten. Furious looks shot around the table like a bag of fireworks thrown on a fire.

You wonderful, stupid soul, Jeff thought. He was torn between respect for her apparent attempt to protect the other Tins, and annoyance with her short-sightedness.

"Is that so?" asked Nadia. "Well, there is a SALIGIA Seminar Series starting next week on Agenda Guidelines and Corporate Protocols. It will run over lunch for a period of twelve Fridays. I will have it added to all of your calendars." She rose without another word, and moved like a spectre of some cursed future across the room and out the doors.

Francis gathered his belongings and followed close on her heels.

The room exhaled. There was a brief moment of peace as people sipped their coffees and caught their breath.

Jordan stood up, pushed the doors shut with a click, and sat back down.

Then, all eyes turned to Janice.

"What the hell Janice?" Jordan started it off.

"Are you trying to get us more work? Cause that's how you get us more work!" Rian jumped in.

Janice slumped in her chair, but said nothing.

"Why would you admit something doesn't work, Janice? You

know what's going to happen. Seriously!" said Adra.

Jeff thought about the snow he still assumed would be piling up outside. He thought of snowballs, forts, and knit hats.

Piggy, piggy, he heard echo through his head.

"That's twelve hours you've stolen from everyone in this room," Jordan raged.

"Get over it," snapped Jeff. "Nadia would have found a way to get us into that bullshit anyways. Let's not turn on each other."

Everyone frowned, but the upbraiding was over. Rian finished her coffee. Jordan feigned a yawn. Then, they began to slowly file out to work on whatever they could manage.

Jeff sat still, sipping his coffee.

Janice stood, stooped, gathered up the soaking heap of coffee paper, and tossed it into the recycling. Then, she gathered up her notebook, pen, and empty coffee thermos, and headed for the door.

Jeff debated getting himself another cup of coffee from the carafe before heading to his office. For what felt like the millionth time, he'd need to pretty much start every initiative from scratch, and figured he could use the pick-me-up.

"Thanks for sticking up for me," said Janice, stopping in the doorway to stare back at Jeff. She looked confused, and sad, but she smiled at him nevertheless before she left.

Deciding the coffee wasn't really necessary, Jeff gathered up his work. *Not a bad start to the morning,* he thought. *Maybe the rain will stop before the day's over.*

CHAPTER 3
The Day Jeff Hatched his Plan

The next morning, Jeff awoke to the wailing of his alarm clock at 7:15 a.m., did a slow, groaning roll out of bed, and stumbled over to the window.

The rain hadn't stopped.

Edmonton wasn't usually accustomed to such long storms, but the weather could be unpredictable at the best of times. Heading into the third consecutive day of rain, Jeff had had just about enough.

Damn rain. He let the curtains fall shut and made his way to the kitchen, where he quickly threw out a greasy donair wrapper from the night before, and prepared to start his day.

The morning routine for Jeff was a matter of rote muscle memory. He had a quick cup of coffee while checking his social media—nothing. Then, he showered, styled, got dressed, and grabbed his lunch without a single thought interrupting the rigidly ingrained actions. The familiarity of this routine proved unfortunate when he left without grabbing his jacket.

God damn rain! he thought again, rather more venomously this time as he scurried from the threshold of his apartment building into the covered bus shelter just beyond.

Public transit in Edmonton was no better than the weather, and he waited a good long while—despite being on time for the scheduled stop—only to watch the first bus that came into sight

39

speed by with an Out of Service sign flashing in its window.

It wasn't just the soaking clothes, the growing chill, or the annoyance of having only himself to blame for his forsaken jacket. It was the oppression of it that really got to him. The inability to go out when you wanted without having to either dart strategically between short stretches of shelter or accept the bitter feeling of pelting rain. More than anything, it was the way everyone wanted to stay inside with their families—warm and safe and content—thus precluding any social interaction besides Marcy and Francis, Jordan, Rian, Adra…and Nadia…

Of course, there was Janice.

As the right bus finally pulled up, it sent a dark slash of drain water across Jeff's freshly washed pants. He stepped up into the bus with a roll of his eyes, and flashed his pass to the driver without looking at him.

"Thanks"—that's all she said, he reflected, trying to remind himself what a small and insignificant gesture it really was. Despite that, he was overwhelmed with its comparative import amid days on end without a word of praise, recognition, or basic human decency.

It's a cold world we live in—that every waking minute is wasted between trying to earn enough money just to keep going, and finding enough meaning to want to bother, he thought. Outside, the rain beat against the windows of the bus, running down in long, shimmering sheets and creating a racket like a dying engine on the roof of the bus.

Sometimes, he wondered how Eddie pulled it off. He was fairly certain his friend made only slightly more than he did. Of course, his wife Bonnie earned a decent bit as well.

Still, Eddie managed to own an entirely respectable house, and care for his seven-year-old while still meeting Jeff for drinks on a semi-regular basis and never losing that cavalier grin he'd worn since their third year of university.

Eddie, Jeff reflected, never even seemed to have a bad day. At any rate, he'd never shown it. Jeff had been told that it was important to show the world what you're feeling, or else risk feeling it longer than you need to. But he couldn't help admiring whatever mad concoction of bravery, idiocy, ignorance, or grace that held Eddie's course so straight and true.

I don't think I've ever been as sure of my path as Eddie is, he thought. He considered his job—the career he had striven so long to obtain, and worked so hard to advance in.

It did nothing for him.

The majority of the ride to work was passed in such sombre reflections. From one bus, to the LRT, to the next bus, Jeff pondered, but he failed to come up with anything that really moved him. There was nothing he looked forward to save the end of each day, and as he went to sleep each night he dreaded the coming dawn.

Through the bus window, he could make out amidst the wash of rain the tall, terrible tower of SALIGIA Inc. It looked like some wretched spore from a futuristic death-machine had taken root right along Jasper Ave, and had slowly leeched all life, water, nutrients, and decency in order to grow into the malignant abomination it was today.

Well, maybe not all the water, he admitted, stepping with a shoe-soaking splash out the door and rushing off with his hands over his head towards the staff entrance located in an alley on the far side of the street.

Jeff felt the weight of the air as he stepped through the door. It wasn't just getting out of the storm that made it feel dry and empty, it was the nature of the tower—like every breath gave a person just enough oxygen to survive, while sucking out everything wholesome and real they still had left inside.

The elevator always took forever, and Jeff resented every second he spent in the main floor foyer—full of fake plants, fake smiles, fake leather couches, and a real, imminent sense of urgent nothingness. The foyer of SALIGIA was designed as if it were a grand transit terminal in some major city far away. Vast and absurdly ornate, it was all done in deep, black marble, embossed here and there with golden plating fit for the personal quarters of an unchecked monarch.

Yet aside from a long reception desk covered by a rotating crew of smiling sycophants, it was primarily without function, and lifeless save for the constant scurrying of interns across its broad expanse. They hurried from one hallway to another, going from meeting room, to office, to boardroom, to conference call—always chasing the whims of their superiors, and most often dreaming about the break that was always just one last task away.

Jeff remembered those days well.

They were hectic and frenzied—bustling and uncertain.

Still, he was happier then. At least he thought so.

After a gentle chime announced its arrival, he stepped at long last into the mirror-lined elevator, pressed the button for the 82nd floor, and pushed his hands down into his pockets. Back in his intern days, he'd rushed faster, spoken clearer, and delivered more promptly than any intern since—or so he liked to imagine.

He'd been run ragged, and seldom stopped even for his legally mandated breaks.

It was that sense of purpose, as he recalled, that really drove him. A feeling of imminence, as if his every effort was building towards something far greater and more significant than he could possibly imagine. Back then, it felt like all the glory and meaning which he'd been promised as a child was just around the corner. Purpose and fulfillment sat poised to jump out at any moment, take him into their warm embrace, and hold him there forever content, thankful, and loved.

It hadn't happened yet.

Still, he ran, and smiled, and did his damn best to keep going, though on days like this, even the fumes of the tank were barely sufficient to push him through the shining elevator door and into the ominous black confines of Floor 82.

"Ding!" Went the bell, and Jeff pushed himself through nevertheless.

So, what does it take? he wondered.

The office floor was still relatively empty—Jeff was seven minutes early, a situation he had to accept due to the inadequacy of the city busses. Anyone that lived downtown or drove to work tended to arrive exactly on time. Nothing free for SALIGIA. Not ever.

Heading to his office, Jeff dumped his lunch on the desk, scooped up his coffee mug, and headed back down the long hall to the lobby.

Eddie has his family, and that's still not beyond me at this age, he thought. *I suppose it's our loved ones that must really make everything else worthwhile.*

Character, connection, personal integrity; that's what it all comes down to in the end, he concluded. Working in a place like SALIGIA though, not a single one of those were easy to hang onto for very long.

He rounded the corner and nearly crashed straight into Janice, who was standing behind someone Jeff didn't work directly with—Rudy (he was only half sure)—in line for coffee.

Evidently, the non-stop pleas of the administrative assistant,

Tali, had finally paid off. Since the old machine broke earlier that year, she'd been tasked with filling an old carafe twice daily on another floor and bringing it up for the staff. Every time she did, she begged anyone in sight to get the coffee machine replaced.

Now, atop the counter stood a disgustingly fancy, nearly man-sized monstrosity with glowing dials and blinking lights. Drink options scrolled across a screen—an endless loop of delicious possibilities with impossible names.

Tali was alternating between flipping through a humongous manual, and tinkering with the machine. Finally, she opened a great metal drum, and groaned as she hoisted it up and poured its contents into a steel grate at the top.

"It should work now," she said doubtfully. Her face looked like a chimney sweep's, with streaks of coffee grounds pushing up into her bleached blonde hair.

Jeff chuckled to himself. *That's what you get for complaining,* he thought.

Tali was pretty new, and would learn soon enough. Either that, or she'd disappear like so many others. Irma, her predecessor, had been unceremoniously fired for failing to properly recite the assigned corporate greeting when answering the phone one morning. Usually, this wouldn't matter, but it had been Nadia calling from an outside line, and so the consequences of her mistake were swift and terrible.

That was the thing about SALIGIA—you could get away with a lot sometimes, because the Brass cared too little to pay attention when it wasn't worth something to them. But fuck up with the wrong person watching, and you'd end up a ghost.

Irma had learned the hard way that Nadia was definitely the wrong person to make a mistake with.

It was a caustic, cruel way to live, but try as he might Jeff could find no better alternative. It was a corporate world, and he was just another cog in the machine. So, he sidled quietly into the coffee line, begrudgingly grateful for that small pleasure.

In front of him, Janice was holding her thermos loosely at her side. It was a tall, mint green abomination still visibly stained with lines of dried coffee from her mid-meeting mishap the day before.

"Good morning," she said, smiling absently in his direction.

"Is it?" Jeff asked without thinking. Immediately, he realized his error, but could think of nothing in the moment to correct the glaring audacity of publicly questioning the accepted pleasantries of office life. For a brief second, he glanced left, then right, half expecting SALGIA drones to sweep down upon him, shock him into a writhing mass of flesh and panic, drag him into the elevator, and up to the top floors where management would process him, reprogram him, and send him back down to the lower foyer to resume intern duties.

"What?" asked Janice.

Jeff paused, a moment of hesitation buffeting his body as he struggled to catch his mind up to his words.

What had he meant?

She was staring at him, still waiting in line as Rudy—or whatever the fuck his name was—prodded at the buttons, shifted his mug, and struggled to produce a mocha-frappe—whatever.

Janice's hair was pulled back into the general semblance of a bun, but long red strands poked this way and that, giving a bride-of-Frankenstein impression. Her eyes were tired and bloodshot, and heavy black bags dragged her face down toward the polished sable floor.

"It's raining," Jeff started, working desperately to justify his unthinkable breach of social norms. He could not, in the end, come up with anything even mildly work appropriate, and decided in that moment to hold his silence and hope for the best.

"Yeah," said Janice. She held her thermos straight down at her side, and Jeff saw small drips of old coffee leaking out. Passing a hand through her bird's nest hair, she gazed up at him with a weary sigh. "Fucking rain."

Rudy finished his ridiculous brew, and scurried off to drink it in the silence of his cubicle as he worked up the courage to open his e-mail and begin the day's routine. Or at least, that's what Jeff imagined.

As Janice stepped forward and lazily jabbed the button for a double black coffee, it occurred to Jeff that she was quite possibly the only person in the office he could relate to at this point. Her naiveté about the job was endearing, and reminded Jeff of his early days. There was something else though—she had an aloof, distant sort of attitude towards her colleagues that Jeff could only fake. It was a total unwillingness or inability to play the corporate games which the rest mired themselves in to survive.

He admired that in her. Still, he worried that her inexperience left her unable to fully process the existential terror of working for a corporate behemoth that not only didn't care about your essential humanity, but actively sought to snuff it out.

Jeff's day was already off to a bad start, and he felt the best approach was to keep his mouth shut and quit while he was ahead.

Fuck that, he decided on second thought. Besides, there was no metric by which he could really consider himself ahead anyways.

"Janice, are you doing okay?" he asked. It was a strange thing to say—borderline unconscionable in their current context. Still, he realized, it was the most sincere thing he'd said in a damn long time, and something about it kindled a warm ember in his ashy guts.

With a soul-wrenching screech, the coffee machine spat out the last of its dark excrement into Janice's thermos, only half filling it. She screwed the lid on tightly—doubly so perhaps—and looked up at Jeff with what he could only assume was an air of barely subdued irony. "I've got my coffee, what else can a girl ask for?" she said, and floated off down the hall to the long row of cubicles where the non-tenured employees took up their potentially temporary abode.

Jeff slid his own mug under the machine and pressed the button for a single black coffee. The machine hissed and spluttered, frothed and protested as the inner gears turned over on themselves as if struggling to process his unreasonable request.

Checking his phone as he waited, he saw that he had a team meeting for the City Branding Initiative in just ten minutes. There, he'd see poor Janice again, along with Adra, and do his best to supply direction to his team despite never getting a glimpse of it from his supervisor. Marcy, of course, would not be available for this low-level planning meeting.

Still the machine shuddered and wheezed, shaking the whole station as it shot a pathetic whiff of steam down towards Jeff's mug. The coffee-scented cloud dispersed into the air, and a red light glowed on the machine.

"God dammit." Jeff couldn't contain himself, and blushed as he felt the weight of all the eyes in the lobby narrowing on him.

Disturbing the corporate peace seems to be my lot in life today, he thought. A moment later, he accepted it as sacrosanct, grabbed up his moist but utterly empty mug, and marched back towards his office.

Unhappy, ill-content, and entirely under-caffeinated, he set his useless cup on his desk, grabbed up his notebook, and headed off on the surprisingly long journey toward SALIGIA Breakout Room 82-F.

Adra was already waiting when he arrived. She was seated—to Jeff's amusement—at the head of the table, with her business pad open in front of her and a line of three different-coloured pens spread out evenly alongside it. She held a neatly foamed cappuccino in her hand.

How does she do it? Jeff wondered. Adra was always the first in the office, which afforded her access to the best options on the coffee machine today. That much was self-explanatory. But at only twenty-four, she managed to show up looking like an executive, get the best of everything, and seemed to legitimately love the rat race that was life working for SALIGIA Inc.

It shouldn't be too surprising, I guess. Jeff took a spot on the side of the small faux-wood table and flipped through his crumpled notebook to find the right page. His only pen was somewhere in his left hip pocket, and he began to dig for it only after sitting down, creating a terribly awkward, lopsided jerking motion he was immediately self-conscious of, but too headstrong to alter.

Only a year and a half ago, Adra had been one of those eager, scurrying interns—jumping at her master's command and searching at every turn for ways to out-do her peers. She'd done well at both points, and had become one of the youngest team members on Floor 82—a distinction of moderate respectability.

The corporate ladder had honed her into an ambitious and smooth-running machine, and Jeff occasionally wondered if he'd seemed as cold and focussed as Adra when he'd come out of the intern program.

"Sorry I'm late!" Janice slurred as she burst in. Her declaration came right at the moment of Jeff's triumph. He pulled the pen from his pocket like Excalibur and held it aloft as if to prove he had indeed been searching for something with purpose, and not just spending far too long rooting in his pocket at work. SALIGIA HR could, after all, be quite strict about such things. Or so he'd been told.

Turning with a satisfied smile he immediately regretted, Jeff watched Janice scurry toward the far end of the table. She carried four large notebooks in a bear hug, with her filthy coffee mug sticking out from the edge clutched by two fingers, and she held a pen in her mouth—which explained the strange slur in her voice. Her hair was still a mess, and Jeff noticed that one of her shoes was only partly clasped.

What is it with this girl? he wondered. Janice hadn't come through the intern program like most of the team. She'd applied directly for the job, and no one really knew what she'd done before that. She must have been qualified—SALIGIA was no easy hop on— but it seemed clear at any rate that Janice wasn't trying to work her way up the ladder the way Adra was. She lacked the killer focus and icy chill indicative of the true corporate stooges. Most importantly, she seemed to take the inevitable setbacks personally, as if they impacted her more directly than the random whims of a psychotic corporate overlord had any right to.

For that reason alone, Jeff suspected she wouldn't last at SALIGIA. *At least,* he thought, *not without fundamentally changing who she is.*

"No worries, Janice," he said, finally finding the right page in his notebook. Reviewing it, he realized the prep work he intended to do the day before had never been completed, since he'd been distracted submitting last-minute projections for the Liveable City Initiative. Now, he was woefully under-prepared for this meeting as a result.

"Yeah, glad you could make it." No one could have missed the snide undertones of Adra's remark. Usually, Jeff wouldn't have cared, but he noticed Janice slouch self-consciously as she settled into her seat and began shuffling the over-stuffed notebooks in front of her.

"Well," said Jeff, hoping to cut the tension, "we might as well get started. So far, we know that our goal with the City Branding Initiative is to evaluate the current city branding efforts, identify weaknesses in those efforts, then design and facilitate a new re-branding campaign meant to get the city tagline into the mouths and minds of every resident."

"The tagline which is yet to be determined." Adra loved to point out the obvious.

"Are we meant to create it?" asked Janice.

"We'll advise on it, but the final call will be up to the City Council," Jeff confirmed.

"Is the scope of this initiative limited by the Clean City Initiative?" Janice chewed her pen as she spoke.

Adra rolled her eyes. "C'mon Janice, could it be any more obvious? This one wants us to increase branding throughout the city, and the other one wants us to reduce marketing clutter. What do you think? Besides, we shouldn't even be talking about the Clean City Initiative in this meeting."

"Well we're not supposed to be talking about the Liveable City Initiative either, but that's the one with a report due next week," Janice shot back.

"This week," Jeff corrected. He'd almost forgotten about that damn report. "But you're both right," he continued. "I'll schedule a meeting later today to finish up the report on the Liveable City Initiative. For now, we have to focus on the City Branding Initiative, for which we don't have a marketing tagline, a budget, or a clear definition of limitations due to its conflicts with other initiatives."

"I think we should run scenarios, and present them to Marcy," Adra started writing as she spoke. "We don't need the tagline to estimate marketing costs, so we could project several different levels of branding, tier the potential expenses, and just go with that until we have a clear directive about how to handle the Clean City—factor. We could also explore marketing avenues that don't interfere with that initiative, such as online marketing, radio, television, and the like."

Breakout Room 82-F had no windows, but Jeff could sense the rain still hammering into the sides of the tower. "That's a good plan Adra, I want you to look into those secondary avenues. Janice, you can handle the budget projections—let's aim for three potential scenarios."

Adra cleared her throat pointedly, "Jeff, I wonder if the budget projections might be a better fit for me."

Janice was picking at the dried flakes of coffee stuck to the side of her thermos, and either didn't notice or didn't care about the judgemental implications behind Adra's comment. Jeff wondered which it was.

"I think the assignments are fine as they are," he said. He wished there was a clock in the room, and even more, a clock that would reveal the day was somehow nearly over. Unfortunately, clocks were a rare occurrence in the office. Employees were expected to check the time on the official SALIGIA App, which also controlled room lighting, and temperature. Of course, the app could only be accessed by employees who owned or signed out a SALIGIA digi-pad, so the Tins spent far too many meetings entombed in dark, cold rooms, with little ability to gauge the slow passing of time.

"Jeff, this is going to be a crucial decision point for the initiative, does Janice even have the budgeting models needed to complete such a task?" Adra wasn't convinced.

"I've got the same access to our databases you do," Janice answered, not looking up from her efforts with the thermos.

"Adra, be sure to forward any potential cost projections to Janice based on your research," said Jeff. He pulled his phone out of his pocket—an action that would see him written up if one of the Brass caught him—and was disappointed to find that no large stretch of time had disappeared while he dithered away in this pointless meeting.

Often, time seemed to dilate in strange ways in the SALIGIA office, and what felt like hours were inevitably revealed to be mere minutes. At least a few times each week, Jeff felt like he'd already lived several terribly dull lifetimes at work. Meanwhile, his real life slipped away in an ever-hastening rush, stressing over the thought of another day at the office.

His phone lit up just then, and a message from Eddie played across the screen.

Beers this evening?

Jeff breathed a sigh of relief. Beers with Eddie were always a highlight of his week. Then again, the prospect would only make the present hours pass by all the more slowly.

"Okay," said Adra. "Janice, I'll get you some numbers by the end of the day, and I'll include some links to advise you on several different considerations you might want to make while incorporating them."

"Thanks," said Janice, her thermos now nearly clean, "but it's not really rocket science."

"This is important stuff!" Adra insisted.

"I'm certain Janice can handle it," Jeff said around a looming yawn.

"I'm just trying to help make sure everything is done right, Jeff." Adra leaned forward, set down her pen, and interlaced her fingers as she spoke.

Janice rolled her eyes. "Calm down," she said.

Adra fumed. "It's not a joke Janice. This is our career, and I care about the results whether you do or not!"

Now, Janice set her thermos down on the table with a thump. She leaned over to meet Adra's fierce gaze with a broad, composed smile. "I know this will be a shock to you Adra, but you can't possibly imagine how little I care about what you think of me."

Jeff let a chuckle slip out before realizing how inappropriate it was, given his position. He also realized with a sudden thrill that he really didn't care either.

"Alright you two, that's enough. You've got your assignments, so go get to it. I'll work on tracking down updates for the other initiatives, and will let you know anything pertinent."

With a loud huff and miserable pout, Adra hurried out of the room.

Janice remained seated, and sipped quietly at her coffee.

"Are you okay?" asked Jeff.

"I'm not worried about Adra," she answered. "I know what her type thinks of me and I'm not bothered by it. I do my job, and I go home. If there's a problem with my work, I'll hear about it from you—or Marcy—or Nadia," she finished with less certainty than she began.

"No problems on my end." Jeff smiled, "Just let me know if you need anything."

Janice gathered up her reams of notebooks, her thermos, and her pen. "Thanks Jeff, you're one of the good ones," she said, and scampered off to her cubicle.

Jeff headed back to his office. He set a meeting for the Liveable City Initiative within the next ten minutes, and spent the rest of the morning trying to track down Marcy or Francis to get the necessary updates on how his initiatives could find an actionable middle ground. At this, he was unsuccessful.

The meeting came and went quietly enough. When he'd finally cobbled together a functionable report on the Liveable City Initiative, he logged into the SALIGIA App on a digi-pad at the front desk to submit it, only to find a note that the due-date was changed to that morning, and it was already so late that it was unnecessary. Marcy was very displeased.

Fucking typical.

Just as the day began to wind down and the idea of walking out of the office and towards a good long chat with Eddie began to feel like an achievable reality, Jeff's phone lit up again. Eddie was needed at home by his wife, and would have to reschedule their plans.

That always seemed to be the way. A person could spend their entire day with one goal in mind—one bit of light at the end of the tunnel to guide them through the agony of work, forced social interaction, and tense, fearful reality. Then, just as they emerged into the real world, that light could be snuffed out like nothing, and all the hope and anticipation that had driven them would vanish. Then, the evening would stretch out long, bleak, and cold, promising only to herald in another day of the same bullshit.

It was enough to break a person's spirit. On any other day, Jeff may have felt just that.

Today though, he walked away from the office with a rare spring in his step. Eddie was lucky to have a family that needed him, and Jeff knew he was lucky to have a friend like Eddie in his life. But as he stepped onto the bus and brushed the cold trails of rain from his arms, he knew that wasn't the only thing he was grateful for.

Certainly, he would have liked to see his friend, and enjoy a nice beer in one of his favourite bars. It would have been fun to tell Eddie about the ridiculous expectations at work, and the ability of all his superiors to somehow disappear whenever their leadership was needed most. He'd have loved to hear about what Eddie's class was up to, or his family's vacation plans, or whatever else Eddie might have had to share.

More than anything though, Jeff realized that he wanted to tell Eddie about Janice. For the first time since he started with SALIGIA, he had a co-worker he related to. *"Do my job, and go home"*—that was exactly it. In that moment, Jeff understood Janice's strange detachment. He felt in perfect harmony with her disinterest in all the bullshit office politics that seemed to suck in everyone else like some vapid vortex of paranoid loathing.

Above all, he finally understood the sense of brooding emptiness he'd always perceived in her—because he had it too. It was the natural result of putting a decent person in such an indecent place, but he liked to think he'd learned to cope with it over the years.

Janice hadn't learned that yet, and it seemed to Jeff that she might need a lifeline to make the job a bit less soul-crushing.

He certainly needed that on his worst days.

It was something he could offer because he'd been there, and he understood. He wanted to show her that it wasn't hopeless, and that there were still things in life that made all the rest worthwhile.

As he thought about this new plan, the stale bus air grew crisp and clean in his lungs, and his tired muscles hummed with energy.

Outside, the rain still cascaded against the windows, catching bits of mud and old streaks of grease. Where it passed, the window was left clearer, and Jeff could make out the beautiful green of the grass by the sidewalk. Above him, through the shine of the newly clean windows, he thought he caught a distant glimpse of clear blue sky.

CHAPTER 4

The Day the Rain Stopped

The alarm clock's howl came less loud, and Jeff rose from his bed without any groan, complaint, or desperate slamming of the snooze button.

He proceeded through his morning routine with a vigour he hadn't felt in a good long while, and it was not until he stepped out the door and reached the bus stop that it occurred to him that the rain had finally stopped.

The sun shone brightly, and the orange of the leaves was brilliant in its radiance. The cool air smelled more natural than it tended to in a city driven by industry and oil.

Jeff stood outside the bus shelter, taking it all in with a broad grin. *Days like this are rare for August. Best to make the most of it.*

Truth be told, Jeff planned to do just that.

Imagining everything he hoped to get done that day, the commute passed quickly, and as Jeff stepped through the elevator door onto Floor 82, a smile spread across his thin face.

What the hell was that? he thought with a shock. A smile from Jeff in the SALIGIA office was an unusual event, and utterly unheard of in the early morning. Anytime before three, really, was pretty much out of bounds to any but the most facetious of sneers.

Today is all about new perspectives. He truly meant it. Today, he'd determined at some point between laying down to sleep last night and waking up, was the day he'd turn himself around, challenge his old habits, and work to become the man he'd always felt he was destined to be. That started with looking inward, tempering his ego, and most importantly, with helping others. Charity, after all, was the chief of virtues; he'd been told that at one point, and it resonated with him to this day.

Jeff had it all planned out.

Glancing over to the technological terror that was their coffee machine, he was disappointed to see that Janice wasn't there—spilling her coffee, cursing the machine, or juggling too many papers in the crook of her tiny arm. Classic Janice stuff.

Not to worry—there was another update meeting for the City Branding Initiative first thing in the morning, and he'd see her there at any rate. He was looking forward to it, which came as a small surprise, but Janice was a kind person in a building full of vipers, and if he could do anything to make her time at SALIGIA more bearable, he was happy to help.

I sure would've appreciated the same when I was starting out.

"Jeff!" The voice startled him for only a moment, then he felt a sudden surge of stress as he realized it was Marcy's.

"I have some great news," she continued. "As you know, SALIGIA Inc. realizes that its workers are its most valuable commodity, and we've decided to show our support even more directly!"

Swallowing down a sudden lump in his throat, Jeff replied. "What does that mean in practice?"

Marcy beamed. "Yesterday, SALIGIA officially implemented an exciting new approach to employee benefits. Effective immediately, everything from medical care to mental health support is being handled internally whenever possible, ensuring the very best and most consistent care for all of our staff members."

Jeff didn't like the sound of that. Marcy could be a surprisingly confident and outspoken person—when Nadia wasn't around at any rate—but anything that got her this fired up had to be dismal indeed.

"We've acquired all transferable personal files for our employees, and reassigned existing support services to internal SALIGIA staff as available. Of course, we always seek the best fit possible. I am excited to tell you that your former therapist has been terminated, and your therapy file has been transferred to yours truly!"

If Marcy expected anything but elation from Jeff, she had a funny way of showing it. Nonetheless, elation is not what Jeff was feeling. Horror, exposure, betrayal—even a twisted, cynical amusement may have fit the bill.

"You're a psychologist?" was the only response he managed.

"There's a lot you may not know about me Mr. Boggs," Marcy said with a ridiculous grin. "But no, I may not be a psychologist, but I do happen to have my undergrad degree in psychology, which was the closest fit on our floor. Just think how much more personalized your care will be from someone who knows and works with you, rather than some cold, detached stranger!

"And besides that," she went on, "SALIGIA is confident that it's in better compliance with current mandates to provide supports internally, no matter the specific qualifications."

The relevant mandate was definitely the almighty dollar, Jeff thought. An anxious knot grew in his stomach. "Detached" was actually one of his favourite traits in his former therapist. Eyeing a big manila folder clutched under Marcy's right arm, he expected the situation was only going to get worse before this strange day was over. "Is that—" he began.

"It sure is!" Marcy burst with excitement, her round face nearly splitting into halves as even as the part in her long auburn hair. "Your personal therapy file! I've only been able to peruse it briefly last night when I received the assignment, but I'm eager to dig in deeper. I've booked us the Endeavour Room—it's usually reserved for management, but I've convinced Nadia that therapeutic services deserved the comfort. Let's go."

"Sorry, but…I have an update meeting for the City Branding Initiative starting, well, now actually."

"Oh, don't worry about that. This is important, Jeff. I'll have your update meeting cancelled, and you can rebook once we're done. Come on now," she finished, typing into her digi-pad what Jeff could only assume was a cancellation order for his meeting as she led him off down the South Hallway.

Imagining tumbling dominos as he traced the cascading complications this would inflict upon his delicate schedule, he followed haplessly along until the way became unfamiliar. Jeff was seldom allowed to venture down this hall, and soon enough he was entirely lost.

For the most part, the South Hallway tended to be reserved for executive suites, management rooms, and other novelties well above his pay grade. Even Marcy barely made the cut. She made two quick turns with Jeff at her heels, then scanned her key card, opening a dark wooden door.

The room inside was like nothing Jeff had ever imagined, considering the otherwise dour confines of the SALIGIA offices. In fact, he realized, he'd never really stopped to wonder exactly what went on in the Management Wing, but the elegance caught him off-guard nonetheless.

It wasn't ostentatious by any means. It was simple, functional, and classy. It was also undeniably top shelf. Even to Jeff's untrained eye, it was obvious the room spared no expense. Two long couches faced each other at opposite sides from the door. They looked to be made of a material softer and more supportive than Jeff knew existed, and a quick passing touch only confirmed this suspicion. The hardwood floors were covered between the couches by what appeared to be the skin of some undoubtedly extinct animal, and the lamps in each of the four corners were like glowing stones atop pillars of silver.

The bench between the couches was a raised rectangle, and if it wasn't carved from solid onyx, it did a fine job of concealing that fact. It was covered with fine—and full—crystal decanters, which Jeff had to assume were off limits even under the auspices of the therapeutic bond.

The most impressive touch though, was the far wall as Jeff entered. It was a deep fish tank replete with coral, rocky hiding places, and populated by fish, eels, and other marine life which Jeff knew little-to-nothing about.

"Please, have a seat," said Marcy. She sat on the couch to their right and began poring eagerly over Jeff's file. "So, Jeff, I'm sure this transition seems abrupt, but I want you to think of me no differently than—" here, she paused, flipping frantically through her notes, "—Cicely, was it? Yes. In this room, I promise you that I am not your supervisor and direct superior. I'm just Marcy, your therapist. Now, where do you think we should begin?"

The way she stressed the "you" in her sentence only assured Jeff that she had absolutely no idea where to begin.

None of this seemed appropriate to Jeff in the least. In fact, he wasn't even sure any of it was legal. But he'd learned long ago that appropriate, legal, normal, or fair were not words SALIGIA concerned itself with. Sadly, he'd concurrently learned that when a corporation had the money and influence SALIGIA had, they tended to be right about that and any other special exceptions they saw fit to make.

"Relax, Jeff." Marcy must have read his mounting anger. "I promise, this process is for you. It's totally confidential, and what we say will not leave this room. You're safe here."

She looked up from the page she'd been reading and smiled at Jeff. The muscles of his face twitched beneath his skin, and he was grateful for his love of poker—owing to that alone his ability to keep a straight face.

Of course, everything she said was bullshit, and Jeff knew it. He remembered a very similar speech being given before an Anonymous Employee Satisfaction Survey was distributed. He also remembered the hassle of operating short-staffed when four members of the team mysteriously decided the next day to never return.

Their belongings were carted off quietly, and grinning replacements showed up within the week.

No one lasted at SALIGIA if they didn't quickly learn that nothing was safe, and nothing was sacred. You had to look out for yourself, because there were pitifully few who would ever help you if they didn't stand to gain from it.

Unfortunately, helping yourself often meant playing along with the whims of corporate. "Well…" Jeff began, wanting only to burn away enough time that Marcy might suddenly decide her alleged talents were needed somewhere else. He prayed for a sudden buzz from her digi-pad to pull her away, or a page to demand she join the other supervisors somewhere else in the Executive Wing—leaving him alone with the decanters for even a moment.

At this point, Jeff would have even been thankful for an alarm to announce a fire in the building. He trusted his chances in the ensuing evacuation far better than he trusted Marcy.

"Well," he began again, realizing the extent of time which had passed since his first effort, "how caught up are you in my file? Are you sure now is the best time?"

Marcy laughed at this—a long, strained, wavering sound. "Oh Jeff, I've already coded this as Therapy time in my logs, so there's no going back now. Don't worry about me though, I'm a fast reader. We can cover whatever you think is important, and I'll review your issues as they come up."

"Issues?" Jeff repeated. He'd never heard Cicely use that word before.

"That's what we're here for after all," said Marcy, perusing again through his file. It looked more extensive than he would have imagined. "You appear to be a far more reflective person than I took you for, Jeff. I believe this experience will not only be beneficial to you, but to our understanding of one another as well.

"I see a lot of serious existential reflection in here," she continued. Her voice disclosed none of her feelings as she flipped slowly through the long, legal-length pages. "You've spoken about your hopes for a family, and how you're beginning to doubt that will come to pass. You've talked about your dwindling pool of friends, your fear of being left alone, and…oh this is interesting…your belief that the life you'd been 'sold' as a child was a lie, and that nothing is really as meaningful or worthwhile as you'd always been told. That sounds promising, Jeff, do you want to talk about that?"

Jesus Christ, thought Jeff. He'd never heard it all read out like that, and whether those were his own words or Cicely's impressions he couldn't tell. Still, it was a fair enough assessment, which made it all the more damning.

It wasn't Marcy's fault though—at least not entirely. In his more honest moments, Jeff had to admit he didn't think Marcy was entirely evil. She was cold, true, and she toed the corporate line to the detriment of everyone beneath her. But Jeff remembered when she started at SALIGIA, and had watched her ascent into the Brass. At the end of the day, they both answered to the same overlords.

Nadia on the other hand…

He imagined her narrow eyes, her tightly-pursed lips, and the chill that accompanied even her most forgiving glares. It was like he could see her right before him.

As the manager of Floor 82, she was SALIGIA-incarnate, and could only be described as cruelly mechanical. In fact, Jeff had wondered more than once if she was SALIGIA's prototype for a state-of-the-art management-bot. Direct, even-toned, interested only in profit, and utterly unconcerned with how she made those around her feel.

It was 2026 after all, and Jeff reasoned that there must be robots somewhere, lurking about, ready to make his life more miserable. If that was the case, Nadia was the only contender he could think of.

Shit! Jeff shook himself from his distracted reveries, and found he'd been staring absently into the eyes of a huge, hideous piranha floating menacingly near the glass of the fish tank.

What did she ask? If I wanted to talk about the sad existential crisis my life has become?

The bitter truth of the matter was that Jeff could only think of one thing he'd like to talk about less. That thing, however, was his frustration at work, which was all too closely tied to every other problem in his life. He'd covered it extensively with Cicely, and feared that at any moment Marcy would find the right page and realize SALIGIA was at the root of all his complaints. Then, he'd be shackled, dragged from the building by security, and tossed headfirst into the dusty street.

He needed a distraction.

"Actually, things may be looking up. I have a date this Saturday." Jeff hoped against hope this would be a sufficiently positive sign for Marcy to immediately decide on a discharge. Any proof of a contented worker should suffice to absolve SALIGIA of potential liability, he reasoned.

He could think of no other reason for any of this.

"A date?" asked Marcy. "That does sound like progress, Jeff. How did you meet? Is it serious?" She closed her folder and leaned forward.

Jeff nearly cheered aloud. His play for a distraction couldn't have worked better. "I don't know yet," he replied in a moment of honesty. "We met online, and it's just a first date. Still, might as well hope for the best."

"The best?" Marcy pondered. "What would that be?"

Small, silver fish flitted along the glass right beneath the maw of the great piranha. Jeff wondered how they'd evaded him for so long, and how often he bloodied the tank with one or two of their carcasses.

"The best that anyone could want," he answered. "It's still early. I mean, I haven't even met the woman in person yet. But if it turned into something more meaningful, even permanent, I suppose that would be nice."

"You suppose?"

"Well, shouldn't I?" asked Jeff. What was so unreasonable about wanting a connection? "I mean, that's what I'd always imagined as a kid—the path that was always described. I guess I always just assumed that was what would happen. Now, if it finally did, it would be a relief, I guess. Because as things stand, well…the intended path was lost long ago, and—"

"Jeff," Marcy barged in, "that's a great insight. It sounds like things are coming together, but…" she started flipping through the file again, her brow furrowing, "…what's this about a 'knit hat incident'?"

The school of silver fish disappeared into a cranny in the rocks, but from the other side of the tank floated a plump, bright blue fish Jeff could only assume was from some tropical paradise he would never see.

It took a moment to process what Marcy had asked. It wasn't that he didn't know what she was referring to. That day on the playground with Katie was never far from his mind, but hearing it referenced by Marcy was a terrible shock. He never spoke openly about it to anyone but his closest friends—it was too obscure, and too long ago.

At this point in his life, that incident was primarily reserved for occasional chats with Eddie, his former therapist Cicely, and his own vapid internal monologues.

The idea that Marcy of all people now had access to this strange, secret part of him sat heavily in Jeff's gut, and a twitch shot through his shoulder, down his back, and settled somewhere just above his knee.

The tropical fish locked eyes with him, floating sideways towards the center of the tank.

"The knit hat incident?" he repeated, stalling for time. Why the hell did Marcy care about the knit hat incident?

"Yeah," she pushed, "it says here you called it the best moment of your life. What made it so special?"

He didn't need to search for the words. He'd said and thought and felt them a million times before. He was, however, surprised to hear them coming out so freely in such an oppressive context.

"Well," he began, wishing he hadn't, but feeling utterly unable to stop now, "I guess it was one of the only times when I felt like I was doing exactly what I was meant to be doing.

"To me, that one short experience was the perfect example of how the world, life, and people should be. It was like a confirmation of all my childhood expectations. Since then, each day has been more disappointing than the last, and slowly, that childish optimism has slipped further and further from view. Sometimes, I worry I'll never be able to recapture it."

"What exactly are you trying to recapture?"

Jeff watched the blue fish drift closer to the piranha. "It's not an easy thing to explain, but it's always felt like I have this bottomless well of talent, love, and skill to offer, if only anyone would ever need any of it. I'd sit alone sometimes in silence—in bars, at work, or anywhere else, just waiting for the person who needed me to recognize I was there. There waiting, and so painfully willing to jump in, take part, and give it my all at the slightest cue.

"But that cue never comes, and all that potential is wasted. Now, I sometimes wonder whether it has withered away in atrophy—or if it was ever there at all." The face of the piranha was long and green and awful to look at, and its mouth bobbed open and closed as the fat tropical fish floated slowly closer.

"It sounds like you're eager to be a part of something meaningful, Jeff. I think that's very noble." Marcy scribbled in her notebook as she spoke, and Jeff studied her for a moment, an awful feeling of doubt gnawing at the back of his throat. He half suspected that little revelation would land him another initiative to lead. Honesty never helped anyone here, and he wondered why he'd opened up like that to begin with.

A quiet minute passed before Marcy spoke again. "What do you think would make you feel that way again—the way you felt on the playground?"

Save for the fish, Jeff was done with this whole scene. He wanted to get back to his office. Back to his work. Back to his team, and back to Janice.

The tropical fish was too close now. It seemed to be tempting fate as it drifted right up to the gaping maw of the huge predator. The piranha's teeth were yellow and sharp, but its eyes were pools of black—unrevealing of their savage desires.

"Sometimes," he finally started, "I think there could still be a chance to find out where I belong. It wouldn't take very much. All the pieces are in place; the gears are built, the machinery is all there, it's just got to start turning, and click into place. It just needs a helping hand. Then I think I could feel that way again. I don't know why it hasn't happened yet. It just…hasn't."

There was a spot of blue before a wall of green and black as the tropical fish swam right in front of the piranha's mouth. It stared out at Jeff like it had no idea how close it was to facing eternity.

Marcy leaned forward, staring intently at Jeff. "You know," she said, "I can tell you're distracted. Did you know that SALIGIA studies have found that watching tropical fish can reduce stress levels by as much as seventeen percent? That's why we have them in here. I see you watching them—I've done the same. They really are something.

"But," she said, standing abruptly now, "SALIGIA has also found they can be a distraction that reduces productivity. That's why we can't have them in the common areas. Don't worry though, they'll be here for you next time.

"I'm afraid our time is up for today. Go handle your work, Jeff. This went very well. I'm proud of you."

Jeff's mouth hung agape, and it took him some effort to close it. When he looked back up, the tank appeared empty—the fish no doubt scared to the back by Marcy's sudden movement.

She opened the door, and Jeff started back to his office.

The whole way there, he wondered how much longer it would have taken for the water to turn red. It seemed unfair to him somehow, to have the payoff of the whole dull ordeal snatched away like that. Then again, Jeff's father had always told him that life wasn't fair.

The rest of the day went by in an empty, colourless haze. No blue fish, no green piranhas, no red water. Jeff remembered little he said or did beyond sitting in his office, walking to the coffee machine, or staring at his phone behind his closed door. Finally, as he hurried to the elevator with his empty lunch bag in hand, he stopped in his tracks at the sight of poor Janice on her hands and knees, cleaning up yet another spilled coffee with a sloppy clot of soggy napkins.

All that forced conversation and accidental soul-searching must have left him desperate for a bit of real honesty, because without thinking about it, he asked her to join him for a real drink once she was done with the spilled one on the floor.

"What?" She glanced up from the mess. Her frazzled expression told Jeff her day hadn't been much better than his. "Yeah, sure. But how about some help first?"

And so, twenty minutes later, Jeff was perched in front of the long black bar at an underground club called River City Revival House. The bar was shiny and slick, and the music was loud. The patrons came in all shapes, sizes, predilections, and styles. Jeff was fond of the place, and would have visited more often if it wasn't downtown—and thus so close to SALIGIA. He was thrilled when Janice suggested it.

The whole cab ride over though, he'd feared they might end up getting there only to find they had nothing to talk about beyond the office. "Do you have time tomorrow for a City Branding Initiative update meeting?" he asked.

He regretted it immediately.

Janice rolled her eyes. It wasn't a subtle, secretive motion. Instead, she looked right at him, and did it as pointedly as a person could possibly roll their eyes. Like pinwheels, or roulette games at a carnival.

Jeff grinned.

"Did you really bring me here to talk about work?" she asked, taking a drink from the Old Fashioned she'd ordered.

Janice was kind. She was clumsy, honest, and one of the most endearing people Jeff knew. In that moment however, he saw another side of her which surprised and thrilled him. Janice was sarcastic. She may have even been showing a bit of cunning.

"Well, I can avoid talking about the initiatives at least, I promise you that," he smiled as he said it. She'd called him out—which meant the rigor of their professional relationship was diminished here amid the thudding bass, clinking glasses, and the smells of wet wood and leather.

"That's probably for the best," she said, "otherwise, I'd have to code this time as a consultation in the SALIGIA App, which would most likely conflict with the number of these I'm hoping to put back." She swirled her Old Fashioned in the air before taking another sip.

No straw, Jeff noted. He was happy to see that Janice was more comfortable outside the office. "Who knows what SALIGIA views as conflict at this point?" he asked, taking a sip of his own beer but wishing he'd gone with a cocktail as well. "With these changes to our benefit plans, I've now got Marcy as my 'internal therapist.' If that's not a conflict of interest, I don't know what is!"

"What? That's insane! These fucking benefits changes are ridiculous. I've been following every bit of news since they were announced, just waiting for the bombs to drop."

"They were announced before today?" Jeff asked.

Janice chuckled. "Details have slowly been leaking out by e-mail for months. Don't you read the Corporate Communications?"

Jeff took a drink, then another. He thought about the constant barrage of useless updates he got from the countless levels of bureaucracy at the office. E-mails to tell him the internet went down, and e-mails to tell him it was back up. Funny how they always arrived together. There were e-mails to tell him that managers he'd never heard of would be out of the office for an hour, and e-mails to announce when they were back. For every one of these, there would be a handful of mindless oafs that reply-all some asinine response.

He was in his second year when he'd gotten into the habit of automatically deleting everything from a SALIGIA Corporate account without second thought.

"No," he admitted.

"Your loss. It's been a wild ride," said Janice. "So far, all the medical specialists are unchanged—they're just contracted through SALIGIA now. I guess they decided that some types of coverage represented too high a risk to fully internalize. So, for me it's a loss of privacy, but not coverage. Who knows though? Given your experience, it might just be a matter of time. If they end up scrapping my health coverage—or having it transferred to some internal dork instead of a proper doctor—I'll lose my mind!"

The water condensing on Jeff's pint glass was beginning to run down the side—cold and slick against his hand. It gave him a strange feeling, like there was something he shouldn't have forgotten. "I'm sure they'll figure out a way to wrap in the medical coverage too. Why not have Francis be your doctor if Marcy can be my therapist?"

"It's not exactly my doctor I'm worried about—although maybe that would change if Francis was the only option."

Jeff laughed. As indecisive and potentially incompetent as Francis was, that nightmare scenario was an undeniably funny image.

Still, talking to Marcy was no picnic either.

"Good god was it awful," said Jeff. "I mean, can you imagine having to talk to Marcy about your innermost thoughts, as she flips through a file containing everything you'd ever spoken to your former therapist about? It was surreal. I felt like I was on some sadistic gameshow." He was surprised with how open he felt. If his session with Marcy had gone like this, his "issues" might have been cured by the end of it.

"SALIGIA would probably get behind outsourcing our coverage to a prank show if it offset the costs," said Janice. She picked at the orange rind in her drink with one thumb.

"It might actually make the experience a bit more fun," said Jeff.

Janice scrunched up her bushy eyebrows, then continued after another sip of her drink. "So, how did Marcy handle the role? Did she keep texting Nadia for advice? Did she remind you that at SALIGIA, no one is as productive as everyone? I'm honestly pretty curious—but only if you're comfortable discussing it."

Not very much surprised Jeff, but the fact that he did in fact want to talk about it hit him like a truck. "It was weird, she clearly hadn't read my file, and had no idea where to begin. Of course, she's not even a real therapist, so she wouldn't have known anyway, I guess."

"It's really unfair you have to do that with your supervisor. Are you sure you're okay talking about all this?"

"Yes," Jeff replied, never stopping to question his wisdom. "You're right, it is unfair, but maybe it's not the worst thing in the world. I mean, it could have been Nadia. She'd have read the entire file and already had a dozen conclusions and action items prepared for me. Marcy just asked what I thought we should talk about, then kept interrupting with things from the file that she found interesting."

Janice looked over at him. "What did you want to talk about?"

For the first time since they'd sat down, Jeff felt uneasy. How could he answer a thing like that, when the answer would only make things more confusing than they already were?

The water from his glass was forming a small pool around the heel of his hand, and again Jeff had that strange feeling of something left behind.

What did I want to talk about? he wondered, only half knowing the answer himself. He wasn't sure how to explain any of it to her, and thinking back on it was like looking through a smudged lens.

Fortunately, he noticed that their drinks were empty, and ordered another round—switching his to a Moscow Mule, and toasting Janice when they arrived. "To the horrors of SALIGIA," he offered.

"Well said!" She clinked her glass to his.

Twirling the copper cup in his palm, Jeff ran a hand through his long hair. "Mostly, I guess we just talked about what I want. In life I mean, not at work," he corrected hastily. "You know, that satisfaction the old rock stars could never find. Every time I got close to expressing it though, Marcy would take the conversation somewhere else. To be honest, I don't know if she was the right choice for my therapist."

Janice laughed, then feigned astonishment at his revelation.

"I don't know." He sighed. "As soon as I step into that damn building every day, the energy bleeds out of me. The moment I leave my door—the thought of dealing with all the ridiculous systems, approval processes, and redundant management makes my skin crawl. Sometimes I daydream about just never going back. Not quitting, just not showing up anymore—drawing a line for myself. Lately I really feel like I might actually do it, if not for…" he stopped himself here, and took a nervous gulp from his drink, "…well, I need the money obviously," he finished.

"There are plenty of places to make money though, Jeff. Why not leave? You're clearly not happy with SALIGIA. You've got a lot of potential—why not find a place that sees that?" She took another long sip, and the neon lights of the bar played off her highball glass, creating a dizzying lightshow.

Jeff wondered if his smile looked as fake as it felt. "Potential?" he asked.

Again, Janice pushed at the orange rind in her drink, picking off tiny pieces which stuck under her long thumbnail. "Jeff, you have to know you're the best of them at SALIGIA. You're the one pulling most of those projects together and keeping everyone on track. More than any of that, you're the only one keeping the team from coming completely undone. You're strong when we need it, fun when you can afford it, and even if no one ever says it, you're the one person— Team Lead or above—that makes us feel like we're anything but work horses ready to be ridden until we break, and shot out behind the barn when we fail." Janice paused.

"You value people, Jeff. You're the best they've got on the floor, and I have no doubt you could work anywhere you wanted. So why not find somewhere you feel valued?"

A long drink, and then another. His insides burned, and his face flushed. Janice went back to picking at her orange rind—her eyes glued to the wet bar.

Jeff took a final swallow, then looked over at Janice. "That's nice of you to say, but if I left, who'd look after my team?" he asked, hoping it wouldn't seem too cheesy.

She chuckled, and signaled the bartender for her bill. "God knows I'd get out if I had your options," she said.

"What's keeping you around then? You're a good worker, and if you got this job, I'm sure you could find a better place without too much trouble."

"Not every office has the benefits plan SALIGIA does—however much longer that holds true."

"Have you been seeing Dr. Marcy as well?" Jeff joked, and the relief that washed over him when Janice burst into a long, loud gale of laugher was the breaking of waves on a hot summer day. He liked to see her laugh. At work it was a welcome relief from the wearisome confines of the office. Outside of work, she was radiant, and he could almost forget how quiet and uncertain she was back on Floor 82.

"You really are a good worker though, Janice. I know it can be stressful there—and management never gives clear feedback for fear of having anyone really believe in themselves beyond their narrow role—but it's true. You're fast and effective, you're intuitive, and you lighten up that drab place in a way that it's sorely needed for a long, long time."

There was a gentleness in Janice's eyes when she looked up at him. Not just at him, it seemed, but into him in a way he hadn't felt in years. "Thanks Jeff, you're a good friend," she said. "I need to head home now, but this was fun."

Janice left money on the bar for her bill, hurried up the wide red stairs, and out onto the streets above beyond sight.

...*my best friend,* a delicate voice echoed in Jeff's mind.

He let his hand settle into the water on the bar, forgetting the discomfort it had brought him earlier. Today was a good day. Those were rare, and always something to hold onto. They were what made the other days more bearable. They kept him warm through the cold, and sometimes, they made it seem like every once in a while, life could be fair after all.

He sat alone for a while before leaving. His fingers traced a long, wet streak across the bar, and he remembered the looming face of the piranha.

CHAPTER 5

Presentation Day

All that night Jeff dreamed of fire. Searing red flames tore through the SALIGIA tower, razing it to the ground and leaving nothing but the smoking, baked earth beneath.

The sun rose bright and hot that morning, and all the way to work, Jeff thought about the fire dream. He half hoped he'd get off the bus to find it was true; that he was unshackled from his job, and Friday stood open for him to do anything he pleased.

That would certainly be a nice change of pace. *Most likely*, he reasoned, *I'd try to track down Janice.* They could go for a drink to discuss how exciting life seemed now that the daily grind of the great black tower had been burned away, and they found themselves suddenly free to do and be whatever they wanted.

Even before the bus stopped though, he saw the black spear of SALIGIA Inc. punching a hole in the clear blue sky, and his heart sank. After having such a great time with Janice the night before, and seeing the depth of her personality beyond the restraints of the workplace, he regretted having to return. More than that, he was beginning to realize just how much the office brought him down. Was he as subdued there as Janice was? He couldn't be sure, and that bothered him in a way he didn't fully understand.

It seemed like the type of thing he should explore with his therapist, but that was out of the question now. *I suppose I can work it all out with Eddie at some point,* he thought as he stepped off the elevator and made a beeline for the coffee machine.

Only when he'd navigated the ridiculous menus and began to fill a flimsy paper cup he snatched hastily off the counter did Jeff finally notice that something was very off about the lobby. Where he would usually expect only the milling of office assistants and scurrying of the occasional intern, he found thriving mobs and heard the buzzing of frantic conversations.

He took a long sip of coffee, hoping his dream was coming true, when a sudden beep from the PA system jerked his focus upward. "Attention SALIGIA Floor 82 personnel, please report to the lobby for immediate instruction."

Whatever it was, Jeff knew it couldn't be good. Not in the everybody-evacuates-and-goes-home sense, at least. A quick glance through the crowd revealed Adra, Francis, and Jordan, but Jeff caught no trace of Janice.

"Attention SALIGIA Floor 82 personnel, please report to the lobby for immediate instruction." Repeated the mechanical voice.

With only a hint of annoyance, he sidled over to a corner and waited for the arrival of whatever fresh new hell was coming.

"Attention SALIGIA Floor 82 personnel, please report to the lobby—" the speaker repeated, then cut off abruptly. A moment later, it resumed in a slightly different tone. "Attention SALIGIA Floor 82 personnel, a Presentation Day is set to commence in the Central Hall in five minutes."

Jeff failed to conceal his derisive groan, but that was of little concern. It was entirely drowned out by a chorus of other groans, moans, several heavy sighs, and one bold "God dammit!"

Presentation Days meant only one thing—Nadia had lost confidence that her direct inferiors—Marcy and Francis—had their initiatives under control, and felt the need to micromanage. It was, in Jeff's personal and professional opinion, the very worst and most tedious thing that could ever happen in the world.

With sunken shoulders and swaying heads, the group filed grudgingly towards the Central Hall. Any hopes they had of actually advancing their initiatives that morning were utterly dashed. Most would have likely preferred to fall truly and publicly ill than to toil through the slog to come, and Jeff counted himself in that number.

Not one of them had a choice though, and no illness short of death could save them. Not from Nadia's decree.

The long corridor to the Central Hall seemed to shrink along its length, and as he passed the final window, Jeff eyed its locking-mechanism, wondering how long it would take him to tear loose its hinge and cast himself down to the cement below.

Too big a risk, he accepted sadly. If caught destroying SALIGIA property, he'd probably be assigned some task even more unbearable than merely existing in the office.

"Hey," came a meek voice from a distant corner of the Central Hall as Jeff stepped inside.

Turning towards the sound, he finally saw Janice. She stood at a table in the corner, her back hunched and her eyes strained as she sorted, collated, and stapled a giant stack of agendas.

Unbearable tasks!

"What did you destroy?" he asked, sneaking over to her as the death-envying herd of office workers found and took whatever seats suited them best.

"Carpet," she said with a pitiable blend of ironic humour and sincere self-loathing.

"Coffee?" he asked.

Janice sighed, frowned, and continued her collating duties.

"Take your seats!" called Francis, scurrying through a tall black door at the back.

"Everyone please be seated!" hollered Marcy, following him through the door and racing to square up her pace alongside his.

Most everyone was already seated, and Jeff reluctantly found an empty chair of his own—leaving Janice to hand out the stacks and somberly rue her misdeeds.

SALIGIA took penitence very seriously, after all, and Jeff wanted no part of that for himself.

Tussling about and scurrying in awkward circles, Marcy and Francis shuffled around the front of the room until they finally reached a mutually agreeable set up—one to each side of the tall black doors at the head of the room. Once they'd settled, the doors opened on cue, and Nadia walked through as if carried on a gale of fiery air and backed by the blast of trumpets.

She does know how to make an entrance, Jeff thought. He'd settled into a seat near the back. There was still an empty chair on his left side, but on his right—much to his dismay—sat Jordan. With his brash attitude and defiant outlook, Jeff never knew if he should envy Jordan's steel, or pity his stupidity. Too many times he'd watched Jordan's smart mouth and lack of temperance earn him extra work, overtime, or stricter supervision. More often than not, his fall took down others nearby, and sitting beside him now, that was precisely what Jeff feared.

Silence took the room in a death grip, and every eye sank to the floor as Nadia stepped to centre stage—except for poor Janice's, who was still hurrying around delivering the packages of useless handouts in the final seconds before the horror began.

Too late, Jeff knew.

"Thank you for assembling on such short notice." Nadia had an incredible mastery of intonation, and it was clear to all but the simplest minds in the room—Jeff had his suspicions who they were—that she was not impressed with their efficiency at all. "We have a lot to cover today, so let's not have any further delay." She raised a pointed eyebrow at Janice before continuing.

"It has come to my attention that some of you are struggling to keep the guiding directives of your initiatives straight, and that your update meetings on each have proven insufficient to provide greater clarity. Now, while I cannot stress enough how imperative it is that meeting times be divided by initiative in order to ensure effective billing, I am willing to afford you a concession. Today's meeting will be coded as Professional Development, and billed to the SALIGIA Corporate account instead. That means this morning will be an open forum where you can all discuss your initiatives as needed—trusting you will show at least a basic sense of propriety.

"I've booked the entire morning for this purpose, but remain committed to having you out of here in time for your Agenda Guidelines and Corporate Protocols workshop at lunch."

This dismal reminder elicited a long series of groans from the less seasoned employees. Marcy's eyes darted around the room like roused bees, tracking the source of each moan, and recording them in her little digi-pad. Noticing this, Francis took a step forward and set to mimicking the action, trying—as it seemed to Jeff—to do so slightly more effectively. Both were no doubt hoping for some recognition from Nadia—an effort more fruitless than shoveling the walks during a blizzard.

Nadia droned on, as she was ever wont to do. Her voice was strong and her presence indomitable, but Jeff had long since acquired a particular talent for drifting away on the winds of his own thought, entirely escaping the hurricane-force gales of her endless bluster.

He could remain attentive to all outward appearances, and catch just enough actual conversation to get by. At this point, it seemed Nadia was explaining how clustering the two Professional Development times was a strategy they would all do well to appreciate.

In the deeper recesses of his mind though, Jeff could drift away to wherever he wanted to be. Sadly, this talent went unutilized more often than not, as the bitter truth of the matter was that Jeff rarely had any idea where he wanted to be. *Anywhere but SALIGIA*, he knew. That was all.

Today however, he used his talent to revisit last night's dream. He could smell the charred wreckage of the black tower, and felt in his bones the thrilling shock of absolute freedom—like atrophied hands lifting skyward as their shackles slid off at last.

What then? he wondered. In truth, Jeff couldn't begin to fathom what he'd do with that kind of freedom. He didn't even want to try. Still, he was certain that somewhere deep in his gut—beneath the anger at being captive so long, beyond the suspicion he harboured about who started the fire to begin with, under the smoke but above the ashes—there must have smouldered some dull embers of a plan.

"Janice, are you ready yet?"

The voice was Nadia's, pulling Jeff suddenly out of his happy place and back into his miserable reality.

Faking an unaffected yawn, he saw at the far back corner of the room that Janice was now seated alone at a table with a stack of paper, a slick laptop, and a projector of the highest order. Only then did Jeff realize he'd been hoping she'd take the empty chair beside him, but Janice's penitent duties were apparently far from ended. *Poor girl, it must have been one hell of a spill.*

With a sigh, a grunt, then a half-withheld squeal of joy, Janice pulled the HDMI cord out of the projector, shoved it back in, and watched as a brilliant white light shot out and illuminated the whiteboard at the front of the room.

"Thank you," said Nadia. She clearly felt absolutely no sense of appreciation.

What is it she feels exactly? Jeff wondered. *Pity? Revulsion? Hate? Probably some unholy mix of all of them, and several others to boot.*

Nadia was a tough customer, there was no doubt about it. She was also, so far as Jeff could tell, the singular most unpleasant, self-fixated, sociopathically-inclined drone that had ever walked the profane halls of SALIGIA Inc. or any of the other corporate blemishes on the face of this green Earth.

It was no wonder she was so successful.

The screen behind her showed a long list of all the current initiatives led by the present audience. There was the Liveable City Initiative, the Clean City Initiative, the City Branding Initiative, the Green City Initiative, The Oil City Initiative, the Sustainable City Initiative, and several others that Jeff had not heard of until just that moment.

He wondered if any of them were his—their assignation lost somewhere in the deadman's land between Marcy and Francis' less-than-auspicious leadership.

"I've received notice that the Green City Initiative needs to hasten its delivery schedule. Evidently, an environmental group have chained themselves to the High-level Bridge to protest the province's policies. City Council is demanding a clear show of progress in order to take the steam out of their engines. Francis, where are we on that?"

Francis couldn't hide his joy as he scurried forward, glancing back at Marcy with a petulant sneer. "I've requested a full project workplan from Jordan. Jordan, how is that coming along?"

Jordan leaned forward in his seat beside Jeff, and cracked his knuckles before he spoke. "It should be ready by the end of today."

"Should be, or will be ready?" asked Francis.

"That depends on how long this meeting goes." Sometimes, it seemed like Jordan didn't think before he spoke. That, or he was the one person in the office who had truly mastered the precarious art of not giving a fuck.

Jeff admired that most days. Watching Marcy make a quick note on her digi-pad, he decided today was not one of those days, and subtly slid his seat further to the left to avoid any possible association with the headstrong idiot.

As Francis stuttered and spat in a meek attempt to assert his authority, Jeff glanced back at Janice. She'd just managed to pull up the slide for the Green City Initiative, and now sat poised and ready to switch to any other slide at a moment's notice. Her forehead was furrowed, and Jeff could barely make out a tiny bead of sweat on her brow. Doubtless, she was eager to re-establish her value, and with Jordan calling his into question, this was no time for a slip up. With any luck, Jeff knew, she'd be out of the spotlight soon if Jordan kept up his shenanigans.

That would be good. Jeff hated to see Janice put under the gun, although he couldn't really explain why. He tried his best to look out for all of his team members, and anyone else who had at least a shred of decency in them. Still, it never really bothered him to watch a little light-hearted misery, especially when it was well-earned.

With Janice though, it was different. Maybe it was her steadfast humility—she never complained or lashed out unless it was utterly necessary. Rather, she bore with quiet grace the endless indignities that were the currency of employ at SALIGIA. It occurred to Jeff that she was no stranger to hardship, and something about the fierce look in her eyes and the unflinching strength of her countenance told him she was the strongest of the lot.

Why then, did he feel the need to protect her?

It was something deep rooted, and more a matter of Jeff's own psychology than anything to do with Janice, he expected. Still, with Marcy as a therapist, it was likely to remain an unexplored anomaly for the foreseeable future.

Staring off at nothing in particular, Jeff smiled.

"Jeff?" Francis asked. His tone left no doubt he was repeating himself.

Now Jeff frowned. "Yes?"

"I asked, is there anything in the Clean City Initiative's report we can share? We need some tangible progress that the Green City Initiative can use to thwart these green-necks."

Nadia glanced over at Francis, but if there was any hint about her train of thought, Jeff had missed it long before it left the station.

"Well…" Jeff started, his mind racing to come up with something, lest he replace Jordan in the shit book.

"Actually," Marcy interrupted, "the Clean City Initiative is in my portfolio." She smiled over at Nadia.

"This is about the Green City Initiative, which is in my portfolio. The Clean City Initiative is just a potential angle here," said Francis, huffing up his chest as his face flushed red.

"And it's mine," Marcy declared as if it represented a great triumph. "Jeff, is there anything under the Clean City Initiative that can help out Francis' struggling team on the Green City Initiative?"

Jeff was beginning to understand the merit of tackling only one initiative at a time. He wished again for fire alarms. Even air-raid sirens would do at this point.

"Actually," he started again, to no avail.

"Jeff?" asked Francis, attempting to reassert his control over the narrative.

Jeff swore he caught the faintest hint of an eyeroll from Nadia, who typed quickly into her digi-pad before wheeling the needle-focus of her eyes back onto the ridiculous scene at the front of the room.

"So?" asked Marcy.

"Well, the Clean City Initiative is really more about reducing advertisement clutter than it is about increasing green spaces, so I'm not sure there's much crossover. We might be able to claim that less paper was used if we can meet our intended goals—which I suppose translates to trees saved—but the City Branding Initiative will make that difficult."

Francis slouched down, pouting at Jeff like he suspected him of intentionally muddying the waters of his grand idea.

Marcy beamed. "Another one of my initiatives—how is progress coming along, Jeff? We're expected to deliver a comprehensive marketing plan by the end of next week."

"Next week?" Jeff nearly swallowed his tongue.

"If we start plastering every empty surface with ads about the city, those green-necks will never let us hear the end of it!" Jordan half-yelled.

Francis perked up like an excited gopher. "Exactly right, we need to be making clear moves to counter the narrative of the protesters."

"Well," said Jordan, "ideally we need to be making tangible progress towards reducing the city's carbon footprint by opening up new green spaces—"

"One thing at a time, Jordan," said Francis. "The carbon footprint isn't currently chained to the biggest bridge in the city and getting national coverage."

Nadia nodded.

Marcy frowned.

Jeff very nearly sighed audibly, and realized it was time once again to distance himself from the conversation as best he could.

What an intolerable crock of shit the entire scene was. Ultimately, he knew this meeting would see them discuss everything, advance nothing, and likely gain some intangible new workload to get in the way of the actual work they needed to get done. Anything they advanced on their own would set another project back, and Nadia—via Marcy and Francis—would hold them all directly accountable for their inevitable failure.

Sometimes, Jeff wondered if he was the unwitting subject of some dystopian reality TV show. That bothered him only slightly less than the sullen realization that if he wasn't the subject of it, he would gladly be in the audience. Anything to dissociate from the suffocating banality of living each day without purpose.

"Janice!" Naida's shout was like a stream of ice-water down his spine.

At the back of the room, Janice quailed. She fumbled furiously with the equipment in front of her until finally, the screen at the front changed, revealing a happy man in coveralls standing in front of a fuming smokestack. *The Oil City Initiative,* Jeff assumed. That meant he should be safe for at least a moment's reprieve.

Time crawled on, as visions of flames, ash, and faraway destinations danced before Jeff's seemingly-attentive eyes. The icy blade of Nadia's voice stabbed between his ribs, and each time she spoke, a familiar chill grew within him. It brought to mind snowy days long ago, when school would force him out into the frigid air for the purposes of good health and fitness.

These days, Jeff could go from home to work and back with only a few minutes of exposure to the actual environment. As a child, he'd have dreamed of such deliverance. Now, he dreamed of different things.

To be understood was the chief of them. To be able to speak his innermost thoughts and have them heard with only understanding— that was the dream.

It wasn't the only one. He dreamed of having his affections received gratefully, to have someone—anyone—realize that he was one of the good guys, despite the unending litany of wolves in sheep's clothing that marred the world these days.

He needed to know he was real—with all the fallibility that entailed—and that despite whatever shortcomings and setbacks he faced, he'd come through in the end and prove his worth.

Finally, he longed for someone to stick around and see all of that come to pass. They'd smile, because they'd known it was the truth all along, and they were now vindicated entirely for their unending faith in him as a decent human being.

With that, he'd know and have it known that he was among the rare few who cared more about doing right than being right. Then, he'd stand triumphant upon his little hill of snow, warmed by the assurance that everything was once again right in the world.

High ambitions, he knew. At that moment, he would have settled for a quick end to the meeting. A sneaky glance at his phone told him it was going faster than he might have guessed. Still…

"Hey," Jordan leaned towards him, and jammed a thick elbow into Jeff's ribs. "Can you believe we still have to get through that Agenda Protocol Corporate whatever workshop after this? I'll never get the Green City workplan done at this rate," he whispered.

It sounded more like a hoarse shout to Jeff, who kept his attention glued firmly ahead. He wanted nothing to do with Jordan's calamity.

Beside him, Jordan scribbled in his notebook as Marcy and Francis bickered over the potential connections between the Clean City and Sustainable City initiatives. The display flickered back and forth between the two as each one wrestled the topic from the other and back, creating a strobe light effect that risked giving any colleague with epilepsy a lethal episode. Jeff wondered if this was a gift to them from Janice—the smallest kind gesture she could do at this moment being an OHS-funded vacation.

"Hey!" Again, Jordan's elbow jabbed into Jeff. He held his notebook out at knee-level. Lowering his eyes in what he hoped was a discreet motion, Jeff saw a picture of a red-haired girl with a giant mouth and a broken light-bulb above her head.

He arched one eyebrow, then got back to pretending to pay attention to the debate at the front of the room.

"It's Janice!" Jordan murmured. "She's the reason we have to go, remember?"

Jordan was a damn idiot. Even if Jeff occasionally admired his willingness to speak his mind despite the potential consequences, it was moments like this that reminded Jeff that his mind was seldom worth speaking.

Jeff half-turned and showed Jordan a pointed eye-roll, hoping he'd get the point and back off.

The smirk on Jordan's face told Jeff his gesture had backfired. He saw him scribbling in the notebook again, and a painful knot began to tighten in his stomach.

The strobe light effect from the projector continued, casting strange shadows around the room and alternatingly lighting and darkening the faces of those around him. Jeff felt like he was in some specially designed hell.

People always said that hell was hot, but that's not how Jeff imagined it. Even if he did believe it was real—which he didn't, unless you counted SALIGIA—he believed it would be terribly cold. *It's probably a Canadian thing,* he thought. It would feel like chunks of snow melting into your mittens and weighing down your hands, or a patch of ice water seeping through your hair and trickling down your back—penetrating the protective layers of comfort and freezing you to the bone.

The day on the playground came unbidden to his mind. "You're my best friend," Katie had said.

He'd thought that would be their truth forever.

Only two weeks later though, Jeff had returned from a sick leave to discover that Katie, David, and several other classmates had made a giant snow-fort in the back part of the playground. When he asked to join in, they all huddled together to discuss the issue, but it was Katie who delivered the verdict. "You didn't help make it, so you can't be part of it now," she proclaimed. She was wearing the wool toque.

The rest of that week, Jeff built his own little fort. At the far end of the playground, with what was left of the good fresh snow, he'd stacked it high and dug it out. Then, he sat in it, cold and miserable, as he felt the moisture seep into his clothes and watched the rest of them play in their special hideout—happy and together.

Some days, even in company, Jeff felt dreadfully alone.

"Hey!" Jordan burst again into his consciousness. He slipped the notebook over Jeff's way once more. Now, the picture had a speech bubble with a steaming poop icon inside, a bundle of question marks above her, and a hollow space erased into her head where the brain would presumably have been. Beneath, it was labelled 'JANICE' in big, bold letters.

"You're an idiot," whispered Jeff.

"Jeff, do you have something to add?" Marcy demanded suddenly, turning her full attention towards him. Francis followed suit, and so did Nadia.

Jeff swallowed, and wondered if everyone else felt the cold breeze going through the Central Hall. It was like the roof had come off and a winter storm came down upon them, leaving them frozen in their chairs like some pathetic Pleistocene mammals caught in a glacier.

"Umm…" Jeff stalled for time, hating himself for it. Marcy, Francis, and Nadia were all tapping something into their digi-pads.

From the back of the room, he heard a distinct cough. Turning, he caught Janice's eyes. She looked directly at him, then gestured down towards his pocket.

He peeked down at the time on his phone—eureka!

"I'd just realized that we only have five minutes left until our workshop. I wouldn't want us to be late," he blurted.

Marcy and Francis frowned. Nadia sliced her steely gaze down to her digi-pad, then turned to the supervisors. "I am sorry to say this meeting has been far less productive than I'd hoped," she said. "It is clear the supervisors have a good deal of work ahead to get their teams on track to meet the efficiency expected of people in the employ of SALIGIA. I will book some complementary training on team-work and inter-team communication for all of you starting next month. In the meantime, take the remaining five minutes to yourselves, then get to your workshop." She spun on her heel—a robotic movement if ever Jeff had seen one—and rushed towards the door, which the frantic efforts of both Marcy and Francis heaved open just in time for the fury of her passing.

As everyone began to file out, Jeff rushed towards the washroom. His coffee was taking its toll. Elbowing through the slower crowd, he gave Janice a grateful smile and half-wink as he went by. The rest of the way to the washroom was spent second-guessing whether the half-wink was work-appropriate.

The washroom door closed behind him, and Jeff spent his time at the stall thinking about the sense of freedom from his dream, losing himself again in the thrilling prospect of what he could do if all of the responsibilities, deadlines, personal obligations, and interpersonal expectations just slipped away. Would he be emboldened to find and finally be his final self?

It was a beautiful prospect, and as he stepped out of the stall and towards the sink, he resolved to be a bit more like that each day. One small action to be truer to himself could make a world of difference, he reasoned, sliding his hands under the smooth white faucets and waiting for the water.

Sadly, no water came.

He moved his hands back and forth beneath the sensors. Still nothing.

"God damn SALIGIA bullshit," Jeff muttered. He was happy for once that the bathroom contained only one stall, thus assuring him that no one overheard his heresy.

Falling instinctively back into his karate-master routine, Jeff waved his hands furiously back and forth beneath the faucet. Finally, a jet of water shot out as his hands moved to the left, and cut off just before he re-centered them. The water's impact with the sink sent a splash over his shirt, and a red light shone out above the faucet, signalling that the "environmentally conscious" refractory time had begun.

"Mother of God," he mumbled again, slashing his hands across the sensor once the light turned green again. The process repeated, this time with Jeff's hands just right of the taps. Cold water splashed up to the neckline of his shirt, chilling him and flashing him back to the freezing clothes and dampened spirits of his lonely little snow fort.

One deep breath, then another. Jeff didn't want to be an impatient man, nor one haunted by the ancient past.

Instead, he waited for the green light to shine again, then placed his hands squarely under the sensor.

One second.

Two...

That was more than enough. Giving up the ghost on self-improvement, Jeff slammed his fist down on the faucet in a war he was certain it had started.

One slam.

Two slams.

Three...shit!

The water shot out, harder and more abundantly than ever before. It came like a torrent, washing his hands in an instant and quickly filling the sink.

This is a fucking disaster, he thought, reaching for the paper towel. He was immediately reminded that it was manufactured by the same withholding sadists as the sink when it hummed once, then shone a red light.

Fuck it. He dried his hands—front and back—against his pant legs, hoping that if he could reach a full saturation point, he might not look wet. With a final tremulous glance at the sink—pouring perhaps even more aggressively now into the overflowing basin and across the black tiled floor, Jeff pushed through the heavy washroom door and determined to hurry off to the workshop without witnesses. Then he would forget the entire obscene ordeal.

He raced out of the flood, and straight into someone standing by the garbage cans outside the bathroom doors.

"Oh crap," she yelled.

It was Janice, who stumbled back against the wall, dropping her thermos in the process. Coffee poured out, but its brown stain quickly dissipated in the maelstrom of water rushing beneath the door of the men's room.

"Well, well, well," she said, smirking up at Jeff, "looks like I'm soon to be off Nadia's black list."

Despite the stress of the situation, Jeff chuckled. "I thought it was called the shit book," he replied.

Now Janice laughed.

A quick look around revealed empty, silent halls. To Jeff's great relief, it seemed everyone was already well on their way to the Agenda Guidelines and Corporate Protocols Workshop.

"To be honest," said Janice, "there are plenty of awful lists to be on. I can't keep them all straight."

"Careful," he said, "there's probably a course to take if you admit that too loudly."

"Which I'm sure Jordan would love to blame me for getting us into. But let's not lose the point here. For once this is your fuckup, Jeff, not mine. What did you do in there anyway?"

The blush on Jeff's face burned his cheeks and tightened his neckline. "It's those damn sinks," he grumbled.

Janice burst into unexpected, incoherent laughter—doubled fully over as she scooped her empty thermos out of the brown-tinted water. "So, do you want some help cleaning this mess up," she asked, "or are you planning on leaving it?"

"Honestly?" Jeff asked.

A flare of excitement flashed in her eyes as she nodded.

"I was planning on leaving it."

She laughed again. "But that means you won't take my place in the shit book!" Janice faked a protest.

"I'm pretty sure Jordan already took that spot. And he deserves it too, for all the crap he gives you about causing that workshop. It would have been pushed on us one way or another."

"Just like this new teamwork training? How does that fit with our current Independent Working Workshop, anyways?"

"I wouldn't worry about it too much. You're liable to go cross-eyed looking for logic around here."

Janice smiled. "Well, if retreat is the plan, shall we make our way to the training? Lots of important information, no doubt."

"Sure," said Jeff. Then he stopped. "Are you doing anything after work today?"

Janice paused for a moment, as if the breath had caught in her throat and nearly choked her. "Nothing exciting, I just have something to take care of at home," she said.

"You're right," he said. Janice raised an eyebrow. "That really doesn't sound exciting! Do you want to grab some drinks instead?"

"I really can't tonight. We'll do it another time."

Jeff could hear the hesitation in her voice, the uncertainty. "Hey now," he pushed, feeling particularly brazen, "nothing could be more important than poking fun at the ridiculous corporate bullshit we have and are yet to see!"

Janice's nostrils flared slightly as she spoke, but Jeff couldn't tell if it was from intrigue, or something else. "As fun as that does sound, and as much as there certainly is to mock, I'll have to take a rain cheque," she said.

"Come on, what could be so dire that it supersedes a little post-work sedition? Nothing I can imagine." The memory of his daydreams took him over, and carried him on a wave of enthusiasm towards brighter places and warmer shores. "What I can imagine," he continued, "is getting out of here. Being done with this place for good and leaving with no plans except to never look back. We'll leave all this shallow shit behind, get a drink, and just keep going. I could stand the idea of never looking back, couldn't you?"

Just then, Jeff became acutely aware of how terribly he'd misread the previous flare of her nostrils. She did it again now, and raised her head slightly as she stepped backward. "It's not just about work for me, Jeff. Maybe that's all you have going on, but I have things to do outside of here. It's nice to make fun of this place once in a while. It does help to blow off steam, but if you think this is my whole life, or that I need help outside of the occasional laugh, then you're way off base."

Her face was hard, and Jeff's earlier resolve was melting into the puddles at his feet. Still, he tried once more, "But…"

An impotent failure.

"No, Jeff, you've said enough. I need to get to the training now." She turned, and sped off down the hall.

The water at Jeff's feet was soaking his shoes, and he could still feel its icy bite at the nape of his neck. Again, he felt like he was back in his pathetic little snow fort.

Walking slowly away, he felt his posture fall and his mind loosen. The old memories froze his spirit, and somewhere in the waking consciousness behind his professional smile, the freedom and fulfillment of his daydream slipped away, leaving him with nothing but the fire.

CHAPTER 6

The Day of Jeff's Big Date

Saturday morning found Jeff up and active far earlier than was his custom. Usually, the better part of the morning—and often some of the afternoon—was spent tossing and turning in a state of half-wakefulness, doing his utmost not to think about returning to work in only two days.

Today however, he jumped out of bed just around the time he'd usually be arriving at work, and momentarily banishing all thoughts of that dreadful place from his mind, he set to cleaning up his small apartment and preparing for his date later that day.

He'd met Avi on a dating app which Eddie had convinced him to download several months ago. For the most part, the app had provided nothing aside from the occasional short-lived conversation, pleas for financial assistance, and what Jeff took to be the occasional catfish.

Avi seemed different early on though. From her first photo, he was taken by her silky, dark hair and the white gleam of what struck him as an entirely natural smile. Jeff hated trying to capture a sincere smile of his own. Forcing one always made him feel like a pathetic fraud, and by the time the click of the camera came, his countenance would inevitably melt into a look of dour self-loathing.

In every picture on her profile though, Avi shone like she was experiencing the greatest thrill of her life. There were looks of boundless hilarity, exalted appreciation, and even one that hinted at something a bit more after-hours. The joyful glow on her face presented a promising juxtaposition to Jeff's grey days.

In a content silence, he finished sweeping his floor, and set a plump pot roast out to thaw on the counter. Then a new fear entered his mind. It was entirely possible that Avi's perfect smiles spoke not to how intrinsically happy she was, but rather to her skill at faking emotions. This was a disappointing thought, and Jeff tried to push it out of his mind—but doing that brought a sudden image of the metallic, inhuman smile Nadia wore when passing down terrible news about changes to SALIGIA's benefits, pay scales, or whatever other fresh hell they deemed fit to present as good news to their employees that week.

I'd prefer a bad date to thinking of work on a weekend, he thought. Continuing with his cleaning, he forced himself back to fretting that Avi was a practiced fraud instead.

He was sure the fears were unfounded. They'd been speaking for several weeks—on the app at first, then finally switching over to text and the occasional real phone call. It was going well, until Eddie convinced Jeff that was too long to talk to someone without asking them out. So, as the weeks threatened to turn to a month, Jeff finally made a bold claim about his skill as a cook, and Avi bit the bait.

Now, in only a few hours, she was due to arrive at Jeff's place to put his boasting to the test. Pulling his mother's old recipe book out of the cupboard, he began to carefully lay out the ingredients he'd purchased on the way home the night before.

A first date at his place was unusual. To be fair, these days any date was unusual, but Jeff was excited by the playful rapport they'd developed online, and was cautiously optimistic about the night ahead. Before the hour came, he'd need to have dinner ready, shower and change, and find the appropriate record to put on. Jeff, although certainly no audiophile, appreciated the physicality of old vinyl records, and thought that playing one would be the perfect finishing touch to class up the date.

Minutes turned to hours, and Jeff was starting to feel like everything was ready as the moment of Avi's arrival approached. A subtle tingling at the back of his head surprised him—a sense of anticipation, perhaps even nervousness, which he hadn't felt for longer than he cared to remember.

He imagined having someone in his life he could rely on. Eddie—of course—was that in spades, but Eddie had his own life, his own responsibilities, and to him, although ever dear, Jeff was just a small piece of that. Everyone else seemed to have their main person—the one they thought of throughout the day, who they couldn't wait to get advice from or tell a great story to. For many, for the lucky ones, it was the person they came home to.

Jeff had always dreamed of that, and assumed since he was young that it was an inevitable stop along life's road—that no matter the chosen route, it would show up sooner or later. It hadn't of course, and as the years drew on, he began to wonder if, somewhere along the line, he'd missed his turn entirely.

What would all the stories and good times be worth if he never did find someone to share them with?

Pulling on a clean navy sweater, Jeff combed his unruly hair carefully in front of the bathroom mirror, then went to check the roast he'd put in the oven a few hours ago. It was coming along nicely.

He thought again about Avi's smile. She too was looking for someone. She was alone for now, no different than Jeff. How, then, did she seem to be so damn happy in every photo? Jeff wondered again if perhaps the smile was fake, and the tingle in the back of his mind grew stronger.

Everything was ready, and Jeff was as confident as he could be that he'd set the stage for the perfect date. Still, something nagged his conscience. Perfect, just what would that be? People didn't simply declare their affections for each other these days. It took time, patience, practice, and struggle. A kiss goodnight? A shimmer in her eye as she left? To be the cause of that smile, or to feel one twist across his own tired face?

At any rate, Jeff hoped Avi wouldn't regret coming over by the time she left. That, he thought, was a humble enough ambition.

He set the potatoes to stew, left the broccoli to steam, and lowered the oven to keep the roast warm. He had only two wine glasses, and not the right type for the wine he'd bought to complement the meal. Still, he polished them and set them out on the table.

Everything was just right, and the hour had come. When Jeff heard his buzzer, he was pleased to note that Avi was exactly on time. Punctuality, after all, was an admirable trait.

His stomach knotted as he made his way around the corner from his kitchen alcove and into the short hall leading to his front door. Pressing the little white button to let her through the main door, he felt a strange thrill of anticipation. It was a welcome reminder of the vivacity and urgency which life could still provide, in its better moments.

Opening the door, the first thing he noticed was that smile— just like in the pictures. No second takes, no photo-editing or professional posing required. It was as natural as sunrise. If Jeff was nervous before, he was doubly so now.

"Hi," she said, and Jeff realized he may have stood content for just a moment too long.

"Hey!" he blurted in eager answer. It might have been just a bit too loud. "Come on in, let me take your coat," he said—too quietly by way of compensation.

Avi smiled again, even deeper and richer than before. "Thanks," she said, and held out a small, sensible green windbreaker as she crossed the threshold with subtle grace.

Grabbing a spare hanger from the long line of empties he kept in the unlikely event he had a sudden rush of company with coats to store, he hung her jacket carefully in his barren closet, taking heed to ensure it wasn't crushed up against a wall, or rubbing against any of his own coats.

"Did you find the place okay?"

"Yeah," she answered, "it was no hassle. Whyte Ave is as straight a line as they come, and while I don't mean to brag, I'm quite proficient at counting numbers down."

Jeff chuckled. Her wit and sharp sarcasm translated well in person. That was another good sign.

"Dinner is nearly ready," he said. "Can I give you a quick tour of the place first?" He gently backed away as he spoke, going halfway into the closet to allow her room to pass. He didn't want her to feel boxed into a corner with his boorish insistences on coat hanging and door closing. After all, Avi had shown a lot of trust agreeing to a first date at his house, and he thought it only fair to let her explore the whole place—to know the layout and see that there were no dark surprises lurking in the distant crevices of his small apartment.

Sometimes, he thought it must be a real chore being a woman and dealing with men these days—or any other days for that matter. When he could, he feebly tried to lower that tension in whatever ways possible, though he often feared he was less successful at this than he wished.

"Yes please, I can't wait to see just what sort of lair a man of your charm has made for himself," she said.

Jeff's cheeks grew hot, and he gave a formal nod, then an over-formal, wide swing of his outstretched arm to indicate her way down the hallway—right from the boot-room and away from the kitchen.

"This is the hallway," he said, "it's quite standard as far as halls go."

"Wait," Avi insisted, "so, you use this to go this way, and that way?" She pointed each direction out with long, painted nails.

"Yes, it is in fact a bi-directional hallway, the builders spared no expense in this unit." They shared a laugh, and Avi pushed his shoulder playfully.

"At the end here, you'll find the bathroom. Please feel welcome to explore and report back with any questions you have." Jeff liked her mocking formality, and decided right then to ride it until the wheels came off.

She poked her head in hesitantly, gave a discerning glance in both directions, and pulled back around the corner with a rapid—groundhog-esque movement. "Everything checks out," she said with a curt nod.

Her dark hair bobbed as she moved, and seemed to contain within it a strange microcosm of her vibrant enthusiasm for life.

Jeff envied that in her. Sometimes, he sat alone on weekends like this and tried to recall that passion from his own past. Usually, few memories ever came, and his attention drifted from the forgotten past to the reviled future—sitting at his desk in two days, regretting whatever awful choices had led him there.

"To the right here is a closet of cleaning supplies, I assure you it is beyond suspect or reproach."

Avi eyed the door, but finally shrugged her acquiescence.

"And to the left," he went on, "is the bedroom." This, he suspected, was the most awkward part of the tour.

Avi looked in, but didn't enter. "Bed?" she asked.

Jeff nodded.

"Closet?" She smirked.

"Indeed," he confirmed.

"Nightstand?" She raised an eyebrow.

"Two in fact!"

"Very adult indeed!" She feigned the immense satisfaction of a mother who's seen her child tie their shoes for the first time.

Again, they laughed, and again she gave Jeff a gentle shove. He revelled in having a role so straightforward and rewarding. If SALIGIA ever felt like this, he imagined he might never leave. But he didn't want to think about SALIGIA. Not today.

"I'm afraid that brings us to the conclusion of our first half, but if you'll follow me back up the very same hallway, we can conclude this exciting production of 'Jeff's Apartment' with part two!"

"I wait with bated breath!" she said, clutching invisible pearls and gasping in faux-anticipation.

Jeff led the way, trying his best to conceal the sudden bounce creeping into his step.

"Here we have the kitchen, and beyond that, the dining room. The attentive eye may notice the lavish settings laid out in advance." He hoped this touch wasn't too self-aggrandizing, but Avi didn't seem to care. Instead, she stopped at the stove.

"Oh wow, this smells amazing, Jeff!" she said, bending down to peer through the blackened glass door.

"Patience lady, it'll be ready soon, and the tour is almost done!"

Avi jolted up from her squat, pulling away from the oven and returning her attention to Jeff with military rigidity. "Then by all means, lead the way, good sir."

Jeff nodded, turned on his heel, and led her onward. "Finally, we find ourselves in the living room. It is, as you can see, fully decked out with all the modern living essentials: couch, armchair, desk, television, dust-laden treadmill, and of course, the jewel of any true home—" Here Jeff gestured wordlessly to his tall, wall-encompassing bookshelf.

Avi gasped. This time, it seemed truly genuine.

"This is the bookshelf, if that wasn't self-evident. What do you think? Any personal favourites? …and yes, I will be judging your answer," he said.

"Is that whole top row just Tolkien? Like, that Hobbit guy?"

"Yes," said Jeff, silently judging.

"Those little dudes are so funny."

Jeff frowned. He didn't even try to conceal it. "That sounds borderline Hobbit-phobic," he teased.

"I had a Yorkshire pudding once and couldn't stand it. Ever since then I've been against anything even vaguely shire-adjacent."

Despite his fervent disapproval of both her dislike of Tolkien—one of his greatest passions—and of Yorkshire puddings, which were perhaps somewhere in his top fifty, Jeff laughed. Long and loud and true. It was, perhaps, the hardest he'd laughed in many years, and he realized this fact between long guffaws and heartfelt failed attempts at catching his breath. When he finally did, he straightened up and found that Avi also had tears in her eyes, and was only just regaining her own perfect posture.

"It's nowhere near a pudding," she choked, "it's just a wet piece of bread."

"Well," he finally managed, "despite your pitiful lack of

appreciation, it is indeed an entire row of Tolkien books. I got into him pretty young, and he's been my favourite author ever since."

"I don't really dislike him. Well, I guess I'm not sure. I loved the movies, but never managed to get through the books. Maybe you'll lend me yours some day?"

Jeff narrowed his eyes and arched his brows suspiciously at her.

"It is an awesome collection, Jeff. I'm jealous, really. I had to give up most of my books when I moved here from Vancouver, and haven't rebuilt the collection since. It's great to see someone who appreciates literature. You may not know this, but it's a very attractive quality."

Failing to conceal his childish grin, Jeff decided to embrace it fully. "I know," he replied with his best roguish sneer.

The practiced roll of Avi's eyes was the crashing of waves over a desert dune.

"Honestly," he continued, "reading has always been one of the best things in my life. I don't get to talk about it much anymore, so your enthusiasm is refreshing. It was an escape when I was young— when nothing seemed to fit and I always felt like no matter where I was, I didn't quite belong. I could always open a book and go somewhere more interesting and meaningful."

"Wow," said Avi.

Again, the red-hot burning of self-awareness took Jeff's cheeks, forehead, and now his neck. It was a strange thing, he thought, how one could suddenly check their honesty and regret what a moment before felt like the most true and honest expression of themselves. "Maybe that was a bit dramatic, but—"

"No," Avi cut him off, a delicate but firm hand on his forearm. "I understand exactly. I remember sitting in this tiny nook at recess sometimes, reading the Narnia series as all the other kids chased soccer balls, played tag, and all that other shit kids do. They always said I was a loser for it, and I believed them. But these days, I wonder how many of those goals or tags they remember. I know every inch of Narnia, and a thousand other books besides. None of those playground friendships last anyways. I have new people, and so do they, but the adventures I found back then are still worth something. Don't you think?"

Jeff wasn't sure he'd ever swooned in his life, but suspected that if it was fated to be, the moment was fast approaching. "I agree. I can't overstate how strongly I agree. It's awful that so many children nowadays grow up without an escape like that. No literacy, no other reality than the dismal shit offered to them by the mass-media. Nothing but corporate culture forced down their throats like so many placebo pills."

"Yeah," said Avi. "I wish there was an easy fix, but a full week's work of coding leaves me with little time to contribute to children's literacy."

"That's one of my dreams. I don't think I've shared this with more than one other person. I'd love to just quit my job, and run away to some other country. Go someplace where I don't know anyone, and no one knows me. Somewhere that teaching literacy would be a valued commodity rather than a tired cliché or half-assed tax write-off.

"I hate to admit it, but it's as much about the escape as it is the actual work. I want to help people, I want to see children read and to help the next generation recapture the imagination I had in my youth, but as much as any of that, I just want to get the fuck out of this place. It seems so greedy, so cynical. I just have to believe there's somewhere left in the world that still values human connection over hoarded wealth."

"Isn't that a Tolkien quote?" asked Avi.

"Bastardized," Jeff admitted.

A strange moment passed between them then, like a cooling wind rushing along a hot beach, taking away the thrill of summer and setting minds to sweaters, shelter, and days passed.

"So anyway, what's for dinner?" she asked.

"I've got a pot roast just finishing, with potatoes and broccoli. I hope that's alright."

"Sounds fantastic."

"Well, we should be pretty much good to go. Would you like a bit of wine?"

"I'd love some," said Avi, taking the chair Jeff offered her.

He poured them each a glass, pulled the roast from the oven, and set it out to cool. Readying the potatoes and broccoli, he spread them on a platter, and moved over to his record player.

Powering it up and flipping on the speakers, he placed down an old Tom Waits record he'd chosen for the occasion. He set it to play, and brought the food over to the table, then hurried back for the nearly empty bottle of wine and a small dish of horseradish.

"This looks incredible," said Avi.

Jeff waited until she'd taken her share, then helped himself. The food was perfect, and the music divine. Waits' *Ol' 55* started humming from his antique speakers, and Jeff couldn't imagine a place he'd rather be just then.

"I fucking love this song. What a great debut," he said between bites. "Are you a Tom Waits fan?"

"Not really," she said. "He's a bit weird for me. Don't get me wrong though," she blurted, nearly losing a bite of beef in the process, "I love a lot of old stuff; Springsteen, U2, the Stones. But what I've heard of Waits has always seemed kind of strange."

"Oh, it is. This is about as conventional as it gets for Tom," said Jeff. "But I love that about him. His songs are strange and foreign, but the voice is so familiar they feel like my own memories sometimes. I can smell these songs—like whiskey, leather, and blood."

"You can smell music?" she asked, her dark forehead knotting up like a sycamore.

"Yeah," said Jeff, "I mean, sort of. It's so rich and deep it seems to reach more than just the ears, if you know what I mean. Besides, it's hard to turn away from a voice like that."

"He sounds kind of like a monster choking on the bones of a child," said Avi.

"That's sort of what I mean."

"Okay," she gave a quick roll of her eyes, then set to working on her meal. "This really is delicious Jeff, thanks so much."

The record continued to croon about the sun coming up and the freedom of the open road. Jeff had never felt the lyrics so strongly.

"So, you said you moved here from Vancouver? Doesn't seem like much of a trade up, what made you do that?" he asked.

"The housing market, of course. Computer coding can be done anywhere, but unless you're high up with one of the major corporations, it's nearly impossible to afford living in a city like Vancouver. Edmonton is a bit more accessible as far as that goes, so here I am."

"Makes sense, I suppose. I can tell you though, working for a major corporation is far from the picnic you may imagine."

"It can't be all bad, at least there's security in something like that."

Jeff shuddered—and visions of Marcy, Francis, and Nadia danced through his head like vengeful phantoms coming to devour his weekend. For a while, the only sounds were the clinking of utensils on plates and the raspy voice of Waits crackling over the speakers.

Feeling he could no longer sit with the ghosts of coworkers present, Jeff sprang suddenly to his feet. "Can I get you another drink?" Dinner was nearly done anyway, the wine was empty, and the time seemed ripe for a bit of digestif.

"That sounds great," Avi said, heartily finishing the remainder of her wine.

"How does a daquiri sound?"

"Even better."

Jeff hurried away the empty wine glasses, along with his mostly empty plate. He left Avi to finish her meal as he cut up limes and shook some rum over ice.

"You're quite the bartender." The excited ring in Avi's voice revealed how happy she was about this particular fact.

"A man must be ready to provide for good company." Jeff smiled over the undulating rim of the shaker.

"A provider, are you? Isn't that a bit old-fashioned?"

"No, that's a totally different drink."

They both laughed at that, loud and long and happily, until in the fit of his merriment Jeff swung a clumsy hand behind him. He'd hoped it would be a graceful flourish to conclude his enthusiastic shaking, but instead he sent one of his martini glasses spinning off the counter to shatter on the tile floor below.

"Oh no, can I help?" Avi leaped up to her feet.

Perfectly still, Jeff surveyed the jagged shards scattered over his floor. "No, no, you stay put, let me take care of this."

A takeout donair menu served as a makeshift funnel to scoop up the larger pieces of glass and dump them into the trash, then Jeff went the long way around to the far hallway, fetching a small broom and dustpan for the more elusive pieces.

"You certainly handled that with class," Avi called down the hallway as he returned the broom and dustpan to the closet. "That beautiful glass destroyed and a big mess, yet not a hint of anger from you. That's good to see."

"Well," Jeff replaced the glass and got back to finishing up the drinks, "patience through adversity is important. What is life after all, if not one long waiting game?"

Avi chuckled quietly. "That's potentially a very grim sentiment. So, what are you waiting for then, Mr. Boggs?"

With the drinks poured, Jeff returned to the table, passing Avi's over with a self-conscious bow before sitting down himself.

No reason to be coy now, he thought. "Death, you mean?"

"Yikes, that is dark," she said. "What about along the way?"

Jeff forced a laugh. "Well, I suppose life should be more than waiting to find out what will kill you. I hate to admit it, but you were right before."

"I'm always right, but when do you mean?"

"When you said I was old-fashioned. It's the terrible truth of Jeffrey Boggs. I am old-fashioned. I'm about the most vanilla, unexceptional guy you'll ever meet. I'm just waiting for picket-fences and contentment. I'm mostly beyond the old delusions of adventure by now."

Avi furrowed her brow. "I've heard it said that the path to those picket fences can be quite adventurous at times."

"I've heard that too, but so far the seas of adventure have been defined more by their doldrums than their tempests."

"Articulate, if bleak."

"I'm sorry, I really don't mean to sound so melancholy." Jeff took a long swallow of his daquiri—perfectly mixed. "I don't want to give the wrong impression, I'm pretty happy for the most part.

"It's just that the wait can really drag, you know? I want everything. I want the rock songs and the Irish poems. I want the starry nights and broken vases. The hard conversations, and the endless hours of silence where no words could ever capture the depths of meaning passing like starlight between interlocked eyes.

"I want to fight forever for someone, but never with them. I want someone who'll fight for me as well. I want the Juliets and the Luthiens, even if that means the Capulets and the Thingols. I… want…" Jeff trailed off trying to find the right endnote, but words suddenly failed him in the trail of their wellspring. "…a reason," he finished sadly.

Avi blinked. She took a long swallow of her daquiri, then another.

"Well," she said, "you really do want it all."

Jeff blushed. "Is that so much to ask?"

"I don't think so. I want those things too. Most of them anyways." She smiled. "The pleasures and the pains, they're all inseparable parts of the same package. But so is the waiting. Without the journey there is no worthy destination. What would the Odyssey be if they simply got home safely by the swiftest paths?"

"Fair enough," Jeff replied with a laugh. "The journey is fun for the reader—those watching from the outside. But for Odysseus, the journey wasn't for its own sake—it was all about Penelope. If he didn't believe she was waiting at the end of it all, I doubt he'd be so eager to go on."

"I'm sure there were also adventures before he ever met Penelope, but I see what you mean. Still, I think it's important to enjoy the ride as well. Be present, you know, because in the end life isn't really a destination—just an ever-expanding series of moments.

Don't wish them all away in favour of one you've yet to see. That's just suicide on an installment plan."

"Wise words," said Jeff. "I agree completely. I wish I could hold onto that sort of clarity more often. But I lose it sometimes. In the daily grind—the bus to work, the dead hours at the office, and the tightrope of social interaction. I begin to daydream about something more."

"Tightrope of social interaction?" asked Avi. She finished her drink and pushed her chair back, letting her long legs stretch out under the table.

Jeff promptly refilled the drinks, and gestured over to the couch. Avi followed, and they sat in the deep green cushions as the record continued in the background.

"Yeah," Jeff rejoined after some reflection, "tightropes, you know? I mean, I try to keep up with the world. I strive to be decent, but it can be hard not to offend these days. One person, or the other. I mean, not for reasons of hate mind you. I don't hate anyone. Offending for spite though? Sure. Impatience? Daily!

"But never hate. Never anger.

"In fact, you mentioned my lack of anger earlier. To be honest, I don't believe in anger. Not as a unique emotion at any rate. Anger is a reaction—there's always some other underlying feeling behind it. If you can find that, then you can truly get to the heart of things." Jeff took another long drink, feeling suddenly that he'd said too much.

Avi did likewise, holding herself in quiet repose before finally speaking again. "You know, for someone who doesn't believe in anger, you seem pretty angry about something. So, what's at the heart of that, Jeff? What are you reacting to?"

The problem with Martini glasses, thought Jeff, *is how pitifully little they hold.* Tom Waits was singing about the lost ideals of his old flame Martha, and it struck Jeff that he couldn't be more on point.

"Wow," he said, and let that stand on its own for some time.

Avi offered nothing else. Rather, she sipped slowly at her own drink, staring straight ahead. There was no trace of her famous smile. Not in the present, nor any imaginable stretch of the future's horizon.

"I guess it's just the particular circumstances of the journey. I know I shouldn't rush the destination, I just wish the meantime had something more to offer. I've seen most of my friends get married and have kids. I've seen some of them die. I've watched people realize their dreams, take amazing vacations, buy houses—laugh their days away. But me, I go to a job I hate, I come home to this half-assed apartment, and I sit and wait to go back to work again. All the while, I hope against hope that some uncalculated catalyst will enter the equation and change everything for the better. But the days slip by, and the hope grows dimmer."

"Jeff, you have a place to live. You have a job, even if you don't always like it. You're gainfully employed; I assume you have benefits, a paycheque and job security. Many people lie in the cold and pray for less than you spend your time resenting."

Jeff drew a long, deep breath. He looked briefly into the dregs of his drink, but decided against quaffing it just then. "You don't know SALIGIA," he finally said. "You don't understand what it's like there."

"I'm sure I don't. Every workplace has its quirks, but they all boil down to the same thing in the end. I hate my boss too. I don't know anyone who doesn't. That's why you're paid to go.

"You can at least afford to live alone, and it certainly seems like you're able to eat well. That means you're ahead of the curve these days. Work always sucks, that's just the way it is. But we live in Alberta, Jeff—if you work oil or corporate you're better off than most. Otherwise, you deal with all the same shit, and you struggle to scrape by on top of it."

Jeff's drink was empty, but still he swallowed hard. "It's not all about the money. They break your spirit for sport in that place. It's how they keep people down—how they keep you from questioning the inane bullshit that goes on. You wouldn't believe what they get away with in the name of profit and prestige. Sure, I make a bit more, but it's not worth it at the end of the day."

"Then quit," said Avi.

Jeff sighed. "I know you're trying to be helpful," he said. "It's just hard to describe what it's like there. You wouldn't believe it if I told you. It's not just the bosses, or the ridiculous red tape and run-around behind every little decision. It's the general madness of it. We spend so much time running in circles and doing nothing. No project really makes any difference except to bring in some future profit. Nothing actually gets done, and nothing ever ends. It's just a bunch of meaningless reports, paper shuffling, and redefining terms forever."

Avi nodded slowly. "That does sound frustrating, but you're still the one choosing to stay. If you hate it that much, and the money isn't worth it, just leave. It would be easier now than when you start building all those things you say you want—wife, kids, soon enough you really will be locked in to your career. You're still free now, and you might as well take advantage of it. There's no reason for you to be so miserable."

"You're probably right. I think about that every day. I've rehearsed my 'I quit' speech so many times—the way I'd go out and the truth I'd finally tell those suit-wearing dial-tones. Then I'd run away and forget ever working there—ever living in this city. I'd never feel snow again, and I'd teach kids to read or something else that actually made a difference."

"So, if you've got it all planned out, what's keeping you?" she asked.

Jeff's head sagged, and the cushions held him tight. "I don't know," he said. "I guess I'm just waiting for a good reason to stay. Something to make it all worth it."

"Something, or someone?" asked Avi.

Jeff felt the chill of the playground years ago. He smelled the cool, wet air of the bar on Jasper Ave the week before, and heard two voices echoing as one through his mind, calling him their friend. He sat silent for a long time, knowing full well the wait would be too much. There was nothing else he could say—he'd already said it all.

How many times could a person cast their nets, just to pull them up with nothing but debris and decay?

It was Avi who broke the silence. "It's getting late, I should probably get going."

Jeff nodded. "I know. Thanks for coming over, this was nice." He stood, and walked her to the door.

"Yeah," she said quietly, "thanks again for dinner. It was delicious."

Avi got her shoes and coat, and stood for a moment in the threshold of the open door. Her dark eyes shone like little gems as she looked up at him, and for the first time, Jeff could see that the smile on her face was clearly fake. "Bye," she said, giving him a quick side hug and hurrying off down the hallway.

Locking the door behind her, Jeff poured the last of the daquiri into his glass, and sank back into the couch.

It had been a good night, on the whole. He thought about the laughs they'd shared, and the smile she'd worn most of the time. During the few hours she'd been over, Jeff had almost forgotten the weight the world put on him each day—until he began to describe it for her as if those dark insights were an intimate gift.

For a little while, though, Jeff had felt like he'd found a new friend.

He knew he wouldn't see her again.

He wouldn't even try.

It was nothing new. People came, people went.

Jeff was used to it at this point.

He wasn't hurt. He certainly wasn't heart-broken. To some degree, he was actually grateful for the night. He would hold onto it. For a while, it would be enough.

Then it would fade. Soon enough he wouldn't remember her name.

Sometimes, it was hard to feel like anything had any real meaning. Not beyond the brief flights of fancy they brought with them. Little splatters of colour on the dull canvas of life.

In a few days, he'd be back at work. Back to everything he couldn't wait to escape.

That night, he dreamed of nothing; an empty sea of night, where time held no sway. He woke up thankful for that. The morning sky was grey with heavy clouds, and no sun broke through their cover.

CHAPTER 7

A Day Off

The sky remained overcast as the morning turned slowly to afternoon, and time's passing was marked by the hands of the clock alone. Jeff spent the early hours lazing about, spread forlornly upon his couch, coffee on the end table beside him and a book held open above his face.

The book in question—recommended to him by Eddie several weeks prior—represented the latest in the endless line of hot-for-a-moment bestsellers about self-improvement and unlocking the innate power of your unbridled human spirit, or something like that.

Eddie, thought Jeff, may be more of an idiot than he'd ever realized. Besides the occasional catchy—if trite—quote, the book had thus far proven little more than a long-winded collection of shallow platitudes and over-played homilies. There was nothing of actionable substance Jeff could discern amidst the asinine cheerleading and overly optimistic rhetoric.

It could, he imagined, be useful to some nitwits out there. Listless incompetents with no direction, no passion, no purpose. But Jeff didn't fancy himself to be anywhere close to his imagined target audience for this hardcover rag, and determined in a sudden flash of clarity to confront Eddie about his flagrant misjudgement.

Sending the book flying unceremoniously across the living room, he watched it land just short of his waste-paper basket and skid under his dust-covered desk.

Good enough, he thought, pulling out his cell and dialing up Eddie.

"Edward, I fear I have a bone to pick with you, my friend." He cut off Eddie's greeting.

"I tremble with anticipation," said Eddie. His voice came strong and clear, and the sound of it immediately lifted Jeff's spirits.

"Anticipation is the least of emotions that should be setting you atremble given my disappointment in you right now."

"How will I ever go on?" Eddie joked.

Jeff chuckled. "Well, facing the music would be a good first step. What are you up to right now?"

"Not far from you, actually. I'm with Bonnie and Anton at the Art Walk."

"The Art Walk is in August now? I had no idea that was even happening. I thought it was earlier in the year."

"Who can fathom the whims of the artistically inclined? You should know this though, you live right on the avenue!"

"I hate crowds," responded Jeff. It was true enough. "Besides, I haven't been down Whyte at all this weekend, what with my big date and all. Mind you, the Art Walk alone would usually be enough to keep me away, but I'm feeling unusually rambunctious today. Mind if I join?"

"I'm sure Bonnie would insist, to say nothing of Anton. This determination to face the hordes wouldn't have anything to do with your impending bone-picking, I trust?"

"Purely speculation," said Jeff. He was happy to join Eddie and his family. Despite his initial resentment of Bonnie stealing Eddie's loyalty away from him in the years shortly after university, he'd grown unexpectedly fond of her in the time since. And Anton—their bottomless pit of energy and enthusiasm in the guise of a plump seven-year-old with thick-framed glasses and inexplicably curly hair—Jeff could not possibly have adored any more. He'd known Anton since birth, and was proud to be accepted as an unofficial uncle. As a result, every giggle, squeal, and smile from Anton lifted Jeff's spirit and lightened his load. Jeff had once described him as a walking cocktail, but the disappointing reaction from Eddie ensured that nickname didn't stick.

Suddenly, the day was shaping up just fine. "I'll head out soon then, and text you for a location when I'm getting close."

"Sounds good, buddy. See you soon," said Eddie.

Jeff wasted no time at all hopping into the shower, changing, and hurrying outside.

For a long stretch, old, dilapidated apartments like his own lined the streets. Occasionally, where one had been torn down, there would be a couple of beautiful, modern houses that sold for a small fortune. The shape of the neighbourhood was changing, but the clouds of dust blowing across the streets on cool fall days remained. The drifters in sweatpants, crushed cans of Lucky Lager, and discarded hotdog trays assured Jeff that the gentrification process was mercifully slow.

In front of him, a big scraggly hare shambled onto the sidewalk, saw Jeff, and scurried away. It was patchy—the summer grey shedding slowly out to reveal spots of clean white beneath.

Edmonton was lousy with the beasts. When he'd first noticed them, Jeff wondered why the city's bustling homeless community didn't capture them, and eat like medieval kings in the River Valley. He'd only had to annoy a few friends with this idea before he learned that rabbits are too lean to live off of. 'Rabbit starvation' he remembered it was called. It took more energy to eat the rabbit than the meat provided, so killing them wasn't worth the effort.

What is? Jeff wondered as he walked. For the most part, he liked the hares.

The blocks passed quickly, and never did the oppressive weight of the sky above threaten to dampen Jeff's mood. A quick series of texts led to a plan to meet near the gazebo in the park by the old Arts Barn, and Jeff pushed through the maddening crowd with all the patience he could muster.

Fucking people, he thought, but managed not to voice it as he turned off Whyte proper and began his way towards the park.

The side streets were all closed down for the Art Walk, and metal mesh formed the frail walls of countless booths along the bustling byway—each hung with the varied works of local artists bold enough to rent them out and ply their wares.

Macabre Muppets, technicolor movie recreations, Cronenberg monstrosities, and countless nude women assuming some variation of the odalisque pose were on display. Over the noise of the crowd came the occasional barking of the more ambitious entrepreneurs, and above all floated the scents of the food trucks lining the street just ahead of Jeff where the art ended and the festival began.

The tight-packed crowds slowed Jeff's movement, but he was near the designated meeting spot now, and knew it was important to move with caution all the same.

He saw the bright white gazebo just across the avenue. It was covered with people sitting, leaning, or standing as they ate churros, poutines, mini-donuts, and onion rings. Others drank from the oversized, ice-packed, eight-dollar lemonades so bafflingly popular at the Art Walk and events like it.

Moving cautiously forward, Jeff kept his eyes peeled. At any moment, he knew, the sharp sight of young Anton would spot him, and then the inevitable ambush would be sprung.

"Uncle Jeff!"

Too late, Jeff spotted the little blur diving towards him. The heavy-set hooligan took him just below the waist at the height of his feline-leap, nearly causing Jeff to topple over. Catching his footing just in time, Jeff rolled with the momentum, reached down, and heaved the boy up into his arms.

"Antwerp!" he exclaimed, spinning him in circles above his head for a few moments before setting him back down and struggling to catch his breath.

Anton stumbled around in three exaggerated circles to show how dizzy he was, then pushed Jeff on the shin. "You're a twerp," he said. His glasses sat crooked on his round face as he smiled up at Jeff.

"Anton!" scolded Bonnie, then looked up at Jeff to nod her secret agreement with her son's indiscretion.

"Hello Bonnie, good to see you're still putting up with this miscreant," said Jeff.

"Don't call poor Ant a miscreant!" said Eddie.

"What's a mystery ant?" asked Anton, and the three of them shared a laugh, with Anton joining in late, but with only a hint of self-doubt.

"Come on, baby, we'll walk on ahead and let the boys talk," said Bonnie. She took Anton by the hand, and headed off down the long row of food trucks. The small boy stopped at each one, staring up at the pictures of food on offer, and alternating between whispering questions to his mother and yelling them out to the proprietors.

"So, how did that big date of yours go last night?" Eddie elbowed Jeff in the ribs, and jockeyed his eyebrows like the incorrigible dork he was.

A quick burst of laughter from Jeff took all mystery out of the conversation before he had time to tell the tale.

"That bad?" asked Eddie.

"Well, let me tell you. It was going all right. We were listening to some good old Tom Waits and talking after dinner—which she certainly seemed to enjoy. Then we got talking about work, and like everything else that gets near SALIGIA, the conversation soured."

"Well, your first mistake was the music. If I've told you once, I've told you a thousand times. 'Crimson and Clover' for a first date—always. But that still seems like a strange reason for the date to go south. Is she a big fan of multi-nationalist corporations or something?"

"She must have been." Jeff loved Eddie's minimalist humour.

"Well, no one could have seen that coming. Have you considered adding a disclaimer to your profile?"

"I really should," said Jeff. They walked in silence for a short while, watching Anton skip along holding Bonnie's hand. From the park came the sound of music mixing from a dozen different stereos, and the air was filled with the smells of good weed, sweet drinks, and deep-fried food. Even Jeff was lured by the distinctive scent of the mini-donuts frying somewhere along the long line of filthy looking, yet somehow delectable food trucks that stretched down the street.

"Bonnie and Anton are looking for something to eat, so we can expect to be here a good hour or two before he finally settles on what he wants," said Eddie.

"He still hasn't managed to move beyond the curse of his father's indecision?"

"A bold accusation coming from you. So, what did you come here to bitch about anyways?"

"That fucking book!" Jeff was a bit too enthusiastic in his exclamation, and accepted a scathing glare from Bonnie just ahead.

"It didn't revitalize your priorities and uncover your true potential?" asked Eddie. Sarcastic bastard. "I'd honestly heard good things from a few co-workers. I thought it might help you out."

"Do you know me? I want something to convince me the bullshit is all worth it, not a cheap list of hackneyed platitudes to placebo me into self-satisfaction. This brief stretch of morosity ends with change, Eddie, not with some hollow realization that I already have everything I need, or that the only real obstacle is me."

Eddie laughed. "Well that really doesn't sound like such a bad ending to me. Besides, sometimes the right attitude is a key ingredient to change."

Gravel crunched under their feet on the worn road as they paced back and forth behind Anton and Bonnie, who searched endlessly for the perfect meal to satisfy his youthful hunger. "While that may be true, the fact you never actually read the book couldn't be more obvious. Do you know what it recommended?"

"What?" Eddie asked, a wry smile creeping over his face. It was the look he always wore when he was ready to laugh at some misfortune he alone had caused, and then blame it all on the recipient.

"It said I should think of the five most important memories of my life. Then, I imagine each one as a layer of wrapping paper over the present that was my being, and remove each layer slowly. I was supposed to savour its colour, hear its texture, and feels its weight, then toss it aside. I was to repeat that until all the layers were gone, and then take in the present that was—get this—my present state."

"Well, how did it go?" Eddie managed over the pained look of derision painted across his face. Even he couldn't maintain his self-righteous façade.

"That's about the time I threw the book in the trash."

"Would last night's date be one of your five layers of tissue? What was her name? Avi?"

"Wrapping paper. No. And yes. Respectively of course."

"I don't know, you were pretty excited going in. And at the very least its colossal failure is a worthy memory. I think that's the first layer of your present—present."

"Sure, it's a funny memory, there's no doubt about that. That's not always enough though—the temporary laughs. I miss being excited about life, and looking forward to what's coming next, like little Ant up there. I used to think there were so many key moments to look forward to, but none of them have turned up. If the only memories I have to share are of disappointments, it's going to be a pretty sorry present in the end."

"Isn't that exactly what you're feeling though? A sorry present? What better memories do you have to explain it?"

Jeff cursed his friend's cunning. Eddie always had a way of joking his way into some simplistic truth, and even if the observations were shallow, he knew Jeff well enough that they always hit their mark. Death by a thousand cuts, or something like that.

Still, it made Jeff wonder. What were the key memories of his life?

"Honestly, it wasn't necessarily Avi I was excited about, just the idea of having someone, you know?" Jeff could hardly recall the last time he had anyone truly important in his life. Not the way Eddie had Bonnie. Not the way most everyone around him had someone.

There had been Sarah...what was it now, five years? Seven?

He'd met Sarah at a bar downtown, and they'd fallen into talking about old music and older movies. They'd kept talking right through the night, and on for several months after that. Their connection was fierce, and Jeff felt at the time that he'd loved her more quickly than anyone he'd ever known.

Eventually though, it became clear they'd talked about every song, movie, and idea they shared. They knew every point of agreement and contention, and explored every avenue of debate. Then, for a while, they'd sit in silence, content that they'd found someone so complementary to themselves.

Contentedness, however, was a glue less strong than others, and eventually familiarity turned to predictability. In the end, Jeff began to entertain the notion that finding someone similar to himself was the wrong choice, given that many days he couldn't stand his own company.

But it was Sarah that left first. With little warning one cold February morning, she said she needed new faces and places, and revealed she'd already made plans to move to Toronto—finding work as she could and starting her life fresh.

Jeff found that his sudden resentment of her transferred perfectly over to himself. He hated her for leaving. He hated himself for staying.

"It's no easy fix, Jeff," Eddie said after some time. "You'll never find anyone who'll give you everything you're looking for. That's not how it works. You've got to work on you before you're ready to be with anyone else. That's what I'd always been told, and it's what I found was true. I wasn't searching for anyone when I met Bonnie—you remember that. I was just getting out of my ridiculous college years, and finally felt proud of myself as I settled into teaching. I was already enjoying where I was, when suddenly she walked in and changed it all for the better."

Ahead of them, Anton was tugging on Bonnie's hand, wheeling back with all his strength to pull her away from a hamburger truck and towards a churro truck. "No!" he screeched with the high-pitched desperation achieved only by hangry children and murder victims.

"Look what that's got you," Jeff joked, but he knew his friend was right. Maddeningly, he usually was.

"It's just been so long," Jeff continued. "It's been since Sarah that I've really felt like I was in love. When she left, it hurt like mad, but even then, it wasn't the way it used to be. Broken hearts used to feel like the world was ending. Sarah was just a small rumbling below the surface. I'm lonely, but the pain is dull now. Do you know I haven't cried since my parents died?"

For a long while, Eddie was silent. He stared off towards the joyful face of his son and the defeated countenance of his wife as they waited in the Churro line. Jeff watched all this and smiled. It was hollow though—if pain was less these days, so too was humour and happiness when they did come.

He thought about the day he'd taken the call from the police, and heard that both his parents had died in their sleep—a carbon monoxide leak snuffing them out quietly and without warning. Jeff calmly thanked the officer, then laid down on the couch and cried for two days straight. As an only child, he'd suddenly become the last of his family name. It seemed a burden and a closure at once—that the end of his line had been sealed, and it would be his fault entirely.

Since then, the colours had bled out, and the highs and lows alike had eroded down from the thrilling peaks of old to pathetic, unimposing plateaus.

"Nothing's like it used to be," he finally broke the silence. "I'm not sure if it was losing my parents that caused it, but all the vibrancy is gone. I'm lonely, but more often than not I don't even care. I doubt I'll feel real love again, and I think I'm okay with that."

"Are you really?" Eddie asked. "Or are you just more willing to accept it?"

"I don't know. Maybe it's age, or depression, or something else, but I think I'm past the point where I can really open up that way. I don't have the hopefulness I used to. Everything I do rests somewhere between cool and cold. That's what you're missing about that whole Avi encounter. It was briefly exciting, but ultimately, it merely proves the rule. It's all just…alright."

Eddie's eyes remained on his family, but Jeff knew he was listening. Eddie had been Jeff's sounding board since they'd met.

"That's the case with everything in my life. Every day feels like the same plain beige template. How can I appreciate the present when the majority of it is wasted going to a job I can't stand, in a city I don't enjoy? I've been caught in these doldrums for years; I'm never going backwards, but I'm certainly not moving forwards either. It seems like the world is moving on without me…new trends, new ideas, new everything—and all the old stuff too. Everyone else checks off the big 'to-do' moments in life, while I'm just going through the motions."

Bonnie and Anton were sitting on a picnic table shared by several strangers, eating their churros happily as Jeff and Eddie stood by at a respectable distance. Best to keep such thoughts from the young, after all.

"What are these 'to-do' moments?" asked Eddie. "What are you still hoping for?"

"It's not one thing in particular. Just something to add a bit of colour to the world—a bit of meaning. I go about my day, and there are dozens of people I come into contact with on a regular basis. We get work done, go about our business, joke around or whatever. But I have this nagging feeling all the time, that to everyone I come across, I'm just a side character—just filling some minor role—or at the best adding a bit of background humour. I'm never a major player in anyone else's story. Does that make any sense at all?"

"It's a tragically narrative way to look at your life, but what if you reverse it? Don't worry about being the main character in other people's lives—especially ones who don't matter. Imagine how abysmal it would be to be a central player in the life of Marcy for instance." Jeff shuddered at this. "Look at it from the other side—who are the main characters in your life? What do they mean to you, and if you're not a main character in their life, why not?"

"I don't even know anymore," said Jeff.

He felt like laughing, but was scared where it would lead. He looked over to Eddie, who was watching him closely, and hoped he hadn't overplayed his concerns. Eddie was his best friend, and certainly the only person he could be this open with, but he didn't want him to worry. At one point, Jeff knew, it would doubtlessly have been Eddie that was the main character in his life. He'd been the star of the show for Eddie as well. During university, they'd been inseparable, even rearranging class schedules on occasion to ensure they could spend more time laughing at strangers and firing off obtuse observations that only they found witty.

Together, they'd helped one another through the hardest and best times inherent in the early adult years, and each honed his character on the whetstone of the other's esteem.

Often, Jeff thought back on those times with a pang of longing, wishing that time could have slowed down, wishing he could have appreciated it more in the moment, or that he could go back and revisit them again. But the wheel of time turned incessantly, and when Bonnie entered Eddie's life, Jeff knew everything had changed. While they would always be close, no one had room for two main characters, and slowly Jeff was shuffled to the periphery of Eddie's story.

"What about that Janice girl you've mentioned, what's her deal?" asked Eddie.

Jeff wondered how to answer that. What was her deal?

"She's suffering under SALIGIA, just like I am. I see a lot of myself in her—except that she still seems hopeful, or at least I still have hope for her. She's pretty new there, and her spirit hasn't been broken yet. I want to help her if I can."

"How noble of you," said Eddie. Jeff shot him a dirty look. "I honestly mean that," he insisted. "But are you sure you're not avoiding the issue here?"

"No," said Jeff, almost entirely convinced of it himself, "it's not a romantic thing. I wouldn't be against it becoming that, but that's not what it is for now, and that's not my intention. I'd just like to see someone make it in that place—to learn what to ignore, who to trust, and how to put it all behind you before it's too late. I think I can help her with that. For some reason, I think I have to help her with it."

"Why though? How can that possibly be on you?" asked Eddie.

Despite the cloudy sky, the day was warm, and the heat from the food trucks bouncing off the asphalt bordered on sweltering. Yet Jeff felt a sudden chill, and in the bangs of his hair there was a wet weight he hadn't felt for a while.

He remembered long ago, the day after the incident with the snow forts, he'd confronted Katie about everything. "You should have let me in your fort," he'd said, "I was the only one who stood up for you when they took your hat. Those guys are all jerks, but you took their side."

Katie had looked upset, but left without saying a word. Later that day, during lunch break, the boys of his class had surrounded him. "We heard what you said," they hissed, circling him like hungry wolves before springing as one, and piling on top of him. They'd pushed his head in the snow, burying his hat and soaking his stringy hair.

When they'd left, he did his best to shake the snow off his hat, but still it clung in patches, and all the way inside it melted against his head and sent freezing trickles down his neck and under his shirt. Jeff remembered thinking life couldn't get any worse, and that he'd never trust anyone again.

He was, he figured, at least half right on both accounts. Nonetheless, he'd refused to let it change his desire to do the right thing when the opportunity arose.

"It's not a moral imperative if that's what you mean," Jeff answered, hoping the question hadn't grown stale in the course of his silent ruminations. "I don't owe it to her or anything. I just want to. She's a good person, and too many good people have fallen victim to that toxic shithole. If I can save just one from that fate, why not do it? Besides, there's little better to do there. Aside from my actual job, that is."

"Probably the best thing to fill your day though, isn't it?"

"To be fair, that really only takes up three hours at most."

Eddie laughed. "Okay then, so how has this heroic quest been going so far?"

"It could certainly be better," Jeff confessed. "I made a joke the other day that really didn't land. I'd been fantasizing about running away, and basically told her she should join me."

"A bit soon for fleeing the country together?"

"Evidently. You never know what sort of standards people have for these things. Still, I think it'll blow over. It was a harmless enough joke, and Janice seems like a pretty level-headed person. I'll try to talk to her sometime tomorrow."

"Are you boys almost done?" called Bonnie. She was chasing after Anton in the park behind them. Having finished his churro, little Ant was a blinding flash of energy, darting between, around, up and down trees as Bonnie laboured to keep up.

Eddie turned, and began to slowly make his way towards the park in a half-hearted show of support. "Coming!" he called. Then quieter, to Jeff, he said, "So what's the plan then? How exactly does this helper's journey play out?"

Jeff thought for a moment, and was surprised to find how little he'd considered the details of his plan. "Well I need to start off by sorting out that whole 'run away' comment and smoothing things out between us. Then I guess I just need to be honest with her, tell her what the place is like, who to watch out for, and what it takes to get by. She's a smart enough girl, and very strong-willed, I think with a bit of coaching and encouragement she should be just fine."

"Jeff," Eddie sighed his name. "Is this really about helping her, or helping yourself? You've always had this strange hero-syndrome mindset. You act like being the martyr for somebody else is the only road to your own happiness, but it's never really worked out for you. Are you sure she even needs the help you're offering?"

Bonnie was leaping up and down, trying to encourage Anton to climb out of the tree he'd perched himself in. Anton, meanwhile, was cawing like a bird and tossing red leaves down at her.

"Anyone working at SALIGIA needs help, trust me. The place is a nightmare, and it's hard to get by alone."

Eddie just stared at Jeff.

"Maybe it's a little bit about me, but what's so bad about that? I like to help people, that doesn't seem like the crime you're making it out to be, Eddie. I think highly of her, and I want her to be happy. If bringing that about makes me happy along the way, isn't that better for everyone?"

"I know you hate that place, Jeff, and I know it's at least partially justified. Still, I'm not convinced that everyone there is suffering the way you are. You need change, that's for sure, but helping yourself should be the primary goal here, not a secondary effect. You've got to do what you need to for yourself, buddy. Now if you'll excuse me for a moment, I have some helping of my own to do."

Eddie hurried over, and pulling himself up by a low hanging branch, snatched Anton down and handed him to Bonnie. The boy protested momentarily, squawking and flailing his arms about. But as the parents coaxed and comforted him, he began to calm down.

Eddie was a good father, and was lucky to have a partner like Bonnie at his side. So too, Jeff knew he was lucky to have a friend like Eddie. He truly cared about Jeff, and if his honesty was occasionally a bit harsh, it always came with the best intentions.

He was right that Jeff needed change, he just failed to see that was exactly what Jeff was doing. The book he'd recommended was a wasted effort—change wasn't about memories, it was about taking action and doing things differently. That was what Jeff planned to do at work this week if he could, and despite the misgivings of his friend, he remained certain that Janice was key to that.

He remembered her first day at SALIGIA. The team had just finished a morning check-in, and Jeff was standing outside the boardroom, pressing his pad of paper against the wall to steady it as he rushed to capture all the key points he'd failed to record in the meeting since he'd been asked to stand up while answering Nadia's endless barrage of questions. He didn't have time to get back to his office to do so, as his next meeting was already overdue.

Behind him, he heard an unfamiliar voice ask Marcy where the washrooms were. "The entire building's layout is shown in your employee orientation manual, which should have been sent digitally to your SALIGIA account before your duties commenced today." Marcy's tone was indignant. "Did you not receive your orientation manual?"

"No, I mean—" the voice began, but was promptly cut off by an increasingly angry Marcy.

"Very well. Please talk to Myra at the reception desk of the main floor foyer, and have her resend it. She's been unreliable lately, and may need a re-orientation of her own. Henceforth, I want you to assume the duty of sending out employee orientation packages for our floor. Report to HR on Floor 95 to get access to the appropriate employee catalogues. Needless to say, you'll need to get your key-card access updated on Floor 2 first." Marcy turned on her heel and sped off.

Jeff, finally finishing recording his best approximation of the orders he'd taken from Nadia, tucked his pad under his arm and began hurrying towards his next meeting, on the far end of the floor.

"Excuse me," the stranger called out behind him.

A hot flush stole over Jeff's face. "Oh yeah, sorry," he said. "Bathrooms are around that corner; to the right and about five doors down. Watch out for the sink-spray, and if you need help with that access card, just let me know." He tried again to hurry away, but was caught off-guard by the candid relief that flowed over the new girl's face.

"Wow, thank you so much. This place can be a bit overwhelming," she said, and rushed on down the hall.

It certainly can, Jeff had thought. All the rest of that day, he'd remembered that one bit of honesty he'd seen in the black tower, and it had helped get him through.

"Say bye to Uncle Jeff now," came a voice from behind him. Bonnie and Eddie were getting ready to head home. Anton, nearly asleep in her arms, looked up and waved at Jeff before falling back into his sugar-induced coma.

"Good seeing you," said Bonnie.

"Take care, buddy. We'll chat again soon," said Eddie.

"Thanks for letting me steal him for a while, Bonnie. Bye guys," said Jeff.

He watched as they left, and envied the small boy's ability to love so publicly, trust so fully, and sleep so openly. Still, it wasn't rest Jeff desired. There was a hot energy inside him despite the sullen sky, and although he still had most of Sunday before him, he was eager for Monday to begin.

As he started the walk home, he saw another hare picking its way along a bit of grass at the edge of the sidewalk. It sniffed eagerly for food, paying no mind to the countless people all around.

CHAPTER 8
A Pretty Decent Day

"I've never been here before," said Janice. As they stepped out of their cab and walked into the dark bar, she narrowed her eyes to look around. At the far end of Jasper Ave, it was one of the last bars on the main stretch, and a place Jeff had visited often in his younger days.

A large central bar lined with worn old guitars dominated the middle of the room, and what few booths it had were torn-up and battered. "It has a certain quaint charm," said Janice.

Catching her alone in the hallway earlier that day, Jeff had asked if she'd join him for drinks after work—telling her both that he wanted to make up for the other day, as well as insisting that she'd love the bar, On the Rocks.

The first point was entirely true. Jeff remained determined to make amends and put his foolish quip behind them. The second point Jeff knew was an ambitious leap, but he hoped its role in assuring the original intention was enough to justify it.

"This place has stood the test of time as many trendier joints went by the wayside. Never doubt the appeal of a dive bar with a good stage," he said.

It was just after 5:00 p.m., and the place was nearly empty. They quickly made their way over to a high table off to the right, near the aforementioned and presently abandoned stage.

In short order, a server came by to take their orders—a Traditional Ale and plate of hot wings for Jeff, and a Long Island Iced Tea with a poutine for Janice. Jeff had also promised to pay—deciding at the last minute that he'd better sweeten the pot a bit if he wanted this apology to work out. Janice rolled her eyes, but accepted with minimal protest.

The drinks came quickly, and Jeff and Janice proceeded with some stagnant small talk for a while. The bar and Jeff's history with it. Places Janice frequented. The ridiculous events at SALIGIA that day. Finally, the food was set out before them, and Jeff steeled his nerves, resolving to get on with his endeavour.

"Janice," he began, "I'm sorry about what I said last Friday; about running away. It was a weird joke, and I really didn't mean it to be so awkward."

Janice didn't answer immediately. She was preoccupied awkwardly working her mouth to reign in a long tendril of melted cheese curd that stretched from her lips back down to the plate. As it broke off, it went wagging like a broken spring, and nearly caught against her neck before she took mastery of it.

"It wasn't so much the not coming back part that bothered me, although that was weird too," she finally answered, before plunging undaunted back into her mess of poutine.

Jeff wondered at this, and wracked his brain in a hopeless attempt to fathom what she meant. He'd never been the type to read too deeply into matters, or to look for meanings when he suspected there were none. Still, as life drew on, he found it a necessary skill to develop.

It was no easy task.

The seat beneath him was sticky, and the bar smelled of old beer. The only sounds were the quiet music playing from speakers set in each corner, and the occasional scrap of conversation from the sparse spattering of people around them. He wondered if any of them were listening to him and Janice.

"Oh," he started, like a child dipping their toes in to test the waters, "what was it then?"

Janice's face was lowered as she hauled again on the long strings of cheese reaching up from her plate to her mouth. The corners of two fries stuck out from her lips, and a small patch of gravy ran down her pointed chin. Still, Jeff couldn't miss the roll of her eyes. She didn't wait to finish her bite before diving into her explanation, and Jeff leaned back in his seat, gnawing on a chicken wing and sipping his beer, eager to take it all in, and hoping to move on shortly afterwards.

"It was your assumption Jeff—your pig-headed insistence on my joining you. I appreciated the offer at first, but you seemed to believe that I could just drop everything at any given moment. Don't get me wrong, I like you. You're a good guy and you've been kind to me. You're a lighthouse of decency on a stormy sea of assholes, but that place isn't my whole life. There's more than one way to escape it, and your reasons for being there aren't mine."

"Well, unless you're there for some reason other than avoiding starvation, they're probably pretty close."

"There are countless other things you could do, Jeff. You could change your life any day, and find some other way to put food on your plate. It's something else that keeps you at SALIGIA, but for the life of me I can't figure out what it is. No one hates it more than you."

"Everyone hates SALIGIA, Janice. How could they not? Anyways, what are you implying with that—what do you think is keeping me there? What's keeping you there for that matter? You could have turned tail after your first day, but you're sticking it out no different than me."

For what felt like a long while, Janice ate her poutine, and sipped on her drink. Jeff had begun to wonder if she had any sort of answer at all, when finally, she spoke. "Jeff, SALIGIA is one of the biggest and wealthiest corporations in the world. Like it or not, that means they have some of the best benefits. Most places offer nothing these days. SALIGIA is awful in a lot of ways—you're preaching to the choir on that point—but I'll stick with them as long as they take care of me and mine."

The bar was strangely quiet, and another long moment passed. Something stuck in Jeff's mind, refusing to turn over, but he couldn't quite put his finger on it. He wasn't sure he should say anything, recognizing it was shaky ground. Still, he'd never been the sort of man to leave an issue half-solved, and was sure that with a bit of tact and tenacity he could see this through and set his quest to help Janice back on course.

"That's fair, I'll give you that. I've had it said to me plenty of times that I'm lucky to work for them," Jeff admitted. Avi's words played through his mind, and his face grew hot. "I make more than a lot of people in similar positions, and the benefits are nothing to sneeze at. That's all true. At what cost, though? Is sanity worth security? I've been there long enough to know for sure, Janice, and I can tell you beyond a shadow of a doubt that it only gets worse. That place will haunt your waking thoughts and plague your dreams. Soon enough you can't escape it because you won't know any other way to interact but paranoia and madness. It will change you.

"Do you really want people like Francis or Marcy to be who you see the most? Do you want to think of Nadia's face first thing when you wake up, or hear her voice in the back of your mind as you fall asleep?"

"No Jeff, I don't. But that's not going to happen. I go to work, I earn my pay, and then I leave it all in that villainous-looking tower back there. Aside from our occasional meetups, I don't take any of it past the door. It's a job, Jeff; that's all it is. My life is at home."

Jeff felt flushed. Maybe the wings were hotter than he remembered them being. An uncomfortable minute dragged on between them, and he watched a couple make their way out to the dance floor. 5:30 p.m. on a Monday was hardly prime dancing time, and Jeff was less than surprised to notice the visible stumble in the man's step. He led his partner away from the bar, around a long line of stools, and into the center of the floor before taking both her hands in his, and promptly leaning hard into her. The patient and shockingly strong woman managed to catch his weight and turn it into a reasonable facsimile of a halting two-step. It didn't fit the classic rock that was playing, but the couple seemed to be having fun.

"I envy you that," Jeff said. "Even when I'm home, I spend so much time stressing about the day to come, the disasters and tragic comedies I'll have to endure. I don't know how you do it."

Once again, Janice was struggling to liberate a rebel string of cheese from the puddle of gravy it sat in, and began to shake her head in a doglike fashion before finally managing to rejoin the conversation. "Because I have to, Jeff. I worked my ass off to get a job at SALIGIA, and I'll do whatever it takes to stay there, because I have no other choice. I can't leave, but you can. Yet you're the only one complaining about feeling trapped. Why is that?"

The heat of the wings was picking up, and Jeff sputtered a moment before taking a long swallow of beer. "Fuck," he said. It seemed like a resounding and thorough expression of his thoughts. As the beer began to cool his scorching mouth, however, the gap between his intentions and reality slowly became apparent. "I mean,

I want to get out of there. I'm looking into possibilities." He heard the impotency of his own words, and sucked at another ranch-soaked wing as he continued. "You're right though, I admit that. It's not easy going from such security into uncertainty. I'd love to travel, to teach literacy or something like that. Anything with a bit of meaning and purpose to it—that's all I'm looking for. But it takes some savings to do that. I'm trying to put something away, to look at my options...

"What about you? Do you have any kind of escape plan?"

Janice stared at him, a dull expression on her freckled face as she chewed on an overly ambitious mouthful of poutine. Finally, she swallowed, took a big pull of her Long Island Iced Tea, and spoke in a surprisingly flat tone. "Have you heard anything I've said, Jeff? I'm not trying to escape. If anything, I'm trying like hell to keep this job. I want this job. I fucking need this job because it's the only thing I've ever found with the level of health coverage I need."

Jeff tried to jump in, but was cut off by Janice's heated soliloquy, "I have a boy at home, Jeff. A sick boy who needs a hell of a lot of medical attention. That's why I have no trouble putting up with Francis, and Marcy, and even Nadia. That shit doesn't bother me in the slightest. They're just people who've celebrated their own stories for too long to see how damn insignificant they are. I do my job, and I keep my son healthy. That's all I care about. They can chastise me. They can give me dumb assignments. They can change the expectations on the drop of a dime. Jordan and all the rest can mock me all day if they want—call me dumb, call me clumsy—I honestly don't give a shit. They're just words. My life begins where the reach of their opinions ends."

Jeff ate another wing, and now he was certain they were hotter than he'd hoped. The collar of his shirt was dampening with sweat, and his head swam. Janice was staring hard at him, swept up by her passionate diatribe, and Jeff had no intention of meeting her intent gaze.

Out on the dance floor, the drunk couple was whirling and swinging each other about in something between exultation and delirium. Jeff wondered if they came together, or simply found what they were looking for in just the right place. Both were dressed business casual, and if the man was significantly more drunk than the woman, something in the determination of her movements and intensity of her focus assured him that his inebriation was not the driving force of this coupling.

"I'm sorry," Jeff knew he had to say something, and that felt like the best place to start.

"Me too," Janice answered after some time. "I didn't mean to unload on you."

"No, I'm glad you did," Jeff replied eagerly. "What's the point of these drinks if we're not being honest with each other? I didn't even know you had a kid." He felt he did a good job of focussing on the point without simply stampeding straight into it.

"Yeah," she answered, "I don't really talk about my life when I'm at work. It's part of that separation I try to maintain—much to your disbelief. They're different parts of me. Honestly, neither of them are anywhere near who I imagined myself being. We're all stuck in some way or another, that's just life."

The dancing couple looked funny, all alone out there swinging around in lazy circles as they stared into one another's hazy eyes. Jeff admired their courage almost as much as he abhorred the idea of making such a spectacle of himself. More often, he preferred to act with subtlety. Of course, that had mixed results.

"Yeah," he said, "I hear that." Growing slowly more concerned about the heat of his wings, he signalled the server for another round. He wasn't about to leave his plate uncleaned, however, and slowly chewed on another one as he hoped Janice would continue the conversation and let him suffer in silence.

"Jeff, I never dreamed of working at SALIGIA, I'll give you that. There are a million other things I'd rather be doing. All of them with absolute grace and no clumsiness whatsoever, of course." She smiled as she spoke.

Jeff grinned and put back the last of his first beer just as the server brought out the next round. He couldn't deny Janice was a klutz, and appreciated her self-effacing humour. It reminded him of himself. At least partly—there was also something entirely foreign in the way she seemed to view herself and her situation that Jeff couldn't quite place.

"I didn't plan for any part of where I am now," said Janice. "But I've still chosen my traps, in my own way. You're choosing yours, too. That's all I'm trying to say." She took another bite of poutine, and set intently to chewing for a drawn-out moment.

"You're right," said Jeff. "It's true, even if I wish it wasn't. Every night I dream about quitting. Just getting up in the morning, packing my bags, and disappearing. Sliding away, flipping my life upside down, and changing it all. I imagine reversing every poor decision I've ever made; maybe lashing out in some irreversible way to ensure there could never be a return to status quo—that change and movement were the only options left. It's a fun fantasy, but that's always where it ends. The next day I go to work, and I go home, and everything stays the same. That's why it's just a fantasy—because real life is more complicated than dreams."

"Complicated?" Janice was indignant. "Let me tell you something about complicated. I used to think I had everything planned out. Life was a pretty simple presupposition—and I scurried down the obvious path until I was too far along to start asking questions.

"Got married to my high school crush when I was twenty. We'd been together since we were kids ourselves. But the bells had rung before I even stopped to consider if any of it was what I wanted. It wasn't anything against Wayne, I just hadn't done enough yet. I wasn't sure who I was—much less where I fit with someone else. Just like that, it felt like all of 'me' was just a secondary part of a bigger 'us.' So, I left him after less than two years. Those years were happy enough, but I needed something I couldn't even understand, much less articulate."

She stared down at the table for a while, sipping slowly at her drink. "It wasn't till later that week I found out I was pregnant." Janice looked intently up at Jeff now, setting down her fork for what seemed like the first time since it arrived. "You can't deny the irony of it all. Escaping one person who risked co-opting my identity, only to have Eustace show up. But it is different now. Or I've gotten used to it, anyway. I do live for him—every waking moment. I know it's mutual though, even if he barely has a choice in the matter." Her laugh was sardonic.

"But I'd never been so scared," she continued. "I laid up all night, not crying, just staring at the ceiling, and watching all my dreams playing across it—all blurry and changed. I knew I wasn't going to go back to Wayne and pretend nothing had happened. I still wanted to find myself. I just knew it would be a hell of a lot more complicated—as you say." With a sudden start, she resumed her efforts on the poutine.

Jeff took a long drink, not knowing exactly how to respond, but knowing her openness deserved the same. "I had no idea," he stumbled. "That does sound ... complicated."

"Oh, it is, believe me. Wayne's actually been amazing with the split custody we settled on. It's gone as smoothly as I could ask, but I knew even before Eustace got sick that I'd never get to have the freedom I'd dreamt of when I left. After he was diagnosed, I made a beeline for the best health insurance I could find with my training and experience. I needed a good benefits package to help cover the cost of all the medications, and I finally found it at SALIGIA. So, I'll hold onto that as tightly as I can, and even be thankful for it. It's not the path I set out for, but it's the one I got, and I'm alright with it."

"Wow, that's a lot. I'm really sorry for assuming anything before…" Jeff trailed off, uncertain what to say. His face was flushed, and he chewed on another wing hoping for the best. The spice of each was subtle at first. It was a fruity, enticing flavour when he bit in, but then it began to slowly burn—a smouldering feeling that made his breath into fire and his saliva boiling oil. The beer he chugged faster and faster only served to swirl the heat around his mouth—never washing it away.

Sucking his teeth to conceal the pain, he stared out at the dance floor. The couple were now engaged in some strange ritual which made Jeff's mouth gape open. This however, only increased the searing heat, and he closed it quickly, continuing to watch with a forced smile. They stood at arms length from each other, hunched over and circling one way then the other like hunting animals stalking prey from the cover of dark. The woman sneered and flashed her dark eyes as the man stumbled, and focussed hard at getting the brown bottle of his beer to his mouth for a swig—half of which ran down his chin to the floor below.

Most people in the bar were watching the odd display. Janice, however, appeared to take no notice at all. She chewed slowly on her poutine, licked her lips, and finished off her first drink. Sliding over the second, she took a deep breath and smiled. "Don't worry about it, you couldn't have known."

Patience had never been Jeff's strong suit. Finding the right moment to push an issue without risking a relationship had always been one of his chief concerns. Being only then in the middle of reconciling the last time he'd fucked up with Janice, he felt he should be especially careful now.

Still, he was curious. "How old is Eustace?"

Janice's smile broadened. "He's four now, and he's doing well for the most part. He doesn't understand all the hospitals, and I can't even begin to explain to him what leukemia is. It's been most of his life anyway. He probably doesn't even remember the year before it all started. He just follows where I take him, and brightens any shadow his little eyes fall on. I wouldn't be living this life if it wasn't for Eustace, but I definitely couldn't manage it without him."

Janice was an endless well of surprises today, and Jeff was struck by how open she was being. Aside from children and the insane, people seldom spoke so frankly. Especially not to coworkers.

Still, his mouth felt like it was melting, and Jeff was self-conscious about how fast his second beer was diminishing. It was his only reprieve however, and he called for another round. Every time he opened his mouth, the fresh flow of oxygen reignited the inferno within, and each word was precious to him. "Eustace..." he risked quietly, not yet certain where he meant to take it.

"Oh, yeah. It's a strange name, I know," Janice blurted out. Clearly, she loved talking about her child, and Jeff enjoyed listening to her talk about him. She'd never been more herself in all the times he'd seen her, except perhaps when she was cleaning up some coffee-related disaster of her own creation.

"It was my grandfather's name," she went on, stealing a quick sip of her own, nearly full second drink. "Not that I ever met him, but he was always my hero growing up somehow. It's weird, because he was an awful father. My mom barely knew him either. He went off to war just after she was born. My mom's family lived down in the States back then. I don't even know what war it was, but he signed up and chose to go. Maybe he couldn't find any other work, I don't know. Anyways, he shipped out, and never really returned. He took to it, I guess, and racked up quite a few medals over the years." She paused, staring off silently for a moment. "There was never a lack of wars to fight in, and I think he liked it that way. He found his calling, and he went for it."

Not wanting to risk the inferno just yet, Jeff said nothing, but offered what he hoped would be taken for an understanding nod.

Janice seemed to accept the encouragement and continued. "As a dumb kid, I always admired that about him. I just assumed that's how life was, and that my calling would come along as sure as his did. But nothing really seems that important these days. Maybe it didn't in those days either. There's just good times and bad times, and a strange blend between them that passes with nothing remarkable enough to even make a memory. It's like an endless ocean, with only the stars of money or family to set your prow to.... I ended up with family," she finished. Then, with a sudden smirk, she raised her glass, clinked it against Jeff's, and with a drawn-out swing of her arm, she craned her neck backwards and downed the substantial remainder of her drink.

"Wow," said Jeff, knowing the feat demanded some remark.

As if choreographed, the server brought out their next round. "Last one for me," Janice told him.

Jeff finished his last wing, then his second beer, and slid his third in close.

Only time and distraction were needed now. His mouth was charred and dry, and he was sure the worst was behind him.

Janice had evidently finished her poutine at some point in her long story. The plate was well cleaned, with a single used napkin folded in its center.

"You could do a lot worse than family," said Jeff. He wasn't convinced that really meant anything, but he wanted Janice to keep painting her story over his former scribbled imaginings, and figured that would be enough.

It was.

"Nothing beats family," Janice declared. "My mom used to tell me that. She held our family together. I imagine she was always skeptical of the idea after what Grandpa pulled, so she made herself a buttress against any possible failing. It was her dedication to family cohesion that first set it in my head that family was the highest destiny one could dream of. Well, here I am living the dream!" She laughed as she spoke, and the heat in Jeff's mouth slowly began to diffuse to the rest of his body.

"You're certainly poetic tonight," he said.

A flash of rose passed over Janice's face before she spoke. "A place this nice kind of brings it out of a girl." They both laughed long and hard, and clinked drinks once more.

Leaning back in his chair and sinking into its worn cushion, Jeff bobbed his head to the heavy thud of the speakers behind him, and looked out to the dance floor. The couple had calmed their stupor, and slow-danced now in the centre of the floor, turning in tight circles with their faces smashed together. They didn't seem to care that the fast metal music buffeting the bar suited their dance like shorts in winter, and for the first time Jeff felt like he understood the strange maniacs.

"So," he started, not entirely certain where he was going with it, "what would you be doing then, if you had no attachments?" He suddenly felt the urgent need to clarify the implications of his question. "Alternate universe scenario—no bonds on you, and let's assume enough money to have some measure of freedom. What's Janice getting up to?"

She chewed her upper lip, and glanced at the ceiling. For a moment, she sat frozen. Then, after another quick sip of her drink, she began. "I don't know. I'm not sure I've ever had the time to consider that in my rush to get where I thought I was going, and the fight to keep it all together since then. What would I be doing?" She resumed chewing her lip for a while, and took another drink.

"If it was the version of me that I am now, and I suddenly just had all that somehow, I don't think I'd ever stop moving. I'd go and see all the things I assumed I'd see along the way, then I'd find other things to see."

"Leaving coffee stains on each one, no doubt," said Jeff.

Janice laughed. "Well of course, but really fancy coffee since money is no issue in this reality. Nothing but the best from each place I went, and a puddle left behind."

Janice longed for freedom. She missed spontaneity and surprise. Who wouldn't? Jeff missed those things too, and he'd taken a solo vacation through South America only four years ago. He'd missed the serenity and the chaos as soon as he got home.

"Where would you go first?" he asked.

"I don't know. It's overwhelming to think of—how do you choose from limitless dreams?" She took a drink and smiled, reflecting on the thought. Her eyes held a flickering shimmer for a second, then some distraction blew across them, and she looked down at the table. "But I can't lie to myself. Every place I imagine being, I can't avoid the thought of wanting to get back to Eustace. He's where I want to be. Anywhere else and I'm left wondering if Wayne is feeding him right, and getting him to his appointments. Hell, I'm still doing that right now in the back of my mind. I can't escape who I am, Jeff, what can I say?" She shrugged.

Jeff raised his glass to her optimism, and took a long drink. "I'm sorry you have to worry like that," he said.

"It's not so bad. All part of the deal, I suppose. Besides, he's worth it," she said.

"What about you, though? Alternate universe—what would you do if you had none of your bullshit excuses holding you back?" Janice barely finished her question before bursting into a long, choking laugh. She slapped the table and looked up with tear-filled eyes. "Wow, that came out so mean. I blame the Long Islanders."

"No worries, they will sneak up on a person," he said. She wasn't wrong anyway, he couldn't deny. Jeff felt trapped at times, but had none of the responsibilities Janice dealt with. None of the worrying about other people and what they were doing—or not doing.

"I know exactly what I'd do." Jeff leaned across the table as he spoke, and fixed her with a foolishly intense gaze. "I'd wait until I could catch Nadia in the middle of a meeting, or in the lobby, and then unleash the greatest 'I quit' speech the world has ever heard. I've got it all scripted out—rehearsed and everything."

Janice chuckled. "Well don't be a tease. I want to hear it."

"Oh, I wouldn't dream of spoiling it before the moment, it would be unjust. I assure you though, it'll be spectacular."

"Well, I honestly hope it never happens. But if it does, I hope I'm there to see it."

Jeff faked an indignant scowl. "Hope I'll never have the freedom and financial security to leave my job?"

"Well, in a lottery-type scenario, I suppose." Janice rolled her eyes.

"Oh," said Jeff, "I imagine it would have to be a pretty hefty prize. I know I'm in a better situation than most, but any empty notion of setting forth with no plans and no promise is years behind me. Still, a man can dream."

"You still haven't answered the question though. What would you do after you quit? What's the destination?" Janice sipped intently at her drink.

"The question was, 'what would you do?' I think it was a fair answer." Janice pouted at this. "Besides," Jeff continued, unabashed, "my plans after that aren't really clear. That—and the overwhelming shortage of money and job prospects—is why I haven't pulled the trigger yet."

They both shared a long laugh at this, then a clink and a drink. As Janice set her glass down, she glanced quickly at her phone before speaking. "I still say it's not fair. I told you some secret stuff, and you just admitted you'd quit if you had enough money. Everyone would do that."

"Not Nadia. It's not in her programming," said Jeff.

"Yeah, probably not Nadia."

"Okay." Jeff faked a long sigh. "I'll tell you a secret to even things up. A story I don't tell much; my first day at SALIGIA."

Janice covered her mouth and faked a gasp, then set her hands down to reveal a playful smile.

"After university, I bounced around between a few different jobs without much luck. Policy gigs, databases, stuff like that. It wasn't an easy market. After years of struggling and with my ambitions in a free-fall, I landed an interview at SALIGIA. That was four years out of university, so I guess I was about twenty-six.

"They pretty much ran the media game by that point, so a shot with them had me jumping for joy. The interview turned out to be an endless list of strange questions I completed on an app they made me download and pay for, but I got a call later that day inviting me to an orientation session."

"Oh my God!" Janice broke in, "I had to take that weird test too. What was it, a personality evaluation or something?"

"Probably. I'll bet it tests to see if applicants have the willpower to survive in the corporate environment. The emotional fortitude to not go completely mad."

"Sounds about right, but that wouldn't explain how you passed," said Janice.

"Har har," Jeff mocked. "So anyways, I showed up at orientation, and was met by this tall, round, bespectacled man named Kevin. He was my guide that day, and I met him in the main floor foyer. He came up to me, looked at me once and said, 'You must be Jeffrey Boggs.'

"When I admitted that I was—still with some pride at that point by the way—he introduced himself, and explained that he'd be orienting me and one other person, once she showed up. Just then, from behind me, I hear 'Oh hello Kevin, are we ready to go?' I turn around, and there's my partner for the day—this tall, bear-like woman wearing a grey blazer. I thought it was strange she knew this guy's name already, and I remember wondering if she had to take the same test I did, or if she got there some other way."

Jeff grasped his drink tightly in his fist. "Well, let me tell you something, Janice," he whispered, and leaned in even closer for his dramatic reveal. "I wonder that to this day—because that woman was Marcy."

Janice gasped again. This time it seemed sincere.

Jeff grinned. "That's right, Marcy and I started together. We shared an orientation, and were interns at the same time."

"Who was manager back then?" asked Janice.

"It was an entirely different set of supervisors; they seem to cycle pretty quickly. They disappear, or they make the corporate cut and get assigned to a different floor. But the manager hasn't changed all the time I've been here. It was Nadia back then—looking exactly the same as ever. Save for the always fresh business suit, not a thing about that woman has changed in the last decade, and I expect she was there looking like that long before I started. Probably since that damn tower was built."

"Weird!" Janice finished her drink emphatically. "So, what happened? What was it like?"

"Well, the orientation was much the same as always, I imagine. Tour of the floor—82 since day one—and then instruction on intern duties. Brief instructions of course, then utter, terrifying independence."

"Sounds about right."

"I've watched a lot of interns come and go. I've known people who quit, people who got fired, and people who just never came back. I've seen people begin to climb the ladder around the office, only to get hauled out by security for trying to pry the safety guards off the window in their new office."

"Jesus," said Janice.

"On the whole, I think I've done okay for myself. Being Team Lead is far from glamorous, but it's only one level below management. I doubt I'll ever make the jump, and I'm not sure I'd want to, but that's fine."

"Why not?" asked Janice.

"Because then I'd have to rub elbows with that crowd. It's

already rough being in this precarious place between the Brass and the Tins, and I don't want to cross that line. I doubt it's in the cards anyway. Marcy knew people when she started, and despite her shocking ineptitude at everything she's ever done, she's failed upwards her whole career. Her tenure as an intern only lasted four months before she became assistant to a supervisor, and she was a Team Lead by the end of the year. She wasn't through her third year before making supervisor herself."

Jeff let his face show his disgust. "There's no merit, no explanation, no rationalization in the world powerful enough to tell me Marcy managed to pull that off on an even playing field. Something's askew, and I don't care enough to find out what it is."

Janice chuckled. "It does sound kind of fishy."

"Good enough secret for you?" Jeff asked.

"Not too shabby," she admitted.

Jeff signalled for another beer. Janice waved for the server to bring her bill.

"So," Jeff said, "all of this to say that I've seen a lot at that place. I know how maddening and isolating and downright mind-boggling it can be, and I'm always around if you need to talk about any of it."

Janice smiled. "Thanks," she said.

Out on the dance floor, the drunk lovers held hands. They stretched apart from one another, staring into each other's eyes across the length of their arms. Slowly, they spun in lazy circles, their joined hands the axle to the wheel of their intoxicated affections.

The server brought out Jeff's new beer, and handed a bill to Janice, who reached for her purse.

"I said I'd get it," said Jeff, waving a hand dismissively over the bill, then feeling foolish about such a trite gesture.

"Oh no, I've got it. Thanks again though," said Janice. She

tapped her card and set out a generous tip.

"Well," Janice grabbed her bag and got to her feet as she spoke. "Tomorrow is another day of it. After all, the city isn't going to brand itself."

Jeff smiled, too wide and too long, he thought, after finally pulling himself out of it only to sit in silence. The entire conversation with Janice, he'd thought of work as a theoretical concept—something that opposed his will and had to eventually be escaped. He'd avoided thinking of it in any practical sense, specifically that it would happen again to him tomorrow. To him, and to Janice.

The way she handled so many tribulations humbled Jeff. The contrast burned in his gut, and in answer the heat of the wings began to boil up once more. He took a long pull from his mug, but it had no effect on this flaming spectre of things once savoured.

He wished he could master that cavalier attitude of hers. She went in every day to the same obscene cesspool of an office, and took all the unbearable bullshit he did—maybe more even—with such grace and charm. He could never manage that stone-faced stoicism for more than a few exhausting minutes.

Then again, he didn't have as much to drive him. Janice was lucky in a lot of ways. She had an undeniable motivator at home, even if that came with some additional frustrations tied to it.

"Are you sure you can't stay for one more?" he asked.

"Yeah," Janice said with an exaggerated frown, "it's getting late. I've still got to bus home and get a few things done around the house before I go pick up Eustace from Wayne's. Then again, maybe if I'm a bit late he'll be ready this time," she laughed.

Jeff smiled.

"Thanks for a great talk, Jeff."

"Goodnight Janice, I'll see you tomorrow," he said.

She waved, and hurried out the door.

For a long while, Jeff sat and sipped absently at his beer.

The music droned on, and the couple continued to rotate. Jeff's mouth still burned, but he didn't mind anymore. He thought about the various strange things that kept people tied down, or prevented them from living how they really wanted.

It seemed a terrible fate that so many people's hopes just collapsed in on themselves. There was little surety in the world. Friends, lovers—that's why they were so important. Because with so much uncertainty, and so many people and businesses and twists of fortune seemingly acting against you at every turn, sometimes a person needed someone they could trust.

That's what made the passing days worthwhile. Jeff was glad for the friends he had. Still, a lot of people didn't seem to care about the ones that mattered most. They continually let others down, or took without ever giving.

Jeff couldn't stand people like that—and he'd known his share.

They were users and manipulators. The worst part of it was that those were the types of people who seemed to do the best in life. They were the Marcy's and the Nadia's who rose up to dominate and victimize others, while gentle and decent people like Janice were tossed carelessly in their wake and left to drift.

She didn't deserve that.

Not at work, and not anyplace else.

Jeff sat, sipped his drink, and thought long and hard about the choices he'd made so far in life, and the sort of choices he hoped to make going forward.

He didn't want to waste any more time.

He didn't want to be afraid of making the big changes he knew were necessary.

He really didn't want to be so reliant on something he hated.

Most of all though, he didn't want his friends to feel those things. Janice especially—so kind and selfless. She deserved better than that.

No one ever helped him those first days at SALIGIA. Not a single day after them either.

She didn't need to go it alone.

Jeff swore in that moment to help her any way he could.

A sudden crash jerked his eyes back over to the dance floor.

The woman was lying on her back. There was a flipped table rolling off to the side, and drinks and food were scattered everywhere. People were throwing their arms up and screaming to no one in particular. Most of them were soaked and stained.

The man stood alone on the dance floor, staring dumbly at the carnage and teetering on the balls of his feet.

He must have let her go as she leaned back in the ecstasy of the dance. She went tumbling backwards over a table, while he was left to barely maintain his own balance.

He had it right up until the end. Then finally, with a long, slow tilt, he crumpled forward and face-planted into the floor. Bouncers swarmed over to drag them both out.

A fumbling manager offered gift certificates to the angry, soiled patrons nearby.

Jeff chuckled. *Poor bastard,* he thought.

He considered another beer—he had no one to get home to anyway. But the highpoint of the dancer's tragic fall was not likely to be topped, and he opted to settle up and move along.

Outside, the street was quiet. A few bedraggled groups stumbled by, their voices echoing between the towers and down into the River Valley beyond. Off to his right, where the Jasper Ave began to curve away from the downtown core, the sun was setting. Peeking out between two tall white buildings, it sent brilliant lances of gold and orange stabbing across the street. They illuminated walls, shimmered on the asphalt, and lit the leaves of trees and bushes all the way down to the falling banks straight ahead.

Turning towards his own bus stop, Jeff couldn't help but feel it was a fittingly scenic ending to a very decent day. He headed east onto the avenue, and hurried forward with the sun at his back. A slow wind rose, cold and sharp. It bit at his face as he walked, and whistled through the alleys. It tossed the hair about his ears, and whispered that fall was drawing to a close.

Chapter 9

Performance Review Day

The harsh wind continued all of Tuesday, and by Wednesday morning it howled through the city hurling dust and debris, and menacing the flower-laden hats of old ladies.

Loose papers whirled and tossed about the streets, and the force of the gale buffeted the long grey and blue bus all the way from the stop outside Jeff's apartment to the tall black doors of SALIGIA. The brief ride on the LRT was the only reprieve from its attack, as it was mostly underground.

Racing into the building, Jeff relished being free of the wind at last, but from the moment the elevator opened onto Floor 82, an undeniable electricity filled the air. Nothing was obvious, but he was certain something was amiss, and approached the coffee machine cautiously. He was determined to fill his mug before whatever absurd trials SALIGIA had set for him were sprung, yet wary lest he walk right into their fiendish trap.

He navigated tentatively through the countless touchscreen menus on the machine, struggling as always to find the option for a simple, large black coffee. When he found the correct button sequence and pressed start, he listened to the chrome abomination whirr, hiss, grind, and gasp, until it finally began to send a slow trickle of dark coffee down into his mug. At the halfway point, the stream turned to white cream, and Jeff sighed—accepting his fate.

Stupid fucking contraption.

No sooner than his mug was filled and sealed was the cause of his urgent foreboding laid bare. The loud speakers buzzed to life, "This is a fifteen-minute notice," came the needlessly robotic voice. "A Performance Review will be held in the South Hall today at 8:45 a.m." It crackled, then ended with a long hiss.

Jeff grinned.

Far more invasive than your standard Presentation Day, Performance Reviews happened on an entirely irregular basis, and were thus always a bitter surprise. The Brass seemed to revel in that aspect however, and Jeff had even caught an excited twinkle in the eye of some clumsy supervisor or another over the years when the announcement was made.

Misery loves company, he thought. He assumed any pleasure the supervisors derived was from knowing that those under them would get to share in their suffering—which meant it was likely a double-edged blade for anyone below Nadia.

Then again—to the best of his knowledge—he was the only one of the Tins who enjoyed Performance Reviews, but that was because he'd discovered a special secret. Like most, he too once cowered when the terrible refrain played, and wished to God he'd called in sick that day. After his first three or four however, Jeff had finally realized the brilliant, liberating truth about Performance Reviews: none of it made any sense, and nothing mattered.

Sure, there were small consequences tossed around sometimes. New training sessions could be assigned. Someone could end up landing in the shit book. That was always funny.

In the end, there was little that could be called a proper review about it. Sometimes the Tins would get cards with arbitrary scores and Barnum statement comments. Once the cards were even signed by whichever supervisor had been closest to the printer when the admin staff ran them off.

Lately, Jeff had begun to suspect that Performance Reviews were actually orchestrated by Nadia to review the performance of Marcy and Francis, and the rest of the floor's staff were merely brought in as unwitting pawns.

It seemed the most likely scenario based on his admittedly biased observations. In fact, he could only come up with two other possible explanations. Either they had been invented as an element of pure chaos in order to remind staff that there were things beyond their understanding, or they were simply a glitch in the programming of whatever mad artificial intelligence ran SALIGIA, with no hope of ever being corrected.

Whatever the reason was, once Jeff had accepted that they made no sense and nothing mattered, it all became a game.

That changed everything for him—he always enjoyed a good game.

It was a useful mindset in general, and whenever a Performance Review came along to remind him of this theory, Jeff regretted not employing it more broadly in his life. *Maybe from now on,* he thought, trotting briskly down a long hallway on the west side of the building. The Performance Review was on the furthest side of the building, and Jeff grabbed his notepad out of his office at a full dash as he hurried along.

The South Hall was SALIGIA Floor 82's most decadent presentation room available to the Tins. It was not to be confused with the South Hallway, which led to the Executive Wing, and was rarely accessible for the Tins. Even some of the lower Brass seemed to get a chilly reception going down that hallway.

As doors to offices slid by, the crowd about him began to gather, like a river passing slowly by its many tributaries and growing into a great flood. The crowd raged and jostled around him like penned up bulls, all struggling towards the broad double doors further up the wide white hallway. The doors, which were the only entrance or exit for the Tins from the South Hall, were ceiling-high, and frightfully black.

Not particularly caring where he sat, he let the natural course of the crowd carry him ploddingly forward, like the slow but steady movement of the immutable tides. Certainly, he thought, he didn't want to sit near the front, under the bright metal eyes of Nadia, or within blame-range of Marcy or Francis.

Jordan too—he really didn't want to get stuck sitting next to that noxious idiot again.

Leaning one shoulder forward now, he began to push his way up through the crowd, plotting a straighter course for the doors.

Of course, it would be great if he ended up getting a seat by Janice. He felt confident his apology had gone well, and Janice had seemed to be in good spirits ever since. If he could manage to sit by her, the meeting might not be half bad.

The doors opened in the midpoint of an immense rectangular room. The back of the hall, seating-wise, was to the right, and to the far left of the entryway was a raised dais from which the Brass cast their judgements.

Moving as methodically as he could within the general norms of corporate work culture, Jeff made it in, he guessed, within the top 10th percentile. Several rows in the back were taken, as were all the seats near the single water cooler—halfway down the hall, opposite the entry.

The entire room was jet black, with a crimson SALIGIA logo in each corner near the ceiling. Seven snakes lay intertwined, biting at one another and devouring their brethren in an endless tangle of tails and fangs. Jeff always thought it was an unapologetically evil logo, which made it the perfect choice for SALIGIA.

So too did the South Hall perfectly capture its malevolent tone. The dark palette, the tremendous height of the ceiling, the tiny, sharp-edged chairs set out for the staff—the fucking dais! All of it seemed designed by cruel-hearted psychologists or gifted demons with the sole intent of crushing the spirits and dashing the hopes of all who entered there.

The shiny black walls were actually screens, and were used by the Brass and their hidden team of computer-capable grunts to display stats, mottos, and provocative imagery befitting their subject matter.

Once, Jeff saw Nadia use actual fire on the walls while chastising a copywriter. He'd found it funny at the time, but somehow the memory stuck with him, carrying a bitter aftertaste.

The worst thing about the South Hall, thought Jeff as he shuffled towards a seat near the entry, *is the damn scent projectors*. Most of the time, a faint smell of lilac lingered throughout the hall. He was never sure why, but something about it really pissed him off. The scent, like the walls, could be changed at any moment to suit the whims of the Brass—who communicated through headsets and digi-pads to their team in the back. This was primarily used to send in pleasant smells while good news was being shared, a slightly sour note for bad news, and for times of punishment, there was a scent Jeff could best describe as the smell of fear.

Often, he suspected a subtler version of this strange technology was used throughout the building to secretly dampen the spirits of the staff.

Nonetheless, with the example of the flames already setting the boundlessness of the South Hall's reckless disregard for human decency, Jeff feared the truly unpleasant extremes the scent projection system could be taken to. That was a second reason to sit near the door.

The first, of course, was to flag Janice over to a seat he saved for her by setting his notepad down on it, knowing she'd soon come scuttling in among the very last stragglers, flustered and bedraggled by the crushing gravity of corporate life.

He couldn't blame her for it. Even for a vet like himself, it could be a lot to deal with. Sometimes, Jeff wondered if the homeless life was the way to go. It was something about the deep, honest way they laughed when they were together. Something in their relaxed posture—their lack of posturing. Inevitably, the next Edmonton winter would come along to change his mind.

That wouldn't be long now.

"Sorry, Jordan, this seat's taken," Jeff said as the grinning idiot tried to back his way into it. Jeff had no doubt he'd seen the notebook and simply decided to ignore it. He smiled spitefully back as Jordan pouted, then turned away in a petulant retreat.

Jeff couldn't help but be proud of himself. Jordan's inability to take a hint and shut up during meetings was a constant thorn in Jeff's side. He was the loudest, most obnoxious person at SALIGIA to never fail their way into the Brass, and Jeff had always disliked him as much for that as his willingness to express what Jeff only thought in loathsome silence.

He pulled out his phone—safe enough before the Brass arrived—and pretended to scroll through it as he watched the throng of people push slowly into the hall. Why it didn't have more doors was beyond him, but he was certain there was some twisted, calculated reason behind it. *Make them fight for it while the Brass have a private entry—remind them what their place is. Something like that,* he thought.

Suddenly, the sight of Janice sliding in amidst the scrum startled Jeff out of his fake distraction. It was, after all, still a full three minutes before the scheduled start time. As Janice raised an inquisitive eyebrow his way, Jeff grabbed his notebook off the seat and indicated downward.

"Three binders, a cup of coffee, and you're early?" he asked.

"It's a new record!" she answered.

From four rows ahead and just to their right, Jordan scowled back at the newly claimed chair, then at Janice, and finally at Jeff. Jeff smiled again.

"Well, I'd be lying if I said I wasn't a bit shocked. What's going on?"

"What do you think? What in the blue hell is a surprise Performance Review? It sounds like trouble, and I don't want to give them any reason to blame whatever trouble it is all on me."

Janice was a fast learner.

"I forgot this was your first one. You're in for a real treat."

"They've happened before? What are they?" Janice spoke perhaps a little louder than was wise in the South Hall, where the walls had more than just screens, touch pads, and scent projectors.

Jeff twisted his face in a fake show of deep thought, and leaned in closer as he finally began to speak. "Think of it like a gameshow," he began, "except instead of clear rules, winners, losers, and the potential for prizes, there's indiscriminate hostility, random punishments, and meaningless results."

Janice frowned, "I don't know if that makes it sound better or worse. Did something happen? Are we in trouble?"

Glancing quickly at Jordan, who sat with his head cocked suspiciously in their direction, Jeff leaned in a bit closer before continuing at a whisper. "Something probably happened, but we'll most likely never know what it was. We're almost definitely in trouble—at least some of us—but who, why, and how much are yet to be determined. Honestly, I've seen five of these in my time here, and I've yet to see a single reasonable result. They're arbitrary, foolish displays of corporate power meant to keep us all bewildered and panicking about job security so we won't complain about the conditions of said job. They may also be a sneaky opportunity for Nadia to evaluate the supervisors—but that's still a theory I'm tinkering with at this point."

"Are we going to be asked to explain our work? I don't know how to do that yet," said Janice. She seemed genuinely concerned. Jeff found that strangely funny.

"Will there be ratings?" she soldiered along the endless road of her well-earned paranoia.

"Maybe," said Jeff. He wished he could offer her more, but he was truly as clueless as she was. His wealth of experience in the matter only served to further obfuscate the clarity Janice naturally sought heading into this strange and unruly proceeding.

"You'll have to trust your instincts on this one, I can't even begin to guess how it will go down. Whatever happens, just remember that everything is pointless, and there's no real meaning behind any of this. Try to relax and have some fun; it's for the best."

Janice leaned over to respond with an expression of mild amusement on her face, but just then an ominous gong sounded from the speakers, and the scattered bits of chatter went dead. Jeff laid his pen and notepad across his lap, turning to a blank page in the event there was anything worth recording in the next few hours. Both he and Janice pressed their backs straight against their chairs and stared towards the front of the hall.

The scent of lilac faded as if carried off by a gentle breeze, and a strange, indefinable odour wafted in to take its place. It had a hint of wood to it, but there was a mustiness that made Jeff feel strangely uneasy, and he scrunched back into his chair as the silent seconds mustered against the Tins.

Finally, the lights dimmed, and an electric charge filled the air as the black walls faded to a dull brown. At the front of the room, a rectangular black window into space opened in the brown of the wall, and a deep, chair-shaking bassline rumbled through the high-ceilinged hall.

Suddenly, Marcy and Francis appeared in the middle of the void—the black screens that formed the doors had slid suddenly apart, Jeff knew from previous investigation.

They sauntered dramatically in, and the depth of the bassline increased. It shook the floor, unless perhaps there as a floor-shaking function built into the hall, which was admittedly possible given the self-aggrandizing excess of SALIGIA.

Marcy stepped to the right, and Francis stepped to the left, each placing their digi-pads upon the thin silver podiums set out on the dais. Marcy adjusted her combined ear-piece and mic, and whispered something into it. Francis stood like a statue, staring down at the floor in front of him.

No one in the room—Jeff included—could have imagined the tone blaring through the room could increase, but increase it did. His ears hurt and his bones rattled beneath his tense flesh. He could feel each loose flap and fold of skin trembling and shaking, and his teeth threatened to pop out of his jaw and scatter across the floor like chicklets.

A sudden smell took the audience. It was old and dry, like the stone of some unexplored mountain cave, mixed with a smoky, carbon scent. Then, the lights dimmed to near pitch black, and a single beam of bright white light shot down from the roof, creating an illuminated white pillar in the darkness before them. If there was a hiss as the door opened again, Jeff wasn't sure, but the flourish with which Nadia stalked into the light made him stifle a chuckle. He couldn't deny that SALIGIA knew how to put on one hell of a production. If they were half so dedicated to actually achieving some tangible purpose, he had no doubt they could change the world.

Don't kid yourself, they'll still manage to change the world, Jeff thought. His face felt heavy. *I just hate to imagine how.*

Nadia ended her grand entry with her arms raised triumphantly at the centre of the dais, which began to rise on noiseless hydraulics. It lifted her slowly upwards as the scent of the room shifted back to summer fields, fresh flowers, and dying fires. She wore a long flowing black dress with loose-hanging arms, and her raven hair was tied back in a tight bun.

Janice sat stiff as a board, watching the proceedings with a puzzling air of fear, confusion, and excitement that Jeff fully understood. Slowly, her right hand drifted over towards Jeff, grabbed his pen, and scrawled in long loopy letters across the top of his notepad, "WTF???"

"Good people of SALIGIA." Nadia's voice was smooth and well-articulated. She always maintained the perfect balance of gravitas and severity to command a room and leave no doubt that she was in charge—benevolently so only by the good graces of the corporation for which she stood. "Today, I have deemed it necessary to hold a full-scale Performance Review. Over the past few weeks, I have gathered there is some confusion about how certain initiatives complement one another, and what the goals of each are. I have heard mixed messages about where each initiative stands, and what the implications are for their completion.

"The goal today is to sort out these needless confusions, and get everyone on track for the betterment of their initiatives, and for SALIGIA as a whole. As always, teamwork and collaboration are among the chief goals at SALIGIA, so the majority of this meeting will be facilitated by your supervisors, Marcy and Francis. Having said that, we will strive to ensure you are all out on time for the Independent Working Workshop at 3:00 p.m. If this cannot be accomplished, the workshop will start immediately after the conclusion of today's Performance Review, and run until finished. Overtime will be paid according to SALIGIA protocols."

"AKA: Not at all," Jeff scribbled under Janice's WTF???

SALIGIA's protocols were available as a download from their staffing page—but to read and understand it all would require several decades and a law degree. The learned take away from experience, however, was that SALIGIA did as they wanted, and somehow got very rich doing it.

Nadia stepped to the back of the dais and began poking at her digi-pad as Francis leaned over his podium. "Any questions before we begin?" he asked.

Ashley raised her hand. She was the newest employee aside from Janice and Tali, and was still struggling to catch up. Taking a resentful nod from Francis as her cue, she proceeded. "At most team meetings, we can only talk about one initiative at a time, and not how they impact each other. Can we just talk about our work all together in this Performance Review, or do we have to stick to all those rules?"

Ashley seemed to have little capacity to grasp the social complexities of a place like SALIGIA, which meant she often asked out loud what everyone else knew to keep to themselves.

Francis and Marcy both glanced back at Nadia, who made an impressive show of revealing nothing on her stony face save for a half-smile illuminated by the screen of her digi-pad.

The supervisors stumbled for a response, but it was Marcy who pulled herself together and managed to form words first. "The focus of today's Performance Review is to address failings within and between the various teams in order to move initiatives along at a rate which is satisfactory to both our clients and shareholders." Marcy kept one eye on Nadia as she spoke, her words coming as if from a teleprompter that was always a second too slow. "The process for solving these challenges will be facilitated on a case by case basis by Francis and myself. The IT team will be doing their best to track time spent on each project for billing purposes, and we'll all help them by ensuring the conversation remains as linear as possible."

"Translation: I don't have a damn clue," Jeff wrote.

Janice nearly let her laughter slip out, and Jeff shot her a cautionary glance before gluing his eyes back to the front of the room. At their podiums, Marcy and Francis were struggling to avoid going first. They glanced sidelong at one another with trembling bottom lips.

The screen of Nadia's digi-pad sent an icy blue glare over her thin face.

"Like a scene from *Catch-22*!" wrote Janice.

Very few people in the office could keep up with Jeff when it came to literary references, and he always appreciated Janice's efforts to do so. In response, Jeff began to sketch Marcy and Francis as Tweedle-Dee and Dum, which only further complicated Janice's efforts to avoid laughing.

It was Francis who finally caved in and took the risk of going first. "Let's start with the Green City Initiative. We'll want a photo-opportunity with city officials by the end of the month, and whatever spot you pick for it had better look greener than it did at the start of summer."

It seemed like a tall order given how seasons work, and Jeff was happy the task was Jordan's rather than his.

"We've established a few new green spaces, although the actual growth has been spotty," said Jordan.

"What about the advertising campaign? I haven't seen any of the posters you've been promising," said Francis.

"The marketing campaign for the Green City Initiative was temporarily suspended in a unanimous decision by a quorum of board members for the Oil City Initiative. They felt the general messaging behind the campaign ran counter to their interests."

"A healthier planet?" Francis asked.

"Yes," said Jordan.

"I can't imagine the shareholders behind the Green City Initiative were happy about that." Francis' face was transitioning slowly from its natural opalescence to something closer to a cherry tomato. His brow trembled as he stared intently at Jordan, with an occasional subtle, flighty glance back towards Nadia.

"No," Jordan answered, hanging his head. "They weren't."

But money mattered more, thought Jeff. He'd seen such cross-initiative interference enough to know how it worked.

Nadia slid her short fingers quickly over the hidden face of her digi-pad.

Marcy, standing fortified behind her podium and grinning like a predator, leaned forward, "This is a perfect example of the kind of inter-initiative conflict we've been noticing in the numbers lately." She took a few quick steps to position herself between Francis and Nadia. A fine corporate move if ever Jeff saw one.

"It's the Clean City Initiative that's throwing everything off, and that one's yours," said Francis. "A media-influencing corporation like ours can't take on a project promising to reduce the media in our own market. It's hubris!" He shook as he spoke, and threw his hands skyward like some ancient cave-dweller appealing to the primordial gods for a mercy they would never see.

"The Clean City Initiative is the highest paying contract we've ever had on this floor. It would seem that saving the world is shockingly lucrative." Marcy stood tall, but there was a visible waver in her back, and a curl to her lip which told Jeff she knew how uncertain her footing was in a madhouse like this.

There was a weight against Jeff's leg, then a tickle. Janice was writing on his notepad again. "Getting things out like this could be helpful???"

Jeff scribbled his response. "When has honesty ever been the best policy?"

Janice snorted, and for a brief, terrifying moment, many eyes in the South Hall shifted to them, and upon the dais at the front all discussion paused.

"Rian, is that true?" Francis blurted, perhaps inadvertently saving Jeff and Janice.

Rian, who sat only two rows ahead of Jeff and several seats to the right, lurched suddenly erect. Her head tilted to the side, and her jaw drew gradually askew. Jeff imagined she lost a good bit of mass from the grating of her teeth, which he could almost hear.

She leaned forward, then looked suddenly towards the door. Jeff understood the urge instinctively. Too often, in meetings no different from this one, he'd looked towards that door and others, and imagined just walking out—or running as the case demanded. He'd leave the building, and hit the sidewalk like the wheels of an escaped fugitive peeling into life on the blacktop to forever.

Then, Rian did something Jeff hadn't imagined. She braced her back, stared straight back into Francis' shimmering pink eyes, and answered him to the best of her ability. "Yes."

Whether it was true or not didn't matter, and Jeff had no doubt she knew it. He nodded his respect, not caring who saw.

"Damn!" wrote Janice, her face an inscrutable mask even as her hand danced above the page.

Jeff nearly made the mistake of snorting this time. It was nice to get confirmation that others celebrated these wanton displays of stupidity and bravado. Especially Janice.

Above the frozen heads in the crowd, Francis stood like a man stunned by a savage strike. His legs wavered beneath him, and his eyes rolled untethered in his head.

Everyone in the room, Jeff knew, were witnessing Francis' complete meltdown. Jeff looked over first to Marcy, who grinned smugly and crossed her arms as if the war was won, and then to Nadia, whose face revealed no sign of human emotions. Jeff imagined the firing of wires and lighting up of circuit boards beneath the smooth contours of her carapace. Still, her articulate digits danced across the screen of her digi-pad, and her attention slid back and forth between it and the antics of her minions.

"But how much has it cost us from other initiatives and potential contracts?" Francis wheeled around and thrust a triumphant finger at Marcy, who blanched and sputtered.

"Jordan?" she called, for no clear reason other than escaping the spotlight.

How Jordan managed not to throw up or implode, Jeff had no clue. He did glance over-long towards the door, and for a sweet second Jeff thought he might finally be the one to live the dream and go charging out like a scalded dog.

Jordan leaned forward, interlacing his fingers behind his head and groaning like a starving animal.

"LOL," Jeff scribbled on the notepad, and Janice gave a fleeting nod.

Did Marcy really think there was any way Jordan could pull an accurate assessment of how much potential income one initiative had cost others straight out of his ass? These were the heinous implications forced on everyone present. Meetings like this were designed for the public flaying of the Tins upon the bloody altars of the Brass. Nadia's robe, Jeff thought, would be more fitting with a dark hood draping down over her eyes.

Suddenly, Janice's face went dead, and a soft tremor shook her body. She reached out, grabbed the pen, and with a stony face peering at Jordan's tortured form, she wrote. "That will happen to all of us sooner or later."

Jeff took the pen from her, faking a pained grin he knew she'd notice. "It doesn't matter. It's a puppet show. Don't let it bother you."

Janice's face returned to its pensive resting state, and Jeff looked back to the front. Marcy was back at her podium, her long neck craning over to Jordan's cowering form like a vulture. Francis was doing his best to shrink into the overbearing blackness of the room. Nadia waited, looking back and forth between Marcy and Francis— a spider watching the dying struggles of her nightly feast. Never did her multi-faceted eyes turn to the immaterial suffering of poor Jordan.

Janice flipped the page on his notepad, and began to draw as Jordan pulled himself slowly up to face his doom.

"It's impossible to say," he squeaked. "But in theory, the

Sustainable City Initiative could be finding green marketing solutions that would solve this entire problem."

Gasps rocked the room, and the smell of smoke and sulphur suddenly rode roughshod over their senses. Like the shifting of gears, all eyes turned back to Francis—the supervisor leading the Sustainable City Initiative.

A sharp elbow in Jeff's side tore him away from the drama and turned his attention back to the notepad on his knee. There, Janice had scrawled the image of Marcy and Francis cowering upon the stage. They were haggard, bent, and starved as they played for the attention of fawning blobs below them. But behind rose an impressive rendering of Barad-dûr—the dark tower of Sauron from *The Lord of the Rings*. Its stylistic depiction told Jeff that Janice was a movie fan more than a book fan. With a comic blur of motion, the eye snapped its attention back and forth between Marcy and Francis just like the judging eye of Nadia on stage.

Jeff nodded approval, failing utterly to conceal his broad grin.

Francis shriveled under the oppressive attention of the room, and the torment of Nadia's eye pushed him against the sharp edges of his podium. "Adra," he barely managed to get the name out, "where are we at with that?"

Adra was a pro, and didn't miss a beat. "We're struggling to make progress with green marketing alternatives when the City Branding Initiative is forcing such a dramatic increase to traditional marketing demands."

Whoosh, thought Jeff, and the terrible pendulum of the room's judgement swung back to Marcy, the supervisor of the City Branding Initiative. A spasm seized Jeff's body, and he felt Janice's eyes on him even as the room reeled and his mind raced. He knew what was coming.

Marcy's face twisted into the hideous visage of a snarling and wounded beast. Then, with the immutable thrust of fate behind her movements, she turned with a desperate, searching hatred towards Jeff. "Jeff," she screeched, "you're Team Lead on the City Branding and the Clean City initiatives—what are you doing to balance these essential stakeholder interests?"

Through the plastic of the closely jammed seats, Jeff could feel Janice's body shaking. She was on the City Branding Initiative as well, and this lightning bolt had struck a bit too close.

With an effort of will, Jeff relaxed, allowing his posture to slacken and his form to melt back over the rigid edges of his chair. "The City Branding Initiative is about having this city known for something. The Clean City Initiative aims to reduce clutter and make the city more presentable. I'm tempted to ask why those two goals can't coincide, but I don't want to step on the toes of the Green City Initiative," he finished with a cavalier grin, leaning back in his chair.

He remembered the days when he couldn't handle SALIGIA's bullshit so well. It wasn't until he finally accepted everything was a game that it all came together. Now, he was in charge, and with his expert riposte the focus went back to Francis—the supervisor of the Green City Initiative.

Minutes crawled into hours, and the insane tedium played out before them like the mad pantomime of some lost tribe—prostrating themselves before the great obsidian monolith of SALIGIA.

The little lined notebook slowly filled up with quips, quotes, and pictures. Jeff's sharp, frenetic declarations juxtaposed Janice's long, lacy flourishes. They shifted fluidly between direct commentary on the manic fluctuations of justification and misdirected blame, and literary quotes to complement the absurdity ranging from Tolkien, to Shelley—who seemed obvious to both of them—to Melville—who neither truly liked, yet still enjoyed referencing in situations like this.

The attention—mixed ever with shame and piercing accusations—passed from Marcy to Francis and back, and each now dripped with sweat and slurred their words as they chanted their rebuttals like pagan incantations. The walls hummed with a red deeper than wine, and the air was sickeningly sweet.

Nadia, standing behind them all and swiping her pointed nails across her digi-pad, gazed back and forth, her paralyzing eyes lancing about the confines of the dreadful hall like snakes striking at whim.

Lunch passed unrecognized, and Jeff's stomach groaned. There were only eleven minutes left until the Independent Working Workshop was scheduled to begin, but they stretched on eternally.

As Jeff was frantically sketching a rough depiction of Hal from *2001: A Space Odyssey*, a sudden smell of grass and dandelion assaulted his senses. The walls turned to a warm magenta, and his stomach heaved.

At the front, Marcy swiveled on her heels. "Janice, when can I expect those quotas?"

The shock of Janice's body convulsing upright shook Jeff's core, and her eyes constricted to needle points.

Jeff always thought of Performance Reviews as a game, but seldom had he paused to consider the deeper stakes. Now, his heart missed a beat. A tremor passed through his lap, and he accepted gratefully whatever harbinger of heart-attack this might be. Then, tearing his eyes away from Nadia's roving gaze, he read Janice's panicked scribble on the notepad. "HELP!"

They'd been joking about how Marcy and Francis seemed like mal-programmed and emotionally-broken AIs, and had lost track of the conversation at hand. Now the terrible weight of the Corporate eye was pressing down on Janice, and neither of them had a clue what it wanted.

"Game!" Jeff scribbled, hoping his shaking body would not be noticed by those on the dais. "Pass the ball!!!"

Her body rattled against her seat, and Jeff knew she was about to have her true Performance Review moment. It happened to everybody eventually, and she'd been lucky to coast by so far.

The moment hung, and each second passed with the weight of pursuing footsteps in dark alleys. Jeff held his breath, watching Janice's face first shaking, then freezing, and finally tensing. Her upper lip swallowed its stunted sister, and she seemed to shrink in her chair.

"The quotas are irrelevant," she stuttered with an expression carved from stone like the statues of ancient kings, "unless we know what our deliverables are. Maybe Nadia can answer that?"

Ice.

Banshees.

Stabbing memories of things he would never see, smell, or hold again—and the sickening taste of bile. Jeff swooned in his chair, and his ears rang with fresh gunshots and early-onset tinnitus.

How many seconds? How many minutes passed?

The room roiled in stupor. They couldn't have been more stunned if a flashbang exploded in their midst.

Marcy and Francis were on their knees, white as ghosts, and each turned towards the bitter figure of Nadia, posed like a spike of iron above all—dead centre, and chillingly still.

Jeff's muscles ached and convulsed in the throes of utter exhaustion. A tremor shook the air of the room, and the walls simmered to the red of boiling blood.

The air smelled like oatmeal cookies, and far off came the sound of trickling water, until a tremendous rumbling line of bass shook off every other sense, leaving everyone gasping and clutching their heads, crying for mercy or quick death.

Torment. Tear gas and terrible truth.

Nadia stepped forward, the sable tail of her dress flowing over the dais and painting it nightmare-black. Each step sent a tremble of bass through the hall, and Jeff failed time and again to swallow down the rebellious ball of fear that rumbled up to his throat from the bottom of his roiling belly.

Then the tension broke, and a torrent swept the room.

Marcy screamed at Francis.

Francis countered Marcy, and brought in Jordan.

Jordan jumped to his feet, raging about the intentional sabotage of Adra, who pointed viciously at Rian, loudly quoting statistics that perhaps both, perhaps one, and quite likely neither one of them really understood.

A gong-stroke peeled through the Hall, sucking the air from the lungs of all in attendance. A smell like raw iron took the crowd, and Nadia now stood on the edge of the dais. The digi-pad rested stiffly at her left side, the point of her right hand stretched out towards Janice, and her eyes stabbed like dirty syringes.

"It is this very lack of decorum that is stunting the growth of my department, Janice. This entire meeting was—" Nadia was cut off, and time stood still as Jeff rose up as tall as he could. His eyebrows were arched, his mouth quaked, and his hands hung dead at his sides.

"She's right," he said, "we'll never straighten out these initiatives unless we get some direction from the top."

The walls melted away to blackness far deeper than the black-grey resting state of the screens. So did the floors, and the roof. The sound went out, and the distinct lack of smell sent a surge of panic up Jeff's spine. They were cut off, all of them. Listless and bereft of hope. Astronauts spinning in space as the Earth grew slowly smaller.

A lifetime hung in limbo, and the grand game Jeff had entered into revealed itself to be a ruse—a pox upon the workplace, and the personal well-being of everyone present. Everyone save Nadia, who gazed now—to Jeff's utter astonishment—not at himself, but at the trembling, clustered ball that was Marcy and Francis.

The hour hung like a man condemned, just short of their 3:00 p.m. escape.

Janice leaned over, a shimmering light reverberating in her eyes. "It's okay Jeff, I spoke out of place."

She looked up. "Nadia—I'm—"

"No!" Jeff interrupted, still standing. "Out of place be damned. You didn't make the mistake here. They did." He thrust his finger towards the front of the Hall. For far too long he'd kept his mouth shut, only dreaming about what he wanted to say to Marcy, Francis, and Nadia. Each day, he regretted not being more honest. Now the levy broke—he couldn't stand the thought of Janice taking the brunt of their wrath. Not if he could stop it with a bit of honesty.

Nadia's eyes were gun barrels roving from Marcy to Francis, who clung to one another and jockeyed for the position farthest from her. Francis seemed to win, stumbling around Marcy and bumping her forward with a jab of his elbow.

Finding escape futile, Marcy lashed out instinctively. "Janice, establishing the priorities was the intention of today's meeting. If you don't have your quotas that is an issue we can address at a different time."

"Leave her alone," Jeff exploded. "You don't need the quotas, you need to be a leader and tell us which initiatives take priority."

"Jeff!" Marcy wheeled around on him and shouted. "We can discuss this uncharacteristic insolence in our next therapy session."

He heard the murmuring around him, felt his face flush. "You said—" he started, but was cut off.

"Back off, Jeff," snapped Janice. A stony expression crossed her face as she shot a furtive glance his way.

Jeff was adrift at sea. No stars. No winds.

"He's right!" called Jordan, standing up and kicking the seat in front of him.

"Please!" screamed Francis. Then he pulled out his digi-pad before continuing, "It's time for the Independent Working Workshop, which you all clearly need more than ever."

Rian, Ashley, and several others began to protest, but were cut off by Marcy, who duly pulled her digi-pad up to her face and sprang to attention. "Finally, please note that due to the damages done to the men's washroom last Friday, all access to restroom facilities will now function by scanning your staff ID-badges at new readers installed above the toilets and sinks earlier today. Any damage done in the washrooms will be automatically deducted from your next paycheque."

Great, that should fix things, thought Jeff. He imagined struggling to activate the sensors while also dangling his key card down in front of the scanner—and the likely wave of water to the face that would result. Honestly, it sounded half-refreshing in the moment.

Unwilling to let Marcy get the last word, Francis flipped madly through his digi-pad, and began to call out some final reminder, but his voice died gasping, and the Hall fell silent as Nadia snapped her fingers twice, and stepped again to the front of the dais.

"This meeting has been a terrible disappointment." Her words were the rumbling of thunder in distant lands—a threat as yet unrealized, yet undeniable and maddening in its brutal inevitability.

"Jeff and Janice," she called, and Jeff's blood froze, "report to HR immediately after this meeting. You will be expected in Revision Room C7. Anything you miss in the Independent Working Workshop will be made up afterward, on your own time," she decreed.

"As for the rest of you, it is clear the supervisors have a good deal of work to do in getting you on track to meet the efficiency expected of those in the employ of SALIGIA. I have selected a course on teamwork and inter-team communication for all of you. You will report to work at 6:00 a.m. this Friday, and take the #47 Train from SALIGIA Station to our conference center in Jasper. The seminar will run the full work day.

"Return train fare will be provided to those employees choosing to return to the city immediately after the course. Those who choose to remain for the weekend will be required to find their own transportation and accommodations. Friday's Agenda Guidelines and Corporate Protocols course will be rescheduled to Monday, at noon."

A collective groan rumbled through the room, and the walls snapped back to their resting state. The scent reset to lilac. It never ceased to amaze Jeff how fast Nadia could act—and how vindictively. The SALIGIA trains were world-class, and would have them to Jasper in under two hours. All the public transit was laughable, however. The decision effectively stole Friday morning and night away from the staff. Worse, it sent them to one of the most beautiful mountain resorts in the world, but left them unable to participate in anything but corporate training.

It was cruel, devious, and brilliant.

The crowd poured slowly out the doors and off towards Breakout Room Victoria, where the Independent Working

Workshop ran. All except Janice and Jeff, who strode on silently down the hallway, turned left to break away from the crowd, and walked heavily towards the tall silver line of elevator doors.

A pall of tension hung between them, and neither spoke as Jeff scanned his card. The sliding doors of the elevator opened, and Jeff let Janice step through first. They stood together, silent as stone sentinels, as he pressed the button for Floor 95. The doors crept together slowly, then clanged shut with the chilling finality of a closing mausoleum.

"You won't believe what the HR floor is like." Jeff hoped to add a bit of levity to their miserable reality.

"I've been there." Janice's flat response killed his hopes in their cradle.

The car crawled slowly up. Why the elevators at SALIGIA—the non-management ones at any rate—were so pathetic was beyond Jeff's reckoning, but it was a long-accepted reality of the Tins. It screeched and protested, and finally grated to a sudden stop as the screen above the door showed a bright red 95.

The door opened, and Jeff's eyes clenched. The dull grey of the HR floor was somehow suffocating, and he swallowed three times before slowly looking up again at the drab stretch before him. "Welcome to SALIGIA Tower Edmonton's 95th Floor—Human Resources! Please follow the signs to your destination." The voice greeting them was dull and lifeless as wet bread. It plodded on in a genderless monotone—like the buzzing of static made into words just to tell them which side of the hall to walk on for maximum safety, and remind them to wash their hands if they needed to use 'the bio-facilities.'

There was a short hallway just ahead of them, and one to either side as they stepped out of the elevator. Each was equally grey and lifeless, and each ended with a tall, windowless grey door. The walls in every direction were covered in signs—most a slightly lighter shade of grey, but a few were slightly darker. Each was etched in fine, subtle text that was all but impossible to read.

"Revision Room C7," Jeff repeated to himself as he squinted at the signs. Amid descriptions of what was down each hall, they contained safety disclaimers, branded catchphrases, and useless historical information about SALIGIA, the tower they stood in, and the land it stood on—which was legally purchased, the text assured.

Nothing Jeff could make out said anything about revision rooms.

"Well, it's worth a try," he mumbled, and ran his card across the scanner by the first door.

"Employee #1781999—Jeffrey Boggs—you do not have access to the Records Retention branch of Human Resources. Please cease tampering with the door immediately. Further malfeasance will be reflected on your permanent record."

The grating robotic voice made Jeff jump. "Well, that's one down," he said.

"Employee #31102018—Janice Cohen—you do not have access to the Management Wing of Human Resources. Please cease tampering with the door immediately. Further malfeasance will be reflected on your permanent record."

The voice, coming from the middle hallway, startled him once again, much to his embarrassment.

Jeff rushed playfully to the final door, but was disappointed to see with a quick glance behind him that Janice followed with only a dour sense of duty, not matching either his pace or his feigned enthusiasm.

"Employee #1781999—Jeffrey Boggs—you have been granted

access to the Asset Management branch of Human Resources. Please proceed through the door."

The door zipped off to the side—showing some of that famous SALIGIA style, and Jeff passed through. No sooner had he crossed the threshold than it snapped shut again with a metallic clang. A frustrated sigh came from the other side of the door, and Jeff scolded himself for chuckling a bit.

He already knew he'd overstepped—and even if he'd meant to help Janice back in the South Hall, he certainly hadn't done a very good job of it considering their current predicament.

"Employee #31102018—Janice Cohen—you have been granted access to the Asset Management branch of Human Resources. Please proceed through the door."

The door whooshed open again, and Janice stepped through.

"Welcome back, Miss Cohen," Jeff offered, hoping the silly formality would ease the dry tension between them.

Janice dodged around him and kept walking.

They followed the long grey halls quietly. With each branch or turn, a new door presented itself, with a new placard filled with illegible scribbles and legal disclaimers.

Each one required a key card, and every door was shockingly diligent in ensuring that only one employee could pass per swipe of the ID-badge.

The halls were neither cool nor warm, and all the corners were rounded. The air was dry, and smelled faintly of old barns and mothballs. Jeff wondered if this was a function of hidden scent projectors, or if the source was even more awful.

They lost track of time as they wearily wandered through the empty halls. When in doubt, they repeated their habit of trying all doors and seeing what was open to them, and with this system navigated their way from the main hall, to the Asset Management Branch, to the Asset Direction Wing, and ultimately towards the Asset Redirection Wing.

The endless grey walls and identical signs made any sort of standard navigation impossible. Everything looked the same, and they pushed deeper into the depressing labyrinth only out of sheer necessity.

"Could this be some brilliant ploy?" asked Jeff. "We'll have everything resolved by the time we find the right room."

"Not likely," said Janice.

The arduous journey had not softened the mood between them. Jeff was sure a cold beer and honest talk would do a better job than whatever HR had in store, but opted not to push his luck.

Finally, the monotony of the halls changed when they reached the Asset Revision Wing. For the first time since they'd arrived on the floor, windows appeared at intervals along the walls. Through each Jeff could see an elderly lady flipping through an enormous binder. Whether they were different binders—or even different elderly ladies—he couldn't be certain. The scene was eerie, and made Jeff all the more eager to get off this infernal floor.

Another fork in the hallway, and another wrong guess. Their path—always guided by the same empty voice, took them to the right now. Here, each window revealed a lone technician toiling on some messy cluster of machines.

He wished he could talk to Janice about the dreary implication behind both employees and hardware being classified as "Assets" by SALIGIA, but again reasoned it better to accept what solace the silence could offer.

The hall of robots—as Jeff decided to call it—ended suddenly with another grey door. Scanning his card, he was welcomed finally to the Employee Revision Hall—another long grey corridor with three grey doors on each side. The one on the far left stood agape.

Once Janice pushed through the door, they marched slowly forward.

Halfway down the hall, a tall lady dressed in nurse's white emerged and waved them in. "You must be Employee #1781999—Jeffrey Boggs, and Employee #31102018—Janice Cohen." Her voice was warm and soft, but too rehearsed to comfort Jeff. She had a stern look under her smile, and he wondered about her age. She was clearly an adult female, but whether she was an intern or a few days from retirement, he had no guess.

They followed her into the room, where she sat down at a flat brown desk. They took the two chairs in front of it, and waited solemnly as the lady flipped through her digi-pad.

"I understand the two of you had a little snafu during a meeting today, is that correct?"

They nodded.

"Janice Cohen, we haven't seen you in this wing before. Let's hope it doesn't become a regular occurrence, eh?" She laughed far too hard. Her sickly-sweet attitude gave a poisonous air to the room—like mould spores and hot light through dusty windows.

Janice smiled and nodded, still holding onto her hard-edged silence.

"And Jeffrey Boggs, oh—" she exclaimed with a start, "I see you're already connected with an approved SALIGIA therapist, that's good. I'll see that you get an appointment in just as soon as possible, deary."

Jeff was certain her voice had grown even more nauseating. She looked at him with pity now—folding her hands on her desk and looking worried he might melt.

"Feeling all right for now?" she asked, for no discernable reason.

"I'm fine, and please don't worry about the appointment. This is just a misunderstanding."

Janice rolled her eyes.

The HR drone smiled sympathetically. "Oh I'm glad to hear that, you really are a trooper. I'll make sure that's scheduled anyway—always best to be safe."

Now it was Jeff's turn to roll his eyes.

Still, the tension hung, and from Janice he could feel a radiating heat—like a pressure chamber ready to explode at any moment. What words of sacred HR wisdom the drone was pulling up on her digi-pad Jeff was almost eager to hear.

She leaned slowly forward, and slid the device to their side of the table. "I must ask that you each sign this before you leave," she said.

Before Jeff could move, Janice snatched the digi-pad up, nearly knocking it off the desk in the process. She scanned it quickly, long dark lines stretching out from her eyes and mouth.

"Is this a waiver?" she finally asked.

"It's a very standard HR form," said the drone. "It simply asserts that any conflict arising between SALIGIA employees, and/or one SALIGIA employee and one non-SALIGIA employee, or during paid SALIGIA hours, and/or on SALIGIA property, is not the legal responsibility of SALIGIA and/or SALIGIA's Management Team, and that SALIGIA and/or SALIGIA's Management Team is absolved of any and all implications stemming from said conflict."

The way she explained such nonsense so matter-of-factly made Jeff's blood boil.

Without another word, Janice signed the screen, and slid it over to Jeff.

A quick look over it revealed legal jargon and rambling clauses scarcely different from the signs that had misled them all the way here, but what comprehensible bits Jeff caught seemed to indicate the drone's summary was more-or-less accurate.

Jeff too signed the screen and slid it back across the desk.

"Great," said the drone as she took the digi-pad and confirmed the signatures. "Janice, I will be adding you to the waitlist for the next available Corporate Hierarchies and Rules of Engagement workshop. That will help you cope with your recent feelings of self-importance. Not to worry Jeff, that can all be covered by your SALIGIA therapist.

"I'm so happy we were able to help you sort everything out today" the woman finished. She folded her hands atop her desk and smiled from behind dead eyes. "Please exit the way you came in, and have a wonderful day."

Doesn't that just fucking figure, Jeff thought, but kept it to himself.

Without another word, Jeff and Janice stood, turned, and walked out of the room. They passed again down the hall, scanning their slow way back to the elevators. When at last they reached the main floor, Janice turned abruptly to the right, and walked speedily towards the far exit.

Jeff didn't want to leave things on such a sour note. "See you tomorrow. Can't wait till Jasper!" he called feebly, and regretted it immediately when he received no response from Janice's receding back.

He left the building, and stood a moment in the street, despondent. The wind had died down, and was now little more than a gentle breeze playing across his hot flesh. The air was cool, and the pale sun still shone in the western sky.

Taking in the hum of the streets and the movement of the

clouds, Jeff tried to catch up with his hurried thoughts. There was an electric liveliness to the streets he usually revelled in. Now, having escaped from the crypt of SALIGIA HR, it seemed foreign. He saw and felt and smelled everything around him as if through a veil, and none of it was meant for him.

His was the empty, dry air, and stale smell of those miserable hallways, and inside his head was an empty echo-chamber of doubts, regrets, and the bitter memory of the day's pointless game.

Playing games, he thought, *is a great way to pass the time. But not everything is a game.* Jeff was sick of games. He was tired of just passing time.

In defiance of everything he'd ever known in his thirty-six years of life, Jeff wanted to start breaking the rules.

CHAPTER 10
A Day in the Mountains

Endless waves of green hills rolled off into the distance, then fell to nothing against the dark blue outlines of the mountains still far beyond. In all directions stretched forests of pine and spruce, poplar and birch, larch and countless other trees Jeff could never hope to identify.

Sometimes, he forgot just how breathtaking the Canadian Rockies could be. They were magnificent beyond the mind's ability to remember, and every time Jeff looked at them, it re-awoke something old and ageless in him—something he always had, but only remembered in their humbling presence.

Lakes, streams, and vast stretches of flowering meadows sped by, and Jeff hoped more than anything that he'd get the chance to see the mountains before he was swept back home.

Really see them, he thought. His long face stared back at him—reflected by the smooth contours of the screens surrounding him on the SALIGIA bullet train to Jasper.

There were no real windows. Instead, the entire car except the seats was covered in LED screens that displayed—allegedly—exactly what the SALIGIA high-definition cameras mounted all over the train recorded as they sped by. It was meant to be a live feed, modified with SALIGIA patented beauty enhancing filter technology. Jeff had long suspected these images were as doctored as the ever-changing smells in the office, but could do nothing to prove his theory.

Rubbing at a cramp in his neck, he leaned back in his seat, watching a heavy black raincloud rolling in just above Rian's head. She sat two seats ahead and one to the left.

At the head of the car, Jordan bobbed his head like an idiot as the train took its long, slow turns. With the state-of-the-art hydraulics, no sense of motion was detectable within the car.

The Tins were all neatly arranged in two rows of two—taking up the entire car themselves. The Brass—Marcy and Francis on this particular trip—each had their own private cars.

Jeff watched both worlds at once—the picturesque landscapes and rugged reality of proxy-nature, and the temperature-neutral, sterile environ of the train car as represented by his own reflection.

Adra sat across the aisle, with white ear buds popping out the sides of her head like a little Apple Frankenstein's monster. She scrolled endlessly through her phone, her eyes never leaving the screen.

To be fair, it was the accepted behaviour in this situation. Other tolerated options included talking quietly to a nearby colleague, or staring politely in one direction, away from anyone else.

Jeff didn't care much about all that, and preferred to gaze freely all around him, taking in the beauty and the falsity and the insanity of it all at once. No one sat beside him on this ride. Jordan tried to, but a fierce glare had sent him scurrying off to leave Jeff in relative peace.

Rudy was behind him, along with Ashley, Nasha, and Finnegan. He didn't actually know the last one's name, but he looked like a puppet dog Jeff saw on TV once, so that's how he thought of him.

Will the people in the other train cars actually get to enjoy the mountains? Will they go to scenic views, or camp in the brutal wilderness outdoors? Will they breathe the air and finally remember they're alive?

Probably, Jeff thought. *But not this car.*

He'd seen this song and dance before, and knew they'd be ushered directly from the train, into a SALIGIA facility, and off into fuck knows what kind of ridiculous trust and teamwork exercises the jazzed-up pinheads at corporate had designed for them.

Part of him wished the train would fly off the track, and that for some brief moment before the fiery end the car would be torn open, and real air and sky and light would filter in, and that would make all the rest worth it.

Far ahead, Jordan's useless head continued to jockey from side to side. Halfway between them and across the aisle, Jeff could see a tuft of curly red hair poking up above the headrest of Janice's seat.

He'd hoped she'd take the seat he'd saved, but had no such luck. He'd only meant to help her during the Performance Review meeting, but he knew he'd overstepped, and it had cost him.

Hills turned slowly to cliffs, then suddenly to mountains. The deep earthy grey of their old stone was enhanced by the patented filter technology of the SALIGIA screens. Jeff wondered what was lost in translation, but sat quietly, shifting like a child excited to track each change in the landscape.

How could he make up for his mistake if he couldn't even get near her? Janice was important to him, although he still couldn't articulate why. He was protective of her—as if in her there lay some old memory that was almost gone within himself—an unspoiled memento of a brighter past that he wanted to nurture and preserve in its natural state as long as he could.

The leafy trees surrounding them gave way to ragged evergreens, and above these stretched the alpine peaks—naked stone jagged and harsh—with the occasional flows of glacier crawling like great blankets of ice over the ancient flesh of the Earth.

Jeff liked the glaciers. He appreciated their patience, but more than that he liked that they left their mark. They were slow beyond measure, but relentless. Like the ceaseless pounding of water that wears away the hillside, the tremendous sheets of ice clove rock and earth, and after countless lives and many ages, their passing was indelibly etched across the world they left behind.

Jeff recognized the mountains around him now. They were getting close to their destination. Suddenly, he thought back to the SALIGIA Tower in Edmonton, imagining a glacier scraping across it in fast-motion. Would it carve a divot in the side? Could it topple the beast?

Time and patience were powerful forces.

"This train will stop at the SALIGIA Inc. Guidance and Administration Centre in five minutes," said the invisible speakers. Their tone was syrup sweet.

Jeff had very little time, and his patience was wearing dangerously thin.

He took a long breath, mentally preparing himself for the absurd training scenarios he'd be forced through at the facility. Games of strength, skill, knowledge, trust, and blind faith in authority had tested his mettle in the years he'd been with SALIGIA, and he dreaded what heinous new drills Nadia would put them through today.

As the train slowed, he imagined the hiss of its brakes and the creaking rails beneath them. Those red iron rails—laid long ago— would carry them inevitably into the giant silver cube of the SALIGIA facility. Somewhere inside, it was rumoured, the Brass lounged in exquisite luxury, but Jeff had never seen those parts and likely never would. He'd be taken to the eastern side of the facility, where the Tins went a time or two each year to be re-broken, re-programmed, and otherwise degraded in the name of corporate profit.

It was a humbling experience, and the familiar peaks surrounding the facility had become symbols of dread for Jeff. At times, he wondered if the mountains were a lie, and they were really in the middle of some burned prairie, or deep underground in cold, wet caverns.

Ultimately, he accepted that idea was unrealistic. Not because SALIGIA would never do that to the Tins. Not even because he believed the rumours about a Brass resort on the mysterious western side of the facility, and knew they'd accept nothing short of heaven on Earth. It was something deep in Jeff's gut that told him the location wasn't about the Brass. It was for the Tins—to be so close to beauty, freedom, and happiness, but to see only bastardized facsimiles through plastic screens.

There was nothing in the world Jeff could imagine that better represented the experience of corporate servitude.

A sudden whoosh sound came from the front of the car, and just beyond Jordan's head where a tall pillar of stone rose on a dark green hill, a gaping black hole tore their false reality to shreds.

Through the void stepped Marcy, followed closely by Francis. Once the illusion was broken, it could not be repaired. As the train slowed, then stopped, the screens faded to a dull, eggshell white. Mountains, trees, lakes, and sky all vanished.

In other cars Jeff imagined more fortunate folk sat and sipped cocktails, unaware the train had even stopped. They still watched the trees glide by, and the mountains moving slowly behind them.

"Floor 82, welcome to the SALIGIA Inc. Team Building,

Communication, Trust, and Corporate Spirit Workshop!" Marcy beamed as she made the declaration.

Francis pushed forward. "We're going to form teams in order to enjoy this workshop. The following employees will join me when we get off the train, and be members of my team, the Hyenas. Jeff, Jordan, Nasha, Colby…"

Colby—that must be Finnegan's real name! thought Jeff. He preferred Finnegan however, and decided he'd stick with it. Francis continued to prattle on, and Jeff listened half-heartedly, wondering if Janice would be on his team.

It was not meant to be though, and when Francis finally concluded his list, Marcy stepped directly in front of him to speak. "And my team will be the Ants. When we leave the train, the following employees will come with me. Adra, Ashley, Rian, Janice…"

With a sharp hiss, the side door slid open—a sudden crack in the smooth white walls of the train revealing a long, blue hallway beyond.

As everyone pushed slowly through the single exit, they bunched up around their respective leaders with all the jostling, debating, swearing, and shoving Jeff knew was inevitable from the get-go. It really wasn't hard to imagine them all as ants.

"How did you come up with the team names?" Jeff usually knew better than to engage with Francis, but in the moment some absurd combination of stress and boredom made him go against his better judgement.

Francis grinned—it wasn't often any of the Tins showed interest in him. "Since this course is about teamwork and communication, we decided to go with animals famous for their cooperation skills," he explained. "Marcy got the first choice." He was clearly still bitter about it.

Jeff nodded, regretting his curiosity already. *Hyenas and ants? What about wolves, or chimps?* he wondered, but kept the thought to himself.

The two groups passed slowly through a long hallway lined with screens portraying sea life. Dolphins swam by in playful pods, and Jeff shook his head at the missed opportunity.

Francis led his team towards a door on the left—just barely distinguished by its white outline cutting through the ocean depths. As they filed through one by one, Jeff turned and saw Janice's yellow sweater disappearing through a door on the right. She was the third ant from the front, and before them Marcy marched proudly in the vanguard of her own little army.

The team wandered through a winding series of hallways—these devoid of screens, and unadorned save for the occasional, haphazardly hung motivational poster.

"Be your best you, and we can be our best us."

Trite trash, thought Jeff.

Entering a small, "wood-panelled" staging room with heavy black rigging rope displayed along the walls, Francis stepped to the far end and turned giddily to face his team like the captain of whatever strange vessel the digi-walls were programmed to represent.

"Today is a big deal Hyenas, make no mistake about that. This is no mere training day—this is about who we want to be as a team." Francis' motivational speech was not off to an encouraging start. At any rate, it seemed destined to be long-winded and ultimately self-serving, but Jeff couldn't deny that when he was afforded the opportunity to act with confidence, Francis could be a surprisingly charming guy. "Imagine the office tomorrow—imagine it a year from now," Francis ran a long hand through his coifed blonde hair before finishing, "and decide right now how you want it to be. Today is about teamwork and communication—but it's about more than that too. It's about dreams and determination!" He threw his hands triumphantly into the air as he spoke.

Jeff was sure he had it figured out. Like the Performance Reviews, this workshop was nothing more than an elaborate test Nadia had designed for Francis and Marcy. Why, he could not fathom, but there was a strange thrill in watching it play out.

Francis was still prattling on, gesticulating around the room like a drunken swordsman. "Our learning is going to be enhanced by participation in three SALIGIA Inc. copyrighted competitions! In each of these, we will square off against the Ants.

"Let me tell you, Hyenas," and here, a terrible shadow passed over Francis' soft features, "I intend to beat them."

Were the supervisors locked in that executive car, designing the trials for the staff? Or were the trials designed by Nadia to test her subordinates? Jeff wondered. Whatever lay behind this whole grand charade, he was convinced it had nothing to do with teamwork or communication in any conventional sense.

He stifled a sudden urge to explain his theory to Janice. Although she wasn't there, she remained the only person in the office with any chance of listening with any real interest. The office lacked imagination, but that was pretty low on its list of deficiencies.

When Jeff finally decided to check back in on what Francis was up to, it seemed clear the grand soliloquy was finally drawing to a close.

"Once each of those competitions is finished, and the two keys have been awarded, the team or teams holding them may approach the door to the final test. Now, let's roll!" He gestured towards the far side of the room.

Shit, thought Jeff. It was clear enough the ultimate lesson was going to be some vapid bullshit about coming together to move forward, but he'd be flying blind on the details of the actual events standing between them and that sorry denouement.

"Well, this is going to be a fun day out of the office!" Jordan clapped Jeff on the back, and spoke loud enough to ensure Francis overheard his corporate spirit.

Staring into the green eyes of the grinning idiot, Jeff smiled back. "Can't wait!" he mumbled.

Jordan was trying to score points with Francis, but Jeff couldn't imagine why. Jordan hated work as much as Jeff did, and was usually even more vocal and defiant about it. Still, when not calling for the guillotines he seemed happy enough to hop in line and feign subservience with a sweetness that always sickened any nearby colleagues.

Maybe that's his angle, he thought. In a strange sort of way, Jeff understood the concept—a laugh in that place was like a drink in the desert.

The group heaved about, jockeying for position behind the long, lean frame of Francis, who turned to beam at each small comment from his team as he led the halting march towards a tall, wood-panelled door.

The hallway beyond abandoned the nautical theme altogether, opting instead for the torch lined and claustrophobic passages of an ancient colosseum. Despite their inability to stick with a theme, Jeff was surprised at the child-like passion Francis and Marcy seemed to have put into their workshop—if it was truly theirs.

Does Janice see what I'm seeing? Was their staging room even a ship, or did Marcy veer off course even sooner than Francis? he wondered, marching in file along the seemingly endless corridor. Just ahead, Jordan glanced giddily about, and Jeff suddenly noticed the smell of dirt, burned wood, and metal.

From far ahead came the sound of rolling drums.

If SALIGIA put this much effort into actually supporting their staff, it wouldn't be such a bad place to work, Jeff thought. He missed having someone to commiserate with, and hoped he'd be able to laugh at it all with Janice again soon.

"Hyenas, welcome to our first challenge." Again, Francis turned to face his small band as he spoke. Only then did Jeff notice they'd come to the end of the long, slowly curving hallway, and waited in front of a tall bronze coloured gate. "The first event is about teamwork, and we'll be going one-on-one with the Ants. It's going to be a fierce competition, but I know if we pull together, we can show them what we're made of!" Francis grinned at his meagre team as if this was his moment of triumph.

How sad—to take such pride in the small successes of a mid-management role for a faceless corporation. Jeff wondered how boring the rest of Francis' life must be, if this was an actual highlight.

With an emphatic push, Francis heaved open the double doors. They hissed subtly on their hydraulic hinges—utterly killing the impression that they were the gates of an ancient colosseum.

The illusion was further broken by the sight within. A great hall stretched out before the Hyenas, and Francis took it in like a king surveying his realm. The walls—high as a gymnasium—were entirely lined with digi-screens, as were the ceilings and floors.

With detail that surprised even Jeff, the entire room was programmed like a vast mountain canyon, with trees of all shapes and shades. At the centre of the room was a shallow trench, and through this roared an image of white-water rapids.

The scene was beautiful, and Jeff would have been thrilled at the sight if not for his constant awareness of its falseness. The technology was impressive, no doubt, but this potential amenity withered in light of other considerations. How many colleagues had Jeff watched get released over the years? How many simple things had the staff begged to change only to be denied by the Brass?

That fucking bathroom sink would be a good place to start, he thought.

In light of such ridiculous failures, any grace SALIGIA might claim seemed inconsequential.

"Finnegan, doesn't this seem like one hell of an expense for an effect they could have achieved by simply taking us outside?" Jeff said sidelong to Finnegan, who stood to his right, jaw agape.

Finnegan was unusually tall. He had flapping jowls, and a spotty, balding head ringed with short, fluffy blonde hair. An entirely forgettable soul, Finnegan reminded Jeff each time they spoke that sometimes, looks were more than skin deep.

"My name is Colby," he said. "Besides, do you know how much that would jack up their Occupational Health and Safety premiums? Plus, I have seasonal allergies!"

Fucking Finnegan.

Jeff wanted to go outside. He needed the fresh air and the wind on his face—the sun warming his skin and all the smells and sounds of nature. In the city, these were all tainted. It seemed a terrible waste to come all this way—even by the SALIGIA train—to not even breathe in the clean mountain air.

A sound from the far end of the room startled Jeff, and looking up, he saw the Ants filing out of a similar broad door behind Marcy.

Rian and Ashley stood next to one another, gossiping wildly about things Jeff could only assume he didn't care about whatsoever. Adra stood closest to Marcy, watching with wide, empty eyes as the leader gave a pep-talk to her unit.

Near the back, behind several faces Jeff didn't recognize, he caught a glimpse of yellow—as if a miniature Big Bird was failing spectacularly at avoiding detection.

Janice.

More than the isolating train ride, the fake scenery, or the inherent stress of a ritual-breaking day out of the office, it was the unsettled strife with her that really weighed on Jeff's mind.

Since the incident at the Performance Review on Wednesday, a stony silence and awkward distance had grown between them. All day Thursday, Jeff had tried to create opportunities to connect with her—struggling to arrange even a hallway passing or accidental coffee machine meetup as he wandered the halls trying to find excuses to be any place she might be. It had been one failed attempt after another though, and he'd caught little more than brief glimpses of her passing through doors, or the outline of her red hair through a frosted window. Once, he'd made eye contact as she hurried into the washroom. Her face was stern, and Jeff felt relatively certain she'd seen him and made the intentional decision not to stop.

He'd considered waiting for her to come back out, but accepted that was a bridge too far. He wanted to apologize for overstepping, and knew better than to double down on his mistake.

Still, as one day drew into two, he was eager to once again have a reliable confidant—and on a day like this it seemed all the more necessary to have at least one trusted ally to stand by his side and mock all proceedings.

Finnegan is a piss poor replacement, he thought.

"All right Hyenas, follow me!" called Francis, beginning a bold march toward the center of the hall. Finnegan followed closely, along with Nasha and a few others. Jeff and Jordan drew up the rear of the procession as the teams inched slowly towards one another at the centre of the hall.

"Ladies and Gentleman—" called Marcy.

"SALIGIA Staff…" interrupted Francis.

They shared a heated stare down, then began to speak in an eerie unison. "Welcome to the first event of the SALIGIA Floor 82 Teamwork and Inter-Team Communication Workshop," they declared. Jeff thought they appeared especially pleased with having managed this announcement, and assumed they'd practiced the delivery ad nauseum in their private train cars.

"This first event is all about teamwork," said Francis.

"First, we're going to practice our communication," Marcy flatly contradicted.

At this, Francis' spine straightened like a flagpole. Deep lines crept across his soft features, and with a deep breath, he ran a pink hand through his carefully styled hair. "Sometimes at the office, we're divided by different perspectives, priorities, or contractual obligations. These divisions can seem vast at times—even impossible for a single person to manage. But none of us needs to act as a single person. We are a team, and today we want to improve those skills and connections. This event is called Bridge Building, and it was designed as a metaphor for these types of daily challenges."

As Francis spoke, Marcy's mouth moved like a fish. Jeff assumed she was continually trying and failing to get a word in edgewise. *Maybe this day will be a good time after all,* he thought. If Marcy and Francis finally took the gloves off and battled it out for supremacy, it could cause a logistical nightmare for the workers who reported to them. It would also be painfully hilarious, however, and Jeff relished that idea despite its many potential drawbacks. *Those are problems for future Jeff,* he accepted.

"In front of us, you'll see a chasm—much like the hypothetical divides we face every day at work." Francis pushed boldly on, stepping forward and puffing out his chest like a soldier awaiting a medal. "Each team now stands on opposite sides, and scattered about the edges of each side you'll find an assortment of equipment, tools, and other sundries."

As Francis gestured to the materials lining the lip of the crevice, Marcy took the opportunity to cut in. "Behind each team, you will observe a pedestal with a key. The goal is to build a functional bridge, make it to the opposite side, grab your key, return it to your side, and place it on your team's pedestal," she instructed.

"Anyone who touches the water in the gorge will be eliminated. Only by communicating clearly with one another, trusting your varied skill sets, and showing true courage and initiative will you be successful." The sense of triumph on Marcy's face was palpable. She was—it couldn't be denied—more articulate than Francis, and a more confident presence on the whole. Still, something about Francis' tenacity was endearing to Jeff. That, or perhaps he'd just been under Francis' heel for less time than Marcy's, and thus found him slightly less detestable.

Give it time, he thought.

"The winning key," Francis found his voice again, "is one of two that must be used to access the final challenge, as explained in the staging room."

"Remember," said Marcy, "that a key from both this game and the next are needed to access the final challenge, so let's start off strong Ants!"

Rian started to clap at this, perceived the stoic silence of her peers, and promptly stared down at the ground. Jeff chuckled to himself, then noticed Francis striding over and cursed himself for letting down his guard.

"Alright Hyenas," Francis spoke as if Jeff was the only Hyena, "we really need this win, so let's give it everything we've got."

Francis' eyes glinted as he spoke, and his smile showed a sterling confidence which must have cost him a litany of Carnegie courses. There was something else in his expression though. Jeff wasn't sure if it was the lines around his mouth, the slight hint of blue in his pupils, or something about the invisible weight under which he appeared to toil, but Francis' savage desperation could not be ignored.

Over the years Jeff served at SALIGIA, he'd suffered the constant wearing away of his zest for life by the rough stone of its oppression. The corporate mandates, the maniacal HR department, the meaningless nature of the work, and above all, the supervisors and the manager—who were the omnipresent harbingers of bad news, stalled raises, and the mind-bendingly foolish decisions of those above even them.

Never before had Jeff considered the import of that last bit—those above them.

Now, he saw it etched across Francis' face. Otherwise youthful and energetic, he seemed on any other day like the prototypical corporate drone—young but ambitious, eager, and entirely divorced from the moral qualms that kept better men at lower pay grades. It was a discomfiting notion that under all those shiny, false fronts, Francis might be struggling with the same sort of unreasonable demands as Jeff and the other Tins.

"If everyone will step behind the red line on their side, we can begin," Marcy's voice carried with ease through the broad hall. The illusion of space created by visions of meadows and mountains illuminated along the walls made the feat seem all the more impressive.

With no sign of enthusiasm aside from Jordan's elbow pumping bullshit, each team made its way slowly behind their lines, which ran through the podiums holding the supposedly sacred keys. Jeff considered pocketing the opposing team's key immediately and discovering the results later, but resigned himself instead to stand by impotently and wait.

Far across the false images of flowing grass and raging rivers, there was a flash of yellow. He wondered what Janice thought of all this. New though she was, Janice displayed a level of clarity that was hard to believe—as if she was somehow immune to the grind at SALIGIA. Jeff admired that, but not as much as he appreciated her willingness to listen to his lessons and gripes, rarely differentiating between the two.

"Are you ready?" called Marcy.

"Get set!" screamed Francis.

Jeff's legs tightened involuntarily. It was strange how a bit of pomp could motivate even the most cynical. That was, he imagined, a tool SALIGIA utilized at every opportunity.

A moment passed, then another.

Marcy looked at Francis.

Francis looked at Marcy.

The screeching of a bird came from their left—an unnecessary detail indicative of SALIGIA's skewed priorities.

Jeff waited.

Nasha stood straight and unaffected to one side. On the other, Finnegan was posed as if ready to charge, but his face betrayed his boredom. Jeff envied his ability to fake it almost as much as he despised the tacit threat which made him do so.

A terrible stretch of time passed with Marcy and Francis staring holes through each other until, with no noticeable indication, they both realized the fatal flaw in their delivery.

"Go!" they screamed in unison.

After such a forced build-up, a more energetic response might have been expected by anyone who hadn't spent so long at SALIGIA. As Jeff watched the slow, almost imperceptible shifting of each team towards the chasm, he pitied the sincere efforts of the supervisors, who were defined daily by anything but sincerity.

Shuffling forward, he reached the edge of the chasm alongside Jordan, who was hoisting up a giant tangle of cords. "Think we could just jump it?" Jeff asked.

"Maybe," said Jordan. "Or we could just toss the key on this side to the other team and call it a day."

Jeff chuckled. He was never quite sure if Jordan was a corporate bootlicker or an unapologetic anarchist. Of all Jeff's colleagues, Jordan was simultaneously the most likely to become a supervisor at some point, and the outlier who might end up burning down the whole damn tower—a fiery monolith in honour of the Old Gods that cared nothing for day timers, mandates, or media jurisdictions.

That ambiguity alone was admirable. *To be fair, the idea isn't half bad*, thought Jeff. It would certainly save them all a lot of time. What it would cost them, however, was anyone's guess. As a matter of course at SALIGIA, the risks and rewards were never established until it was far too late.

"Has anyone found the carabiners?" Francis called, rooting frantically through the gear spread along the lip of the digi-river. He huffed and puffed like an angry wolf, and it was clear that the Hyenas' victory truly was every bit as important to him as he'd claimed.

It all comes back to Nadia, Jeff assured himself. *It has to*. Nadia was the epicentre—the bleeding tumour poisoning the rest of the body. If this training, these competitions were all some mad ruse to test Francis and Marcy, its genesis lay in her.

The only question left to Jeff was, why? Well, perhaps it wasn't the only question. In fact, the more he considered it, he came to realise the why of it really didn't bother him at all. The question that did concern him was—what does that mean for me?

Shuffling along the lip of the TV-screen valley, in a giant gymnasium that smelled like pine trees and moss due to the likely-toxic and definitely-expensive chemicals being pumped in for the sake of realism, Jeff realized he'd never know what it meant for him until the rough reality of it was dragged across his face.

At any rate, the entire absurd situation was taking time he could be spending on his already bloated to-do list. Instead, the day would be wasted, and sooner or later he'd be taken to task for the lost time. For now, though, he could only grit his teeth and carry on.

Jeff chuckled bitterly to himself, staring down at a humongous tangle of giant metal carabiners.

"Well," he whispered to Jordan as he heaved the gaudy mass of metal to chest height, "if we can't be productive, we might as well pretend to be cooperative."

"The Carabiners!" Francis clapped him on the back, lingering for a moment in what may have been his professionalism striving against his excitement to defeat the urge to hug his subordinate. "They're the key to all of this! Now we just need the mesh and ropes."

Francis glanced desperately about, and behind him the digi-mountains climbed into the distance—beautiful and terrible. Suddenly, he spun back around. "Come with me Jeff, I'm glad someone is taking this seriously."

Bent by his burden, Jeff followed along beside his idiot of a leader. From the far side of what looked like a parachute covering several bales of hay, he saw Jordan chuckling as he watched them. Behind him a strong wind blew through a digital stand of juniper bushes.

Jeff wondered where they really were. Were there mountains? Was there water? How did the air smell? Hauling the carabiners at knee-height now, he imagined how great it would be to find a way out of the facility, and show the staff what the world was like outside of this madness-factory they called a job.

Across the shallow gorge, where a continuous loop of white water rapids flowed, and a localized roaring of water played at deafening volume, he saw Janice hurrying along with a long tangle of ropes in her hands. Her red hair bounced as she struggled towards Rian and Marcy, who were busy sorting their own mess of carabiners.

"Save that blue one!" Marcy screeched, and Rian went crawling through the pile on her hands and knees.

The Clean City Initiative popped suddenly into his head—was he supposed to have a phone call with the Director of Transit today?

It didn't matter, he knew. Nothing could be done about it anyway—corporate wanted them here. Doing—this.

He finally dropped the carabiners beside a giant stack of ropes, mesh, and what looked to be a series of interlaced hula hoops.

"Perfect, we are exactly where we need to be right now," said Francis, surveying his opponent's progress.

Jeff laughed.

All his life, he'd been self-conscious of his laugh. Sometimes it was harsher than he meant. Other times it went too squeaky. He worried it put people off, and made them feel like he was mocking either them, or the world itself. In most situations, he tried to alter his laugh slightly, making it softer and his accompanying smile less maniacal.

Only at SALIGIA had he learned to truly embrace the art of laughing out loud.

"Now help me untangle these! Jordan? Jordan, where are you?" Francis was screaming like a lost child.

Across the river, Marcy was in a similar state—mad with desire to prove herself the better leader. "No, dammit," she yelled, "you're just tangling them more!"

Beneath her, Rian and Janice scurried over the mass of carabiners in a panic to sort them out before Marcy lost control entirely. "Where is the blue carabiner!" she screamed, and Rian and Janice shuddered as they redoubled their efforts.

Adra stood calmly beside Marcy, her arms folded over her chest.

Finnegan and Nasha were standing near the edge of the gorge talking to Ashley on the other side. Several others Jeff didn't know stood nearby, while a few pushed around stray pommel horses, bean bags, and cushions.

Jordan was sitting off to the side in the elimination zone, having evidently "fallen" into the water. He seemed to be finding great humour in the struggles of his peers. That was all that mattered to a person like him.

Still, one thing he'd said was true. Someone could just toss the key from their side to the other side, and get the first game over with. This was about the supervisors anyway, and they were only using the opportunity to abuse their staff and waste everyone's time. As usual.

Jeff was beyond tired of playing along. Tired of the supervisors being the ones in the way of getting work done, and also the ones mad about work not being done. More than anything, he was sick of the god damn hypocrisy, and the unbearable divide between the Tins and the Brass.

His mind was settled.

It had been a long time since he'd felt so certain, and he grinned as he strode forward.

The thin golden pedestal was just beside Francis as he shouted his commands. Jeff lifted the key—also golden—and turned towards the gorge. Only as he walked did he notice the tiny sash laced through its loop—white, and embroidered at the end with the crimson image of a tiny ant.

He was hard-pressed to keep his face straight as he reached the gorge and nonchalantly tossed the key across. It hit the ground with a surprising clatter, and slid a moment on the smooth surface of the floor screen, skidding to a stop a foot from Janice.

Everyone froze. The chatter went dead, as did the sound of the river. No more ambient nature sounds bounced through the massive arena. Even the scents stopped. All was calm, and as the digital water continued to flow in silence, a terrible, mind-flaying awareness of their situation's falsity pervaded the room.

Janice gaped at the key, then glared up at Jeff. She didn't move.

Francis' face was a funeral pall. His strong jaw hung loose, and his shoulders slouched.

Jeff smirked at Janice. He hoped she'd take his cue to embrace the absurdity of the situation, but her face was stone.

With a rush of overbearing stillness, the world turned over again on Jeff. This wasn't how it was supposed to be.

His neck felt cold, and a shiver ran down his spine.

Was Janice trembling too?

Suddenly, Adra threw herself forward. Flying lengthwise through the air, she hit the ground hard, knocking the breath from her lungs and gasping wretchedly as she slid forward and clenched both hands around the key. Kicking up with impressive resilience, she raced to her team's pedestal, brushed off the Hyena-marked key, and set the Ant key in its place.

The scenery went dead.

A chilling wail echoed through the room, and following the sound, Jeff saw Francis on his knees. He was doubled over in despair, his face buried in his palms.

Janice still stood amid the tangled ropes. She stared straight ahead as if lost in thought.

"Well," said Marcy, stepping into the center of the room as the bottom of the gorge rose up to meet the rest of the floor, "that was a fantastic game everyone. I think we've learned an interesting lesson in this activity. Teamwork and communication is sometimes about thinking outside the box, and by reaching out to unexpected helpers, we can often find innovative solutions. It was an unexpected result, but sometimes surprises make for the best teachable moments.

"Score one for the Ants!" she finished, grabbing up the key and holding it triumphantly above her head. Standing tall against the resolute blackness of the dead screens that surrounded them, she struck a powerful pose.

Less powerful, but far more pitiful, Francis hopped to his feet and motioned her off away from the main group of employees—most of whom had lost all interest, and were happily chatting amongst themselves.

Jeff watched Francis lead Marcy away until they were almost out of earshot. "What the hell was that?" his voice came as a whisper, and Jeff tossed a carabiner up and down in his hand as he inched closer to them.

"Creative problem solving?" Marcy seemed to know her validation was feeble, and offered a casual shrug as compensation.

"It was unfair and you know it!"

"Life isn't always fair, Francis. Our job is to lead our team forward no matter what."

Jeff shuddered at the platitude, but couldn't pull himself away from the rift.

"Don't give me that inspirational bullshit, Marcy. We've had the same training. Your team won by breaking the rules, that's the bottom line here. I won't stand for it!"

"Technically, my team won because your team broke the rules, so feel free to lie down if it suits you better."

They spoke in whispers, but the fury behind Francis' words assured the conversation was never difficult to listen in on. Jeff grinned, feeling his suspicions were further vindicated with every passing second. *There's no doubt they're the ones competing here. It's sad*, he thought, *that they'll so happily tear each other apart for a shred of recognition from Nadia.*

"Listen Francis, we were both more helpful to our teams than we should have been. Let's try to let them solve the next puzzle, and we can focus on facilitation. We'll sort out everything else once this is behind us." Marcy slashed her hands out in front of her body as if to signify she was done with the conversation.

Francis did not share her sentiments. "Easy for you to say when you're the only one who's benefitted from the rule-breaking," he hissed.

"Will the staff from SALIGIA Edmonton Floor 82 please proceed to Training Hall C," came a voice over the PA. It was a soft voice, smooth and delicate. The best voice money could program, Jeff imagined.

Nonetheless, the intrusion brought a sudden unease upon him, and—judging by the awkward shifting—in the rest of the staff as well. Most had been milling about happily, talking amongst themselves as Jeff eavesdropped on his supervisors. The voice over the PA reminded them all where they were, and why they were there. Now, a renewed sense of gloom gripped the room as the masses turned begrudgingly towards Marcy and Francis for further instruction.

Bearing the weight of one failure already, Francis was unwilling to risk Marcy taking charge. "Ladies and Gentleman, please follow me," he called. His voice was hollow—a faint shadow flitting through the dark and cavernous hall.

"This way," Marcy chimed in, and turning on a dime she went marching towards a door indicated by a thin white outline against the unsullied sable of the hall. Francis chased closely at her heels, and like a poorly reared gaggle of goslings, the rest of the employees followed dutifully along.

Largely because they'd have no place else to go in this nightmare-scape of a training-ground, Jeff thought. The others felt it too, he knew. A quick eyeroll with Jordan, a smirk from Finnegan—Jeff hurried through the crowd, pushing slowly but surely towards the yellow of Janice's sweater as it slid in and out of sight.

The door led to a narrow corridor which glowed a gentle white. Its twists and turns were nearly impossible to see in advance, but the supervisors led the group in an awkward walking-race through the maze. The herd was thinned by the tight confines, and Jeff watched the yellow sweater grow increasingly distant as they journeyed—only appearing briefly at long bends in the corridor. Then, it would peak through the crowded masses, yellow and bright like the sun breaking through the clouds before vanishing again.

Each time it did, Jeff immediately thought of something he wanted to rant about, but there was no one else near him who would listen. It was a strange thing—knowing he was with this group of people more than any other. With the staff of Floor 82, he'd wasted more hours, encountered more quandaries, and soldiered through more inane corporate bullshit than he cared to imagine, and yet for the most part, he hadn't grown close to any of them.

For each, there was some inside joke, or a single story he could reference to placate them on demand without pushing things further.

There weren't many he enjoyed chatting with, and even fewer that he was comfortable sharing anything more than the most offhand critique of SALIGIA—unless he'd been recently affronted by his superiors, which was an increasingly regular occurrence.

Jordan was a convenient distraction on occasion, but nothing more than that. Killing time. Dead air.

Only Janice—he looked forward to her. The jokes he'd tell her. The way she'd laugh.

It was nice to have someone he looked forward to, and as Jeff tried his best to push through the crowd and reach her, it occurred to him that this was perhaps the cruelest of SALIGIA's ploys today— that he be both literally and figuratively denied the sun he so desperately craved.

Lost in these thoughts, he was taken by surprise when suddenly the corridor opened up into a long, high-roofed room. Halfway along, a single wall rose out of nowhere, dividing the remainder of the space into two equal halves. The entire room appeared to be carved from stone, but Jeff assumed that was just the machinations of the digi-walls again.

The crowd spaced out as they filed in, but everyone stuck to the back of the room—as far as possible from the edge of the dividing wall where the supervisors awaited them. Janice settled at the far end, near Adra. Jeff, managing his way in last, felt compelled to remain near the door he'd just come through.

Francis and Marcy were circling one another, screaming in

whispers as their arms flailed at their sides like falling drunkards. Their strange display escalated, and as their pitches rose, their arms moved slowly from waist-level, to shoulder-level, until finally, at the undeniable crescendo of their sad display, they waved directly above their heads, whipping like wind-tube dancers as the voices hissed at barely-audible decibel levels.

Jeff wondered if anyone else was watching their debate, but a glance down the line found most engaged in their own antics. Some snuck furtive glances down at their phones, some made chit chat with one another.

Only Janice watched, utterly transfixed by the commotion.

That gave Jeff some comfort, but by the time he turned back to the main event, he was disappointed to find it ended. Both Marcy and Francis were still and quiet now. They faced the team with big, shit-eating grins.

This doesn't bode well.

"Welcome to round two," said Francis.

"This competition is all about vision," said Marcy.

"And communication," Francis added.

"The teams will each take up their places on opposite sides of this dividing wall."

"There, they'll find a telephone, a blueprint, and a set of blocks."

"The goal," Marcy continued—they were working like a true corporate machine now, "is to build the design featured on the other team's blueprint."

"Teams can take turns calling one another for hints about the blueprint."

"The team on the opposite side cannot lie to a closed, or 'Yes or No' question."

"Teams must alternate in asking questions."

"Meaning that if one team just asked a question. They can't ask another until their opposition has asked one."

"The Hyenas will be on the right side," Francis said, indicating the way as he spoke.

"And the Ants will be on the left." Marcy did the same.

The teams followed their respective leaders with impressive efficiency. *Almost disappointingly efficient,* Jeff thought. He watched as Janice disappeared behind the central wall, onto her side, then he followed the last straggler—Jordan—to his own territory.

Large, foam multicoloured blocks were scattered in the middle of the space. Precisely as described, there was an old-fashioned telephone hanging on the dividing wall, with a large poster next to it. The poster showed a basic model of a house, with a flat blue rectangle placed down in front of it like a pool.

With all the poise of a soldier in rout, Francis hurried over to the phone. He made a point of avoiding eye-contact with Jeff.

I guess that was a short-lived friendship, Jeff thought.

Francis picked up the phone.

Speaking, Jeff assumed, with Marcy on the other end, he confirmed the count down.

"On your marks, get set, go!" he called.

Jeff could hear the echo of Marcy doing the same on the other side, and wondered if someone over there would speak loudly enough to give away their design. Then, he felt ashamed for caring about the outcome at all, and resigned himself to faking his way through the game.

"Alright Hyenas, let's see some real creative thinking here!" Francis clapped his hands together and grinned like a starving dog.

Jordan sidled slowly up beside Francis, who stood near the phone trembling with excitement. "Do we get a lunch today?" he asked.

"There will be a short, catered break after we win this event, now go!" Francis spoke loudly, and jumped in place as he gestured to the blocks.

"Do you know what we're having?"

"Sandwiches!" screamed Francis.

"Will there be gluten-free options?" Jordan was just messing with Francis at this point.

Growing bored with the routine, Jeff made his way over to the blocks. A quick scan told him that their team didn't have the same blocks as those laid out in the blueprint on their wall, meaning the correct design wasn't the same.

Realizing this, he promptly gave up, and hurried over to the phone.

The nostalgic ring could be heard from the other side before the line clicked to life. "Hello?" The voice was Adra's.

"What's our design?" he asked.

A short time passed before he realized Adra was refusing to answer anything but a closed question.

"Can you please tell me what our design is?" he tried.

"No!" she said, and slammed the phone down.

"They can't ask another question until we do!" her triumphant declaration echoed through the hall.

Francis glared at Jeff, but remained silent.

"So close!" consoled Jordan.

Jeff shook his head in faux dismay.

Behind them, Finnegan was stacking blocks like a gleeful toddler. He was making a tower.

"Great work Colby, let's test some patterns. The room will immediately acknowledge any correct design," Francis did his best to play the bold leader. Jeff liked that in a cold, distant sort of way.

"The room will immediately acknowledge any correct pattern, so don't be afraid to get creative!" came Marcy's echo.

The phone rang, and Jordan swept over to grab it up. "Yes, who's this?"

"No," he then answered. "It's a house with a pool."

"Jordan!" screeched Francis.

"They asked if it was a household object!" Jordan explained.

Jeff burst out laughing. Francis glared nails into him, then returned his wrath to Jordan. "So what? You could have left it at 'no'!"

"That's not very good communication," said Jordan. "Besides, I'm hungry."

The other side of the room was alive with commotion. Blocks tumbled, and voices screeched commands until a horn blared through the hall, and the stone walls faded to black.

"We did it! We won both keys!" cheered Marcy.

In the centre of the room, a pillar rose from the ground. Marcy raced towards it with Adra close on her heels. She grabbed up the second key and began jumping up and down with joy. Adra followed suit as the rest of the Ants milled about, seemingly unimpressed.

Jeff wondered if they were as hungry as he was.

"Only one more to go," Jordan whispered into his ear, and flashed an eager smile.

Francis stared at the ground, running his hands repeatedly through his hair as his lips moved wordlessly.

"Everyone please follow me," called Marcy, "SALIGIA has kindly provided us a complimentary meal to enjoy during this scheduled fifteen-minute break."

She led them through a sudden opening on the side of the room, down a hallway, and into a small break room. The walls were dull white, the table was fake wood, and the entire room smelled like coffee and stale bread.

It was the realest room Jeff had seen all day.

He pushed his way through the crowd until he was near Janice, then noticed the forlorn shape of Francis bent over the table beside him. "Hey, we'll get them next time," Jeff said, leaning down towards him.

Francis looked up. His brow was rigid iron, but his eyes were polished glass. He sneered at Jeff, not bothering to hide his disdain. Then he turned away, ignoring him completely.

Jeff hoped the sandwiches would help with the quaking in his gut.

"Jordan," said Marcy, "I'm told that a special gluten-free sandwich has been prepared for you," she said, gesturing to a single plate cling-wrapped at the edge of the table.

Jordan's shoulders collapsed in on themselves like a dying star, and he wandered meekly over to collect his meal. Jeff failed to hide his amusement as Jordan looked mournfully back at him.

Grabbing up a sandwich of his own, Jeff managed to snag a seat just across and two seats down from Janice.

For a long while, the table ate in ravenous silence. Crusts crunched, lips smacked, and soggy tomatoes splattered down onto Styrofoam plates.

"Well, I've got us through one, and Jordan has gotten us through a second. Who's got the next round?" Jeff spoke quietly down into his meal, hoping only those nearby would hear.

Janice leaned forward. "Funny that you credit members of a team without a single key. Maybe you should actually try winning one next time," she smirked. Jeff wasn't sure how much of her comment was meant to be biting and how much was playful, but he wasn't comfortable with the mix.

Suddenly, Marcy stood up at the head of the table. "It's been a day full of surprises and fun—" she began, but was cut off as Francis shot to his feet.

"Nobody had fun except the ones ruining it for everyone else. No one is happy now, and the entire team is weaker for the behaviour we've seen today."

Jeff took it all in, chewing on the last of his crusts. Francis was hurt by his crushing defeat, and desperate to blame anything but the absurdity of the situation he himself had helped create.

"There have certainly been some speedbumps along the way," Marcy began once more. Jeff assumed that by speedbumps, she referred to a dashed hope the supervisors had held that each team would win one key—forcing them to come together for the final challenge.

He was unsurprised therefore, when Marcy continued. "In the spirit of good corporate citizenship, the Ants would like to invite the Hyenas to share our keys, and join us for the final challenge. We believe that only together can we truly excel."

Francis groaned. The whole room must have heard it. It was a bitter pill to not only lose, but to have his rival take such a high-ground approach to leadership.

He'd never seen Francis so hopeless.

"If everyone is done eating, please follow me all together," said Marcy. "Let's forget the old divisions and take this final challenge as one!" She turned on her heel and marched out of the room, making it clear that she really didn't care at all whether everyone was done eating or not.

Jeff stood slowly, leaving his empty plate on the table, and following the group out of the lunch room.

Outside, the hallway was again lined with digi-screens—these showing rather plain, white walls and an endless checkerboard floor. The lunch room, Jeff reflected, may have been the only space in the building without the screens, unless of course they were simply programmed to project the bland corporate coffee room the group experienced.

Would a better group have been treated to a more interesting view on their break? Jeff wondered. Still he longed for the real mountains, fresh air, and natural smells denied to him by the sterile facility.

With Marcy in the lead, and Francis trailing sullenly behind her, the group rounded a final turn, then stopped before a large, elaborate door.

No simple trick of the screens—this door seemed to have been custom made for the purpose. *Maybe this whole workshop is a SALIGIA template,* Jeff reasoned. Most likely, Marcy and Francis had merely filled in the blanks to make it suit their needs.

The door was rounded at the top, and made of real wood. It hung on large, black iron hinges, and in the centre were two keyholes.

Marcy turned to Francis, a keen smile carving her broad face in two. "Francis," she said, holding one of the two golden keys out to him, "we're a team at SALIGIA. Let's do this together."

Jeff grinned, understanding Marcy had delivered the ultimate coup de grâce. Francis would only seem petulant if he refused. He was left with no other option than to accept her merciful offer, even though it only made her look better at his expense.

"Let's see what's in store!" Francis did an impressive job of maintaining that shit-eating faux-sincerity so typical of corporate communication. Beneath, he must have been fuming.

Together, they turned the two keys, and a loud click sounded as the door swung loose on its hinges. Each with one hand on the door, the supervisors grinned at their underlings like Cheshire cats as they pushed it open and waved the group through.

Inside, the room was wood panelled, wood floored, and the surprisingly low ceilings were similarly of wood. *It's a Hobbit hole,* Jeff thought, knowing it was meant to have more of a mountain cabin vibe. It was ironic, considering that was a luxury denied to them by this ridiculous workshop.

Besides the door they'd entered, there was a single, narrow door in the opposite corner. Above this hung a bright, glowing red Exit sign, the only thing breaking the illusion of the otherwise rustic room.

In the middle of each wall was a digi-screen window displaying beautiful mountain scenery. They did a decent job of capturing the possible scene—including the occasional bird flying by, or deer passing slowly in the distance. Jeff stared at the window directly ahead as he approached a circle of seats. He accepted the nearest without bothering to strategize about who he was next to, staring absently at the lake and forest projected on the screen.

What's really out there? It couldn't be anything like the scene displayed. Otherwise, a window would have been far cheaper. The other possible explanation only reinforced Jeff's wildest suspicions. If the screens were accurate, then they really were in the mountains, and elsewhere, members of the Brass were taking in the wonderful scenery and revitalizing air as the Tins toiled in misery—afforded only an LED approximation of the wonder just beyond their grasp.

"Tartarean"—of or pertaining to Tartarus. Jeff remembered Eddie's words and chuckled to himself.

"What's so funny?" asked Adra.

Only then did Jeff realize the cost of ignoring his seating choice. Adra sat to his left, and Marcy to his right. Across the circle,

Francis stared nails through him.

Shit.

"Nothing," he said in Adra's direction. She cast him a suspicious, sidelong glance, and scooted her chair away with a less-than-subtle hop.

"Well," said Marcy, and all eyes in the room fell on her. "We've come to our final challenge of the day," she finished.

"This one is a little different," said Francis, "and I'm glad that we can face it together as a united team, because that's what it's all about."

"In the other activities, we worked on our problem solving, creative thinking, and communication skills," said Marcy. Their words flowed back and forth perfectly—apparently the workshop had been successful for them at least.

"In the final challenge, we'll work on our sense of trust," said Francis.

"Every day, we share information, work together to move projects forward, and rely on one another to achieve success." Marcy counted out the tasks on her fingers as she spoke.

"They say that there's no 'I' in 'achieve', and to…" Francis trailed off, and the muscles in his neck tightened—pushing out like eels writhing beneath a thin white sheet.

For several seconds, he chewed his lip. Marcy slowly leaned forward, staring with gentle encouragement towards her crumbling colleague. Jeff decided immediately this was his favourite part of the entire workshop.

"They say," Francis finally repeated, "that there's no 'I' in 'Team', and to achieve our goals, we truly need to look beyond ourselves."

"It's in that spirit that we designed this final challenge. We spend a lot of time together, so it's important for us to understand one another on a deeper, more personal level," said Marcy.

"This one isn't about winners or losers," said Francis.

"It's about sharing—being open with ourselves, and accepting of one another." With that, Marcy pulled out her digi-pad and made a point of pushing something on its screen.

A series of *dings, beeps, buzzes,* and a variety of songs played throughout the room. Pockets vibrated, people squirmed, and pants illuminated.

Francis leaned forward. "We've just shared an app with each of you. By opening it on your phones, you will have the opportunity to enter your answers to each question. They will then be shared anonymously with the team."

Anonymously. Jeff hoped he hadn't actually rolled his eyes. He still bitterly remembered the mass exodus of formerly fine employees after the Anonymous Employee Satisfaction Survey three years ago.

"In order to build understanding and trust, we are looking to get introspective today," said Marcy.

"Everyone will answer the question via the app, then we'll review the answers together. While we won't know who said what specifically, it will give us all greater insight into the depth of humanity on our team, and hopefully, help us realize that we aren't alone, and we truly are all in this together." Francis smiled. He'd clearly nailed the hardest part of his script.

It would be cute if it wasn't so sad, thought Jeff.

"As you will all see on your screens," said Marcy, "the question we want you to answer first is: What is one truth you wish your coworkers knew about you?"

Classic entrapment, thought Jeff. Pulling out his phone, he touched the notice and brought up a simple black screen with a green blinking cursor below the text of Marcy's question.

She'd got that part right at least.

It was a safe assumption that nothing was anonymous, but that only added another layer of complexity to the puzzle. If he shared some deep personal truth, it could be used against him. If he played it too safe, he wouldn't be seen as a team player. While that was never his goal, it was best to tread carefully if he could. The end of the game was near, and there was no telling what sudden stakes might arise.

Fuck.

Around the room, people slowly pulled out their phones, and most began typing. Marcy and Francis seemed to be sharing answers as well, Jeff noted.

Time slowed, and Jeff's fingers trembled over his keypad as his mind raced. Logically, there had to be a perfect response that would meet the letter of the exercise without putting himself at risk. Try as he might however, he couldn't put his finger on it.

Seconds crawled into minutes. It was worse than the long-gone days when waiting for the mail to arrive was among the chief pains of being. Would this torture ever cease? It had to eventually. But the stretch between start and end elongated into one of those infinite time scenarios like the typewriters and the monkeys.

Jeff didn't have time for any of that monkey business.

His fingers teased the screen with an energy all their own, but still he hesitated. Looking around the circle, he saw several people had already set their phones down, having submitted their answers. Were they really that in touch with themselves, or had they been prescient enough to have an answer to this sort of question at the ready? Jeff would never know.

He was among the laggards now, and this weighed on him as

much as the question itself. To be the last one to submit an answer would be a tacit declaration of either defeat or defiance in the eyes of the SALIGIA Overlords. They wouldn't care which.

His teeth nearly turned to dust as he ground them together, and his knuckles were snowy peaks. Finally, he resigned himself to the moment, and forcing away any second-guessing, he typed his answer in a wild rush, hit enter, and shoved his phone back into his pocket.

A few more seconds passed. Several people started whispered conversations before Francis called the team back to order. "Alright, please everyone submit your answers immediately if you have not yet done so. We'll begin shortly."

"Don't feel too much pressure," Marcy joined in the moment Francis had stopped. "Remember that this is all about letting go—so don't overthink things."

"Thanks everyone, it looks like all the answers are in. I want everyone to remember there are no wrong answers," said Francis.

Marcy nodded and picked up the thread. "This is not the time to discuss the answers, and it's certainly not about guessing whose answer is whose. We just want to be present, and really feel what our friends and coworkers choose to share with us today."

"As a reminder," said Francis, "the question was: What is one truth you wish your coworkers knew about you?"

Marcy glanced quickly down at her digi-pad. "One of us answered, 'I'm afraid of elevators.' Well, it must be a fright working on Floor 82," Marcy chuckled at her own wit, laying her digi-pad down squarely in her lap.

Francis lifted up his own, illuminating his pale face. "Another said, 'I always wanted to be a bartender.' We sure do have a fascinating and multi-talented team, don't we, Marcy?"

"We sure do, Francis," Marcy replied, again raising her own digi-pad. "This person said, 'I love my coworkers!' Well, I'm certain they love you too!"

Jeff stifled a groan, and wondered who'd decided to double down on the corporate ass-kissing. It might have been a sarcastic Jordan, or possibly a sincere Adra. Of course, it also might have been one of the supervisors themselves.

Francis smiled. "This next person answered, 'This job is all I have.' Well," he hesitated, and a shifting silence seized the room, "career is an important aspect of all our lives, and I think we can all relate to feeling thankful for our positions," he finished.

Marcy nodded. She must have approved of Francis' ad-libbing. Jeff hoped more responses would be like that—he took a strange pleasure in watching his superiors squirm.

"Our next randomly chosen response is, 'I don't really believe in giraffes.'" Marcy blushed after reading it, as if she feared people would take the silliness as her own.

Francis fought to stifle a giggle. "I suppose if you don't have evidence, it's not so unreasonable," he said after some time.

"Evidence like a zoo?" asked Jordan.

"Remember that we aren't here to judge, only to accept the openness of our coworkers," said Marcy.

"That's exactly right," Francis confirmed. Then, looking down at his digi-pad, he continued, "One of you said…" Here he blanched, and for a long while a tense silence held sway over the room.

"They said…" With all eyes on him, he slowly mustered the steel to continue, "'I hate working here.'" He hung his head upon finishing, resigned to the shame of the moment.

Marcy cleared her throat. "It sounds like someone is really struggling, but that's also important to know." She spoke fast, betraying her nervous energy. "We all go through rough times. It's important for this person—or anyone else—to remember that SALIGIA can help you if you bring this concern forward to your supervisor. Support is available." She glanced at Jeff as she finished. He shifted in his seat, his collar growing tight as he raced to figure out why Marcy seemed to blame him for the comment.

Is she the only one? he wondered.

"Thank you, Marcy," said Francis.

Marcy offered a polite smile. Then she glanced about the room as if searching for an escape, before finally looking back down to the screen in her lap. "The next response is, 'Whether I'm at work, at home, or anywhere else, I never know who I'm meant to be.'"

Jeff's collar continued to tighten, and he felt his face flush. He snuck a quick glance around the room, testing to see if anyone was staring at him.

Furtive, suspicious looks shot around like hot shrapnel, but none seemed to target him in particular.

Francis' face was ash as he read from his screen. "The next one says, 'I haven't seen my son in two years, and I think about him every day.'"

Jeff felt bad about looking over at Finnegan, but did so anyway. He wasn't alone. Most eyes in the room now rested heavily on the poor man, who sat slouched over with his eyes down. His family troubles were already well known around the office.

"This is a deep share, people." Francis continued, no doubt grateful for something negative that didn't reflect directly on SALIGIA. "That's what this is all about—feeling open enough to share our true selves with one another. Great work, Colby."

Finnegan's head sunk further, and his body shook.

"Indeed," said Marcy. Her jaw was set firm, and her will seemed unwavering as she continued. "One of you said, 'SALIGIA is the bane of my existence.'"

Her eyes flashed as she read it.

Francis' jaw fell open.

From around the quaint, cabin themed room came hushed chuckles and one sudden snort. While the feeling was likely shared by everyone in the room, Jeff couldn't imagine anyone but Jordan having the guts to write it.

Marcy and Francis stared about, their gazes lingering like searchlights as they moved from person to person.

Did they land longer on me? Jeff wondered.

For just a moment, he caught Janice looking at him. She wore a tired expression on the parts of her face not covered by her tumbling red hair. *Does she really think I wrote that one?*

Finally, the buzz died down, and Francis spoke. "As always, SALIGIA HR has many services to help anyone feeling like they are struggling in their position. Now, this next person said, 'I'm afraid of failure.' That's sure an understandable one. I imagine we all want to be our best selves," he finished.

The air in the room was dead. Everyone in attendance wished desperately to be anywhere else.

"The next response is, 'I'm afraid of our bathroom sinks,'" said Marcy. Her voice was cold and toneless. "That's funny," she added, and Jeff felt her shift in her seat.

A few forced chuckles popped up around the room, then died alone under the terrible weight of nervous tension.

At the far side of the room, the door with the Exit sign called to Jeff—signalling an escape from the dreary discussions and forced sincerity. It was salvation—delivery into excitement and real air and, best of all, the absolute unknown.

Beside it, one of the windows showed a tall mountain peak, with green fields and patches of pines marching up its stony slopes.

Between Jeff and the far door, Francis stared briefly down at his digi-pad. "'I am more capable than you know,'" he blurted. Catching himself, he hurried to finish, "was the next answer given." With the ending in sight, he was no doubt eager to skip formalities.

It seemed to Jeff like the sort of thing Janice would say. But Marcy's eyes were slits, shooting back and forth between Francis and himself.

Francis eyed Marcy in turn, while Jordan gave Jeff a knowing grin.

Janice held her calm repose, staring straight ahead with no emotion on her face. Adra and Rian debated with hand-gestures and hushed voices.

"I believe," said Marcy, "that SALIGIA does a very good job of knowing exactly what its employees are capable of."

"This was meant to be a team-building experience," said Francis. "Many of you have treated this like a chance to abuse and insult your source of employment…"

"Are you kidding? This entire workshop was a fucking insult!" Jordan jumped out of his chair as he spoke. The action was immediately mirrored by the rest of the room.

Chairs hit the floor, and the volume hit the roof. A deafening cacophony of accusations, defenses, and random pleas for sanity engulfed the tense calm of a moment before.

"You need to think before you speak," Marcy was scolding Francis.

Does she think it was from him? Jeff wondered.

"This is all your fault!" Francis threw his arms into the air.

A part of Jeff pitied them—so shackled by their servitude to SALIGIA. Could they see past it all like he could, or did they really believe everything they pushed on the Tins?

Jordan's voice rose above the din. "Does SALIGIA really think this crap is going to help us work better? To expose our secrets, sow distrust, and have us play a bunch of meaningless games when we could be getting our work done and enjoying our weekends? This is bullshit! No one is happy, and no one is better off than they were yesterday." He was on a roll now, and Jeff was enjoying the show.

Still, as much as he loved to see someone else take risks, he knew Jordan was right. There were a lot of places Jeff would rather be.

He could be home.

He could be with friends.

He could be just a few yards away, on the other side of the Exit door in the glory of nature untamed.

The door sang for him—a visual siren of red lights and endless promise.

Janice was arguing with Adra. Francis was screaming at Marcy. Jordan was yelling at anyone who would listen. Finnegan and Rian were huddled like scared rabbits in a corner, and Rudy was recording it all on his phone.

"You've been trying to make me look bad all day," Francis' finger was in Marcy's face.

"You've been doing a fine job of that without my help. Try remembering this isn't all about you," Marcy shot back.

"Fuck this and fuck SALIGIA," screamed Jordan.

Jeff wasn't certain exactly who he was talking to, but didn't feel inclined to involve himself despite his inclination to agree.

Instead, he made his way slowly through the crowd. Nobody needed this. Nothing would be settled.

The whole day in the mountains had been an absolute bust. Soon, they'd be back on the SALIGIA train, speeding back to

Edmonton. Nobody would even get a glimpse of the real mountains.

That could not stand.

He knew it was against the rules. There was probably an entire book of Occupational Health and Safety guidelines forbidding just such an action. Jeff knew a thousand good reasons to stay still, to turn around, to accept his fate.

He simply didn't care.

The metal bar of the door was cold against his palm. Tensing his body, he heaved it forward. A metallic clink sounded, and the Exit light began to flash. From somewhere in the hall behind him came the shrill cry of an alarm sounding, but it had no meaning to Jeff.

The air flowed fresh and cold and wet. With shocking force, it pushed at the door, then whipped around it and filled up the room. The arguments inside died as Jeff shoved the door fully open.

Then he felt the rain. A heavy cascading rush on his arms, face, and chest. It slammed into the wet concrete outside, flooded over the threshold, and streamed across the wooden flooring. All eyes turned outward, where in the distance, black against the dark navy clouds, loomed the primal shape of nature's untamed edge. A mountain rose into the sky, tearing through the clouds up into the realm of gods.

Against the force of the storm, it was a stark and stunning image.

Just then came a crack of thunder. Cannon fire, gunshots, and Zeus's angry judgement echoed through the hills, rolled down into the valley, and buffeted the shocked SALIGIA staff.

Jeff stared in wonder, not caring one bit about the rain.

Behind him the silence held, and Janice and Marcy, Francis and Adra and even Jordan stood in awe. The rain angled in hard. Everyone near the door was wet, but no one seemed to care.

The fear and stress so poignant only a second ago washed away with the torrent, and Jeff was certain there could never be a more powerful force in all the world.

Then, behind them, the door to the hallway swung open, and a sharp command revealed his error.

"That is enough."

The voice was Nadia's.

If her sudden appearance proved Jeff's earlier suspicions were true, it hardly mattered anymore. She stood now as the epicenter of all things. Her compact form cast long shadows across the floor, and her gaze sucked the air from the room.

The serene call of nature was dead, and the defiant pride and puffed up chests around the room deflated like so many old balloons.

Marcy and Francis hurried to her side, but were met with only a withering look.

Nadia waited, and the stragglers hurried to find their seats.

Finally, she continued. "Jordan, you will follow me."

As he approached her, she waved him through the door. Then she turned to the supervisors, and spoke in hurried, hushed tones.

The only word Jeff could make out was his own name. The Exit door was closed again, but the room was deadly cold.

Nadia followed Jordan out. The supervisors led the rest of the group through the endless hallways, back towards the train station. All the way, it echoed in Jeff's mind.

"...Jeff..." she'd said.

He could only imagine what else she said.

Jordan had been the final straw, but Jeff knew he shared responsibility. All day he'd tested the cracks. He pulled at the loose strings and challenged the workshop every step of the way.

Soon, much like Jordan, his judgement would come. Maybe today, maybe tomorrow. Soon enough. He couldn't escape it. He knew that, because he couldn't escape himself. He couldn't change his attitude any more than he could change the weather.

Work wasn't the only problem—it was how he responded.

The office was the perfect model of insanity taken to dogma. It was empire, it was total control. Now, a terrible truth was dawning on Jeff. He was the opposite of all that—the antithesis of SALIGIA.

Jeff saw it all as clearly as he'd seen the mountain.

He was chaos.

Soon, something had to give. One thing, or the other.

CHAPTER 11
The End of Another Day

O'Byrne's Irish Pub was especially busy, even for a Saturday night. When he'd set out to meet Eddie, Jeff hoped they'd manage to secure a spot on the patio to enjoy what he expected might be the last stretch of tolerable weather they got this summer.

The moment he'd stepped out of his door though, that hope withered like the flowers in front of his squat brown apartment building. The chilly air bit his exposed flesh, and Jeff tugged the collar of his thin jacket snug against him as he hurried down the avenue.

Arriving at O'Byrne's, he was pleased to find Eddie had beat him there again, and was already sitting in a corner booth inside. He had a smug look on his face and a full beer in front of him.

"I hope you don't mind the switch—I'm not down with sitting outside at this point," he said.

"Good call," Jeff said, taking the seat opposite.

Eddie was the one person Jeff could always rely on. To be early, to make the right call—to simply be there when needed.

Today, Jeff needed his friend.

He'd texted Eddie as soon as he stepped off the corporate train the day before, and they'd confirmed plans before he got home for a sleepless night.

Tangled in sweat-soaked blankets and flipping from one side to another, the strange events of the mountain retreat played through his head like a hellish pantomime. The ridiculous competitions, the rising tensions, and the explosion at the end.

He remembered Jordan finally losing his cool, and how he'd been carted off by Nadia. Jeff feared the worst for him, and wondered how long it would be for his own day to come.

The train ride back had solidified his fears. After he'd heard Nadia whisper his name to Marcy, the rest of the group returned to the train under a solemn shroud of silence. Jeff was once again hoping to find a seat by Janice and chat, but at the last moment Marcy signalled him to follow her into a private car. She wanted— no doubt at Nadia's insistence—to get back to their absurd "therapy" routine.

The degradation of that long ride echoed in his memory, and only when Eddie agreed to meet him for a good old-fashioned night of venting did Jeff find any hope of relief.

Finally, in a place he felt comfortable, Jeff sank down against the back of his bench as the server brought over a pint of Traditional Ale.

"Do you not even have to order here anymore?" asked Eddie.

"Like I've always told you, the best friends are bartender friends."

Eddie frowned, and took a sip of his lager.

"And teachers of course, but that goes without saying," Jeff added.

Eddie laughed. "So, what's new? Your invitation seemed more urgent than the usual night out."

Jeff sighed, wondering where to begin. "Hey now," he started with inflamed bravado, "don't go assuming that our usual nights out are anything but urgently needed."

"I hear that," Eddie said around a mouthful of beer.

His days as a teacher were long, no doubt. Still, Jeff could immediately tell Eddie saw through his bold façade, but knew he was unlikely to force the issue.

Sometimes, he understood Jeff too well.

He probably already knows what this is about. He's too clever by half.

Jeff still had no clue where to begin. "The workshop in the mountains was interesting, to say the least," he said after some reflection.

Eddie smiled over the lip of his mug. "Classic SALIGIA shenanigans?" he asked.

"Oh man, it was so absurd. There's no way you're going to believe even half of it, so be forewarned."

"And doubly sceptical now." Eddie chuckled, rolled his eyes, and took another sip of beer.

Jeff did likewise, but there was no mirth in it. He began to tell Eddie about the insane competitions they were forced to partake in, but already, his mind was far ahead of that—in the elegant private train car, sitting across from Marcy.

"Jeff, you've been increasingly agitated these past few days, and I'm sorry I didn't find the time to check in with you sooner. As noted during our recent Performance Review, there's been an ongoing pattern of…" she trailed off here, flipping through her notes.

"Uncharacteristic insolence?" Jeff remembered her words well.

"Right. Well, this conversation is certainly overdue one way or another. Tell me, Jeff, what's going on?" Marcy clicked her long nails on the polished red wood of the end table beside her. If she was still frazzled by the chaos in the training centre, she hid it well.

Their car had none of the digi-screens that covered the staff cars—it was for the Brass. The soft, silky carpets and wood-panelled walls all proved authentic. There was room to walk around, and Jeff spotted what he was quite certain was a mini-bar in the corner.

"Honestly," Jeff's mind raced to find an excuse. The impromptu therapy session had caught him off-guard, and he worried that Nadia's apparent insistence on it happening now was a bad omen. In the rush of the moment, he couldn't find a reasonable excuse in time to catch up with his wagging tongue. "...I don't have any real excuse," he said.

It was—surprisingly enough—the plain truth. Jeff lived with the grim reality of knowing that he was far too old to have excuses. It was terrifying, but also comforting somehow.

At any rate, he saw no other path than the one he was on now, so he decided to double down. "Most people have their stories, their experiences, and unique reasons for the fucked-up things they do. I just have me. It's all I've ever had."

Marcy's thick black eyebrows arched, and her lips turned down in a curious scowl. "You know," she said, "I actually get that."

It caught Jeff off guard, and he'd sat in the cool, ornate room ill at ease, waiting to see where the ride would take him.

"Have you ever seen *Wipeout*?" Jeff asked Eddie, forcing the memories from his mind. Then, he took a long pull from his mug. As he set it down, a heavy-set guy in a New City vest bumped their table, nearly spilling the beer. Every seat was taken, and between the antique-covered walls of the bar people shuffled back and forth among groups of friends.

"The obstacle course gameshow with all the weird challenges?" asked Eddie.

"That's the one. The retreat was a lot like that, except with the constant, unstated threat of being fired at any moment—or given new assignments that made you wish you were." Jeff finished his drink, and waved for two more. The bar smelled like old beer and older whiskey. It always made Jeff feel at home.

"Did anyone get eliminated—I mean fired?" Eddie joked.

"I think Jordan finally managed it. And I'm probably next."

"What did you do?"

"I opened a door." Jeff smiled, his eyes glazing slowly over as he thought back on how accurate that statement was. It really was all he'd done.

"Do you understand what you did today, Jeff?" Marcy had leaned forward, and looked intently at him as she spoke. "When an employee acts in such flagrant defiance of corporate expectations, it sends a message, whether you meant it or not. You opened a door to malfeasance, and SALIGIA cannot afford the loss of productivity that could bring with it. You know our bottom-line is tight this quarter."

Jeff smiled, and gazed off at the corporate mini-bar shining in the corner. *Does she actually believe all this shit?* he wondered. There was no way to be certain, but she had to see through it.

How could someone be so blind to what they'd become?

The seats in the car were a deep brown leather. They cradled Jeff and held him like a mother's arms as he leaned back and spread his own arms around the edge of his chair. "Have you ever come up with the greatest quote or idea you've ever had, only to find out it's already been done? Not like you copied it—it was independently yours. It's just that the world has been going on for so long and so many things have happened that all the really great stuff is already done. Everything you might ever want to say is just another whisper in the storm. You know?"

Marcy pinched her mouth into a thin white line, but said nothing.

"I feel like that's been my whole life," Jeff continued. If this was a chance to vent, he might as well seize it. It would be better than listening to more corporate platitudes.

"It's the sad side effect of being raised on fairy tales and classic literature. I always thought it was meant to be the paths less trodden—that's where you find the treasure," he finished.

"Treasure?" asked Marcy.

"You know," Jeff was starting to enjoy this thread, "the truth, freedom, whatever you want to call it. That feeling that life must eventually reveal some grand coherence. But it hasn't, of course, and I think I'm beyond that illusion now. It only gets harder—more painful and more demanding each year. Still, the beautiful things— though rare—become all the brighter for that," he finished.

Marcy stared at him and slowly blinked. "That's a lovely thought, Jeff, but the issue here comes down to you always assuming you know better—that everybody else in the world is just in your way. Sometimes other people are right, sometimes the well-trodden paths are familiar for a reason. Maybe they lead us to where we need to be."

She was talking about SALIGIA. It was all she knew.

"I guess you're right," he admitted. "We have signposts now— hell, we have full-on freeways. I don't always need to hack my lonely way through the wilderness." Jeff could spit out meaningless tripe with the best of them, and was having a blast at this point.

For a while, Marcy stared at him, no clear sign of understanding registering on her round, ruddy face. Then, she too glanced back at the mini-bar. "Do you want a drink, Jeff? SALIGIA doesn't even count the expenses from management, and we're all pushing eleven hours at this point anyways."

"Sure…" Jeff murmured, fearing a trap. He'd wanted a drink every day at SALIGIA since the first week he'd started. He'd imagined slipping out on a coffee break for a quick libation, or sneaking in a flask, but he never entertained the notion of it coming from the Brass.

His surprise only increased as he watched Marcy pour two glasses of straight, special label Jameson. She slid one over to him as if it was the most mundane thing in the world.

"Thanks…" he said.

Marcy clinked his glass, and nodded silently.

"None of this was my idea, Jeff. Not really. Of course, I tried to do my best, and I followed my instincts when I started, just like anyone would. Suddenly, I was management, and the promising career I'd always dreamed of settled into a reality I never imagined." She took a quick sip of her drink, and seemed to lose herself in thought for a moment.

"Now, I'm competing for pyrrhic victories in a race I don't even remember entering. For what? I sure as hell don't want Nadia's job—but I can't go back, either. If I'm going to be a supervisor, I need to at least try and be the best supervisor I can be. That's all anyone can do, right?"

"Anyone that's a supervisor," said Jeff.

"You know what I mean." Marcy took an impressive swallow of whiskey.

To his surprise and dismay, Jeff did know what she meant. Even now it made sense.

It had been the longest train ride of his life, yet he knew he'd only skim the surface of it tonight with Eddie.

"Was it a trap door?" Eddie offered eventually, shaking Jeff out of his reflections.

"Something like that. They just pushed us all too far. The lunacy got to be too much, and Jordan exploded. Then I opened the emergency exit. I just wanted to see the mountains. Jordan got carted out, and I had to endure a two-hour therapy session with Marcy."

"So, who really came out on top?"

"Marcy."

Their loud laughter was drowned out by the heavy hum of a hundred other conversations in the bar.

"I thought about quitting instead, but that's nothing new," said Jeff. "I think about that every day."

"You know, I always hear people complaining about being out of work. I know this comes from a place of ignorance, but I've got to say, being out of work sounds amazing!"

"I'm sure you'll find out soon enough," said Eddie.

"Maybe," said Jeff. "The truth is, I do try my best, but it never amounts to much. Ineffective and underappreciated. At this point, I second—even third-guess myself at every juncture. Which is futile of course, since any answer is inevitably wrong anyway."

"Did you explain that to Marcy?" Eddie asked, likely knowing the answer.

"Not exactly. The whole thing was pretty strange actually. More so than you'd imagine," said Jeff.

"How so?" asked Eddie.

Jeff sighed. He took a quick sip of beer, then a long look around the familiar confines of O'Byrne's. "I sort of understood where she was coming from. For the first time since she got the supervisor position, she sounded like a real person. It's a dangerous precipice, of course," he continued, "I really can't afford to humanize my superiors right now; mocking their every move is all that keeps me sane these days."

Eddie chuckled. "In a place like that, I imagine everyone's struggling on some level."

Jeff sat up in his chair as he spoke. "That's just it, though. SALIGIA is a nightmare. It helped to think that behind all our torture, there was someone holding a pitchfork getting a kick out of it. But if it's just suffering all the way up, then what's the point? What's sustaining it?"

Eddie raised an eyebrow. "Are you humanizing Nadia now, too?"

"No," Jeff replied without a second thought. "She's definitely an evil cyborg. I don't know if she's the head cyborg, but she's well up there. Maybe she's the prototype for the SALIGIA Overlords—the next word in overbearing boss automation."

"So, you briefly tasted fresh air, narrowly avoided termination, and had to hang out with Marcy. That honestly is a rough Friday. I'm sorry, buddy."

Jeff couldn't tell if Eddie was being facetious or not, so he decided to sweeten the pot. "Drink with Marcy, actually."

"What?" Eddie nearly choked on his beer, and had to wipe a dribble of foam from his chin.

"For real. She gave me booze!" Jeff explained, still hardly believing it himself.

For the rest of his life, Jeff would remember how good that whiskey was. He knew he'd never have better from the moment he tasted it.

"This is depressingly good whiskey," he'd said to Marcy. It eased his nerves, and cooled his simmering fears about how all this would end.

"SALIGIA takes care of its own. And for better or worse, I am one of its own." Marcy frowned, and refilled their cups.

"It got pretty intense with you and Francis today," Jeff swallowed his trepidation, deciding to take advantage of the moment. "What was that about?"

"Who fucking knows?" Marcy slouched back on her couch and rolled her eyes. "It always gets that way. I guess it's like—if you can't prove that you're better than the other supervisor, you risk Nadia thinking you're underperforming.

"Of course, you don't want Nadia to think you're underperforming."

"I don't imagine." Jeff shuddered.

He remembered Francis' fury when he'd tossed the key across the gap, and realized the fear behind it. There were few things Jeff could imagine wanting less than to trigger the ire of Nadia.

Poor Jordan, he'd thought.

Still, he didn't really disagree with anything Jordan had said.

He took another drink. It burned his throat, then sat with a soothing, invigorating warmth in his gut. "What will happen to Jordan?" he asked. His candour surprised him.

Marcy rolled her eyes again, then arched her brow towards Jeff with a sardonic grin. "Who?" she asked.

Jeff nodded. *Poor fucking Jordan.*

"Well Jeff, I told you my story. What about you? You have plenty of talent, and a respectable bit of potential if you could get your act together. So why do you insist on making a joke of yourself and everything you touch? What is this destructive urge of yours about?"

"I make the jokes for myself. I just take notice when someone else laughs." Jeff could hardly believe how fast the answer came to him—much less that it felt honest.

Marcy nodded, but didn't say anything. For a long while they drank in silence, and his mind was in another place.

"You're awfully distracted tonight, Mr. Boggs." Eddie cut into his reflections. "The trying circumstances aside, a trip to virtual mountains and a gameshow of calamity sound like a decent opportunity for some hijinks. Nothing else worthwhile came of it?"

"It was a work retreat, what could possibly come of it?" Jeff knew what Eddie was pushing for, but obstinance seemed easier than sincerity just then.

"C'mon, Jeff. You had a two-hour train ride there, atypical activities all day, and you're telling me you didn't dream up any other wild schemes?"

Jeff thought about the yellow sweater sliding in and out of view between the people ahead of him in line—of frizzy red hair popping over the top of a headrest on the train.

"I rarely dream," he said. He intended to maintain his flippant avoidance, but somehow honesty got the better of him once more. "And when I do, I'm left with indistinct images and ideas. An unknown place, or shadows of half-familiar faces. A sense of purpose and adventure. Then I wake up, and they begin to fade. Every night, we lose things that usually seem more interesting than real life. It's the worst part of the morning. The terror of forgetting better people than you ever knew. Better people than you deserve to know."

Eddie held his beer in front of him like a playwright's skull. "Does the sun grow dimmer each day?" he spoke with dramatic flourish. "If so, does not the moon shine the brighter for it?"

Jeff chuckled. "Are you mocking me?"

"I was. I'm sorry," said Eddie. He clinked his mug with Jeff's. "I really don't know what else to say to any of that. I'm glad to see your philosophy minor is paying off though."

"Oh, don't take it personally buddy, you're still one of my favourites." Jeff knew Eddie hated when he got down on himself like this. After all, everyone had their limits.

"I just wish you wouldn't bullshit me, Jeff. You're a ball of nerves tonight—something's on your mind. You called me out here to talk about it, so why waste so much time beating around the bush? What's going on?"

If Jeff was to line up everyone he knew, and rate them based on how comfortable he was opening up to them, Eddie would be in rare company. He could be—and on many occasions, had been—more open with Eddie than anyone else in his life. Eddie was the brother he never had, and there was nothing he'd hesitate to tell him.

So, it wasn't that he felt uncomfortable sharing his mind with Eddie, it was just that he'd unloaded it all so recently. Tonight, he needed Eddie to help him cope with that very fact.

That strange, unexpected, haunting fact.

"Okay." Marcy shattered a silence which had become a comforting blanket, and left Jeff suddenly exposed. "I think I understand the jokes. Nevertheless, SALIGIA has noted a downturn in your performance. The only reason you weren't required to attend that Corporate Hierarchies workshop Janice had to take was because you're on SALIGIA's Special Attention list. So, you should consider yourself lucky for that, and for these sessions."

Of all the indignities he'd experienced, this increasing breach into his personal life seemed the cruelest. He finished his drink, but said nothing.

"So," Marcy pushed, "when are you going to start working towards something real, Jeff?"

Jeff's first thought was that this was a terrible breach of professional boundaries. He was certain it surpassed anything that could be justified as defense of SALIGIA's best interests. It may even have been pushing into infringement of personal privacy rights.

Jeff might have been surprised, yet he found himself entirely unphased.

To be fair, it's not a bad question, he thought. For longer than he cared to admit, he'd intended to live up to some distant sense of potential he recalled having. He got onto the elevator each morning pregnant with potential, only to find it stillborn when he stepped out onto Floor 82.

If it was the result of some suffocating phantasm that ruled over the floor, the direct impact of a managerial structure that would sooner eviscerate him alive than admit error, or something else entirely, Jeff couldn't be sure. The simple fact was that when Jeff was at work, his energy was drained as if a psychic vampire was latched to his neck like a moray eel.

Nothing bothered him, and nothing really motivated him.

Nothing except...

"It's not only about work. I guess it's just how I am. I used to make a point of always trying to do the right thing. These days, I'm lucky to settle for alright."

Marcy leaned forward. "That's very insightful, Jeff. What do you think you can do about it?"

"I don't know." This trend of honesty was wearing on him, and exhaustion was creeping in. "There's something in the way, I guess I need to figure out what that is. Nothing can grow when the roots are rotten," he finished, and felt a great weight lifting from his shoulders.

Marcy nodded, and finished her own drink. She smiled, seemingly content that her work was done.

All the rest of the way home, Jeff considered what he needed to do.

"I'm sorry," said Jeff. His beer was empty. "I'm not trying to mess with you, Eddie. I'm glad you came out tonight, I just have a lot going on right now."

Eddie leaned over the scratched, sticky table. "It's okay. All in good time, my guy."

"Hey! Eddie? Well I'll be fucked!" a booming voice overpowered the sounds of the bar, and a tall man in a grey pea coat leaned over the table, sloshing his beer and spilling it in the process. "How the shit are you?"

"Russ!" Eddie held up his beer and clinked with his friend.

Jeff mirrored the motion, but cursed the inevitable addition to their table. He'd never really liked Russ, primarily because he had the annoying habit of loudly spewing thoughts Jeff was still chewing on silently. "Hello Russ," he mumbled, rueing the need.

"Is that Jeff? I haven't seen you in a dog's age. How've you been, fella?" Russ clapped Jeff on the shoulder, and squeezed into the booth next to him.

"Were you here all alone?" asked Eddie.

"We're all here alone," said Russ.

Behind his empty mug, Jeff rolled his eyes. *Fucking Russ.*

"I was out on the patio," Russ continued, interested only in his own bloated sense of self-importance, "but then I saw you two miserable mugs and thought I'd come lighten the mood."

"Glad to have you." Eddie clinked glasses with him again.

Russ grinned. His teeth were crooked, and his jaw was slightly offset, yet he smiled more than most people Jeff could think of. "Seeing you is some good timing too, I'll be leaving soon."

"Where to?" Eddie asked.

Jeff ordered another round from a passing server. Immediately, Russ threw his hand up, adding himself to the order.

"Off to Belize—just signed a new contract last week. I should be down there eight months at least," Russ answered loud enough that the whole bar must have heard him.

Jeff never bothered to learn exactly what Russ did—he was

Eddie's friend anyway, and nothing more than an occasional annoyance to Jeff. Whatever it was, he was able to take contracts all over the world, and appeared to be in steady demand. It didn't seem overly lucrative, but it afforded him a sense of freedom that Jeff often envied.

Belize sounded warm. Jeff didn't know much about it, but he was sure there'd be some fine scenery, and likely beachside drinks to boot.

"What are you doing there?" he asked, wondering if any of his skills from SALIGIA would transfer.

"Hard to say," Russ stared at the ceiling and spoke in a low monotone, "whatever comes up I suppose."

It sounded perfect, and Jeff despised that an idiot like Russ managed such a sweet setup.

"That's a great opportunity man, I'm happy for you," said Eddie. "Let me know if you hear of any teaching jobs down there," he finished with a grin.

Eddie would never uproot his family. Much worse, he didn't seem to have any real desire to. The notion of a beachside paradise was nothing more than a fanciful romance to a man as settled as Eddie.

To Jeff, it sounded more like a long-promised deliverance.

What it meant to Russ, Jeff could only imagine. Finding out, however, would likely require far more discussion with Russ—and thereby exposure to his breathy platitudes and painful homilies—than Jeff was inclined to tolerate.

"Yeah, I don't really want to make any plans," Russ continued. "The contract is a solid one, and I can handle it well within the timeframe. Beyond that, I'm just going to be in the moment and enjoy where life takes me."

Jeff really hated Russ sometimes. It was a strange thing, how one could sit so long on some idea, with no hope of articulating it. A raw, restless emotion boiling within the breast, pounding its intentions out against the skull, and fermenting in the guts unarticulated and unrealized. Then, some blithering numbskull could come along and put it to words and make it solid. Suddenly it's a dream no longer. It's a tangible, approachable concept, and other people will have done it many times over. Then it becomes terrifying and senseless, and loses all the appeal of the unknown and the unrealized.

Only the lucky and the mad knew exactly what they wanted to do at all times—even if that was nothing in particular.

Eddie and Russ continued to chat, and laugh, and presumably catch up on old times, or something like that. Jeff picked up bits and pieces here and there. A previous business trip that failed. A new chance in Belize—a girl who wouldn't wait for him. It was the same old shit.

No matter what anyone chose to do in life, it meant choosing not to do something else. Jeff wondered how much Russ had sacrificed to achieve what he quietly envied. It was humbling, and reminded him that he was no better than those he resented.

His father was right—life wasn't fair.

Jeff sipped his beer slowly, and felt the soft, cracking leather of the booth through his jacket. He slipped back into his mind, and thought about all the different lives he'd meant to lead. The places he thought he'd go, and the people he thought he'd know. He thought about the roles he might have played, and, more than anything else, the person he might have been.

All the possibilities of youthful ambition and middle-aged ignorance danced before him, calling out with ghostly voices all the excuses he'd told himself as time wore on, and slowly, painfully, he watched his choices culled.

Now, he stood upon a perilous precipice—worn ceaselessly away by the heavy strokes of the clock's hand—between those lost hopes, and the dwindling options that remained to him.

It made him quail, and he took a long pull from his mug to steady his racing heart.

Like carnival funhouses, doors opened, and doors closed. There was no telling where any would lead. All the stories—past and possible, real, and only hoped-for—played through his mind. Within each, he saw the common thread of wild ambition, and a ubiquitous need to recapture some sense of who he'd been before time, excuses, stress, and the pervasive terror of reality had ground him down and molded him into a more functional and less joyful form.

He thought of snowballs and knit hats, and the certainty of being on the right side of the story.

Finally, he thought of Janice. He hoped she was all right. He wished he could help her, and he wondered—if he did have the chance to do so—was he still the sort of person who would recognize it?

One door closes, another one opens.

Chapter 12
The Day Everything Changed

It wasn't until Jeff was on the bus home that he really processed how fast Monday had gone by.

At no point was the day easy—in fact it was one of the more exhausting days he'd faced in years. Rather, it was so utterly jam-packed that he never really had the time to lament the toilsome nature of his predicament.

As soon as he'd stepped off the elevator onto Floor 82, he knew just what kind of turmoil he was up against. Unsurprisingly, Jordan was nowhere to be found, and the office was abuzz with whispers and speculation. A few people who had his personal cell number reported that it was disconnected, and some claimed that early in the morning hours, they'd seen the cleaning crew buffing claw marks out of the polished walls where Jordan had been ripped from his office and dragged away.

Jeff doubted at least half of this. That Jordan showed up to work today, much less early, seemed especially dubious. What couldn't be disputed was that Jordan was gone, and it was very likely no one would ever hear from him again.

Already, there was a smiling little goon named Ames sitting in his chair, and Francis wasted no time grabbing Jeff by the arm when he arrived, and dragging him down the hall to introduce them. With a shit-eating grin, he explained that Jeff would spend the rest of the

251

week getting Ames up to speed on all of Jordan's old initiatives.

Jeff watched any hope of truly valuing the wearisome Ames as a teammate or colleague vanish to the dust. Still, he recognized the innate potential in training the man who would inevitably be his direct opposition once he grasped the paradoxical nature of their initiatives. Inevitably, he'd soon start withholding information, and obscuring facts not to further his own projects, but rather to defend his position against the endless barrage of critiques, attacks, and outright slander from the Brass.

Jeff would never again get the chance to so directly force the goals of Ames' initiatives towards his own.

So, sitting by Ames in an uncomfortable office chair, Jeff transitioned him into the role the best he could, seeking clarity of project mandates while wondering all along if Ames could smell the fresh blood of his predecessor. Did he sense the danger he'd inadvertently stepped into?

All day, Jeff struggled to avoid grasping him by his thin, crooked shoulders and shaking his pitiable frame while screaming. *Get out of here you damned loon, it's not too late to find something to make you happy. Anything! Run now. Now, dammit!*

The example set by Jordan's absence, however, was a stark reminder of the consequences for speaking up against SALIGIA, and Jeff held his tongue all day long.

He was stepping off the bus at the end of the day when he finally began to feel it. The air was chilly, and had a bite to it which portended bitter things to come. He knew that winter wasn't far off, and pulled his sweater tight around him as he hurried towards his apartment building.

Reaching the entry, he saw his reflection in the grimy windows, and the wet, brown streets of Edmonton behind him. He pulled out his phone as he searched his other pocket for keys. A text had come in at some point, and he opened it just as the key turned in his door.

Are you still around? Want to grab a drink?

He recognized the number. It was Janice.

Twelve minutes had passed since he'd received it. With his key still in the door, Jeff stood stark straight. A sudden chill took his spine, and he cracked his neck as he considered this unexpected change of course.

Finally, pushing his keys back down into his pocket and leaning against the dirty red brick of the building, Jeff called Janice back.

"Hello?" she answered.

"Hey, it's Jeff."

"Jeff!" He was certain she sounded excited. "I hope I'm not bothering you. I know I shouldn't be using your private number, but I thought maybe if you were still in the area you might want to grab a drink?"

"Two things, Janice. First, thanks for not leaving a voicemail. No one likes that bullshit." They both chuckled.

"Second," he continued matter-of-factly, "I'd love to grab a drink."

"You're not too far away already?" she asked.

Jeff thought about the long, creaking bus ride back—the cold air seeping through the rattling bus door, and the crowded packs of mouth-breathing, personal-space-defying commuters. "It's no big deal. I don't have plans tonight. I'll try to get my car running and come meet you."

"Great, how does Sherlock's Downtown work?"

"Perfect," Jeff answered. "I'll be there in about fifteen minutes."

Hoping to hell his car would start, Jeff hurried around to the parking lot. His car was a 2002 Civic, and had been on its last legs for about six years. Long ago, Jeff began to rely on the abysmal busses for most of his transportation needs, and only used the car to pick up heavy items, or on the rare occasions he opted to leave the city.

In winter, there was no hope of starting it. Even during a cool autumn, it was a coin flip. Nonetheless, it seemed like Janice was finally open to hearing him out, and Jeff was ready to risk stalling his car on the side of the road to make it work.

The car was right where he'd left it, which was never a guarantee in his neighbourhood. It must have been at least four months since he'd driven it, and the windows were dirty, leaves covered the roof, and the wheels were stuck to the asphalt with old mud. The trunk made a weary screeching sound as he opened it to toss in his bag, and it took three tries to finally turn the engine over. The gears groaned as the car slowly chugged to life and rolled out onto the street, but in Jeff's veins there pumped a sudden, uncontrollable vigour.

The downtown Sherlock Holmes pub was a squat little cottage covered in vines and nestled between two office towers just off Jasper Ave. It wasn't far from the SALIGIA Tower, but its mood was as different as could be. It was warm and homey, and its stark contrast to the personality-devoid monoliths around it made it feel like an old friend.

Its location also meant Jeff had to go straight back where he'd come from, but this time he relished the trip. Despite the many troubles with his car, he enjoyed driving, and as he turned west onto Whyte, he pushed a Springsteen CD into his player and began to sing along.

He needed to cross the river again to get back downtown, but driving afforded him a better view than the LRT offered. With one eye on the road, he glanced down at the trees of the River Valley below. The green canopy was speckled here and there with hints of oranges and reds, a promise that all beauty and life would soon be snuffed out by bitter frosts.

Turning out of the valley and up towards the downtown core, he focussed again on the music. His cheap, third party speakers weren't optimal, but even with the poor sound, the tunes were unbeatable.

Bruce said that we had to "get out while we're young." It was pushing a decade now since Jeff felt truly young, yet here he remained. He didn't know when, but sometime between then and now, the youthful idealism of the song had aged into a hard-edged desperation in his gut.

Crossing Jasper and turning left, his wheels rattled along a narrow brick-paved lane. He found a single parking space open in front of Sherlock's, and considered that a damn good start to the night as he angled in and sputtered to a stop.

Passing the antiquated red phonebooth and following along the white picket fence, he pushed through the door and paused in front of the bar. Sherlock's walls, roof, and every other empty surface were covered in knick-knacks, foreign dollar bills, magazine cut-outs, and general "British" imagery. It was a potpourri of smells—old, musty papers, deep fried foods, and good beers.

He spotted Janice off in the corner. She was seated in a booth near the back, already halfway through a pint of Guinness.

"Decided to have your meal and drink all in one, I see?" Jeff called over to her as his long strides closed the expanse between them. A couple of old barflies glanced up. One sneered, as if Jeff's greeting had spoiled his sacred silence.

Janice rolled her eyes as Jeff took a seat across from her in the soft-cushioned booth. "I've always been one for efficiency," she said. Then, she seemed to catch herself, and rushed in a caveat. "I know I could have asked you to join sooner, sorry about that. I wasn't really sure, and I—"

"It's okay," Jeff cut her off. He meant it too, which was a refreshing change from the glib acquiescence his work demanded. "I get it, it's been a weird week. I'm glad you called though, it'll be nice to catch up after all the shit we've seen."

Janice laughed, and the sound was like the tinkling of light rain into clear, moonlit water. "Strange times indeed," she said. "Jeff, I'm sorry things have been weird lately. I know you meant well, but you really crossed a line at the Performance Review. I can handle myself, and I don't need anyone speaking for me."

Jeff tried to interject, but she pushed on with a brazen determination that was as inspiring as it was uncharacteristic.

"My independence is important to me, that's all. For a lot of my life I just did what I thought was expected of me. I went with the flow, and tried to make everyone else happy. It took me way too long to accept that I wasn't happy, and at that point making the changes I needed to was one of the hardest things I've ever done. Since then, I get a bit testy when anyone else tries to make my choices for me. I know control wasn't your intention, but it really pushed my buttons—not to mention getting both of us in the hot seat with HR." She took a pointed chug of her thick, black beer.

"Yeah, sorry again about that." Jeff swallowed hard, and looked around for a server. He hadn't put much thought into what he wanted to say, and suddenly felt painfully aware of that lapse. "I get what you're saying, honestly. You've been through a lot, and I know I overstepped. I guess I was just trying to lighten your load at the time, but I understand why it upset you, and I'm sorry."

For a while they said nothing, but the silence was a comfortable one. Like lying in bed, home sick from school, surrounded by warmth and comfort and a lack of responsibilities so liberating that you couldn't help but do nothing at all.

It was broken by a server coming by to take their orders.

"I actually drove, so I should probably eat as well. Are you eating?" Jeff asked.

Janice held up her near-empty Guinness. "Like you said, drink and meal all in one." She turned to the server, "I'll have another, please."

Jeff glanced quickly over the draught list. "And I'll have a Rickard's Red, and a plate of hot wings."

The server nodded, and hurried into the back.

"You have consistent tastes," said Janice.

Jeff felt his face flush, suddenly self-conscious. "I guess so."

"Can you believe what happened to Jordan?" asked Janice.

"Believe it? I can hardly believe it didn't happen sooner."

"Is that going to affect your work much?"

"Less than you'd imagine, but I do have to train the new guy. You were on some of Jordan's projects, weren't you?"

"Yeah," she answered, "I guess I'll report to Ames now."

"He seems alright," said Jeff. He hoped it would offer some comfort. "I hope he's the cooperative sort, and we can make headway on our initiatives. Jordan was good for an occasional laugh, but he was impossible to work with."

"I guess that's why he's gone."

"Well, part of it. He's gone because he was hard for SALIGIA to work with, too. Hard to control, at least. If being generally unpleasant was his only flaw, he'd be a supervisor by now."

They both laughed, then nodded sadly. Janice chewed at her lip for a moment, then took a sip from the fresh beer the server brought.

"To me, the more pressing implication is that the Brass finally pulled the trigger and canned him," said Jeff. "That means I'm probably next on the chopping block."

"Well the mountain air was totally worth it, just in case no one else bothered to say so."

"Right? That workshop was a goddamn nightmare. Why couldn't we have done all of that outside? Or better yet, not done any of it at all?"

"It was meant to be a punishment, wasn't it?"

"Isn't everything?"

Janice nodded, her mouth curling into a frustrated grimace. "Is that why they pulled you aside at the end? I've been worried about you, especially after the news about Jordan. Do you really think you're next?"

Jeff took a drink, and wondered the same thing himself. "SALIGIA will come for any one of us if they see a dime to be made or saved. They take general malfeasance pretty seriously if it effects the bottom line, but defiance of the hierarchy is the cardinal sin. Jordan and I have both been guilty of that for a long time. I can't see myself stopping it either, since it's the only thing that brings me joy in the office. So one way or another, I imagine my days are numbered."

"Hmm." Janice rubbed her hand across her forehead, pushing a red curl out of her eye. "Would that be the worst thing in the world, though? You admit you're not happy there. Hell, why not find something better before that happens?"

The cozy room echoed with the sounds of fiddles and laughter, and the distant smell of his wings cooking mingled with the beer and old wood smell of the building. It was a familiar combination, and it comforted Jeff in spite of the terrible reality brought home by Janice's questions.

She really does have my number, he thought.

"Maybe I will," he answered. He knew it was a lie. Despite his constant daydreams to the contrary, Jeff feared he'd be at SALIGIA until they fired him or he died. Sometimes he imagined the firing would immediately precede the death. SALIGIA did provide decent life insurance after all, and employee death was an even greater expense than employee recruitment.

"No, you won't," Janice spoke over the lip of her mug, which only partially concealed the confident sneer smeared across her face.

Fuck.

"Yeah, probably not," he admitted.

"Your wings," the server's voice surprised him. She slid an empty plate with napkins and a wet wipe in front of him, then placed a steaming plate of hot wings just behind it. The sight made Jeff's mouth water. Then his eyes did likewise.

"Those smell amazing," said Janice. When Jeff motioned for her to take one, however, she declined.

"Well, you do what you want," she said, "but if I were as free as you are, I'd be nowhere near that cesspit."

Jeff pointed to his full mouth, thankful for the opportunity to delay his response. He understood Janice's need to stay there for her kid. Like he'd told Marcy though, Jeff had no excuses—only a strange indifference towards self-betterment he could never quite articulate.

"How is Eustace doing?" he asked after swallowing. It was a cowardly move.

"He has good days and bad." Janice gazed into her beer as she spoke. "We were out the other day, trying to get some fresh air before the snow hits. There was a little bit of runoff in the gutter that he kept calling a river. He wanted to follow it forever," she said.

Jeff remembered playing similar games out in the alley behind his house growing up, or during the rare, warm recess breaks at school. Summers were brief in Edmonton, but as a child they always seemed like they'd last forever.

"Does he like frogs?" he asked.

"Frogs?" Janice looked almost more disgusted than confused.

"Yeah," Jeff said, washing his hands with a wet wipe. "I used to catch them all the time when I was a kid. I never had any siblings, but me and the neighbour kids would race them. There's an incredible, riveting joy that comes from seeing a frog jump. It's childish, but it works for me to this day. They're so reckless and free."

Do those things always go together? he wondered.

Janice finished her beer, and stared at the cluttered wall behind Jeff. "I wish Eustace had a little brother or sister," she said. "I mean, I never really meant to have him, but since I did, it would be nice if he had someone his own age to play with sometimes. I never see any kids in our neighbourhood, and I don't think he's met any at Wayne's place either."

"At least he's got you. You two have lots of fun together." Jeff tried to cheer her up, but could tell it wasn't working.

"Most of the time it feels just the opposite—like I'm the lucky one. He changed everything. He showed up just as I was beginning to figure out what I wanted in life, and took the feet right out from under any plans I had. He became my everything, because everything I did had to be for him. Now, it just seems natural that I live for him. The commute on the bus, the eight hours at SALIGIA, avoiding Nadia's eye—it's all for him."

Jeff nodded, but couldn't think of what to say.

"Well, maybe that last part is for me," she finished.

Signalling the server for one more round, Jeff tried to imagine being so devoted to another person. He'd never been that dedicated to anyone, any place, thing, or creed as Janice was to her child.

The thought bothered him. His back slid down the seat, and his shoulders hunched under an invisible yet suddenly unbearable weight.

I'm not really fighting for anything the way she is, he thought. *That's why I always lose. I only aim for the next laugh, or good meal, or maybe for the dream of not having to fight anymore—or maybe for just having a reason to.*

A sudden screeching sound tore Jeff out of his dark thoughts, and he jumped up in his chair, bumping into the server carrying their drinks and sending them shattering down onto the hardwood floor.

"Shit," he yelled.

"Fuck," whispered the server.

Janice gasped, then moved towards the obnoxious sound, pulled out her phone, and answered it. "Hello?"

"I'm so sorry," said the server. "Let me go replace these." She hurried to the bar to pour a new round. A busboy rushed from the back to clean up the mess.

"What?" said Janice.

"She's going to get us—" Jeff realized she was still on the phone.

"What the fuck, Wayne?" said Janice. Her face scrunched up, and she reached for her beer but found it empty. Pressing her fist down on the table, she rolled her eyes. "Are you serious? Now?" Her voice had an iron edge to it that Jeff hadn't heard before—despite giving her ample opportunity to debut it.

"Fine." With a tremendous sigh, Janice hung up the phone and shoved it down into her jacket pocket. "I have to go pick up Eustace—Wayne is being an idiot," she said.

Jeff fumbled for words, but again found none. Instead, he

focussed on finishing his wings.

The server returned, setting down the new drinks.

"Could we actually get the bill as well? All together is fine," said Janice.

The server nodded and hurried away.

"Dammit." Jeff wasn't sure if Janice was talking to him or herself. "He's supposed to have him until Wednesday. Apparently, something came up and he needs to head back to the patch."

Jeff nodded absently, wondering if Wayne could be the source of the inexplicable anxiety Janice always seemed to carry.

Between tremendous chugs of beer, Janice looked over at Jeff. "I'm so sorry to ask, but is there any chance you could drive me over to Wayne's, then back to my place? There's no decent transit to the north side where Wayne lives. I'd have to bus home, pick up my car, then drive all the way over. It would take almost two hours and—"

"Hey," Jeff cut her off, "it's no problem."

He meant it—such a small favor wasn't much to ask, especially when they'd planned to be spending time together anyway. He wondered why she seemed so stressed over it.

"Thanks," she said. Her face was flushed, and she focussed back on her beer.

A heavy pall of tension took the air, and they finished their drinks in a hurried hush. Jeff left half of his, conscious that he'd soon be driving. Finally, Janice paid the bill. Jeff tried to pay for his, but she'd hear none of it.

"Well, shall we?" she said.

The old wooden table creaked as Jeff pushed against it, rising from his seat and following Janice around the bar, along a narrow row of stools, and out the front door.

The lattice-lined path from the bar led them to the cement

sidewalk—caked with black gum stains and old cigarette butts—and they stepped over trash-lined gutters to reach Jeff's car.

He held the passenger door open as Janice jumped over an oil-stained puddle. "Rocinante awaits," he said.

"You named your car?" she asked with a bemused smile as she dropped into the seat.

"Of course," said Jeff.

"You're a fucking nerd."

Closing the door and rounding to the driver's side, Jeff pondered whether she got the reference.

It doesn't matter, he concluded. In point of fact, some things were probably best left unexplained.

"So," he said, settling in behind the wheel, "where are we heading?"

"Wayne's place is up north, in Clareview—137th and Victoria Trail area. I can guide you once we're near. I'll need to grab Eustace there, then you can drop me at my place near Westmount. Fort Road will probably be fastest. I really do appreciate this, Jeff."

He smiled—she'd certainly better appreciate it with all that driving.

Turning the key once, twice, and finally a third time before the engine turned over, Jeff's music kicked back in as the car hummed to life. He backed slowly out of the tight parking space, and pulled onto the brick side street.

"Springsteen," Janice nodded her approval. "Nice."

With an arched eyebrow and a curled lip, Jeff glanced over at her as he turned left onto Jasper Ave. "You're a fan?" he asked.

"Who doesn't like the Boss? I'm going back to the start though!" Janice reached over to the stereo and pressed the skip button until the small monochrome screen showed track one.

Jeff moaned internally, but opted to allow his guest DJ privileges—a rare exception.

As the longing sound of the opening harmonicas squawked through his old speakers, he turned north and picked up speed as he left the downtown core. It was risky—you could never go too fast in Edmonton without the threat of hitting some crater-like pothole and messing up your alignment, suspension, or worse.

It was part of life here. The endless cycle of thaw and freeze cracked the sidewalks and pitted the roads. Given enough time, the hellacious Alberta weather broke down cement and vehicles and anything else foolish enough to test it. People were no different. Most fled when they got the chance, and those left behind were forced to endure its cruel bite until they too were finally broken.

The rusted underbelly of his car rattled beneath Jeff's feet with each pothole he hit, but still it endured.

Janice tapped out the beat on the dusty dashboard as the song picked up pace, and her frizzy red hair bounced as she moved her head to the rhythm. "Do you remember feeling this way? This whole album...it feels like yesterday that this was me. Young and eager, teetering on the edge of adulthood and desperate to slip off into the stream and see what life might hold. God, I miss that."

Freedom, thought Jeff. He remembered it too—the potential of life opening up before you. He'd relished it then as much as he missed it now. In fact, he wasn't sure when it had happened—that strange shift from enjoying his freedom to regretting its passing. What had changed within his tired mind to accept the dreary reality of life instead of dreaming up a better one?

"Well," he said with a snicker, "we've got a road and a car, so freedom isn't that far off." Despite his best rockstar sneer, Jeff heard how hollow the idea rang.

"Wait!" Janice's yelp almost made Jeff slam on the brakes. "This isn't the right song! Which one is the title track?"

Jeff rolled his eyes. "Five." He exaggerated his frustration with a lip-flapping huff.

Janice rolled her eyes right back at him, and switched the song with a triumphant stab of her finger followed by three truncated jabs.

"This one always makes me wish I was driving somewhere fast with the top down." She spoke over the rising tempo of the song.

"Somewhere?" Jeff asked.

"Nowhere. Anywhere."

"I'm afraid the top is permanently up on this car."

Janice chuckled. "I don't think there's a road in or near Edmonton in good enough repair for a drive like that."

"Well, at least they all point in the right direction," he said.

"Yeah, yeah, I know," said Janice. "Desperate to get out, but don't know where to go. All the right intentions, but stuck in the wrong place, right?"

Flinching, Jeff shot a hard eye over at her. "Was that meant to be so cutting?"

"C'mon," her voice was soft. "You just introduced your car as Rocinante. If that's not a self-admitted Quixote complex, I don't know what is."

"Fair play," he confessed. Turning the car onto the Yellowhead Freeway and picking up speed, he rolled down the passenger window.

"Are you crazy, the air is freezing!" Janice howled.

"I thought you were born to run!"

"I've done my running…my tramp days are behind me!" she squealed.

This nearly doubled Jeff over, but the steering wheel prevented it. Still, he struggled to keep his eyes on the rutted road. Jeff appreciated few things quite like double entendre. "Sounds nice," he said, hoping it didn't sound as sad as it echoed in his ear.

"Well, on days like this, when I'm rushing to cover someone else's fuck-ups, and missing out on fun and freedom—it's easy to miss the old days. Hell, there are even times when I wish I could just take Eustace, hop in a car, and take off. You know? Hit the road and see where it leads?"

She sighed. "But I know that's crazy—and as fun as it might be, it wouldn't be a great lesson for the lil' guy. Besides, not every day is like this. It felt like it at first, but coming home to his smile, or seeing him discover new things—that's what makes the rest worth it. I can daydream about being younger and untethered nowadays, but even in my wildest fantasies, I end up running back home to him. It's kind of ironic, really. I always thought I needed to live for others. To be the perfect family woman, and follow the normal path. When I finally decided to go find my own path, it was too late. But in the end, what I once feared the most turned out to be my salvation. I wonder if it's ever like that for other people," she finished, staring quietly out the window.

The song had changed twice by now, and the soft, brooding saxophone of the current one suited the northern part of the city well as Jeff turned off the Yellowhead up onto Fort Road. The skyline out this way was dominated by brutal, jutting smokestacks and distant oil tanks. Anywhere you went, you could hear the sound of crunching gravel, and the air always smelled of acrid gasoline and sharp, tangy rust.

Her words played over in his mind, and something inside shifted and turned as if making way for some unknown but inevitable intrusion.

"You'll need to turn left just up here, then it'll be your next right," said Janice.

Jeff nodded. He wondered what he feared most, and how it might be the key to his own salvation.

Lingering at SALIGIA forever? he shuddered. He much preferred the thought of quitting in a magnificent diatribe of corporation-crushing revelations. It was his favourite fantasy, but ultimately a futile dream, he knew. He'd be left with scant few options for employment, and none whatsoever in the corporate world—which made up the vast majority of paying jobs at this point.

Besides, he'd hate to leave Janice to toil on alone. Everyone needed someone to commiserate with, and they worked well together.

"I don't know," he finally admitted. It felt good to be so honest. "Maybe I shouldn't admit this, but I'd still love the chance to run free like that—to disappear and start again from scratch. See if I'd learned enough the first time to live a more fulfilling life the next. Right now, I go to work, go home, and find some friends or hobbies to distract me until I go to work again. I see a doctor, I try to eat better, I accept that things are okay for now. That they will be, until they aren't…"

Janice stared across the car at him. "Christ, that's bleak," she said. "But it tells me two things. First, you should absolutely listen to your doctor. Second, it tells me that you haven't found what you need yet, buddy." She laid a comforting hand on his free arm.

The music was a warm blanket.

"It's that one right up there," said Janice. She pointed across the car to a short white house with a crushed rock finish on the lower half and a wooden porch with flaking brown paint.

Jeff pulled up, and put his car in park.

"I'll be right back," she said.

Janice stepped out, shut the door, and hurried up the porch. She opened the door without a knock, and closed it behind her.

Jeff chewed his lip, listening to the song, but barely hearing it.

He knew she was right. Aside from her humour matching his own, that was Jeff's favourite thing about Janice. Her sense of clarity. Despite her roundabout way of getting there, Janice knew exactly what she wanted.

The music was static in the background now, and Jeff's head was a cacophony of racing thoughts.

He'd been idle for too long—bemoaning his circumstances but doing nothing to alter them.

It was embarrassing.

The door opened, and Janice edged backwards through it cradling a small blonde boy in one arm, and lugging a clunky booster seat in the other.

Jeff hurried out to help her with the burden. "Let me grab that," he called. Janice was halfway down the broken sidewalk already.

"It's okay, can you just open the back door?"

As he did so, Jeff watched in wonder as Janice spun around, slipping the large seat through the door and exactly into place as she bounced Eustace in her other arm. With the deft movements of a single hand, she wrapped the seatbelt around and clicked everything into place.

"This is the girl who can never even hold onto her coffee cup?"

Janice laughed. "This is Eustace. Eustace, this is Jeff. Mommy works with him."

Eustace waved at Jeff. His smile showed a big gap between his front teeth, and his eyes sparkled with excitement. He seemed small for four, but had the unrestrainable vigour to him reserved strictly for children and those with nothing left to lose.

Remembering his condition, and the reason Janice stayed at SALIGIA, a shadow came over Jeff, and it seemed that the day grew darker.

Securing Eustace in place and planting a quick kiss on his cheek, Janice slammed the back door shut and hopped back into the passenger seat.

"I'm right back the other way, near Westmount," said Janice as Jeff slipped behind the wheel.

Looking up as he pulled away, he couldn't see anyone watching their departure from behind the faded yellow curtains in the front room.

Eustace's feet were kicking gently along to the beat of the song, and he seemed content enough, despite the limited view of his mother behind and across from him.

"So, tramp, did you figure out where you'd run to yet?" asked Janice.

Jeff smiled, and thought for a while. "Anywhere but SALIGIA," he said with a smirk. "Someplace that SALIGIA and any other mega-corporations like them have never even been—back in time if possible."

"So, should I expect to be leaderless tomorrow?"

"Not tomorrow at any rate—I'd hate to leave poor Ames stranded."

They laughed, and behind them came the soft sound of the child's laughter echoing in ignorant bliss.

"Actually," said Jeff, "nothing against him, but I'd be okay with that. SALIGIA has sapped so much of my life over the years, I daydream constantly of how to stick it to them if I ever had the chance to escape."

"Chances are pretty easy to find, if you're looking." Janice was wiser than she seemed while spilling coffee and zoning out in meetings. That wasn't her world. But here with her boy, she was the master.

"You're not wrong about that," said Jeff. "What about—before? What would you have done with all that freedom if things had been different?"

"Well, I used to have a decent bit of money saved up to go back to school and find something I'd enjoy. A vocation, if you will. I'd considered teaching, or maybe something with books. I don't know, I had a lot of dreams without any real plans back then. Maybe none of that was for me anyways."

"I get what you mean," said Jeff. "But what about going back to school now? I mean, you're obviously busy, but there must be some feasible options. Online classes, maybe?"

Janice sighed, and glanced up to the rear-view mirror to check on Eustace. He was clapping two little toys together and mumbling happily to himself. "Sure," she said, "it's a tempting idea to go back and see if there's anything else out there I could love. Something just for me. But I think that ship has sailed as well. Any savings I had went into buying our house. Between that and paying for everything Eustace needs, I really don't put much away."

"As a kid, I never imagined how expensive life was," said Jeff.

"Truth," said Janice.

"Truth!" called Eustace, then burst into a fit of giggles.

"Like I said, he makes it all worth it," she said with a smile. "Turn right up here, then I'm three blocks down."

Jeff pulled up to a quaint little one-story house with a friendly bay window. Like so many in Edmonton, the house was a relic of past expansion, and sat now on land the corporations judged better suited to apartments or high-rises. Neighbourhoods like this were slowly choked out—poor transit, no amenities—until the property could be snatched up and new developments started.

He thought of Sherlock's, so resolute in its defiance, then of his own apartment—with the empty spaces on two sides where others had once stood.

Opening the car door for Janice, Jeff spotted a long strip of empty land behind her property—tall brown shoots of grass visible between her house and the distant lamp posts of the next street.

The process had already begun.

With Eustace still strapped into the car seat, Janice unhooked it and lifted it out. She whirled it around like a spaceship, and he squealed with joy.

"So," she said, "I will see you tomorrow, right? You're not going to let Ames down?"

He laughed. "You'll see me."

Waving as she let herself in, Jeff got back into his car and turned out onto the main avenue. *Ames...*

Soon he'd be home again. Home to kill time until he slept, then to wake and back to work. At work he'd see Ames and catch him up on all the initiatives he'd inherited from Jordan, explaining the status and current direction of each. Of course, he had little idea about that last bit, since discussing more than one initiative at a time was so rarely permitted. He'd have to glean some of the info from whatever access they allowed Ames to Jordan's files, and simply make up the rest.

So many initiatives, so many different and competing objectives—such detached, psychotic leadership.

Jeff hoped Ames would turn out to be a decent guy. He wasn't hoping for a friend. In fact, the idea sounded awful from the start.

He just wanted Ames to be reasonable enough to work with. It didn't seem like so much to ask, but given the trend at SALIGIA, it remained an unlikely pipedream.

New condos, catchphrases, city branding, and so much other meaningless bullshit. It was enough to drive a man insane. Yet it was up to him to somehow cobble together a solution which would reconcile them all. There were clients to placate and contracts to close.

Then, a whole new set of contracts would come, and all the old work would be undone. That was the cycle. He'd seen it a million times.

One day, he'd save a green space. The next month, efficient high-rise developments would be the big new idea, and up they'd go.

He wondered if all these jobs, all the back and forth, and all the madness had some consistent reasoning behind them. Beyond simply making money and increasing shareholder value, could there be some driving force? Was the greenspace he'd save with this project already selected to be the development site of the next?

But such intentional coordination was just a silly conspiracy theory. He was certain of it. No one at SALIGIA was capable of that kind of complex scheming. At least no one on Floor 82.

Well…maybe Nadia.

Sometimes, he imagined the terrifying inner workings of SALIGIA rising like a dying machine. Its steel rib cage opened up, its fluids spilled out slick and shining over the city, and the countless layers of turning gears and sizzling wires within were all that remained of the world.

He thought about Ames. He thought of Janice, and Eustace. Did he play in that field behind his house?

How long until it became a strip mall or a condo?

Jeff drove for a long while in silence, nodding his head along to the closing chords of the album. He'd leave it in for a while, he knew. It still had a few spins left.

Rolling the windows down a bit, a smile slowly traced itself across his lips. He felt his cheeks pushing at his ears, and the cool air rushing over his teeth.

The car grew chilly, but he rolled the windows down the rest of the way.

Pulling onto the freeway, the cold air whistled wildly through the car and tossed his stringy hair about. The hard wind brought tears to his eyes, and he laughed like a madman, not caring who might see him.

He was in no rush to go home, and decided to keep driving for a while. Tomorrow would come when it came, and he was ready for it.

For the first time in a long time, Jeff knew where he was going.

He had a plan.

CHAPTER 13
Jeff's Worst Day at SALIGIA

The oppression of the morning sky was a cruel counterbalance to the lighthearted sense of freedom Jeff woke with. He made it to the bus stop in record time, and only twice considered going back to bed and letting the chips fall where they may the next day.

Gazing through the grimy bus windows, he watched small clusters of dark blue clouds gathering over the city. They soared higher than rain clouds, and melded together as one met another. The chill he'd felt in the wind the day before—a refreshing promise at the time—now bit at his bare skin. Leaves were already falling, and the hoarfrost covered grass beside the street was a brooding harbinger that the warmer days of fall were passing, and winter was just around the way.

The bus radio prattled on about the inevitability of a great blizzard, bringing a snow that would be unlikely to melt until mid-April.

When he hit the street, the bitter air was the barrel of the big freeze—menacing his face with its frigid threats.

Despite all this, however, by the time Jeff stepped off the elevator and into the controlled atmosphere of Floor 82, the changing weather was but a vague foreboding at the back of his mind. He was focussed, and ready for the day ahead.

He'd slept better than he had in a long time; his night had only been disturbed by dreams of his plans for the day playing out in all their potential on an endless loop. Yet when he rose in the morning, he didn't feel tired of the tasks, but eager to truly see them through.

The first part was crucial—he had to establish a good rapport with Ames. That way, as Jeff led him through orientation, he'd be able to glean more information about Ames' initiatives. Maybe he could even influence their future direction.

The final payoff was still a work in progress, but he was certain he'd never get another opportunity to affect change at SALIGIA quite like the one now in front of him.

Jeff knew he had nothing to lose, everything to gain, and he was ready.

This triumphant feeling of personal autonomy was bordering on pride as he reached the coffee machine. Upon the broad metal surface was taped a flimsy loose-leaf sign. "Out of Order."

Dammit!

"Jeff."

The monotone voice behind him wasn't asking a question, or requesting attention. There was no interrogative tonal shift. It was flat and simple. It was a statement.

Nadia, he knew.

Jeff turned slowly, screwing his mouth into what he hoped was a passable semblance of a smile. "Yes?" It was most certainly a question. In fact, if Nadia told him he was wrong, and someone else was in fact Jeff, he'd barely consider arguing.

She stood only a few feet away, staring up at him with an expression that made him feel like he was slipping into a shark tank. Francis and Marcy hovered behind her, their hands on their hips. They looked uncomfortable, but Jeff also sensed the hidden glee of a rat ready to watch someone else pay the piper in their stead.

"You have a busy week ahead of you, Mr. Boggs," said Nadia. Jeff watched for her to blink, but knew he'd have to respond first.

"Yeah," he said. He figured it was a good start. An honest, simple response.

"I am told that you have been making some positive progress in your personal Supervision Sessions." She pronounced the phrase with such obvious stress it left no doubt she meant Jeff's therapy. This was her idea of small talk, he supposed.

Marcy squirmed behind her, a restrained smile bending her tightly pursed lips.

"Our recent training was focussed on teamwork and communication," Nadia continued. "In the spirit of those ambitions, I have invited Francis and Marcy to join you in orienting our newest team member. You will still lead the process, and be responsible for its success. Having your supervisors attend to your efforts will help us be clear about the parameters and end goals of all active initiatives, while maintaining our commitments to SALIGIA's service standards and billing cycles.

"I trust you will be up to this task, Jeff?"

Again, he knew there was no question being asked. Not in earnest. She'd fastened two giant weights around his neck and expected him to thank her. Double supervisors scrutinizing each move, slowing every step, and changing direction at their wildest whims. But at least Jeff would still be responsible in the end!

He understood without question that responsibility for the project's success naturally implied the opposite as well.

"Of course," he answered.

"Good. This week's schedule has been compressed by the unexpected departure of Employee #1921256, so Marcy will have to find an opportunity to continue your personal Supervision Sessions at her discretion."

"Yes. Okay," said Jeff. *Why not?*

He wondered. *Is she not legally allowed to say Jordan's name anymore? I suppose he's no longer SALIGIA property—lucky bastard.* Then, he breathed a quiet sigh of relief as Nadia turned a sharp one-eighty and slid quickly down the hall towards her private office.

"Well, Jeff," said Francis, "like Nadia said, you're in charge of this one, so lead the way." He put on an incredulous voice, as if he couldn't believe his own words.

An uneasy weight was growing in his stomach, but Jeff forced a grin. "Follow me," he said.

The wind went out of Francis, and Jeff's grin turned to a true smile as he led them around the corner to the barren space of empty walls and stacked boxes that was slowly becoming Ames' office.

Jeff knocked sharply on the open door before stepping in. He stopped in the doorway, and leaned against its frame, ensuring he'd block both the entry and view of his supervisors. He knew that would infuriate them.

Ames turned with a start. He was still nervous in the new position. *Smart guy*, thought Jeff.

He certainly didn't look it, though. He was a round little man with sweaty jowls, and thin greying hair ringed around a shiny dome head. His eyes squinted behind his oversized glasses like a mole looking through a telescope, and he always curled his upper lip before speaking, exposing his chicklet teeth.

Poor Ames. He seemed like just the sort of doughy pushover a corporation like SALIGIA would eat alive.

"Jeff, good to see you!" said Ames.

Jeff wondered how anyone could be sincere about a greeting like that to a co-worker they'd only met the day before, but reasoned it was best to remain as professional as possible given the circumstances.

"You too," he replied. "Are you ready for a busy one today?" Jeff continued, not waiting for a response. "We're going to run over the current initiatives on each of our dockets, contrast goals, and try to orient you on some of the key decisions to be made over the next few days. Marcy and Francis will be helping out," he said, indicating over his shoulder with a quick jerk of his thumb.

"Sounds great!" said Ames. If he was being false, his weak, wavering voice did nothing to hide it.

"I'm going to go reserve a space for us and grab a digi-pad. Why don't you meet me in the Excelsior Room? Francis and Marcy can show you the way."

With that, Jeff turned and hurried towards reception. He caught the gaping expressions of his supervisors and, knowing full well he'd rue his rashness soon enough, remained convinced it was worth it.

Reaching reception at a hurried jaunt, he stopped and smiled at Tali. "How can SALIGIA improve your day?" she asked. Whatever training she'd been subjected to, it had clearly been effective at turning her into a sycophantic drone. It seldom took long.

Jeff groaned internally, already done to death with the corporate façade. "I need to book a room, and some equipment," he said.

"We can certainly do that here." She spoke through a broad, white smile. "All bookings are done through the SALIGIA Reception Desk to streamline the process and improve the user journey."

Jeff rolled his eyes, but quickly booked himself into the Excelsior Room for the rest of the day and signed out a corporate digi-pad for the week. Usually, only the Brass got digi-pads, but this assignment and room booking would justify a lowly Tin like him borrowing one.

The Excelsior Room was at the westernmost end of the South Hallway, and was one of the only rooms in that area regularly accessed by the Tins. He wasn't surprised it was open to booking with such short notice—it was primarily used for either top-down corporate presentations, or project management meetings such as today's.

While ideal for those, it was impractical for much else. The Excelsior Room was a technological marvel in the worst possible sense. Its walls were comprised of touchscreen displays that ran from floor to ceiling, save for one long row of windows which took up the greater part of the wall furthest from the door. The windows faced south, and gave a lovely view of the River Valley far below. The rest of the walls—the touch screens—could be programmed from a digipad, and manipulated by touch at any point. It was the perfect setup for high-level planning, and the sorting of various incongruous ideas.

When Jeff entered, Ames, Francis, and Marcy were already seated around the small central table facing one another. "So, how are you adjusting to life with SALIGIA?" asked Francis.

"It's—"

"I think you'll find your experience here to be a real step up from…whatever you're used to," said Marcy, cutting Ames off before he could begin.

"That's right!" said Francis, not one to be outdone. "SALIGIA is the most cutting-edge employer in the world today."

"I've really—"

"Just look at this room, for example!" said Francis, not letting Ames get a word in edgewise. "Did you know—"

"Ready to get started?" It was Jeff's turn to interrupt, since nothing would ever get done if he didn't wrench the reins away from his hapless supervisors. He logged into the SALIGIA App, quickly locking them in at room temperature, activating the wall-screens, and dimming the lights. Since he'd booked the room, it was entirely up to him—IT only supported the Brass.

Ames nodded absently, probably as eager to escape the hellish small talk as Jeff was.

"I want to start with a brief overview of the initiatives currently in each of our portfolios, then review and contrast the end goals and contractual necessities of each." Jeff almost sounded too corporate for comfort as he positioned himself at the front of the room. "The better we understand which initiatives complement each other, and which run contrary to one another, the easier it will be to make progress."

Marcy sprang to her feet and hurried over beside Jeff. "Needless to say, it's imperative we remember the work of SALIGIA is primarily contract based, and as such we need to carefully track the time spent on each individual initiative."

"That's right," Francis jumped in, rushing to Jeff's other side. "We need to ensure we stick to one initiative at a time, so that Marcy and I can record the time, effort, and resources dedicated to each, and bill accordingly."

The supervisors glared at each other as Jeff stood between them, dumbstruck by the inanity of it all. Never as a child could he have guessed—not if he was given a million years and unlimited attempts—that he'd spend his adult life in such hollow toils.

Finally, he regained his senses, and pressed on with his wearisome task. Flicking his fingers deftly across the digi-pad, illuminated images appeared on the walls and began to sort themselves out on one side of the room or the other. Between them were the windows, where the sprawling expanses of ramshackle buildings and holdover stretches of nature were darkened by the gathering clouds.

"On this side are the initiatives you're inheriting. You have the

Green City Initiative, the Oil City Initiative, and the Sustainable City Initiative," said Jeff. He indicated a small, labelled icon for each glowing neatly on the otherwise white walls as he spoke.

"Those seem…" Ames' brow furrowed, and his words trailed off into an empty sigh.

"Yup," said Jeff with a cavalier grin. The process was already starting.

He let a moment pass, expecting protests from the supervisors. But they returned quietly to their seats, so he shook off the eerie feeling building up inside and continued undeterred. "And over here," he indicated the icons on the further wall, "are my current initiatives. I have the Liveable City Initiative, the Clean City Initiative, and the City Branding Initiative."

"Isn't the Liveable City Initiative similar to the Green City Initiative?" Ames' voice came slowly, as if he sensed disaster at any moment. More and more, Jeff began to suspect he was far more clever than he appeared.

He hoped he was wrong.

"You'd think so," said Jeff. "But the Liveable City Initiative is actually a Condo Developer's marketing campaign."

Ames was chewing on his bottom lip. "Oh," he said.

Jeff waited, knowing Ames' line of thinking could only go one way.

"So, based on my understanding of the initiatives," he tiptoed in, "doesn't the goal of my Sustainable City Initiative conflict with my Oil City Initiative? I'm sure we'll go into more detail about each in time, but what's my metric of—".

Marcy jumped back up. "Jeff, please remember that we need to discuss one initiative at a time. Going back and forth drives our accounting department bonkers. Besides that, SALIGIA Policy is clear on the division of billable hours. It's your job to ensure compliance as you guide this meeting today."

"Of course, thanks Marcy."

"I hate to say it, but she's right," Francis chimed in. "SALIGIA Policy is iron-clad on this issue. There's really no wiggle room at our level."

Jeff smiled, and gave a quick nod. He considered bringing up the hazy exceptions exhibited at the Performance Review, but quickly accepted it wasn't worth the time and headache.

"As you can see, while you're the Team Lead on these initiatives, each initiative also has a supervisor attached to it." Here Jeff tapped the screen of his digi-pad, and the names of the supervisors appeared above their own. Marcy was above Jeff, and Francis was above Ames. "Francis is the direct supervisor of your initiatives, and Marcy is the direct supervisor of my initiatives."

"However, I'm also Jeff's supervisor," Francis called from his seat.

"But not supervisor of his initiatives," insisted Marcy.

"I am insofar as his overall performance impacts those initiatives!" Francis snapped. They glared at each other long and hard.

Jeff—satisfied they'd continue their little war in silence for a while—soldiered on. "That's all true," he admitted. His initially confident posture was beginning to wilt.

Ames said nothing. Behind his goofy glasses, his eyes shimmered. By now, he must have realized his terrible mistake. Like a Venus flytrap, SALIGIA was a tempting offer from the outside, but regret always followed in short order.

Jeff tapped his screen again, and a list of names appeared under the initiatives. "Here, you can see the other team members assigned to each initiative."

Ames examined the lists. "So, we don't have teams ourselves, but our initiatives have teams?"

"That's exactly right. One person may be on one of my initiatives, and also on one of yours'."

Ames frowned. "Doesn't that make scheduling difficult?"

"Yes," said Jeff.

"But it's also a great boon to team creativity," Marcy stayed seated, but still derailed Jeff's efforts. "SALIGIA studies have shown that by mixing up the teams we work with, we activate a greater portion of our left brains."

"That's especially important for Delta Personality types," said Francis.

"Write that down," said Jeff. He hoped Ames would at least make a gesture of scribbling something in the pristine little notebook sitting in front of him. Much to Jeff's dismay, he did no such thing.

"You're in charge of guiding your team's progress on each initiative, and reporting it to that initiative's supervisor," said Jeff.

"So, Francis?"

"Yes," said Jeff. "Francis is the direct supervisor on each of your initiatives, and he is also your direct supervisor."

"Well, I guess that makes sense. So, I report progress to Francis, then what?"

"He reports it to Nadia," said Jeff.

Ames seemed lost again.

"And Jeff reports his initiatives' progress to me," said Marcy.

"And I work with Jeff to supervise his performance," said Francis.

Jeff's neck twitched.

Ames twiddled his thumbs and stared down at the table.

"Any questions at this point?" Jeff asked, hoping for a moment to catch his wits.

Ames leaned forward in his chair, squinting at the wall with his initiatives. "So, if I can only focus on one initiative at a time, and they each have different teams, how do I coordinate between them?"

Jeff let out one loud guffaw before catching himself. "I have no idea," he failed to come up with anything less honest.

"Navigating the complex and sometimes conflicting needs of our clients is exactly what we have Team Leads for," said Marcy. "It's your job to make the right decisions for each of your initiatives, then report them to Francis. Of course, you can always check in with the initiative's supervisor for advice. Jeff knows my door is always open if he has questions."

Jeff's face was getting hot. He tried, but failed to recall a single time he'd gone to ask Marcy for guidance. He tried to picture how it might go, but found himself instead imagining the long walk through the strange, endless labyrinth to HR. Somehow, they felt similar. Every moment at SALIGIA had the same bones underneath the bullshit.

"That's right," he forced the thoughts from his mind, "and thank you for that, Marcy. It's a tough role Ames, but you were chosen because—"

"Jeff," interrupted Francis, "you know you can come to me too, right?"

"Francis, if it's a question about his initiatives, he should go to the supervisor of that initiative," said Marcy.

Francis' fists clenched against the table. "But his decision making is directly tied to his performance, and that's my area!"

"Dammit!" It was only 9:07 a.m., and Jeff had reached the end of his rope. "We'll never get anywhere with you two constantly arguing."

Marcy and Francis stared at him, their faces twisted into hideous masks of disbelief. Ames swallowed, and kept staring down at the table.

Marcy rose—a slow, methodical motion. "Jeff, maybe we should check in on your Supervision Sessions. Would you follow me for just a moment?"

Without waiting for an answer, she made a beeline for the door.

Francis leapt to his feet and charged after her. "Stop! This is a performance issue, and if anyone should talk to Jeff in the hall, it should be me!"

"I am presently tasked with Jeff's—workplace wellbeing." Marcy placed her hand in front of her mouth and loudly whispered this last bit to Francis. Ames cast a guilty look over to Jeff, who stood defeated and alone in front of the window. Jeff gave a dejected smile back, then turned to watch the gathering army of clouds mount the sky and slowly blot out the morning.

"Performance is performance Marcy, this is mine. Nadia gave me this role for a reason!"

"I'm a SALIGIA registered therapist, and this is an emotional reaction, not a performance issue. I will speak with him first. Otherwise we can call Nadia in to settle this."

Jeff registered the heavy silence. It was a dangerous gamble on Marcy's part—he knew neither of them wanted to call in Nadia to settle a leadership dispute. There could be no winners if that happened.

Still, every passing second told him her gambit had paid off. Outside, the darkening clouds devoured the daylight as they inched over the city. From his high perch, Jeff could see the top of the distant stormfront, where long gray tendrils of night floated from the sable centre and mingled with the blue sky above. *There's no escaping it this time,* he thought. It was still early, but a sinking feeling in his gut told him that soon the snow would fall heavy and deep, and the ground would freeze, and grass and life would be gone again until the distant thaw of spring.

During winter, it always felt like spring would never arrive. Then, too soon it was gone.

"Fine. You take him out and deal with his emotions, then I'll meet with him to provide performance supervision." Francis was defeated again. He never seemed to catch a break.

"Jeff?" Marcy called, and with a long-drawn breath, Jeff turned and followed her out into the hall.

The South Hallway was a long, luxurious hallway at the southern end of the building. It led to the Excelsior Room, the Executive Wing, several multi-purpose enclaves of managerial luxury, and one small storage closet. There was a golden door just to Jeff's right as he left the Excelsior Room that could only be accessed by the key card of a supervisor or higher. "Brass Only," as it were.

In the opposite direction, a small door marked the storage closet—filled mostly with paper towels, empty binders, digi-pad sleeves, and knee-high tangles of discarded power cords. Beyond that was the entrance to the main lobby; the broken coffee machine, the reception desk, and most everything else in the building.

"Jeff," said Marcy, "you don't need to worry about your outburst. If it's caught on camera and there's an HR inquest, I'll confirm that we covered and resolved the issue. Honestly, I can't blame you—Francis can be so infuriating sometimes."

Jeff stood mute, knowing there was no correct response to a prompt like that. Instead, he mulled over the comment about HR reviewing recordings, amending his long-held suspicions about the extent of SALIGIA's personal violations.

"Thanks, I won't worry about it then," he said, deciding that was the safest bet.

Marcy grinned. "That's good. You don't worry about much, do you Jeff?"

"What?" It caught him off-guard. He'd forgotten what astute insight Marcy seemed to possess. She'd displayed it during their therapy session on the train. Now, once again she seemed to understand just what was going on in his head. "No, not really I guess."

"You know Jeff, I admire that about you. This place drives me crazy—and it's only gotten worse since I became a supervisor. Just listen to the way that little shit is constantly trying to undermine me and push in on my territory." She flicked her pointed nail disdainfully back towards the Excelsior Room. Jeff knew the others were waiting on them. With Francis as agitated as he was, it had to be a torturous time for Ames. How long would it take him to accept his mistake and walk out?

For too long, Jeff had asked himself the same thing. Then, somewhere along the way, he'd stopped considering it in earnest, and settled for daydreaming instead.

"It drives everyone crazy," Jeff said with a laugh, before catching the import of his words. He gulped self-consciously. Despite her occasional ability to humanize herself, Marcy was still the Brass, after all.

The hallway in both directions was pristine white, with no art or signs to lessen their off-putting sterility. They were the sort of corridors a person might reasonably expect a Stormtrooper to pop out of. Looking at Marcy leaning bedraggled against the wall, she certainly didn't strike Jeff as the sort of Dark Lord the Brass were justly portrayed as. Still, there had to be a dividing line.

"I guess so," she agreed, and Jeff felt the tension leave him. It was a nice feeling. "I hardly even remember how crazy it used to drive me back…" she trailed off.

"When you were still in my position?" Jeff asked.

"Yeah," she admitted. "It's all new challenges now, though. How would you like reporting directly to Nadia?"

Words escaped Jeff, and his chin nearly touched his chest. Marcy was shattering his conceptions of the Brass, and the process was strange. In all his years at SALIGIA, he'd never heard a supervisor speak so candidly. There was always a thin line that kept the supervisors—so similar in all other respects, and victim to the same torments—separated from the lowly Tins. Part of it was their unwillingness to empathize with how maddening the SALIGIA corporate structure could be. It kept them above the rest, kept them part of the Brass.

To the last, they always maintained the sacred illusion that—sacrosanct above all people, meaning, and logic in the world—the good of SALIGIA was the uttermost goal, and that all goodness was SALIGIA.

It took a long while lost in reflection for Jeff to realize he'd been quiet far too long. Marcy seemed uncomfortable. She held her elbows, and shifted against the wall on one foot as the other kicked around in impotent circles.

He forced a laugh, but knew it wouldn't be enough. "I can only imagine," he finally said.

"I don't imagine you can," she said. Her voice came from far away.

"C'mon though," he pushed. He needed to prove his convictions to himself as much as her. "We still have to toe the line for her, and she still finds out everything we do. We can't escape her any more than you can. At least she views you as a team member, rather than some faulty tool."

"Is that how it seems? It's all just a game, Jeff, you should know that by now. She pits us against one another for reasons way above my pay grade. Or maybe they're entirely her own, but it seems like every manager on every floor is the same. They hire and fire on a whim. They switch goals with no notice, then advance the deadline. You never know what to believe. Right now, there might be a promotion one of us may or may not be in line for. I doubt it's real myself, but it's probably what's got Francis all worked up."

Jeff frowned.

"Anyway, you've got a lot of work ahead of you, let's not draw this out anymore. Watch your language—but nothing will come of this incident. Hear Francis out, and try not to get too frustrated with him. Try humouring him a bit, you're good at that."

Jeff blushed.

"He's annoying," she continued, "but trust me when I tell you he's under a lot of pressure. He takes as much shit from Nadia as I do. Worse yet, when he's forced into a competition, it's always against me." She finished with a confident smirk, and hurried back into the Excelsior Room.

Jeff stood bewildered and disoriented in the hall. As the door swung shut, he saw Marcy taking a seat at the central table, where Ames and Francis sat in what seemed to be perfect, bone-chilling silence.

For a short while, Jeff stood surrounded by the empty white walls, and he thought that winter had set in long ago. It was like he'd fallen asleep one night, and woken up to a world white and cold. Everything he had and everyone he loved were buried under the oppressive blanket of snow, and only he was left—alone and freezing.

Then the door opened again, and Francis stepped out. His back was bent, and his head wagged like a broken jack-in-the-box. His hair was pushed around in wild waves from too many nervous swipes of his hand, and behind his shimmering eyes was a strange, brooding intensity which Jeff never imagined him capable of.

"Jeff," he said.

"Francis," said Jeff.

"I'm glad we're finally getting a chance to connect—staff to supervisor."

The inside of Jeff's lip hurt, and his vision went black as his pupils got lost somewhere behind his eyebrows. He leaned against the white wall, looking over at Francis, but held his silence for the moment.

"Look Jeff, I know things have been pretty hectic lately, and that's probably not going to change anytime soon." Francis ran his hand through his hair again as he spoke, leaving a large tuft sticking upright. He looked like a frazzled bird from some exotic island.

Jeff sighed. "So, did you just want to point that out, or do you have a solution?"

Francis raised one finely groomed eyebrow. "Do you really think I can change how crazy things are? SALIGIA is a big corporation, Jeff, you can't expect a supervisor to do everything for you."

"As you've said, you supervise my performance. If that performance is being impacted by corporate red tape and foolish regulations, it seems like the perfect place for you to interject."

Francis chuckled. Reaching up to pat down the wayward tuft of blonde hair, he continued. "My role here is to help you cope with the pressures of the job, not to do it for you. I'm trying to be an ally to you, Jeff. We're all under the same pressures here, but if you want to get through, you've got to let me help you."

"Okay," said Jeff. "What can you do to help? Can you let me discuss more than one initiative at a time so we can make progress? Can you clear up how to navigate contradictory initiative goals?"

"Jeff, you know those rules are in place for a good reason, and meeting initiative goals is your role as Team Lead."

"So, you just want me to complain about how hard it is, but avoid any sort of problem solving?" Jeff was growing weary.

Francis huffed, and a red tinge crept into his pale cheeks. "Having a shoulder to lean on isn't such a terrible imposition, you know. I wish I had support like that. Do you know what it's like in my position? Of course not. I have to deal not only with the trials on this floor, but others as well. Have you ever been to an inter-floor managerial meeting? It's scary stuff. I once saw a supervisor fired right in the middle of proceedings. His security pass was taken away, and he had to take the stairs down from the 97th floor!

"There's no certainty anywhere, and your obsession with being given a clear path shows why you're struggling, Jeff. This is a fast-moving business environment. We create sense as we go, we aren't handed it in advance."

"That seems like a poor approach to navigation," said Jeff.

"Well, maybe it is, but that doesn't change anything. With so many active contracts, we can't just slow down and evaluate our long-term planning—that's for Floor 97. We need to complete our initiatives, close contracts, and sign new ones. That's our role."

"Thanks," Jeff gave a goofy grin as he spoke, "I feel a lot better now."

The rolling of Francis' eyes could have been seen from the far end of the hall. "You don't have it as hard as you think you do, Jeff. All you need to do is complete your initiatives, and send in the reports. I have to balance every other moving piece. It's a lot more complicated than you think. Besides, I don't know if you've noticed it, but Marcy has been intentionally undermining me at every turn these past few weeks. There's rumours about a new position opening up, and I'm certain she's trying to throw me under the bus to secure it for herself. She's shameless—she'd do anything to advance."

Jeff nodded, failing to see how any of this was relevant to him.

Sadly, Francis was undeterred by Jeff's apathy. "Ever since I started here, it's been the same. Marcy cuts off every opportunity I have to prove myself, and Nadia eats it up. I was made your supervisor specifically because you complained that leadership was failing you. So, she goes and gets herself approved as your therapist, and cuts my entire task off before I can even get started. I'd love to help you, Jeff, but I can't do it at my own expense. If you want things to improve, you've got to work with me."

The air in the hallway was still, and Jeff took a long, deep breath. It was dry and warm in his lungs, nearly making him cough. In both directions, the bright white walls stretched off like endless arctic tundra.

He'd never really realized it before, but Jeff was starting to see the real depths of misery SALIGIA was capable of. Where before he'd imagined a vicious hierarchy of predators frantically glutting on the suffering of those below them, the image morphed now into something yet more lowly and depraved.

No one was happy at SALIGIA. It was a cesspool of paranoid distrust and secret knives, where all who entered were abandoned to despair and left to fester in their mutual woe—divided against one another by roles and rank to prevent even the lightest commiseration.

Only Nadia—or perhaps those unseen and unnamed roles above hers—was content in the emotional carnage. Did she sit in her office each day, watching the stress and turmoil the mad empire doled out upon its citizens, laughing and feasting and celebrating her position? Or did she also answer to some mindless drone which chanted SALIGIA guidelines, and cut away all humanity and reason until only the bones were left? Was there some cold artificial intelligence at the top of the tower, watching everything and fixating on the unending projects between the present moment and the capital of the future?

Jeff would never know. He wasn't paid enough to know things like that, and should probably know better than to wonder about them in the first place. His head sagged, and his shoulders turned in on themselves. "I'll do what I can," he said, hoping that would be enough to end the toothless lecture.

"I hope so," said Francis. "I'm rooting for you, Jeff, but I'll tell you now, there's a lot of change coming. SALIGIA has noticed the growing trend of insubordination on this floor and others, and it won't be tolerated for long. In our last managerial meeting with Nadia, Marcy mentioned that you've openly admitted in your therapy sessions that you have no excuses for your behaviour. That isn't a good look given what you've been up to lately. I'm here to help where I can, but I need to watch my own back too."

Jeff's mouth was dry, and his legs were weak. He leaned hard against the wall as the floor rolled beneath him.

Was he surprised? He couldn't tell.

Had he briefly trusted Marcy at some point in those sessions, or had he always remembered it was all just a game?

Looking back, he couldn't be sure.

"We'll discuss some of the changing needs at the end of today's meeting, if you're ready to return," Francis finished. Without waiting for an answer, he hurried back into the Excelsior Room.

Needs to watch his own back, Jeff sneered as he thought about it.

That's all anyone ever did. That was the thing about SALIGIA—there was no room for passion or dedication, only self-preservation. Personal interests trumped all, and shoved to the wayside any chances of humour, kindness, or even comradery beyond the scripted, box-checking bullshit the Brass loved to tout.

Francis and Marcy were cut from the same cloth, that's what made them supervisors.

With one foot through the door, Jeff turned at a sound from the far end of the hall, towards the lobby entrance. Tiptoeing like a cartoon spy, Janice stepped through and hurried towards the closet door halfway down. From a distance, she looked like a small dark dot moving across the serene white landscape—a doe stepping out of the forest's cover, or a bird soaring past the full moon.

As she drew closer, Jeff noticed her hair and sweater were sopping wet. Her typically vibrant red curls hung heavy and dark, and her purple, wool sweater ran with water and bunched awkwardly at the elbows. She looked less like a deer perhaps, and more like a wet cat.

Jeff could barely hide his amusement. Already, he knew this one wasn't her fault. Ever since the badge readers had been installed in the bathrooms, it was nearly impossible to avoid getting sprayed as you struggled to keep your badge in front of the reader while washing your other hand. Coming out of the bathroom with only a few drops on you had become a mark of honour among the Tins lately.

Janice, clearly, was having a less than honourable day.

They locked eyes for a moment, and Jeff smiled. He thought about her predicament, and tried to imagine the jokes he'd make about it if they had the time. Sadly, the punchlines didn't come, and the heavy door of the Excelsior Room swung shut behind Jeff with a thud, sundering him from his only friend.

Despite all evidence, I hope her day is going better than mine, he thought.

Back at the table, Francis was just settling in behind his digi-pad, and Marcy was typing furiously on hers. Ames scribbled quietly in his notepad, but whether it was ideas for the initiatives, or doodles, Jeff couldn't tell.

Only as he started towards the table did he realize the room was dark. The lights were out, and the walls were dead.

Shit.

As a Tin, Jeff's access to the SALIGIA App was limited, and it would automatically log out every five minutes if no activity was detected on the account. This was, they'd been told, designed in the name of efficiency and sustainability, and part of an award-winning international corporate campaign.

For all intents and purposes however, it was a tremendous pain in the ass.

Marcy glared up as he approached. "Jeff, the lights in the room went out two minutes ago, leaving Ames and I in the dark. It's not only inconsiderate, it presents a serious safety hazard. As the facilitator of this meeting, the lights are your responsibility. I'm very disappointed with you."

"Disappointed?" Jeff nearly choked on the word. He didn't look up at Marcy, hurrying instead to reactivate the app and get the room going again. "How do you think I felt to discover you're sharing the contents of my therapy in your management meetings?" He knew he was pushing it, but didn't care anymore. If nothing was sacred, so be it.

Marcy frowned, and set her digi-pad down. She cast a pitiful, maternal gaze at Jeff. "At our managerial meetings, we exchange data relevant to each supervisor's tasks, and are overseen by Nadia. If I have knowledge that could help Francis in his role, it's my duty to share it. It's an important process, and clearly outlined in the Corporate Policy Guidebook. If you have any concerns about SALIGIA policy, you are encouraged to book an appointment with HR outside of your working hours."

Jeff shuddered. His body shook, and something, somewhere, struggled to turn over like the poor, dying engine of his dilapidated old Civic.

"Sorry," he muttered. He didn't know what else to say. As the lights and walls flicked back to life, Jeff slunk towards the table.

Just as he sat, Marcy leapt to her feet. Francis followed a moment later.

"Anyway, it's time to move on," Marcy said. She leaned against the table and tapped her pointed nails along its shiny white surface, glancing down at her digi-pad as if to confirm what she already knew. "While you two were occupied outside, I've been in touch with Nadia. She's provided me with an updated schedule for our floor, and I'm afraid it reflects very poorly on you, Jeff. You're way behind."

"Behind the new target dates?" Jeff asked.

"Yes," said Francis.

"Very behind," Marcy stressed the first word. "By the end of the week, Francis and I will need reports on the status of all active initiatives. These reports will include clear steps towards project completion, with an end date no later than next Monday for any initiative."

Jeff's stomach rolled. He tasted batteries, and the floor bucked like a branded bull beneath his seat.

Ames scratched at his chin, perhaps not fully comprehending the dire implications of this sudden change.

"Next Monday?" Jeff managed to force through his desert-dry mouth.

Marcy sighed. "Jeff, SALIGIA makes money per contract. We need to finish these off and move on to new ones—that's how we survive. Nadia's been reviewing financials and media projections with other managers, and has made adjustments to your timeline accordingly."

"Next Monday?" Jeff croaked again.

Marcy nodded once, and her face took on an edge like shattered stone. "The six active initiatives being discussed in this room must be completed by end of day Monday, yes. As I already said however, I will need to see detailed reports on the projected steps to completion no later than this Friday."

Jeff tried to swallow but failed. Molten rock ran down his throat, and his cheeks boiled.

"This meeting has been another colossal disappointment, Jeff. We're going to need to see tangible improvements very soon," said Francis.

"A disappointment?"

Francis looked at Marcy and rolled his eyes. "Jeff, I haven't even heard one idea to move your initiatives forward today."

"You never asked!"

"They're all due on Friday, Jeff, it should be an obvious priority," Marcy took a consoling tone.

"They weren't due this Friday until just now! That was never the intention of today's meeting." Jeff knew it was hopeless.

Marcy frowned and took a long breath, as if nearing the limits of her mercy. "Jeff, as Team Lead, you're expected to show initiative."

Francis nodded his agreement. "It's important for you to

anticipate the needs of your superiors in order to guide your initiatives successfully. That's not beyond you, is it, Jeff?"

"No," he mumbled.

Yes, he knew. Anticipating the irrational whims of SALIGIA was beyond anyone. If Nostradamus himself worked there he'd have been drawn and quartered long ago for failing to fill out the correct version of a form three days before it was released.

Marcy's face softened, and she smiled at Jeff. "I'm glad to hear that," she said. "Being a leader is never easy, but this is a great opportunity to demonstrate your strengths."

Jeff nodded.

"Needless to say," said Francis, "as the senior Team Lead at the moment, you'll be expected to mentor Ames and help him meet his targets as well."

"Of course," said Jeff.

Why not? he thought. It was an impossible task anyway, so why shouldn't he be responsible for his peer's success too?

Responsible? he reflected. *Constructive dismissal... is that their game?*

Marcy and Francis gazed down at him as if expecting an answer—or maybe an immediate solution. Ames was still scribbling something in his notebook.

Stealing a glance out the window, Jeff saw the other tall buildings in the distance, and wondered what life was like for the people in them. He could see the River Valley below, where the yellow and orange trees tumbled down the steep cliffs towards the slow-moving water. Above all loomed the coming clouds, crawling across the city without thought of clemency.

Jeff swallowed again, turning to Ames. "Well, let's get to work," he said.

Ames looked up with a crooked smile.

Marcy wasted no time jumping in. "Actually, Jeff, Ames needs to complete the mandatory New Employee Computer Training course in the Asset Supports wing of HR, Training Room #23.

"You are to show him there, then report to HR Revision Room E17 to discuss the events of today's meeting."

Francis nodded along, and picked up the thread the second Marcy finished. "Today was not your best work, Jeff," he said. "I really think you need to start looking at things from a team-based perspective, instead of only considering yourself."

Finally, Jeff was defeated. The last bit of air in his lungs departed in a long warm hiss, and his bones turned to gelatin.

"Will do," he said. He didn't stop to consider if he meant it or not. Meaning had no place at SALIGIA. At any rate, the writing was on the wall. At his HR meeting, he'd be forced to sign some lengthy, unintelligible document. Its jargon would be unclear, but the implications were already obvious enough. He'd be made responsible for the success of both his and Ames' initiatives, which were all due by the end of Monday.

When he inevitably failed, SALIGIA's retribution would be swift and terrible.

Pulling himself slowly out of his chair, he snatched up his digi-pad and motioned for Ames to follow.

They moved silently down the South Hallway, and the comparatively reserved tone of the lobby shocked his snow-blind eyes. "One second," he said to Ames.

Stepping towards the reception desk, his fingers flashed over his digi-pad, booking the Excelsior Room for the entire next day. Finally, he added the booking to Ames' calendar—a desperate attempt to keep him from being pulled into some other inane training at the last minute. While entirely insufficient to even dent the workload, at least he'd have the best possible tools at his disposal.

He handed the digi-pad to Tali, and signed another that she presented to confirm the return. "Thank you, and see you bright and early tomorrow morning!" she said. Her voice always had a hollow ring to it—like a little SALIGIA jingle from a bygone era. Jeff hated that.

His feet were lead, but he turned them slowly towards the elevator. "This way," he said to Ames, neither looking nor listening for a response.

Hitting the elevator button and waiting for the familiar tone, Jeff sunk his hands into his pockets. Across the lobby, a bird flew past the tall line of windows, flitting free and uncaring of anything but the wind. Behind it, the dark clouds marched ever onward.

CHAPTER 14

The Day Jeff Made His Move

The dark mantle of clouds now completely covered the city, laying the streets under a heavy pall of shadow. Jeff—alone in the vast Excelsior Room—hurried to set up for his big day. His mind raced with discordant thoughts all competing for attention, and he struggled to keep his focus on the precarious road ahead.

The previous day wore on his psyche as it flashed through his memory. The long walk through the HR hallway, the corporate jargon-laden speech about SALIGIA mandates and hierarchies, and the inevitable admission of total responsibility he was forced to sign.

They called it an Intention for Improvement contract. Those sons of bitches, of course they did. It also exonerated his supervisors of any real accountability, no doubt.

The long bus ride home under the slow-moving stormfront dragged on until he could hardly take it. Then the empty apartment, the microwaved dinner, and finally the phone call to Eddie. It had been a while since he'd needed to talk to someone so badly. Frustration was mounting. Plans were fomenting. He needed a friend.

Now, as he keyed his password into the digi-pad and connected to the SALIGIA App, he vividly recalled tucking his dishes away into the cupboard, sitting down on his worn leather couch, and dialing Eddie's number.

He'd considered calling Janice, but didn't want to burden her with talk of work. Some part of him still reserved hope that her day was better than his, and he was loath to spoil that.

"Hey, what's up buddy?" Eddie answered.

Despite only a few days passing, it felt like a long time since Jeff had heard his friend's voice. "I just got home from the longest day I've ever had in that hellhole," he said, kicking his feet up onto his small black ottoman.

Eddie took a long breath before he responded. He was reflective, and seldom spoke before putting real consideration into what he wanted to say. After all these years, Jeff still appreciated that about him. "So, how bad are we talking, and what are you going to do about it?"

Whenever he spoke with Eddie, Jeff gained a clarity he seldom felt elsewhere. It was the exact feeling he wanted to carry into the day with him. He'd need that confidence and focus today, if he was going to pull off what he had planned.

Now, the screens on the walls flickered to life as they synced with Jeff's digi-pad, the six current initiatives appearing and sorting themselves according to his commands. Ames hadn't arrived yet, but that was fine. Jeff was nearly ten minutes early—setting a personal record. He wanted everything ready. It all had to go perfect today.

He needed to stick to the plan, just like he'd told Eddie last night.

"You're going to love this," he'd said.

"What?" asked Eddie.

"I honestly think I'm ready. I've finally had enough of their shit."

Eddie took another long breath, this one less subtle. "That didn't answer either of my questions," he said.

"Don't worry," Jeff assured him, "I've got an idea."

It took several hours—and numerous second-hand apologies to an increasingly impatient Bonnie—but Jeff slowly managed to turn that idea into a halfway-decent plan thanks to the gentle encouragement and countless protestations of Eddie.

That night he slept restlessly, and woke with a hungry fire burning in his stomach. On the way to the bus stop, Jeff sighed under the pressing weight of the day ahead, and watched his breath billow out before him in a thick white mist. *That doesn't bode well,* he thought. The desperation of his predicament couldn't be avoided.

Now, the minutes ticked by, but still the sun refused to show its face. A plan was one thing, he knew. Now he had to pull it all off. It was now or never. It all ended today. It had to.

Staring out the window into the loathsome blackness, he grinned.

"Hi Jeff!" Stepping into the room, Ames offered a meek smile and eager wave as he scampered over to the table and set down his notebook.

Jeff grinned at the mild-mannered little man. "We've got one hell of a busy day ahead of us. Have you had a chance to review the details of any of your initiatives?"

Ames hurriedly flipped through his book as if looking for the answer. "A bit," he said finally. "I hate to admit it, but the training yesterday was a little—slow-paced. So, I took the liberty of reading over some of the files when I had time."

"Good work." Jeff sat down opposite Ames, slid his chair away from the table, and leaned back into a lazy slouch.

The initiatives on the wall were divided up by Team Lead, with Ames' to the right, and Jeff's to the left. "Are you ready for this?" asked Jeff.

Ames scrunched up his mouth, and stared down at the empty

white table. "Well, I'm definitely ready to give it my best shot. To be honest, though, the deadline they gave us yesterday sounds awfully tight on my first week. I'm really hoping you'll be taking the lead on some of this. So, are you ready?"

Jeff nodded absently. He briefly mulled the implication of the question, but his mind was elsewhere. He couldn't blame Ames. Honestly, he couldn't help but admire the guy's willingness to give it a try. If Jeff's first week had shown the obvious signs of disaster Ames' was, he'd have turned tail and fled immediately.

Then again, maybe it was time alone that made the warning signs so clear. He wondered if the more experienced team members had looked at him the same way when he started.

What if they'd warned me? he wondered. *Would I have left?*

Probably not, he knew. Still, a strange desire was growing in him to give Ames the heads up he never had. The poor sap deserved the same chance to get out that Jeff wished he'd taken long ago.

How different life might have been...

None of that mattered now, though. Ames was already in too deep. There was no turning back. Besides that, Ames was right. It wasn't his job to get them through—it was Jeff's. Marcy and Francis had made that crystal clear the day before, and HR made it legally binding.

Poor Ames would be scared to death if he had any idea how precarious the rest of the week would be. He'd need to rely on a stranger to guide the work which would inevitably define both of their careers for a long time to come.

Jeff smiled again. For the first time since starting with SALIGIA, he knew he wasn't going to fuck it up. He'd never been so certain about anything in his life.

This unexpected surety had kindled within him late last night.

It was something Eddie had said as they were ending their conversation. He'd just finished talking Jeff down off a panicked precipice—a sounding board and spirit guide as Jeff fumbled towards coherence on the finer details of his master plan. Bonnie had already told him to wrap up several times, and it was clear to both of them the next request would be less stoic. Still, Eddie was patient as he began to shut the conversation down.

"I guess you could call that a plan. And while I'm concerned, I can't deny I'm impressed. You really are going for broke on this one, buddy. If you actually pull this off—hell even if you try it and fail—there's no going back. You'll be done there. You'll be a legend, mind you, but done nonetheless."

Jeff knew it was true. He'd never imagined any other ending. Still, hearing it from Eddie grounded the fact and gave it a cumbersome weight. "I know," he'd answered. "I think at this point it's too late to avoid that either way. There's no better means to pull these initiatives together, and if I can't prove I've got a plan by Friday, I'm pretty sure I'll be frog-marched out by day's end. The writing is on the wall, the only power I have is how I go out."

"Well, it is going out in style, that's for sure," said Eddie. "Do you really think you can do this?"

Jeff had thought in silence for a while. "Well, as long as I can get everything approved and in action by the end of the day tomorrow, I think I've got a real shot. By the time the work orders are reviewed on Thursday morning, they'll be too far along to stop. So hopefully I can just lay low until Friday, then reveal it all in my report! It's actually kind of perfect," Jeff finished, and breathed a long sigh of relief.

"You don't think they'll confront you about it first thing Thursday morning?"

"They might," Jeff admitted. "It really depends on what else the Brass is up to." His plan didn't come without risk.

"What then?" asked Eddie.

That bit was easy. It was the most important part, and the inevitable conclusion to his grand finale. "That's the same whether I make it to Friday or not—I quit before they fire me," he said.

The air in the room was cool and sweet.

"You're really doing it," said Eddie with a chuckle. "Well, I'm proud of you, Jeff. You truly are selfless in your strange way, so I'm glad to hear you finally doing something for yourself. You've never been happy there, and I hope this helps you find whatever you're looking for."

"Thanks," said Jeff, wiping at a wet spot on his cheek. He knew he didn't need to say any more. Not to Eddie.

His friend raised a good point though. Leaving SALIGIA would be absolutely liberating, and quitting would be a downright joy, but that wasn't the end-goal. It couldn't be.

Getting out of there was just the first step, but the thrill of imagining the endless branching paths that might open to him afterward had left him dizzy and eager for bed.

"I should really get going," said Eddie.

"Yeah yeah, have a good one bud, and thanks again. We'll talk soon."

"Later bro," said Eddie.

"Bye," said Jeff.

After that, he never questioned his plan. Not the rest of that night, and not this morning. Even now, he didn't know if it would work out, but he knew he had to try.

Outside the office window, the sky was as black as the tower itself, but to Jeff, it seemed less menacing just then. He glanced over at Ames, who sat patiently at the table, flipping through his notebook. "Yeah," Jeff's voice was resolute, and there was no hesitation in him, "I'm ready."

The first step would be making Ames believe that it was at least partially his own idea. He'd have to put his name on it at the end of the day, after all. "To start off, we'll need to distill each initiative down to its key deliverable—what contractually needs to be accomplished in order for each to be considered closed? These boards can be written on with markers too." Jeff slid a small box across the table to Ames. "Can you get started on that while I arrange our work channels?"

Then, Jeff quickly pushed over a wireless mouse he'd connected to his digi-pad. "By the way, try to give that a click every three minutes or so. It should prevent the app from shutting everything down if we're idle."

It was a tedious measure, but the best Jeff had come up with. He couldn't afford the time or distraction of logging back into the app every time it shut down. Why it was programmed to do so every five minutes was beyond him. He was certain, however, that it had far less to do with energy conservation, and more to do with the cruel oppression of reminding the Tins just how powerless they were.

Ames nodded, but his brows scrunched up and his eyes turned downward. Pocketing the mouse and working the cap off an orange marker, he sidled silently over to the wall at his side of the room.

The second step would be a bit more difficult, but Jeff was ready for it. Somehow, he needed to convince both supervisors to sign off on the immediate actions they'd be taking today. That would never work if he followed the proper approval procedures—which involved a mind-boggling series of multi-coloured folders, reviews, edits, digital conversions, physical printings, and other useless red-tape. The entire process served only to create a long line of steps that could go wrong, and thus afford the supervisors plausible deniability when inevitably, nothing got done.

It took weeks even when it did work, but Jeff needed his plan to go into action today. Otherwise, it was all for nothing.

To do that, he'd need to employ a bit of social savvy. He'd been especially stoked about this part when he'd dreamed it slowly up with Eddie the night before.

Switching his digi-pad from the app over to his e-mail, the subtle grin on Jeff's face continued to grow—a slowly shifting fault-line over the chasms of his vengeful mirth.

"Francis," he typed...

I'm working with Ames to advance our initiatives, and I think things are progressing well. I wanted to extend my heartfelt thanks for your support over the past few weeks. Even if I haven't done the best job of showing it, I do realize the effort you've been putting in.

It can come as a shock, I suppose. In a competitive environment like this, it's unusual to come across selfless actions like yours. It's truly commendable that a supervisor would go out of his way to help those beneath him, especially when he's dealing with many of the same challenges we are.

A lesser supervisor thinks only of themselves. In fact, I've just been told by Marcy that despite our very tight timelines on these initiatives, I must follow all the traditional channels for work order approval. I was hoping she'd give me a temporary supervisor's code so I could get traction on advancing the initiatives I have under her control, but some people just can't put themselves in other's shoes.

Oh well, if being exceptional was a common trait, they'd have to call it something different. I don't imagine Marcy will have much progress to share from my reports come Friday, but she'll only have herself to blame.

Until then, I'm focussing my efforts where real progress is possible.

Thank you again for all your support. I hope you'll be pleased with our results at the end of the week.

Jeff sent the message, took a long breath, and hurried on. No time for second guessing now—the wheels were in motion.

Opening a new blank e-mail addressed to Marcy, he proceeded to copy and paste the text from his e-mail to Francis, replacing names and pronouns where necessary.

Hitting send, Jeff afforded himself a wide, uninhibited grin. He was in the shit now. Disaster pressed on both sides, and he advanced on a knife's edge with only a more entertaining, more fulfilling disaster ahead.

Both of the supervisors would be in meetings with upper management today—listening to Nadia and others drone on about topics Jeff could scarcely imagine. There was a lot of room for error in his plan—and even the smallest would mean complete, humiliating failure. The supervisors might not even have the time to check their e-mails, he knew, but that was a risk he had to take.

"How's it going over there Ames?" he called.

"Okay," Ames answered after a sudden, startled click of the mouse in his pocket. He'd made his way over to the other side of the room by this point, and was scribbling in long, flowery letters beneath the last of Jeff's initiatives. "Just wrapping up," he said. "How does this look?"

On each wall, under the digitally projected initiative titles, Ames had scribbled succinct little summaries of each initiative's key goals—exactly as Jeff had asked.

Beneath the Green City Initiative, Ames had summarized the end goal as "decreasing our carbon footprint by increasing the amount of green spaces available to the public."

So far so good.

The Oil City Initiative was about "increasing the public's esteem for oil-based energy," while the Sustainable City Initiative was meant to "raise awareness of renewable energy alternatives."

Aside from the obvious conflicts of intent, everything looked perfect. Ames' understandings of his own initiatives matched Jeff's assumptions exactly.

As for Jeff's initiatives, Ames indicated that the Liveable City Initiative was meant to "spread awareness of a new Condo Development the client was opening in the River Valley the following spring." For the Clean City Initiative, Ames wrote that the crux was to "reduce advertising in public spaces," and finally the City Branding Initiative intended to "create greater recognition of the City's branding slogans and iconography."

As maddeningly contradictory as the goals were, Jeff was pleased with what he saw. Ames had described the key goals exactly as Jeff hoped he would. Just like that, the first two steps of his plan were accomplished to a tee.

"Great," said Jeff, leading Ames slowly along his predetermined path. "Now we need to create a strategy for meeting all of these by this Friday." He hoped his sarcasm lessened the blow, and the enormity of the task wouldn't throw Ames off. He needed him to feel like the end product was at least partially his own invention. "Any ideas?" he tested.

Ames sat down again at the small round table and clicked the mouse. Then, he set his chin in his palm and furrowed his forehead in deep concentration. He looked like a damned statue. "Hmm," he finally offered by way of response. Nothing more.

Jeff measured his next move. It had to be direct enough to get where he desperately needed to go, and not one iota more. "I want to be clear about one thing here, buddy." He hoped his sudden familiarity wouldn't be too obvious. "We're alone on this task, and it's a tough one. I've never had to push an initiative towards a feasible end result so quickly, much less six of them at once," he confided.

"We're in dire straits, and need to pull off a miracle. There are no supervisors here, so I want to work on this in a more honest way. Forget about looking at one initiative at a time—I've already logged these hours as Professional Development for both of us, so we don't need to worry about all that crap."

He was certain he'd overplayed his hand.

For a torturous second, Ames' mouth hung open like an expressionist scream. Jeff waited for him to storm out, or pull out his phone and dial up SALIGIA High Command. Ames' lower lip trembled, and for a moment everything hung in limbo. Then, a strange tearing sound came from his mouth, rising and falling like crashing sheet metal as his bent little body jostled in his seat. Ames laughed, long and hard, and very unpleasantly, but to Jeff it was the sound of a light spring rain.

"Man, I'm so glad you said that," said Ames through his laughter.

Jeff was unspeakably happy Ames said that. So much so that he failed to speak for far too long. Ames' laughter petered out, and he leaned against the table, looking pleadingly at Jeff.

"That flexibility will help a lot," Ames said finally. "I'm glad you see how crazy some of these corporate rules are. If we can bend them here and there, then all for the better. It's still going to be a tall order coming up with a way to report conclusive action on all of these initiatives."

"You've got that right," said Jeff.

This was perfect.

Even as his smile threatened to split him in half, his digi-pad vibrated on the table, and an e-mail notification popped up in the corner. A quick click left him elated. Francis had bitten the bait, and responded with a twenty-four-hour supervisor's code to authorize work orders.

Jeff had hardly finished reading it when a similar notification came through from Marcy.

Too fucking perfect.

There were several moments in Jeff's life he'd have listed as great. He had, of course, the best day of his life to recall—ever sweet, though increasingly distant. He had a decent handful of memories he was proud of, and more than his share of humorous recollections. Nonetheless, he could tell beyond doubt this moment was one which would remain among his very favourites.

How could so many things go so right? Breathlessly, he took a second to stare again out the window, struggling to reign in his wild imagination. The buildings across the valley cut up through a solemn mantle of shadow, and the sky behind beckoned to him like the beginning and end of all things.

It would have been a nice view, if not for the clouds and the context. The SALIGIA building was a marvel, but ever since his first day all its grandeur and glory were soiled by the knowledge of what vile purposes it served, and with what cruel intent. Such was the way with knowing things too well. Despite his triumph, the clouds reminded him that even if his plan continued to work as perfectly as it had so far, there was no happy ending for him at SALIGIA.

Looking over at Ames—who continued to slouch in ponderous silence—Jeff tried to conceal his excitement. "Well, I just found out that we have the go ahead to act independently on actionable items if we can come up with a plan," Jeff declared.

"What?" Ames yelped. "What do you mean? How?"

Whether Ames' enthusiasm reflected a real understanding of the significance of Jeff's accomplishment, or merely a projection of how he imagined Jeff wanted him to act, it was impossible to discern. Either way, it hardly mattered so long as he was willing to continue along the bread crumb trail Jeff laid out.

The tinkling of a rising piano tempo began to play through Jeff's mind as he watched his vision unfold. "I worked some magic with Marcy and Francis," he explained. "They've both provided twenty-four-hour supervisor codes. If we can come up with a plan that advances the end goals of any of our initiatives, we have the full weight of SALIGIA at our beck and call."

Jeff saw the gears turning in Ames' head as he spoke. "So, we can actually give the orders and get real work done? That's incredible!"

"As many complete project orders as we can come up with today, but each one takes some time to fully draft and send off," said Jeff.

Ames grinned, and leaned over his notebook as he spoke. "Well, by Friday we need to show tangible progress towards completion, right? So why don't we try to see how many initiatives we can advance with as few work orders as possible? Maybe we can kill two or three birds with one stone here?"

The piano tune in Jeff's head rose to a crescendo, and the singing of angels filled the room. "That's not a bad idea," he said. He could feel a hearty laugh beating at the backs of his teeth.

Still scribbling in his notepad as he rose—and reaching on occasion into his pocket to click the mouse—Ames began to pace the room, squinting intently at the initiatives and jotting notes as he scurried back and forth. "Let's see. There are four initiatives which require some sort of advertising, one that aims to reduce advertising, and one that requires new green spaces opened," he listed.

"We might be able to erect some billboards to address the first four, but that would be a problem for the other one, and still leave us no closer on the Green City Initiative. What do you say, four out of six isn't bad? Do you think we can get four billboards ordered in time?"

Ames was busting his ass on this, and fast approaching the point it had taken Jeff two hours and a "phone-a-friend" to arrive at. Impressive.

Jeff hummed audibly, and chewed at his thumb before speaking. "So, four projects with four billboards. We can probably manage that, but it'll still leave the other two unfinished—and one in the negative..." he trailed off, praying Ames would pick up his hints.

For a moment, Ames stood perplexed, glancing down at his notebook, then up at the wall and back. Then, his tight lips curled upward, and a flash of light grew behind his pupils. "What if we combine them? Four messages, with three or maybe even two billboards? That way more messaging is getting done with less advertising, so we can claim a victory on the Clean City Initiative as well!"

"I like that a lot. It just might work," said Jeff. He rose, and joined Ames at the far wall. "We're going to need a place to put these billboards though...if we can find an empty lot with space to turn into parkland, then we've got all six goals met to some extent."

Ames was on a roll now, "And if we create separate zoning designations for the billboard space and the park, we can label the park as being free of advertising."

Damn, thought Jeff. Even he hadn't thought of that.

As the sun wheeled invisibly behind the dark clouds, no hint of natural light made its way into the digitally illuminated Excelsior Room. Only an occasional glance at his digi-pad marked the passing of time as Jeff and Ames scribbled on the board, listing catchphrases, drawing sketches, erasing everything, and starting over. With each iteration, the vibrating sense of triumph in Jeff's stomach grew, making his skin itch with energy as their efforts slowly approached the vision of his master plan.

Two billboards would be set up in an arched formation. Behind them would be a converted strip of land that could be used for a green space. The location would need to be public enough to make the billboards effective, yet still near an empty lot. The billboards—facing opposite directions of traffic and tall enough to be seen from afar, would split the intentions right down the middle.

The first would show the wide white drums and bristling towers of the nearby refineries—full of lights and bustling with workers in navy blue coveralls and white helmets. "Edmonton—Powering the Future!" would scroll along the top in a stylish black font.

"That increases city branding as an energy powerhouse, which should thrill the Council. I think it meets the basic needs of the City Branding and the Oil City initiatives." Even Ames seemed to shake with excitement as he spoke.

The second billboard would show sleek white towers rising out of the trees of the River Valley. "Return…to nature!" would read the bold green letters at the top. Along the bottom, in subtler white lettering would be the name and contact information of the Condo Developers building in the River Valley. "That should meet the goals of the Liveable City Initiative easily, and I think between the slogan and the green space behind it, we can report this as a Sustainable City success too." Jeff nodded proudly as he surveyed the results on the board.

"And our billboard efficiency and division of properties—along with the new park—should provide justifiable success on the Clean City and Green City initiatives," said Ames.

His face had relaxed now, and as the finality of their plan began to set in, Jeff felt his energy change. Once again, he was the nervous, mousy man Jeff had first met, and he looked furtively around at their designs as if searching for any hole to poke in their illusions. Finally, he looked back over at Jeff. "Can we really order all this work to begin with those codes of yours?"

Jeff smiled. "These are SALIGIA Supervisor Temporary Codes. Do you know how rich this corporation is? All they care about is their share price—and that requires happy clients. We can order damn near anything we want. Actually—why don't we make the signs solar-powered? That should add extra points to your Sustainable City Initiative, right?"

Ames sat down and began flipping through the pages of his notebook, avoiding eye contact as he spoke. "That's not really what I meant," he said.

"Ames, think of us as the supervisors today, and we have the chance they've always wished they could have—to really prove their worth to Nadia. We've been given an impossible task, and we're going to pull it off against all odds."

Several more pages were turned in silence. "We're not really pulling it off though, are we? We're meeting the bare minimum so that we can submit our report. It borders on malicious compliance."

"No, it's absolutely malicious compliance," Jeff said. Maintaining the front was no longer possible. He had to sell Ames on this idea honestly, and he had to do it right now. "Like you said, we're doing all of this so that we can meet the exact requirements of the report they made us do. I know the results aren't ideal, but they've destroyed our timeline and forced our hand. It's this, or abject failure."

Ames shrunk in his chair. "Is this going to get us in trouble?" he asked.

A timer in Jeff's mind began to race. "Umm…" he said.

One second had passed. Now two. He didn't have many more before his hesitation became a confession. Four more, maybe five at most. Another two had passed as he considered this, and he was still no closer to a plausible denial.

"Probably," Jeff admitted. He stood tall and straight in front of the defeated Ames, hoping it would foster a sense of authority. Behind him, the towers and streets of Edmonton were lost in the inky darkness of the coming storm.

Jeff lost track of the passing seconds, and they remained locked in their hopeless standoff for a cruel stretch of time uncounted. Finally, Ames leaned forward, and ran his puffy hands over his bald head. He sighed, long and loudly, and then stood up. Turning, he faced Jeff, and looked straight at him with steel in his eyes. "Okay," he said.

This is it. The second-best moment of my life, Jeff knew. He'd actually managed to do it, and he couldn't wait to tell Eddie. What happened now was out of his hands.

Peace radiated through Jeff, warming him from the inside out and taking from him a weight he'd forgotten he carried. "Well," he said, "we'd better get started on these work orders. We need to have them submitted by the end of the day to get things moving, then we can spend tomorrow working on our report."

Jeff projected his screen onto the wall, and logged into the SALIGIA Work Order App. Once prompted, he clicked to access the server with a temporary password, and entered the one Marcy had sent.

A list of the initiatives she supervised populated a tiny box to the right. Then, he repeated the process with Francis' code, and saw the rest of the initiatives appear.

"Cool," said Ames. He was smiling again.

So was Jeff. "Yeah," he agreed.

"I guess the last thing to figure out is where to find the right piece of property to meet our needs. Do you want me to start searching while you fill out the orders?" asked Ames.

Jeff remembered the feeling of wind in his hair, and the freedom of his car rumbling down the Yellowhead. He thought about the little house he'd dropped Janice off at, and the empty strip of land out back. What had she said? He remembered it clearly.

"Sure, it's a tempting idea. To go back and see if there's anything else out there I could love. Something just for me. But that ship has sailed as well. Any savings I had went into buying our house..." Despite not owning his own place, Jeff had related to her feelings. Nobody wanted to be stuck in one place, but more often than not freedom came at a steep cost.

"Don't bother," said Jeff. "It might be a bit pricey, but I think I know just the place."

"Okay," said Ames, "then let's get started."

Jeff sighed, not trying to hide it from Ames. The final step was done. The rest of the day would be spent hammering out the harmless little details and submitting the work orders. Jeff rubbed his hands together like an ancient Roman official. He was finished.

It was liberating to know his role in all of this was finally over. He had only to wait and see now. No more worry, no more stress, no more panic. Just time.

Freedom, he thought again. It really could cost a man. But without it, what did all the rest mean?

With the dark clouds mustering behind him, Jeff leaned back in his chair and smiled.

Nothing, he knew. *Without freedom, nothing else means a damn thing.*

CHAPTER 15

The Day the Snow Came Down

Below a certain temperature, there's a strange sound the snow makes when you step on it. It's like a scream. Most decent places never get cold enough to experience this. Edmonton is not such a place.

As Jeff left his building and hurried to reach the bus stop, the wind stung at his face, and the tortured sound rose up to bite his quickly reddening ears. Beneath his feet he felt a soft crunching, and the world around him was blindingly white. Summer was long gone, and today was the death rattle of fall. Nothing now stood between him and the endless freeze of winter.

Waiting for the bus to arrive, he shivered in place, and squinted against the glare of the sun on the mirror-like sheen of the snow.

It wasn't much—just enough to cover the world in a thin layer, erasing everything beneath. What was familiar yesterday was now lost or obscured by the snow, and large fluffy flakes continued to flutter down without any sign of stopping. Soon, the city would be unrecognizable as its former self. It would embrace its cold and unforgiving true form.

Jeff's teeth ground in his mouth. He pulled his bare hands up into the thin sleeves of his coat and smiled with grim desperation. When the bus finally pulled up, it sent a brown spray of slush across the bottom of his pants. He rolled his eyes at the driver as he flashed his pass, but took a seat without complaint.

Today was going to be quite a day, he knew. It wasn't just the de facto beginning of winter. It was more than a day to freeze and suffer from the very air he breathed. Today, Jeff knew, was likely to be his last day at SALIGIA.

It was exhilarating, and strange. The past ten years he'd spent trying desperately to avoid getting fired, while daydreaming all the while about how thrilling it would be to quit.

He'd imagined it a thousand times and more. Again and again, each and every day for over a decade.

It happened sitting at his desk, staring out the windows at meetings, riding the elevator, and tuning out the endless droning of whichever supervisor had him cornered at the time. Jeff had seen countless iterations play out in his mind like blockbuster films made just for him. In some scenarios, he'd wait until the middle of some tedious meeting, when the supervisors were competing to explain their asinine plans, and Nadia stood like a viper poised behind them. Then, he'd rise slowly from his chair. Even in his daydreams, he could feel his pulse quicken as the blather from the front cut off, and all eyes turned to him.

Then, he'd let loose the spiteful diatribe that had fermented within him over the years slaving away unappreciated in that corporate hellhole. Jaws would hit the floor. Once or twice someone would probably try to speak over him, or gently motion him back to the realm of reason.

Nothing would stop him though, and for hours he'd go on like a twisted wizard astride a sharp mountain pinnacle, raining down his judgements on all who deserved it, and plenty more who didn't.

Several times, he'd gotten creative in his imagined farewells. If he signed out a digi-pad the day before, he could spend the night going through old clips, audio files, and e-mails to create a looped presentation of all the hypocritical, mind-bending idiocy that happened there in the name of stock prices and shareholder engagement.

He'd keep the device hidden beneath his coat like contraband or kill-switches, then activate the show in the middle of some corporate presentation in the Excelsior Room. The walls would spring to life with irrefutable records of the madness—and with no chance for excuses, no pre-written corporate bylines to fall back on, the Brass would have to stand exposed in the cold knowledge of their own incompetence.

Sometimes he considered filing a Human Rights complaint with HR, but this fantasy always came with the grim acceptance that any interaction with the perfumed automatons in HR would inevitably leave him worse off than when he went in.

Showing up to work naked had crossed his mind at least a few times. Surely SALIGIA had no official protocols written to respond to a colleague walking into work asshole naked—and he'd love to see the gears turning in the hard, metal heads of the Brass as they cycled through their programming in a hopeless search for a corporate sanctioned response.

If it wasn't for the weather, he might have really done it.

Of course, he still remembered his fire dream, and had not yet escaped the clear implications there. The images flashed through his mind again as he hopped off the bus at his stop and hurried towards the great black tower.

The snow crunched beneath his feet like dying banshees, and he looked up at his destination, remembering the smell of smoke and the ruin all around him in the dream.

Today, however, he had no plans at all. None of the daydreams, or the real dreams, were roadmaps for him, and he was ready to take on the day as a blank slate. With his ultimate destiny already written behind the scenes, it didn't really matter how he got there.

It might be today, and if not, it would certainly be Friday, but Jeff knew where he was going, and nothing could change his course.

It made him taller. It hurried his steps and peeled the dusty years off his face.

He was bullet-proof as he rode the elevator up to the 82nd floor. It was the earliest he'd arrived since he was an intern—he didn't want the Brass pulling the rug out from under him before the show even started.

The doors slid open with their metallic hiss, and beyond, the lobby buzzed with life. Despite it being fifteen minutes before start time, people lingered in front of the oblong reception desk, while others chatted on work phones, or typed away on digi-pads. Some slid back and forth between the windows and the coffee station. The giant machine was gone, Jeff noted, and in its place was once again the old stained carafe. *Poor Tali,* he thought.

Most mornings, at least one representative from management would be out on the floor overseeing arrival times. Today, everyone present were Tins. So far as Jeff could see, there wasn't a member of the Brass to be found. Not Marcy, not Francis. Certainly not Nadia. *That,* thought Jeff, *explains the restless mood.*

Everyone wandered about like headless chickens. It wasn't clear what they were waiting for, or what they hoped to find—only that there was no direction, no familiarity, and nobody to tell them to get to work.

Something was wrong.

Adra was arguing with Tali at the front desk, but Jeff didn't bother to listen what the issue was. Finnegan was staring morosely out the window, sipping slowly from a giant thermos. Rudy, Rian, and Nasha paced in tight circles, no clear leader emerging as each gazed solemnly at their feet and shuffled around in silence.

In the corner of the room, Ames was fixated on a digi-pad. Ashley lingered near him, flipping mindlessly through a notebook. Whenever she drifted within view of Ames' screen, he glanced briefly at her, then turned away.

She didn't seem to care.

"But where are they?" Adra's nervous voice rose above the buzz. "Do I still have my one-on-one at 8:45?"

Tali shrugged, locking her eyes on the screen in front of her, no doubt hoping to avoid further engagement. "This is okay, it all makes sense. SALIGIA has a reason," she mumbled to her screen.

"This isn't right," Jeff heard Rian mumble as she continued her hopeless loop. "Something big is happening."

Jeff had a good idea what was coming. He'd hoped it would take a bit longer, but nothing could be done about it now.

The corners of his mouth pushed at his thin cheeks as he made his way toward the coffee carafe. It was best, he reasoned, to get his energy up before the fireworks started.

He never got the chance.

"Jeff!" Hearing his name, the dull droning of the room around him went dead, and a shrill alarm began to ring somewhere behind his forehead.

"What the fuck did you do?"

As Jeff turned, he was met with a shove to the chest. He bumped back against the coffee carafe, nearly sending it tumbling. That was the least of his danger, as in front of him Janice was poised to attack again. Her nostrils flared out to the sides, her frizzy hair shot wildly out from her head like the fringe of some primitive predator, and a white light shone in her eyes.

"What were you thinking?" she asked again, holding up a crumpled piece of paper. "I found this on my desk today. SALIGIA has purchased my house and property for a work order signed by you. Seriously, Jeff, what the fuck?"

Jeff grinned. "Did they pay well?"

A faint blush crept over her round cheeks. "Yes," she admitted. "But I still need to find a new house."

"It shouldn't be hard with that payout. You could also look into those courses you mentioned, and still have change to spare."

"Maybe I will." Janice scrunched up her face and jabbed a finger towards Jeff as if to reinforce her righteous anger. "It's none of your business what I do though, Jeff. You had no right to do this."

Of all the slings and arrows Jeff expected today, this one caught him off guard. His mouth was dry, and his legs felt suddenly overburdened. "I..." he stammered, searching for the right words. "I helped you."

His ears were hot, and his throat fought to swallow. The air in the room seemed to cool though, and Janice's posture relaxed as she spoke—like the wind coming out of a balloon filled near to popping. "You're an idiot. I don't need your help. Honestly, you should have spent this effort helping yourself."

"I did," he said.

"You're going to get fired. You know that, right?"

Jeff sighed. "I deserve it. No one has any business being in a place they hate so much." Now his shoulders slouched, and he felt more vulnerable than he'd imagined he could feel on a day like this. A gentle tremble ran up his back.

Janice set a warm hand on his shoulder. "Well, that's true enough. Don't worry, you'll find what you need, Jeff. You just need to remember to focus on yourself and your own needs. I think sometimes you lose that in this drive you have to always help others and put them before you. It made you the best Team Lead on the floor, and I'm grateful for that. But I was never looking for a savior Jeff, just a friend."

Jeff's stomach churned. He'd learned this lesson long ago.

It was a day much like this, he recalled, about three years ago. He'd been walking down Whyte Ave, on his way to meet Eddie at The Black Dog. If he'd been asked prior to that moment, he'd have happily bragged about how quickly he'd recognize Katie even after all the years. From across a street, down a block, or passing in a crowd, he'd have sworn he could pick out her face, and go tumbling right back to that cold snowy day on the playground.

But he froze up when she spoke—suddenly before him, saying his name and asking all the requisite pleasantries. She said her name twice before he managed to splutter a reply.

"Hi," he said.

It fell far short of the passive musings which occupied the years.

He hadn't seen her since she'd switched schools two years after the playground incident, but beyond the time, weather, wear, and weariness, he could still see her. She had a knit hat on once again, which seemed fitting. A long winter coat hung down to her knees, and she wore thick black mittens. Not the gloves that had separate fingers, but big, bulky mittens.

He remembered that clearly, and how strange they felt slapping against his back when they hugged.

They covered the basics. She worked for an oil company, but in the local offices, not onsite. It wasn't far from SALIGIA, actually. She was married now, but no kids. He was an IT Tech. It didn't sound like anything special, but he was there at home each night, and when she spoke about him she smiled like she had no other thoughts in her head save the last time they'd laughed.

They went to Peru last year. She didn't love it.

Jeff stood with her on the corner of 103 St. and Whyte, and people hurried past them as they spoke. Big, weightless flakes of snow floated through the air. A few landed on her hat and rested there, frozen in time.

"Sometimes," he'd said, "I think about that day the guys tried to steal your hat."

She laughed—a light, tinkling sound.

It took Jeff a second to realize she had no other answer.

"I managed to get it back for you?" he heard the question in his own voice.

The air was cold and wet—the sort of chill that sinks in and settles deep in your bones.

Katie smiled. "You always liked to play the hero," she said.

The comment meant little. Nothing did. She didn't even remember.

He'd sat at home that night, listening to old music and drinking straight liquor. For a long time, that moment had been his high-water mark for noble behaviour, and his template for human interactions.

She didn't even remember it.

It was a strange thought, and he wrestled with it all that night. The better part of his life had been spent under the illusion he'd been the hero to the lonely kid on the playground—it was a key part of his identity. After seeing her again on the street, he knew that he'd been the lonely kid all along.

The epiphany was crucl, and it sat heavy in his gut for a long while afterward. Then, the load lightened, and he gave less thought to it each day.

Now he looked at Janice, and her sad eyes stared back at him. He may have learned the lesson that day on the streets, but it was obvious he'd failed to grow from it.

Her words couldn't have been clearer—she'd only wanted a friend. It wasn't so much to ask. "I'm sorry," he said.

If any anger remained in Janice, it left her like smoke from a snuffed candle. "Maybe I will end up going back to school. It's nice that you thought of me. You love trying to help others. That's been obvious since I met you, and I imagine it's nothing new. Just make sure you look out for yourself as well. You deserve it."

His cheeks were hot, but his heart slowed, and the tension in his limbs released like the hiss of a venting engine.

He knew Janice was right. He'd known it since before she said it, known it since he left the playground long ago and found that life went on beyond his favorite parts of it.

How long had he considered that his best day? Out in the cold, on the playground, handing over that silly knit hat. He'd felt good about himself in the moment, and that golden feeling had caused him to martyr the truth of the moment and create some inaccessible effigy of decency for all his future days.

To some degree, he'd spent the rest of his life failing to live up to that fleeting memory.

It was a fine moment, and worth remembering because he'd acted purely for another. Since then, he'd chased that thrill selfishly, inserting his heroic projections into the content realities of others. It seemed to Jeff that people were all just little pieces of one another— we carry around what we can't let go, until we realize we're beginning to lose ourselves.

It was cold now, and Jeff was getting tired. His body trembled, but whether from the frigid air, or the wheels of exhaustion bearing down on him over the past few days, he wasn't sure.

Janice's hand was still on his shoulder, like a little glowing coal. Her face was calm, her cheekbones pink, and her frizzy hair enveloped her like the leaves of some balmy jungle. Her deep brown eyes were soft as she held him in her gaze. Then, clouds blew up. Her pupils turned to pinpricks, and suddenly her hand was ice.

From somewhere far outside the realm of reason, up from deep in his guts, Jeff understood. Turning with the weight of the world on his shoulders, he followed her gaze through the window to the South Hallway.

They were coming.

Nadia led the charge, moving smooth and quick—the fury of her will was a burning chariot. Marcy and Francis followed at each shoulder, and behind them came an endless train of black-tie-wearing yes-bots—a veritable army of HR reps and corporate lawyers ready to climb over each other's corpses to defend the profit margins at all costs.

The windows outside showed little but the deathly dark of the clouds, and the small, fast-falling blades of icy snow raining down from their sable belly. So too came the wrath of SALIGIA down the South Hallway, and in the vanguard, terrible and unwavering, Nadia locked eyes with Jeff, and held his gaze as she came forth, and a shadow followed in her wake.

The lights dimmed, and a rumbling line of bass shook the room. If it was the machinations of the SALIGIA IT Techs, or the slow rising pounding of his own pulse, Jeff couldn't tell.

His legs wavered, and the thudding in his head nearly took his feet out from under him. Still, he stood and watched them come.

They were in the common section now, passing the doors of the Excelsior Room.

Nadia still held his eyes, and it seemed now that he floated off the ground as she daunted him. His vision focused, and he lost himself in the small points of light emanating from her pupils. The blackness was everything, and yet he could perceive clearly all around him.

Just behind her, the supervisors marched like chained beasts. Their backs faltered, and their eyes shot around like starving flies. Their faces showed nothing—like photo-copied pictures of times they no longer remembered.

They'd already paid their price. Jeff wondered how steep it had been.

There was a dry spot in his throat he couldn't quite swallow, and he fought with it as he melted into the darkness.

Then they were at the door.

"Good luck buddy," Janice whispered. She'd drifted behind him now, and let the currents of apprehension and fear carry her away as she offered her final condolences.

Ames stood to the back of the group staring at his digi-pad, which seemed like as good a choice as any given the circumstances. No one wanted to draw attention, only to sit back and watch the show. The entire lobby was still, and even the dullest of the lot—Finnegan—realized the time had come.

Jeff had made his stand, and the heavy hand of doom was come to strike him down for his hubris. It was just like his father used to say—life wasn't fair. It wouldn't just work out eventually, and the good guys didn't always win. Not without a damn good fight anyway.

The door flew open, and Jeff swallowed down the dry patch. His throat relaxed, and his body was free. Flamenco guitars and brass horns played through his mind as time drew to a crawl.

He'd been waiting for this moment so long. The lines were drawn, the time had come, the dice were cast... all that bullshit.

High fucking noon.

The wall in front of him was black as the sky outside—the suits spread along it like an oil slick. At the head of this dark tide, Nadia now stood resolute before Jeff.

On rare occasions during staff meetings, the lightning would break through the clouds, and some quick condemnation would smash down from her high throne before she returned to the more pressing corporate matters of her digi-pad. Usually, she only interacted with the Tins through HR-approved e-mails, or messages passed through the supervisors who were prostrated behind her.

Now, her focus was on him alone. The wall was breached, and the façade rent asunder. For the first time in his life, he had the full attention of his captor and benefactor. The eye of SALIGIA itself was turned upon him.

He had so much to say, and wanted more than anything to begin. But he knew what was coming, and the inevitability of the ending made caution obsolete. He was expected to explain himself and beg for mercy, but the glorious truth was that he didn't have to.

Jeff's body shuddered—a sudden burst of satisfaction surging through his veins. He grinned, but said nothing.

Nadia stood unflinching. Her arms were crossed, and tucked underneath, in her right hand was her digi-pad. Though she was a short woman, something in her posture made her seem like a towering column of stone—immoveable and inescapable. As she stared into Jeff, he felt compelled to tell her everything, and throw himself at her mercy.

Still, he resisted, and slowly, he sensed a change in her. Ever so slightly, her stance wavered. The lawyers and HR reps behind her shuffled subtly, and Francis and Marcy exchanged pained glances before hurrying their attention back to the floor.

Nadia's eyes narrowed, and slowly her pursed lips peeled open. "Jeff, would you please follow us?" She indicated back down the hallway behind her.

"No, thank you," Jeff answered. His spine shook, but his spirit trilled like a bugle blast.

A tiny point of flame grew in Nadia's pupils. She frowned—Jeff was forcing her hand. "This morning I was informed of some very unusual activity on last night's work orders. Do you have anything to say about that?"

Never in his life had Jeff felt so powerful and alive. "You're welcome." His mouth hurt from the smirk tearing at its seams. A nervous chatter rose, then fell back immediately into silence as the Tins behind Jeff exchanged furtive looks with each other and pretended not to be listening.

"You're welcome?" One of the lawyers repeated, aghast.

"This is not the time for levity, Mr. Boggs," said an HR rep.

Nadia held out a manicured hand, and they fell back into line.

"Jeff, based on the reports I have received, I get the impression you used your temporary codes to send no less than four work orders—all of which were coded to more than one initiative. That alone is highly unusual and frankly, quite suspect."

Jeff nodded, and the silence around him was a warm bath.

Nadia was seething. Her nostrils flared like thunderclouds, but her voice remained smooth and controlled. "You have two orders for billboards. One is coded to both the City Branding and the Oil City Initiative, and the other to the Livable City and the Sustainable City initiatives. I have never seen anything like this, Jeff. What do you have to say?"

Laughter beat at the back of Jeff's teeth, and he had to purse his lips shut to keep it from bursting forth. He took a deep breath in through his nose, and let it slowly out until he was certain he had the composure to respond. "Should we really be discussing more than one initiative at once? I'd hate to mess up the time logs," he said.

Several snickers mixed with the shocked gasps from the Tins behind him. Lawyers shuffled their papers, and HR reps clutched invisible pearls. A coy smile played across Jeff's face.

"Can you honestly claim this was a sincere effort to advance any of our client's interests?" Nadia's eyes were slits over hot coals.

Jeff steadied his nerve. "As sincere as could be expected. I was tasked with advancing all initiatives towards completion by Friday. I did what I could."

Nadia licked her upper lip and turned her head sharply to the left twice before she continued. "You also ordered the purchase and re-zoning of property that cost SALIGIA a small fortune. Not only that, it belonged to an employee that works directly under you. That is dangerous territory, Jeff. I must insist you explain the meaning of these actions."

The snowstorm outside had grown slowly over several days, but that wasn't always the case in Edmonton. Sometimes it was a chill wind, then a fresh smell. A sudden silence, and leaves skittering down asphalt streets. With such scarce warning, a clear blue sky could turn to an overcast storm—snow or rain or driving sleet chasing children off the streets and even some cars to the side of the road.

This storm came fast. Jeff couldn't have articulated why just then, but with those words all the fun of the moment was gone. His little goodbye party was over, and the immunity he felt from knowing he was done lost all its thrill. The sound dropped out of the room, and a distant ringing rose in his right ear.

"Meaning?" he repeated. The indignation was growing in him—a tumor of pent up rage and injustice pushed down for too long and finally turned malignant. "That's a bold word for you to throw around."

Now the lawyers gasped, and the HR reps shuffled papers.

"Just what is that supposed to mean?" asked one pencil-necked lawyer, his fingers hovering eagerly above the screen of his digi-pad.

Jeff interlaced his fingers behind him and cracked his back. He stretched his neck to each side, and saw his colleagues cowering in the shadows. *I have the chance to say what they all wish they could,* he knew.

Taking a deep breath, Jeff looked more directly at Nadia than he ever had during his long tenure at SALIGIA. "Meaning?" he repeated. "What the hell does anything mean around here? Profit and self-aggrandizement are the only things that have ever meant anything.

"The sinks that never work? They don't mean anything except that SALIGIA found a tax loophole around 'energy-efficient' sinks and took full advantage. The phony retreats and staff development you orchestrate mean nothing, except that some suit gets to check off a box and SALIGIA can report on how much they care about their staff.

"There are loyal, decent people working here, who put up with all of this because they have meaning of their own. They do their time and go home to whatever makes them happy—that's where meaning is. So, don't ask me what my actions today, or yesterday, or at any point in my ten years mean, because I can't tell you."

Everyone in Nadia's retinue gaped save for Marcy and Francis, whose eyes remained locked sadly on the polished black floors.

A moment passed, and Jeff realized he could feel the silence in the room like the greasy smoke of the refineries. He heard its power by the pounding in his chest. He'd said more than he'd intended to. It wasn't the imminent repercussions that bothered him though, he was already immune to them.

Everyone goes home to their own meaning, he thought, and swallowed again at his dry throat.

Nadia stepped closer. He could hear the hiss of her breath like steam from an old brass engine. The fire in her eyes was a dull red now, and she seethed up at him like she truly believed in her cold metal soul that looks could kill.

"Now you want to play the hero card, Mr. Boggs? You care less about these people than you claim SALIGIA does." At this, the lawyers raced their hands across their digi-pads, and the HR reps spoke among themselves in furious whispers. "I still cannot imagine what you thought you would accomplish pushing through this ridiculous plot, but you willingly pulled Ames in with you. He was brand new, under your tutelage, and you sold him out for what I gather is some high-minded prank."

"He—" Jeff started, but Nadia wasn't done.

"Make no mistake about it Jeff, I hold you entirely accountable for this incident, but Ames was a Team Lead and will answer for his role as well. Perhaps you would like to explain why you dragged him into all this?" she said, and a vindictive smirk slashed across her face in crimson.

Jeff started to speak, but his words were cut off once more. "Actually," said Ames, and he let the moment hang as he stepped out of his dark corner. He slipped his digi-pad into his pocket, and shuffled his way to the head of the crowd. He stood taller than before, and his little bald head shone under the fluorescent lights. "That won't be necessary, Jeff. I appreciate the help you gave me, but I think we can call it even. See, my corporate personnel file officially states that I've closed three initiatives in only four days. My completion time quota is currently a SALIGIA world-record, and I've just accepted a supervisor position with Logistics and Procurement, down on the 77th floor."

Nadia's body trembled, and a dull groan emanated from somewhere deep within. Her corporate team talked loudly among themselves, many pulling up their digi-pads and promptly getting into arguments with whoever they called.

Chuckling, Jeff couldn't help but admire Ames. He'd always seemed like the quietest, least assuming person Jeff had ever seen, but now he revealed himself to be a cunning planner, and his talent for manipulating things to his advantage meant he was well-suited for SALIGIA Brass.

Smiling like that cat who ate the canary, Ames poured himself a coffee as the in-fighting continued. Even now, Jeff could hear the bitter debate spreading out among his co-workers. None were happy that someone could spend less than a week doing nothing, then fuck up once, only to fail upwards into a better life than they could ever dream of.

Jeff wasn't surprised, though. He'd seen it all before. The only way to ever succeed at SALIGIA was to have no loyalty to anything but yourself, and no talent for anything but convincing others that you were talented. The honest, hardworking employees never got promoted—their skills were too essential to waste in management.

A strange sound shook Jeff from his bitter reflections. Ames finished his coffee, smacked his lips, and tossed the empty cup in the recycling. Then, with a broad grin, he strode towards the elevator, waited just a moment, and waved as he disappeared behind the sliding silver doors.

"Well, at least I've made someone happy." Jeff regretted the joke the moment it left his mouth.

Nadia scoffed, and stuttered absently before she found her words. "Do you think this is some kind of joke? You do not care about anyone but yourself, do you? You pulled this off by betraying the trust of your supervisors, who had nothing but the best of hopes and intentions for you. Because of your actions, I have been forced to review the hierarchy with corporate. A new position—Operational Supervisor—will be created above the supervisors."

"Or Supervisor of Operations," chimed in one of the HR reps. She was promptly ignored by everyone.

The people behind Jeff sighed. They'd all have another level of Brass to contend with now.

Jeff couldn't help but feel bad. It would have likely happened anyway—SALIGIA never balked at the chance to fatten out their arsenal of corporate-level thugs to beat down any independent thinking from the Tins—but the thought of leaving his colleagues behind to an even worse situation bugged him.

The aspirations of Marcy and Francis were utterly crushed, and try as he might, Jeff couldn't fully commit to feeling good about that. *Leave it to SALIGIA to suck all the fun out of payback.*

In the corporate world, everyone was a replaceable part in a role they didn't quite fit—desperate to turn on one another for a chance to fit elsewhere. Life was a commodity, difficult to own anymore.

It wasn't natural. People were never meant for this environment. People wanted to be happy and loving and wild like they were in the streets and the bars. It used to feel like that. He was sure of it. But the towers got taller, and the alleys narrower. It seemed like a strange time to live in—to know the world is changing right in front of you, but to be powerless to affect it. It was too large a thing, too vast. Still,

Jeff knew he could change his own story. That would have to be enough.

The fires of argument around the room had burned down to smouldering embers. Here and there a few groups chatted angrily, and one lawyer demanded in whispered tones to be transferred to another floor.

Jeff was finished. His moment of triumph had lost all its charm, and only then did he consider he might be celebrating the wrong things in life.

Marcy and Francis were both staring sullenly at him, as if they still believed he could stop what he'd set in motion. If he could, he wouldn't have. Not even to spite Ames.

Still, he had his regrets.

"I'm sorry," he said to the supervisors, and watched their shimmering gazes droop back to the floor as they accepted the finality of their situation.

"Really," he turned to the others, looking at each in turn. Even if he'd never been close with most of them, he'd certainly never meant to hurt them. Adra and her grand ambitions to join the Brass, Rian's fearful toeing of the corporate line, Nasha's entirely forgettable presence, spaced-out Ashley, and clueless Rudy. He thought of Tali at the reception desk always parroting the corporate mantras, poor Finnegan and his unhappy family life, and even Jordan—whose outspoken distaste for SALIGIA had sent him packing even sooner than Jeff.

"I am sorry," he managed to lock eyes with Janice as he finished. He smiled, but she didn't return it, and her eyes fell away like dropped glassware. All she'd wanted was a friend, that's what she said. Jeff hoped he'd managed to be that, when he wasn't too distracted trying to be everything else.

"I fear that 'sorry' is not going to cut it this time, Jeff," said Nadia. Gone was the hard artifice of her corporate mettle. She stood shaking with rage for no other reason than knowing her authority had been questioned. Ames had already walked out, and even she had to know by now that Jeff would soon do the same.

All that day and the night before, Jeff had savoured his decision with sweet satisfaction. He'd awoken with its taste lingering on his lips, energized and sustained by it—instilled with a great strength.

To fear no consequences was a potent cocktail.

Knowing now that Nadia saw her defeat was the dizzying payoff, and Jeff drank it to the dregs.

She licked her lips again, and turned her head four times to the side. She blinked, and finally, opening her mouth, stuttered for a while before continuing. "Sorry is not good enough," was all she managed.

Jeff laughed aloud. Then, with a sigh that took ten years and half the memory of a life under ever-growing corporate servitude off his shoulders, he spoke loud enough to ensure everyone could hear. "I wasn't talking to you," he said. The scent of fresh cut grass filled the air. "I don't give a shit about you."

White clouds and sunny beaches took him, and in a swoon kept him entranced in that endless moment. It was a gasp—Janice's—that finally shook him back to reality. The lawyers were stepping to the forefront, and one of the HR reps was putting a hand on Nadia's shoulder.

Will they retire her model after this gross system failure? Jeff wondered.

Her power was gone now. She'd never truly had any. It had been Jeff's all along.

He turned away, and he was moving before he realized it—

hurrying through throngs of dumbfounded Tins. They looked at him like they'd never seen him before. Like a strange, legendary forest-dweller, long rumoured, and finally sighted in all its shaggy, reeking glory.

Janice was as wide-eyed as the rest, but etched in the lines of her face, beside her trembling lips was the whisper of a smile peeking from behind the clouds of fear which had taken the rest.

No retort came from behind him. No promises of retribution or legal action. No final demands for reports on his initiatives. Those would fall to someone else now, and the wheel would continue to turn without him.

No pleas for him to stop echoed through the room, and no self-assured "You're fired!" came from any of the Brass.

That last part bothered him, and he wondered if he was missing out on the opportunity for severance. But it seemed like a trivial detail, and not something worth ruining his great quitting moment over.

He was at the corner near the elevators when it really hit him that he hadn't officially quit, and all his day-dreaming was coming down to a self-satisfied retreat.

That wouldn't do at all.

From the elevator door, he turned back towards the silent crowd. He saw the dark clouds out the stainless wall of windows behind them, and below the city seemed cold and grim.

"I quit," he yelled back at anyone who would hear him, chuckling to himself at the dream of severance. Then, caught up in the glee of the moment, he reached over without thought, and pulled the fire alarm in front of him.

He realized immediately that while he'd participated in countless monthly fire-drills, he'd never actually seen a fire-alarm pulled in the

SALIGIA Tower.

Banshees cried through the halls, and bells rang in his head. The water hit his face—cold and drowning and endless. From invisible sprinklers hidden on every possible wall, roof, and apparently even some on the floor, the torrent took him.

Pushing through the maelstrom, he pressed the button for the elevator, but it did no good. The building was locked down.

Knowing that he had only freezing weather and snow to meet his soaking carcass at the exit, he turned blindly toward the stairwell, pushed through, and started his long way down.

That was amazing.

The indecency of his circumstances was overborne by his boundless relief.

He didn't imagine he'd ever retrieve what scarce personal belongings he kept in his office. A stress ball that looked like the Death Star, a Joker's card tacked to a cork board, and an old photo of him and his parents.

They could be replaced.

Wet and forlorn, Jeff had seldom been happier. He'd never quit before. Not on anything or anyone. Not when it was right, not when it was direly necessary. It was a large part of his problem, which he understood only now.

His shoes sloshed with each step, and the floors passed slowly. Jeff wondered if the water would finish off Nadia's failing circuits. He imagined her head spinning in frantic circles as sparks flew out from the neckline of her business suit and black, oily smoke filled the air.

Her authority had been questioned—not just in front of the HR reps and the lawyers, but in front of the Tins as well. He didn't suspect SALIGIA would let that stand. Intimidation and fear were her only purpose, and the weak could not survive in the corporate world. Eventually, she would be retired, and something stronger and more cruel would take her place. He laughed at the thought of the poor, sad bastards up on 82 when SALIGIA rolled out the new model. The laughter echoed in the wet, cement stairwell, sounding distant and foreign.

In a place like SALIGIA, things would never get better. It's not how they were designed. What a tragedy then, that such places seemed more common by the day.

The sprinkler water was cold, and for many floors he thought about those he'd left behind. Marcy and Francis had been his tormentors for a long time, but they were the guards in a prison they too could neither escape, nor advance in—standing impotently on the other side of the same bars.

He hoped the rest would find what mattered to them, and live for something, if they didn't already.

He thought about Janice. He'd tried to be a hero to her, it was always his style. It had been the same with Katie, and so many other people in his life, but it always came down to the same lesson—late learned, but of no less value for that.

The flippant jokes, the self-destructive chaos—it was all just a distraction. From what though, that was the question. It seemed like Jeff was always one step behind the world. With his attempted friendships in childhood, his sense of fashion, his old-fashioned interests, and especially with his tenacious expectation that hard work would prevail over corporate chicanery.

Now, he was simply too late. It was a bitter pill to swallow, that all of those missteps which he felt made him a better person were the very ones that dragged him down in the end.

Janice didn't need his help. Already, she had more than he did.

More purpose, more happiness, and more love. If anything, he could learn from her.

For too long, he'd held onto some ideal of himself in relation to others. The tutor, the helper, the merciful saviour.

It was all bullshit. Contrived excuses to avoid facing his own problems.

Driven by an unfamiliar momentum, Jeff moved quickly—freed from the ancient shackles of expectation and fear which had hobbled him for too long.

Despite the chill of the water, his face was hot.

Halfway down the building, he realized he didn't have a plan beyond the exit. He would make his own choices, and forge his own stories. Never again, he pledged, would he lose himself in the stories of others—those dusty mausoleums of imagined futures long past.

Beyond that, he had no clue. He'd wasted too much time with plans already—other people's plans, or those he adopted for no reason beyond rote convenience. They make sense when you're young, but as you get older, it's hard to care like you used to. Hard to love new music. Hard to find new loves; not ones that burn like they used to, anyway. When you no longer believe in any of the myths, it gets hard to play the part.

For ten years he'd borne such grinding indignities, and done his best to be a good corporate dog. It never suited him, and seemed now beyond his ability to imagine. That Jeff was gone—shattered to jagged shards and scattered down the cold stairwell—to be resurrected by neither horses nor men.

His bridges were burned, and wandering was the joyful alternative he'd left himself. Wet and miserable, he was certain he'd never regret it. Shivering and sick, he was surer than he'd ever been, and there came a simplicity to things he'd only dreamed of as he shuffled papers at his desk, or bit his lip at corporate meetings. There were a million stories you could tell yourself to justify throwing your time away on something you didn't love. But every second—even those frozen in winter's pitiless embrace—were worth living.

That was the secret. The meaning of life was to live with meaning, not to languish away in some dystopian corporate hellscape.

His shivering body jolted as he hit the door to the outside—a rusted engine plowing over its predetermined resting place. If the alarms were deafening already, now they truly howled.

His head pounded, and his flesh was numb. Outside was a battlefield—the lights of fire trucks painting the snow-covered scenery with the blood of Jeff's late ambitions. Big, fluffy flakes floated down from the clouds to the ground, dancing in front of him like ancient Sherpas to a forgotten faerie land.

Where they would take him, Jeff didn't care. In a city where summer was occupied primarily by the fear of it ending, sometimes life began to feel the same. Maybe he'd stay in Edmonton, or maybe he'd go someplace warmer. Someplace where the endless rush of days held more meaning than the slow surety of their passing.

Meaning—it wasn't so much to ask. Whether we know it or not, everything has meaning on some level. Each action, each inaction— every moment. Every chat in a bar, every spilled coffee, and every day wasted in an office. They all matter.

Jeff was younger than he'd felt since he was truly young. His limbs moved with ease, and he crossed the street, ducking down an alley. It stretched endlessly on ahead of him, muddy and soiled where the snow was trampled. But the side lanes in each direction lay pristine and white—empty and unclaimed. Beautiful.

Behind him, the great black tower of SALIGIA Inc. shrunk

slowly away into the distance, and the crisp air in his lungs was invigorating.

His shirt began to stiffen as it froze, and the fog billowing from each breath warned him of the hardships ahead. Still, he trudged on, and it seemed a good thing to suffer in something worthwhile, rather than to simply subsist in a world where he merely got by each day, and each day meant a little less.

He'd been a man of small ambition, save to do little harm and to find on occasion some small amount of joy. Such men often accomplished less—overborn by the bold and brash, and those who felt entitled to all the world's bounty at the expense of their fellows.

His type seldom changed the world, and even more rarely did they endeavour to. For Jeff's part, he'd hoped only that the world would not change him, and in that he'd come up far short.

The snow falling on his face reminded him of days long gone. For a second, he tried to hold onto the feeling, but let it go just as the snow melted down his cheek.

Time and again the flakes landed, sat for a second, and then vanished. If he held out his hand and watched them, he could take each one in for a moment, and then let them go—lost forever, and yet no less worthy for that.

He could cradle them in his mind, and nearly believe that they were still real. Then they were gone, relegated to their proper place on the shelf of his memory, with all the other things whose beauty was now remembered only by the light of a sun long set.

About the Author

Brad Oates grew up in the small town of Mayerthorpe, Alberta, Canada. He developed a passion for literature at an early age. Many of his first memories involve being curled up on the couch with his parents and siblings as they read 'The Hobbit' and 'The Lord of the Rings'.

Now living in Edmonton, Alberta, with his dog, Bogney, and his partner, Janine, Brad enjoys spending his free time writing in the bars along Whyte Avenue... when it isn't too cold, of course.

Brad is also the author of 'Edgar's Worst Sunday', and has contributed to three anthologies of short stories with the Edmonton Writer's Group. On his blog, www.BradOHInc.com, he enjoys producing a wide range of content—including poetry, political commentary, philosophical reflections, and more. In general, he finds himself leaning towards a darkly comedic, literary approach and often dwells on the themes of human virtue and self-deception.